Praise for *This Side of Night*

"Mr. Scott, as it happens, has been a federal agent with the Drug Enforcement Administration for more than twenty years, which surely contributes to the authenticity of this convincing saga. . . . In *This Side of Night*, [Scott] demonstrates the Texas-size writing talents to which his protagonist aspires." —*The Wall Street Journal*

"Scott's twenty-year career as a DEA agent infuses his work with realism, and his writing chops will make readers wonder why he waited so long to launch his literary career. . . . Better yet, his descriptions of dry, stark Big Bend country are so vivid and poetic they approach the beauty of James Lee Burke's passages about Louisiana bayou country. The result is a fine novel that is suspenseful, action-packed, literary, and thought-provoking." —Associated Press

"The author exploits his decades of experience as a federal agent to create a powerful, realistic picture of crime along the southern border. Thriller fans will enjoy this absorbing and disturbing book." —*Kirkus Reviews*

"The stellar third volume in Scott's epic Texas border series (after 2018's *High White Sun*) draws its inspiration from a real-life tragedy. . . . Scott, a veteran federal agent, writes with authority and gravitas about complex border issues. Fans of Don Winslow and Cormac McCarthy won't want to miss this one." —*Publishers Weekly*

THIS SIDE OF NIGHT

J. TODD SCOTT

G. P. PUTNAM'S SONS || NEW YORK

PUTNAM
— EST. 1838 —

G. P. PUTNAM'S SONS
Publishers Since 1838
An imprint of Penguin Random House LLC
penguinrandomhouse.com

Copyright © 2019 by Jeffrey Todd Scott
Excerpt from *Lost River* copyright © 2020 by Jeffrey Todd Scott
Penguin supports copyright. Copyright fuels creativity, encourages diverse voices, promotes free speech, and creates a vibrant culture. Thank you for buying an authorized edition of this book and for complying with copyright laws by not reproducing, scanning, or distributing any part of it in any form without permission. You are supporting writers and allowing Penguin to continue to publish books for every reader.

The translation of Juan Ramón Jiménez's aphorism used as the epigraph is by Christopher Maurer, from *The Complete Perfectionist: A Poetics of Work*.

The Library of Congress has catalogued the G. P. Putnam's Sons
hardcover edition as follows:

Names: Scott, J. Todd, author.
Title: This side of night / J. Todd Scott.
Description: New York : G. P. Putnam's Sons, 2019.
Identifiers: LCCN 2018010782| ISBN 9780735212916 (hardcover) |
ISBN 9780735212923 (epub)
Classification: LCC PS3619.C66536 T48 2018 | DDC 813/.6—dc23
LC record available at https://lccn.loc.gov/2018010782
p.   cm.

First G. P. Putnam's Sons hardcover edition / July 2019
First G. P. Putnam's Sons premium edition / May 2020
G. P. Putnam's Sons premium edition ISBN: 9780735212930

Printed in the United States of America
1   3   5   7   9   10   8   6   4   2

For Mom and Dad
Sorry it took so long.

Lo malo de la muerte no ha de ser más que la prima noche.

The only bad part of death must be the first night.

—JUAN RAMÓN JIMÉNEZ

PROLOGUE

NOCHE

I

CHAYO & NEVA

When they shot Castel in the face, Chayo knew they were going to kill them all.

Castel had just pulled off his dirty T-shirt and was waving it over his shaved head, screaming they were students, *normalistas*, all unarmed, when the shot rang out. It was a high sound, clear and cutting, nothing like Chayo had ever heard before.

A church bell ringing.

Castel looked surprised, staring upward into the softening sky, when he fell.

Moments before, he'd stepped off the bus right into the burning bright headlights of the municipal police truck that had blocked their way. Chayo had marveled at how pale Castel was in those lights, his skin smooth and perfect and shiny like a new peso. How small and thin he looked, too, though he was three years older and ready to graduate. His glasses had sat crooked on his face as he yelled, big old ones his *abuelo* might have worn, and they were just as shiny as his skin, reflecting everything and nothing at all, since beyond that circled glow the intersection—the whole of the world—was nothing but shadows. Shadows so deep that the men surrounding them were only the barest hints of secret movement.

It was like the night itself was sweating, breathing hard: black lungs and an open, swallowing mouth.

Chayo knew that some of those men circling them in the dark wore uniforms, their faces covered with bandannas or old shirts, in shame and fear, and that unlike the *normalistas*, all of them were armed.

Everyone was then yelling, warnings and names that made no sense. All these *policía* or men pretending to be so, and the students they threatened.

At the next intersection, so far away it was like looking up to the moon, a red streetlight blinked on and off.

On and off.

A heart beating.

Despite the calming words of their own driver, when the other truck had first appeared, Chayo and Castel and some of the older students—Ernesto, Iker, Juan Pablo—had been angry and eager to pile out of the bus and confront it, make it get out of their way. But it was Neva who'd held him back, her small hand trembling yet holding his tight. Whispering, "No, please," begging him with her eyes to stay, so that when he looked down into those eyes that for weeks had been making his heart trip and stumble—always tying his tongue—he'd hesitated.

He'd sat back down. *For her* . . . for them both.

And he wasn't the only one, not after Iker—with his round, pockmarked face pressed against the window—had called out that the truck was empty anyway. *Abandonado*. Its driver having quickly vanished into the dark to join the swiftly circling shadows, the truck left idling in the intersection.

Only its lights alive, pointed at them like cold, staring eyes. Seeing nothing.

Ojos de los muertos.

Holding Neva's hand, feeling her heartbeat in his fingers, Chayo had thought he could hear the empty truck's radio still chattering to itself, ghostly voices from far away. A mouthful of static. *Fantasmas* whispering in the hot night and the empty air, murmuring about *them*: two busloads of young students, trapped in the street.

So it was Castel alone who'd stepped down from the bus to face the truck, calling out to the rest of them still huddled on the bus—all those like Chayo who'd sat back down, afraid:

". . . It's nothing, we'll push it out of the way. Have heart!"

¡Tener corazón!

Castel, who was going to teach in Chiquero later in the year, who liked navelina oranges more than anyone Chayo had ever known.

Castel, from Meoqui, who also wanted to be a poet, someday.

Castel, who had never listened to anyone about anything and made everything an argument, smiling as he did so, the gap between his two front teeth far too wide.

Castel, who took off his shirt to wave wildly in front of him.

Un pequeño torero.

Only Castel . . . whose voice was far too big for that small, exposed body.

Surrounded by light.

Naked.

"We are unarmed. Who do you think you are? The night cannot hide you! We see all of you."

¡Los vemos a todos ustedes!

But Chayo couldn't see anything, not really. The night *was* too dark. It had become this living thing, with its black lungs and beating red streetlight heart and hot, open mouth.

And . . .

Ojos de los muertos.

The night had come alive to swallow them whole and make them disappear.

Or Chayo hadn't *wanted* to see, as Neva buried her face in his arm, turning them both away . . .

. . . when the shooting began.

Leaving Castel alone in that pooled light, looking up into the night sky, searching for that mysterious church bell they'd all heard and Chayo would never forget.

Castel, still calling out, "It's okay. No fear, my friends. They're shooting in the air."

But they weren't.

THEY'D TAKEN THE BUSES two hours earlier outside Ojinaga, bargaining with the drivers until they'd agreed to take the thirty-five students of the Escuela Normal Rural Librado Rivera to Chihuahua City. It was the way of things, a practice that had been going on for as long as the rural schools had existed. With no funding from the government, the *normalistas*—all teachers-in-training for Mexico's most remote farming areas—had become accustomed to making deals with local bus and van drivers, borrowing and begging and offering them food and lodging and what little money they had in exchange for help. Sometimes it was easy, sometimes not, but they took the buses all the time to visit the remote schools they would eventually be responsible for or to pick up supplies . . . and of course, to go to protests. On this occasion they were going to Chihuahua City to join other *normalistas* in a great rally against government corruption. Next fall they'd need them again to make their way to Mexico City itself, to commemorate the 1968 massacre of students and civilians by government security forces in Tlatelolco, in the great Plaza de las Tres Culturas. They'd sing and draw chalk outlines of the dead and bleed fake blood on scribbled doves.

Carry signs and chant.

"¡Yo no estaba allí, pero no voy a olvidar!" I wasn't there, but I won't forget!

Again, it was the way of things. All the *normalistas* were going to be teachers, but most were activists, too, at heart. They loved their country and wanted better for it.

Chayo, a first-year, along with Castel and Juan Pablo and Batista, was responsible for getting the buses for the trip to Chihuahua. They found the first at Calle Segunda, near Federal Highway 16. The bus had been empty and the driver had been lighthearted. A big man, round and ruddy as the navelinas Castel liked so much (so Chayo called him "Naranja"), drinking two warm Cokes and eating an empanada his wife had made; laughing easily at Juan Pablo's jokes. He told dirty stories of his own youth and they all liked him. They found the second on Calle del Pacífico, but this one had been less enthusiastic. He already had paying passengers, a handful of old *abuelas* and teenagers no older than the *normalistas* themselves, and only agreed to their request if he could first drop them at the bus station and then talk with his dispatch.

He had to make arrangements for the rest of his shift and have the tires checked for such a long trip.

He didn't tell jokes or laugh. He was as thin as the other driver was fat, with a pinched and sour face (so he became "Limón"), and sparse hair too small for his head. It looked painted on, badly colored like a child's drawing. Juan Pablo made a joke about it, and although Chayo had tried hard not to laugh, he joined in with the others until the driver stared at them all, glaring, as if counting or memorizing their faces.

At the station, Limón got off his bus and spoke for a long time to a security guard. An hour passed, and no one seemed to look at the tires. Instead, Limón made calls from a small cell phone, one after another, pacing back and forth and smoking four or five cigarettes— taking so long it made Chayo nervous—until he finally returned.

That was the only time he smiled at them, as he stepped back up onto the bus. He grinned wide to reveal dirty yellow teeth, winking in slow motion in the last of the late-afternoon light, as if they were all just sharing another of Juan Pablo's jokes.

But no one else knew what the joke was.

And then they were rolling down the dusty road to join Batista, who waited with the first bus.

———

NEVA WAS BATISTA'S YOUNGER COUSIN, and she was not a *normalista*.

She went to the Catholic school in Ojinaga, but proudly told Chayo the first time she saw him she didn't believe in God, laughing out loud as she said it, twining her tiny wooden rosary around her fingers. She claimed she'd believe in God when He did something good for her, and He hadn't done a damn thing yet. Chayo wasn't sure if she meant that or not. She was small and dark, always in motion like a delicate bird, and everything made her laugh. She'd gotten an iPhone for her *quince* the year before and loved all other things *americano*: music and pop stars and bands that Chayo had never heard of. She talked endlessly about television shows and movies, and sometimes Chayo tried to find out about them so he could understand all the things that seemed so important to her, to truly understand *her*. Most afternoons after school she'd change into a small T-shirt and put on some bright makeup and then appear with a carload of other laughing and smoking girls outside Librado Rivera, supposedly to visit Batista and bring him food and other things, although she somehow always ended up talking to Chayo, too, who felt tall and strange and awkward around her in those moments, as if he were put together from mismatched wood and old nails. He *wanted* to be funny like her friends, or like Juan Pablo, but he didn't know any jokes, and oftentimes said nothing at all.

Smiling like a fool as she circled him in cigarette smoke, humming melodies to her songs.

They once walked together along the dirt road by the school, near the fields the *normalistas* had worked so hard to plant, and for each song she sang, he pointed out for her a different plant, tree, or flower: the dahlias and the lechuguilla and the guayule. The candelilla and the drooping molina and bright red splash of ocotillo. He showed her the sideways S of a rattlesnake's passage drawn in the dust, and pointed out the difference between the footsteps of a mule deer and a javelina. He told her that at one time jaguars had hunted these areas, but they were long gone, or no one had seen one in such a long time that it was much the same thing. She asked where he was from, and although he was embarrassed, he told her anyway—near Blanco—and when she admitted she did not know that place, he said no one did.

And then she had laughed, though he wasn't trying to be funny, and it was still the most beautiful sound in the world. She even put her hand on his arm—for a heartbeat—to let him know she meant no harm.

It was the first time he'd felt those fingers on his bare, tanned skin, and although he was ashamed of how filthy he was from the fields, he couldn't shy away from that slight brush of fingertips . . . letting her touch work all the way through him. Right into his blood and bone. For hours after she was gone he'd still felt that brief contact—heavy and hot and beating in time with his heart—leaving him both happy and terrified that he would always feel it.

That it would never go away, or worse, never come again.

It wasn't just that touch, but also what she'd said: how she'd smiled and put her head next to his as if they were sharing a secret, sharing one breath, and whispered that she *liked* his seriousness. He'd wanted so badly then to tell her that she was beautiful—the most beautiful thing he'd ever seen—but she'd already pulled her hand back from his arm, dancing away down the sunlit road, taking all his words and breath and heart away with her.

NEVA DIDN'T WANT TO CHANGE THE WORLD, she wanted to leave it.

She talked about it all the time: going over the Río Bravo to Los Estados Unidos to stay with *familia* she had in Dallas or Houston (Chayo could never remember which). In two years she planned to leave Ojinaga for good, or so she promised, and get a job and see the *americano* bands that she loved and shop in the stores that she'd read about. She believed trying to change things in México was as silly as trying to move a mountain, and when Chayo once told her that such a thing could be done, one rock at a time, she'd said *maybe*, *maybe*, but that would take too damn long and she had too many other things to do. Plus, rocks were sharp and heavy, and she didn't want to hurt herself. She pretended not to care with such practiced ease that she almost believed it herself, but Chayo knew better. She was afraid of what change demanded, of its high cost. In the past few years everyone had lost someone, something, to the narcos and their corruption and a government that had no will to stop either. Everyone had a story, as many stories as all the songs she sang.

She was right; she just didn't want to get hurt.

———————

SO HE WAS SURPRISED when they returned to Naranja's bus to find her there waiting with Batista and the other *normalistas*. He thought at first she'd only come to see them off, but no, she was going with them. She needed to see for herself what all the fuss was about, take some pictures on her iPhone, and share her grand adventure with her friends. She even leaned in close to him (not as close as that day on the road, but close enough) and said maybe she'd carry a rock or two of her own, a couple of the lighter ones. Her eyes were bright and shining and forever, and he knew then that he'd carry *her* all the way to Chihuahua City and back in his arms, if he had to. He wanted her to come more than he'd ever wanted anything in his whole life, so it was good there was no talking her out of it anyway.

She marched onto Naranja's bus with a smile on her face and Chayo had no choice but to follow her.

"IT'S OKAY. NO FEAR, my friends. They're shooting in the air." Castel was waving his shirt, about to adjust his now crooked glasses, when his face disappeared.

Chayo saw *that* clearly.

It was there and then it was gone, only a reddish mist left hanging in the air like a bloody thumbprint. Shattered glasses falling to the ground. Then Castel himself was gone, too, all of him, as if he had never been; vanishing completely. The night that had been stalking them took him just like that, just like a pouncing jaguar. Juan

Pablo shouted, pointing at the place where Castel had been standing, as another bullet came through an open window and punched him in the throat. He looked down at his hands, opening and closing them like he was trying to hold on to something he couldn't see, before falling backward into his seat. His steaming blood hit Iker in the face, who screamed and scrambled to wipe it off, but not before three fingers of his frantic left hand were clipped off by another passing bullet. Then the whole bus was filled with them: bullets from every direction, like heavy bugs battering at the inside of a glass lamp, each as big as the pale leopard moths Chayo had collected in jars as a boy. The *normalistas* began screaming and throwing themselves down between the seats and on the floor to escape them.

Chayo saw the driver Naranja stand, his great bulk eclipsing the light from the truck in front of them. It was like he was lit from within, the tips of his hair burnished by light. He waved his fat arms as if waving the bullets away, trying to shield a boy Chayo did not know well, until the funny and brave bus driver took one, two, three bullets in the stomach and chest and the bus's windshield buckled, flecking his falling body with glass.

An hour earlier he'd been eating an empanada and laughing with them.

Él sólo murió por nosotros.

No . . . no . . . we killed him.

Limón had already abandoned his bus, leaving Naranja's pinned between the other two vehicles. Both buses were under heavy fire now, bullets ricocheting off their metal skin, hot sparks dancing in the air. Glass was breaking and blown tires were groaning like old men. *Normalistas* were crawling over one another and fleeing the buses, making a wild run across the intersection, some waving cell phones in the air, either trying to make calls or film what was happening to them. But they were only beacons, as bright and telling as flashlights, and the men hidden in the shadows used them to track the fleeing students over the dark streets.

Chayo saw one after another go down, their phones left bouncing across the pavement.

And that's when he knew they were going to kill them all. He didn't know why, or what crime they had committed, but now that the shooting had started, it couldn't end without all of them dead. Dead and buried and rotting somewhere in a deep hole, piled on top of each other and covered in dirt or sand or trash or shit. The men out there would see to that.

They had to, to bury the shame of what they'd done.

This night would never end until it swallowed them all.

Neva was screaming, both his name and Batista's, and this time it was he who grabbed her hand, holding it tight. He told her over all the noise that it was going to be okay, that he would get her out of there no matter what. Nothing would happen to her.

She looked into his face and he saw that she believed him.

A bullet gently moved the air, nearly kissed his face. Like soft wings against his skin. It reminded him of Neva's touch, that very first touch.

These are only moths like those I used to catch in Blanco. They cannot hurt me.

Nada me puede hacer daño.

He told her to stay low and behind him, to move only when he moved. If he fell, she was to keep running and not look back. He couldn't help himself and quickly kissed her between the eyes and whispered that he loved her, but he wasn't sure she heard him, and that was okay. At least he'd said the words, finally releasing them. Their weight would no longer burden him or slow him down and he would not die with them heavy on his lips.

Voy a volar por los dos de nosotros.

He squeezed her hand again, not to hold her back as she had done for him, but to let her know it was finally time to run. To run and never stop.

To fly. Para volar.

And they did.

Juan Abrego Carrión kissed his little Zita and thought about murder.

Death. *Muerte*.

She was in a new dress and had come out to the porch to show it to him, turning in circles by firelight. It was a pretty thing, pink and lace. The sort of thing when she was older she would wear to her *quince*, and what a fine party that would be. He did not want to touch it with his hands and get it dirty. He'd found himself staring at his hands more and more lately—they sometimes shook on their own now—unable to get them clean no matter how much he washed and scrubbed at them. There was always dirt beneath his nails, thick and rich, worked into the creases of his old, leathery skin. Sometimes it even looked like *sangre* . . . blood. He did not know if he was imagining this, or if he truly was forever stained. Was it possible he still had the soil of his father's fields ground into his skin, buried in his heart? Fields that had once grown marijuana, and now poppies? He had memories of long stretches of rolling green under a hot, hot sun, standing stripped to his waist and tanned as dark as cowhide, drinking water from a wooden bucket. But he wasn't sure how real those were, either.

Maybe that was *another* boy, another place. Sometimes he wished that boy had never grown up to do the things he'd done.

He motioned to Luisa, who was not Zita's mother, to take the young girl gently by the hand and lead her back into the main house. Moths circled them both, winging against the naked bulbs. When Luisa moved, a man with a gun moved behind her, a shadow on the ranch house's simple walls. Wherever Luisa and little Zita went, men with guns followed. There were so many he did not know them anymore, and they all looked the same. Young, dark-skinned, thick-mustachioed. Their eyes were all flat, unreadable, like they were hand-painted on their skulls—blank and mirrored as the sunglasses they often hid them behind. They pretended to be like the great men who had come before them, the true narcos, but these *buchon* gangsters were nothing, replaceable as the money it took to buy them. No one would ever know their names, no one would sing *narcocorridos* about them, and their clothes were richer than they were. Here in Cuchillo Negro they wore jeans and boots and Stetson palm-leaf cowboy hats that had been sent down new from El Paso. But when they were in Mazatlán or Juárez or Mexico City they wore Z Zegna suits, like those his own son favored, although Martino himself never came to Cuchillo Negro anymore. He didn't like the dirt, the smell, the sun. Martino had never worked fields the way he had, and said it wasn't safe for them ever to be together anyway, and he was probably right.

He'd last looked on Martino's face a year ago, not

recognizing the boy he'd once been or the *empresario* in the expensive suit he was pretending to be.

The man with the gun fell in step behind Luisa and his Zita. He had never seen this one before, or maybe he had, but he didn't like the look of him anyway. He was one step too slow, too nonchalant. Like he was distracted, listening to music only he could hear. Maybe he was thinking of a girl he'd had in Mexico City. *Who was choosing these men now?* Martino, or his *segundo*, Gualterio? He would have to ask. He would have this one replaced with another. There was always another.

He knew that as well as anyone, even if Gualterio liked to tell him: *There will only ever be one El Patrón.*

What his oldest, dearest friend truly meant was that he, Juan Abrego Carrión, had outlasted all the rest. For one more day, he yet remained standing.

Él estaba solo. He was alone.

Now, with the girl safe and gone, he rose from his rocking chair and made ready to go down to the barn, where a man waited to die. As much as he wanted two fingers of Tres Quatro Cinco in a cool glass and his bed, and the slow touch of whatever woman they'd brought out to the ranch for him, he still had work to attend to.

There was always more work, and because he took it seriously, so personally, maybe that's why he had lasted so long.

As the old man—and he was old, *too old*—finally stepped off the porch to make his long walk to the barn, more than a dozen other men, with shoulder-strapped Mossberg Tactical AR-15s, walked with him.

———

THE BARN SMELLED THICK OF HORSES, although the animals themselves had been moved into the fields because the fire in the barrel would scare them. He'd once owned Andalusians, Arabians, and Trakehners, and years ago funneled nearly ten million dollars through a quarterhorse farm in Texas. One of his finest animals there, Hay Fuego, won the All-American Futurity at Ruidoso Downs, New Mexico. But the horses here now were farm breeds, no different from those in the surrounding valley. He kept them simply because he liked them. On the coolest mornings, he always took his black coffee in the barn to spend time with them, rubbing their coats, listening to them talk to each other, watching their breath plume that was so much warmer . . . so much more *alive* . . . than the air around them. He wondered what they said to each other, what they thought of this life.

What did they think of the old man with his coffee, watching them and calling them by name?

This ranch at Cuchillo Negro—one of his favorite places—was among dozens he owned, so many he could not remember them all. It reminded him most of where he'd grown up right on the edge of Durango, although that place no longer existed. On a night like this when he could see every star ever made, when the sky glowed thick with them in all directions above the blackened curves of nearby hills, and when the small fires of distant farms also burned, he imagined hearing the wind itself lost in the trees. He could feel, too, the soft step of unseen animals moving under them. It was *vida* everywhere, all around him. But as much as he liked it here, he could only spend two or three days at the most, sometimes less, because of the *americanos*. Las Tres Letras . . . DEA. He could never stay anywhere for long. His life had become disposable, cast away, everything in it ready to be thrown out or discarded at a moment's notice. He used a cell phone two times and it was replaced with another; fresh laptops and satellite phones were always appearing out of plastic and Styrofoam; new cars and stolen and repainted trucks came and went by the score, changing or disappearing as frequently as the men who drove them and protected him. No longer was he with the same woman twice. No one could know too much, or get too close, except for Gualterio. Not even Martino, who chose to stay away anyway. This was his life now: all these things he could have, yet everything slipping almost untouched through his fingers.

The lyrics of a *narcocorrido* once boasted that Juan Abrego Carrión owned the world, but that was far from true.

He could *buy* the world, but he could own nothing.

No longer.

HE WANTED TO STAND outside the barn door for a moment more, gather himself for what would come next, but it was never good to be outside, uncovered, for long. Martino, who had studied two years at a university in California, had talked to him of satellites and drones and all the things the *americanos* were using nowadays to hunt him. No, he truly did not own the world. *It* owned him, and even the sky held him prisoner.

That's why they had to light the fire barrel inside the barn, and do this thing he needed to do beneath its roof, so there would be no image of it flashing across the night's horizon, captured by a camera hidden among the stars.

But in some ways, it did not matter. God saw all anyway, and He knew all that Juan Abrego had done.

THEY HAD THE MAN TIED TO A CHAIR, his hands pinned back with copper wire.

There was no blood on him, not yet, because Juan Abrego had given the order he would not be harmed. And there was a bottle of water that his men had been giving him mouthfuls of as a small mercy, next to his shoeless, bruised feet, and another filled with sour goat's milk and cayenne pepper for Juan Abrego to spray up the man's nose, if he chose to do so. There was also a bag of pepper in a small bowl ready to push directly into the man's face as well, to force him to breathe in deep, like inhaling raw flame. The barn was brutally hot from the burning barrel and the man had sweated twice through his shirt. It clung to him, revealing a thin body, the very count of his ribs. He had been brought here in a hood, but that had long been tossed aside in the hay, which should have terrified the man as much as anything; a fresh understanding that it did not matter what he saw at this ranch, even if it mattered very, very much what he said here.

Then there were all the other items Juan Abrego had ordered to be made ready: more copper wire, two machetes, a bag of broken lightbulbs and glass, a hammer and nails, and a brand-new set of medical implements. Scalpels and saws and specula of all sizes and shapes reflecting the men standing in the shadows. All these things had been carefully, specifically, laid out on a horse blanket in front of the man, and his eyes roamed wildly over them.

There was a real doctor sitting in a car outside the barn, driven in from Ciudad Jiménez wearing a hood of his own, with a bottle of Juan Abrego's favorite Tres Quatro Cinco and two freshly cut limes, grown right here at the ranch, on a tray in the passenger seat to help steady him. He'd been brought here not to use the new medical instruments, but to keep the man in the barn alive as long as necessary.

Juan Abrego knew terror intimately, knew the very curves and contours of it as well as he knew those of any woman he'd ever had, so he stood in front of the bound man for a long minute, watching him. Watching him breathe faster and faster and then piss himself as the terror took hold. He let it embrace this man, when Gualterio appeared at his side.

Gualterio was big, solid. His chest pushed against the pearl buttons of his shirt and his stomach hung handsomely over his jeans. He remained as strong as ever, his size alone menacing, though there was some gray in the thick hair at his temples that Juan Abrego suspected his friend was thinking about coloring. It was in the way his hands went unconsciously to his hair all the time now, continually pushing his fingers through it, as if he could rub the signs of his age away. Juan Abrego would say nothing about it, having learned long ago that a man's vanity was a dangerous thing better left unchallenged, even between old friends. He was ten years Gualterio's senior and they had known each other their whole lives. Gualterio had always liked his rich food and his women and his beer—it showed in his florid face and stomach—and on Juan Abrego's orders had killed more men than either of them could count. There was no one he knew better, and after the death of his own brother Rafael—who everyone had called Nemesio—no one he trusted more, and that included his five remaining half brothers and one sister and his own son.

It was sometimes hard to remember that Nemesio had died thirty years ago.

But here, now, in front of the other men with guns, even Gualterio knew to stand silent until he'd been addressed.

"Is this the bus driver?" Juan Abrego asked the darkness gathered in the barn, although only Gualterio would dare answer.

"*Sí,*" Gualterio said. "It was all done as you asked." Gualterio paused to light a cigarette; again, the only man who had the license to do so in Juan Abrego's presence. "There are others. We will find them." Gualterio ended with a shrug. It was both a statement and a threat. *Una promesa.*

So many had made promises in the dark in front of Juan Abrego Carrión. Men had died trying to keep them. More had died failing.

The bus driver.

Two nights ago there had been an attack on two buses of *normalistas* in Ojinaga. It was still unclear how many had been killed or injured, although a few seconds of cell phone video had already surfaced and now the whole world was watching, listening, waiting. Hundreds of *federales* had flown in from Mexico City, as well as forces from the Secretaría de Marina. Children had been shot in the street, so *el presidente* was constantly on TV promising that something would be done this time, and perhaps, this time, he thought he spoke the truth, although promises would not make this thing go away. No threats would ever make those videos disappear or return those children who had vanished.

No one knew who had ordered the attack, but Juan Abrego suspected who was supposed to answer for it.

No one knew . . . except maybe for *this* man, this bus driver tied to the chair. There had been two buses and two drivers and somehow this one had walked away unhurt, smart enough to abandon his bus moments before the shooting began.

There had been cell phone calls back and forth. This man had been warned.

Although Juan Abrego had long ago learned there was a limit to what any one man could truly promise and deliver to him, there was no limit to what he could learn with enough money, terror, and time, and a willingness to use all three.

It was important also that not only children but students had been the targets, for Juan Abrego had once dreamed of being a teacher. He and Nemesio had been *normalistas* like those in Ojinaga, and he did not believe this attack was a coincidence, because he did not believe in such things. It had been a lesson for him alone.

A declaration of war.

He bent down in front of the bus driver, feeling not only age in his knees but something worse: he'd been sick for months now and had said nothing to anyone, although Gualterio suspected. His legs trembled and his arms were weak and there was a dull pain all the way to his groin, but he wanted, needed, to look this man in the eye.

He coughed, spit, and Gualterio, in respect, looked away.

"I'm going to ask you questions, my friend. Many, many questions. And you are going to answer them all. Not because you want to, or because you believe you will live when I'm done, because you will not, and it is important that you know that. I will not give you that false hope. If you answer truthfully, quickly, you will die honorably. Your wife and your two daughters will never lack for anything again. I will see to that. They will be able to say your name proudly. But if you lie or deny, if you try to protect those who did this thing, then you will die painfully. I will have these men here rape and kill your wife, the mother of your children. Then your oldest daughter will be whored out on the streets in Culiacán, and your youngest will be sold to another man I know in Camargo, to do as he wishes. He is a *pervertido*. He makes movies, I think. Horrible, horrible movies that decent men cannot stomach. These are not threats or promises, but simple truths. *The only truth.* Do you believe me?"

The bus driver started crying, whining like an old dog, but nodded. His whole body shook as if electric current ran through it, and he pissed himself again. It was a high, ripe scent. *Agrio*. Juan Abrego had seen this all before. Terror now held the man close in her skeletal arms, whispering in his ears, saying things Juan Abrego did not have to.

"Do you know who I am?"

The bus driver shook his head, squeezing his eyes tight.

"Yes, yes, you do. Pretending otherwise will not change this. It cannot. Open your eyes and say my name. I cannot yet take your tongue, but I can make you use it. And I will."

Gualterio stirred next to him, ready to step forward and force the man to comply. He'd seen all this before as well, but many of the others in the barn had not. They knew El Patrón only as an old man, confined often to his chair; prone to falling asleep in the late-afternoon shadows of the hottest days. A man who enjoyed telenovelas and his Zita's dancing. Perhaps they mocked him behind his back. Maybe one of them thought to betray him.

This display was as much for those men as the one tied to the chair. Juan Abrego was now the teacher he'd once dreamed of being, and this was his lesson.

The bus driver finally opened his eyes, took a deep, deep breath. "You are Fox Uno."

Juan Abrego shook his head, although the man was not wrong. It was a silly name, given to him long ago, the way they now called Martino Tiburón; the way Gualterio had always been known as Oso Ocho. Such things stayed alive mainly in the press, in the *narcocorridos*. Many people believed "Fox Uno" had no true meaning now and that such a person no longer existed. Only the name itself lived on, carrying an immense weight . . . an impossible burden.

Fox Uno was little more than a horrible dream, *un espantajo*—a terror. Something to frighten children.

And when Juan Abrego remembered the boy he had once been, the boy he had left in his father's fields decades ago, he could almost believe that, too.

"No, I am Death, my friend . . ."

After the bus driver finally answered all his questions—after he was broken and all his secrets poured out—Juan Abrego would strangle him to death with his bare hands. *Fox Uno's hands.* Those same hands he was afraid would dirty Zita's dress and that he dreamed were permanently stained in blood. He would then have Gualterio help him with the *guiso*, putting the body in the burning barrel, where it would fold in on itself and melt and stink so bad that the barn itself would never be rid of it. He might later decide to give his horses away, or cut them loose to run free, and burn all the buildings here, never to return to Cuchillo Negro. But before all that, he wanted every man in this barn to watch him kill this bus driver and stare into the barrel until the body was only embers and ash and grease. No matter how long it took. He wanted them to learn this lesson well, and never, ever forget it.

Juan Abrego Carrión, better known as Fox Uno— leader of the Nemesio cartel—picked up the hammer from the horse blanket.

He weighed it up and down, turning the clawed end toward the driver's face.

His hand was old, but it did not shake now.

Yo soy la Muerte.

I am Death.

PART ONE

RÍO BRAVO

ONE

I
t started with two eggs and an iron skillet, and went
downhill from there.

TAKE-OUT PEERED THROUGH THE BROKEN GLASS,
his face a watery blur. If he recognized Danny Ford, it
wasn't immediately obvious to either man. Danny
watched Take-Out's eyes watching *him*, searching him up
and down and all over before they disappeared again.

Blink, blink, and they were gone.

That was the thing about a place as small as Murfee,
Texas, and as large as Big Bend County: everyone kind
of knew everyone else, so the question wasn't whether
Take-Out *knew* Danny, it was whether he *remembered*
him. And Danny was counting on a lifetime of Take-Out
scorching his brain with about every pill and powder
known to man that his memory wasn't worth a damn
anyway. Sketchy at best, as full of holes as his trailer.

The flimsy door wasn't opening though, which wasn't a
good sign. Or maybe it didn't mean a goddamn thing at all.

Take-Out—Eddy Lee Rabbit—was notoriously paranoid.

"Open the fuck up, I'm not standing here all damn day . . ." Danny called out to the closed door, measuring the distance between it and the top porch step, sliding back and to the side, so if Eddy was in a fighting mood, Danny would have some room to operate. He wanted to put his cold hands in his pockets, but needed them free, too. It was early September and the Big Bend was cool in the mornings until the sun cleared the mountains to heat things up, and that was just as true down here in the canyon by the river. The trailer was still painted in the long shadows that stretched all the way down to the water that Danny couldn't see, where the giant cane and salt cedars—the tamarisks—grew wild and big and blocked his sight. He'd read somewhere that neither were native to the area, having escaped domestic cultivation in the 1800s, but since then the sprawling plants and athel trees had almost taken over the riverways, stealing all the land's water and salt. That didn't make them much different from a lot of other things in the Big Bend: men like Take-Out who weren't native either and who'd moved in to claim their piece of it. There were groups of people called "tammywhackers" who spent their summers pulling the invaders out by their roots, trying to clear and reclaim the riverbanks and waterways, but to Danny's unpracticed eye, it looked like they were losing the battle.

At least they were trying, like he was here trying, with Eddy Lee Rabbit.

The old single-wide was worth about five hundred dollars, with a two-million-dollar view. Bits of junk gleamed here and there: old bikes and cans and beer bottles and engine blocks and rusty pieces of rebar that were out here for no reason at all. An old refrigerator. But it commanded the flats of Delcia Canyon, with desert stretching into the distance and river gorge walls rising south to the horizon; dark striations of sandstone, quartz, and gypsum that changed color with the season and the sun.

Across the desert floor, after the recent rains that had swollen the river for three days, Danny could pick out more splashes of color: bloodred ocotillo, the yellow of desert marigold, white and purple Texas sage, and the sunset fruit of the prickly pear—the tuna. Most people dismissed the desert as a dry, desperate place. Colorless and lifeless. He'd learned that it was neither.

Although Danny Ford wasn't a native either, that didn't mean he hadn't come to love the Big Bend and the Chihuahuan Desert in all its moods and seasons, even if he didn't always understand them.

Maybe Eddy loved it, too, in his own way. Maybe.

Danny was about to hammer on the door when it opened, revealing Eddy with something in his hand. Not a Colt .380 or a Buck Woodsman or a Louisville Slugger—all plausible options—but just an old iron skillet, like Danny's mom used to own back in Sweetwater. Eddy was forking what appeared to be scrambled eggs out of it—eggs and chorizo—and keeping the door open with a scabbed knee. He was shirtless, his dirty, thin hair shadowing his eyes, calmly eating his goddamn breakfast.

King of his castle.

But . . . those eyes were bright, too bright, bouncing up and down and all around . . . *popping* . . . barely staying still in his skull. He'd been on a meth bender and his skin shone with its acid sweat.

"It's too goddamn early, so what the fuck you want?" Eddy asked around a mouthful of eggs and chorizo.

Danny hadn't woken Take-Out up, not even close. He'd probably already been awake for a couple of days.

Eddy Lee Rabbit, aka Take-Out, was forty-one years old, and supposedly named after *the* Eddie Rabbitt, the famous songwriter and singer. Eddy had grown up around Floydada, drifting southward after high school before finally washing up in the Big Bend ten or fifteen years ago. Take-Out had come by his nickname honestly— he was *the* drive-thru-window guy, selling his first bag of weed out of a Beto's Taco Shop along with three street tacos. He then moved on to coke, heroin, meth, pills; like he moved on to Arby's, Wendy's, and Kentucky Fried Chicken. You just had to wait for his shift and know what to ask for when you pulled up to the window to get your order.

He'd wrap it in some napkins and slip it in with some extra ketchup or honey barbecue sauce.

Eddy was arrested twice for drug distribution, dividing his time between the Texas Department of Criminal Justice's Preston Smith and James Lynaugh units. Neither stint had been very long, but the facts laid out at both sentencings all but guaranteed he'd never work at another Big Bend fast-food restaurant again.

That's when Eddy started selling out of his own place down by the river, and from the look of it now, using a hell of a lot more than he was selling. It was all pretty much the same as before, though. You called or stopped by to place your order and took it with you when you left, because Eddy Lee Rabbit *never* tripped with his dope— he never delivered and never would.

Small-time, small-town stuff.

And if that's all there was to it, Deputy Danny Ford of the Big Bend County Sheriff's Department might have left Eddy alone out here in Delcia Canyon. Sheriff Chris Cherry knew Eddy's local history well enough not to want to hang a third arrest around his neck, so he'd given the word to all his deputies to leave him be.

But unfortunately for Eddy, that wasn't all of it.

Not according to Charity Mumford, Eddy's on-again, off-again girlfriend. Last weekend they'd been off-again, *real off*, after Eddy had spun a cue ball upside her head. He'd thrown it at her from across the trailer, and after-ward she'd driven herself—still a bloody mess, needing stitches—up to the urgent care in Murfee, where they referred her instead to the Hancock Hill Medical Center, since it was clear she was still very high and screaming her damn head off the whole time. *All about Eddy.* The sher-iff sent Deputy America Reynosa to Hancock Hill to fig-ure out what all the fuss was about, and that's when Charity had started going on and on about the Mexicans.

All about Eddy *and his goddamn motherfuckin' Mexi-cans* . . . so that Eddy's small-time "stuff" suddenly didn't sound so small anymore.

It sounded damn serious.

The next morning, after Charity had come down a bit—and figured out what she'd done—she'd refused to discuss it again. More than that, she took it all back. Said she got hurt falling against her car, and claimed she'd made the rest of it up; it was all tweaker bullshit. The sheriff didn't want to get a warrant based on the shaky word of a recanting meth addict—maybe the stuff about Eddy *was* bullshit—but the twelve stitches across Charity's scalp were not, and the sheriff couldn't ignore those. He had America take Charity over to the family crisis center in Artesia, and finally relented and told Danny and Amé to take a long, hard look at Eddy Rabbit.

To get inside his trailer.

And that was how Danny found himself now standing in cool morning shadows on Take-Out's porch, watching him eat eggs without a care in the world.

"I got an order . . . I need something . . . an eight-ball. Speed. You got it?"

Eddy held his fork in his mouth a long, long time, balanced there without his hands, clenched in his bad teeth. When he finally took it out, he did it in one smooth, slow motion.

Other wheels, though, were turning furiously behind those already spinning, too-bright eyes.

"That ain't me no more, brother. I don't do that. Don't know what you're talkin' about."

Danny shrugged, spit. "C'mon, that's not what I heard."

"Says who? That man's a goddamn liar."

"Who said it was a man?"

"Really? Interestin' . . ." Eddy took another mouthful of eggs, the same slow fork routine as before, like he was afraid if he moved too fast his head would fall off and roll around on the ground between them.

Fucking tweakers. Danny wasn't unsympathetic to

whatever pain or problems or life's fuck-ups drove some-one like Charity or Eddy to start getting high in the first place, but he had zero tolerance for the consequences, since he was the one who had to deal with them. When tweakers were using, they only saw the world through the holes that shit had burned through their brains, like circles cut into a bedsheet for a little kid dressing up as a ghost for Halloween. Their whole world turned into these brightly colored fragments that didn't quite fit together anymore, all light and sound and fury. A silver spinning ball above an empty dance floor. It made everything mag-ical or mysterious to them, or worse, dangerous.

It also made them unpredictable, because even they didn't know what they were going to do next. Looking out through the ragged holes that circled the world, they just couldn't see that far ahead.

Not that he couldn't sympathize with that, either. Ever since his run-in with a skinhead piece of shit named Jesse Earl, Danny had suffered lingering trouble with his own vision. Only his left eye, where Jesse had hit him again and again with the butt of an old Ruger Nighthawk. Danny had kept the eye (and a vicious scar as a souvenir), but it was like there was an electrical short in there some-where, his sight coming and going. It would start at the edge of his peripheral vision, something dark and furious coming at him with great speed, followed by a squall of gray static and a sharp pain, before correcting itself. A light switch flipping off and on again fast inside his head, disorienting, a bit scary. But so far it had affected only that one eye, and he'd gotten used to it. Or rather, he'd learned how to ignore it. Sometimes he'd go two months without an episode, then he might have two in a day. After his surgery and recovery, and long after he was tired of dealing with doctors, he'd decided not to say anything about it, and he hadn't told the sheriff or Amé, both of whom would have made it a big deal. A serious deal.

To Danny, it was just another problem to manage, one of life's little fuck-ups, and something he was willing to accept.

Like Eddy Rabbit—it was just the way he saw the world now.

Danny glanced past Eddy's shoulder, trying to gauge whether the other man was alone in the trailer. He couldn't see anything, hear anything except a radio, playing some music in there somewhere. He couldn't make out the song.

"Look, I'm not here to fuck with you. This is business. All business. I talked to Cody at the Comanche, and Mike over there, too. You know Mikey, right? He damn well knows you."

The Comanche was Murfee's cattle auction, and faceless guys came and went through there all the time, grabbing seasonal work. And everyone, everywhere, knew a Michael or a Mike or a Mikey . . .

Eddy considered it, trying hard to keep his bouncing eyes on Danny, or a spot on the ground behind him. It was hard to say.

"Money?"

Danny moved slow, keeping his hands more or less visible and away from his body, and pulled a small roll of dirty bills from his jeans. He and Amé had roughed them up in the street in front of her apartment yesterday. It was the sort of money a full-on tweaker might beg, borrow, or steal.

Eddy focused on *that*. His whole world narrowed down to it. He moved when it moved.

"Mikey's a piece of shit to talk about me that way. It ain't fair, man. Today was the day I was really gonna try to go straight, get clean. Goddamn, I'm tryin'."

Danny nodded. He winked at Eddy, smiled big. "Brother, aren't we all?"

This was the moment. Danny had learned both as a soldier and a cop, there was always *a moment*.

Yes, no.

Go, no-go.

Run, fight.

Shoot, don't shoot.

Life was made up of these moments.

Eddy thought about it, and then laughed. It came out of nowhere, a quick bark, echoing across the canyon. It startled some scaled quail nesting out by an old tire in Eddy's yard, and they ran around in a noisy circle before settling down again. Eddy showed his bad teeth behind a not-quite-there smile and tapped his fork against the edge of his skillet in time to music only he could hear, not whatever was playing behind him. "Well, there's always tomorrow, right?"

That moment.

Danny laughed, agreeing with him. "Yeah, tomorrow."

It was good . . . they were all good.

"And tomorrow's a motherfucker," Eddy said, still laughing, still in the moment, when he swung the skillet at Danny's head.

IT DIDN'T GET HIM CLEANLY, but it got him good enough, and he couldn't blame his bad eye. He didn't see it coming, didn't expect it. In that moment when they'd been laughing, he'd gotten too comfortable, let his guard down. He goddamn knew better . . . he'd always known better. Knowing better had kept him alive for two years in Afghanistan, and mostly safe while working all those months undercover with those skinhead gangs. Never take your eye off the ball: the shadowed corner of an artillery-blasted hotel in Wanat or a gun shoved down in some teenage skinhead's jeans. Or even an old fucking skillet. But that meant you had to be looking for it to begin with.

That goddamn moment.

Because a moment was all it took to get you killed.

He ducked fast, still felt the skillet sharp across his neck and shoulder, greasy eggs in his eyes. Eddy had swung it wide like an ax, snake-quick, and if Danny hadn't pulled back it might have opened his head from jaw to scalp. He stumbled down the stunted porch but stayed upright, catching a last glimpse of Eddy as he tossed the skillet overhand at him and disappeared back through the trailer's open door in a full run. The throw was wide, not close, and the skillet bounced into the ocotillo, chasing the money that Danny had flung away and that was now blowing across the ground.

Danny wasn't sure exactly how much of this Amé and the other deputy, Dale Holt, were hearing. The desert and the canyons could play hell with the KEL recorders, which is why he hadn't been too concerned about wearing one to begin with, but neither the sheriff nor Amé would've allowed him to do the deal without one, so he hadn't argued about it. However, Amé and Dale were a hundred yards or more back in her truck, past a knotted stand of mesquites and the sightlines of the trailer, so Danny had known—hell, they'd all known—that if things went south (like they were going now), it would take them too long to get to him. Too long to do much of anything at all. And Eddy was on the move, *now*. Danny listened for the rev of Amé's big Ford, for her sirens, but there was nothing. Not yet.

That moment . . . again.

Go, no-go.

Run, fight.

Goddamn.

Goddamn if he was going to let Eddy Rabbit nearly beat him senseless with a skillet and then bolt like his namesake.

Danny yelled "Go go go" into his shirt where the KEL mic was hidden and started back toward the trailer. It wasn't his official "Fuck, I'm in trouble" signal—the silly phrase he was supposed to say if things got bad with Eddy—but it was clear enough.

And besides, that moment had passed anyway.

DANNY PUSHED HARD through the swinging door, looking left and right and clearing the corners. What few windows there were had been haphazardly spray-painted black so it was like falling into dark, fetid water.

The trailer smelled bad, too lived in, or maybe where something had gone to die. There was a futon here, an old cut-up recliner there, a mess of busted lightbulbs everywhere that crunched beneath his boots, and what looked to be a whole porcelain sink sitting in the middle of the main room, filled with crushed beer cans and spent cigarettes. Eddy and his buddies had been using it as a trash can.

There was also the thick, animal odor of weed. A whole lot of weed, and the stink of it clung to the walls Danny brushed against as if the plants themselves were growing there behind the particleboard.

He kept moving.

Ahead, Danny could pick out patchy sunlight pale as mold on the floor and walls, blooming where the kitchen screen door was still hanging open from Eddy's passage. He'd run straight through the trailer and out the other side.

Danny paused for a heartbeat, crouched, before coming at the kitchen low and fast and at an angle to make sure Eddy hadn't kicked at the screen door and then backpedaled into a corner to wait for him.

He could still have that damn fork or whatever else he might have grabbed.

But the kitchen was empty. Mostly empty. The original stove and fridge and dishwasher had all been yanked out, probably sold, leaving rotting holes like pulled teeth. Some of the linoleum had been peeled back, and torn-up strips of burlap were scattered all about. However, there was a leaking mini-fridge on the floor, a dented microwave and a rusted hot plate on the counter, and finally the source of the music Danny had heard earlier: an old Sony boom box.

Also, a police-band scanner and a couple of Motorola handheld radios in a small crate in a corner.

Now that he was here, Danny could finally make out that damn song. It was by Metallica, "The Day That Never Comes," and that song threw him all the way back to Afghanistan, where he wasn't chasing Eddy Rabbit anymore, but instead clearing some shitty mud house out in Nuristan Province; batting away flies crawling into his mouth and his eyes, and baking in his Interceptor body armor even in the deepest shadows, waiting for something to explode and someone to die. Always waiting. All the guys had listened to that Metallica song back then . . . *back there*. It was like their national fucking anthem.

He was eighteen, nineteen years old again, and scared shitless.

His bad eye flickered, threatened to go out.

He realized he was shaking.

He had to get outside. He had to get this place off his skin and out of his head.

He was running full tilt through the kitchen door when the sirens started.

EDDY WAS MAKING HIS WAY down to the water.

Danny could see where he'd stumbled along a thin path that had already been cut through the giant cane—which squared with Charity's story—and maybe thought he could hear him breathing hard, stumbling and cuss-

ing up ahead. Danny kept after him, gulping big mouthfuls of the morning air and letting the sunlight strike his
face; feeling better after shedding the dark and stink of
the trailer, after leaving that ominous music behind.
He'd never experienced anything like that before, but
knew plenty of others who had. Guys who'd never quite
left Afghanistan, friends who still felt like they were forever trapped in one of those mud houses. Like parts of
them had been entombed there, and for some that was a
certain, terrible truth—all the arms and legs that had
never come back to the United States with them. Danny
knew how lucky he was, but also knew he hadn't survived
all that shit only to come back home to Texas to get hurt.
Not here, not now, not like this. He could just stop, not
chase Eddy down into that thick foliage; let him disappear and try to track him down later. It wasn't like Eddy
had anywhere to go or the means to get there.

But he couldn't, wouldn't.

Because there was a part of him—there'd always been
a part of him—that simply wouldn't take no for an answer. It was a compass in his head always pointed in one
direction. And Eddy Lee had plenty to answer for. Not
only braining him with a skillet and smacking Charity
around, but also all those radios and the scanners in his
kitchen. Since getting out of Lynaugh, Eddy Rabbit had
moved way beyond selling dime bags out of Arby's or
Steak 'n Shake. He'd graduated to something else altogether.

Fortunately, Eddy made the decision easy on him
when he suddenly reappeared out of that green curtain
of cane, reversing his course and now running full speed

right back toward the trailer . . . toward Danny. He still had the fork in his hand, but it was long forgotten, because whatever he'd seen out in that cane, down by the water, was suddenly scarier than having the Big Bend County's deputy sheriff he'd just assaulted catch him.

They met in the shadows of a salt cedar as Danny hit him full force, using his forward momentum to lift Eddy clean off the ground. Eddy made a noise, not quite a cry or a grunt, and he barely weighed anything. It was like picking up a bundle of sticks wrapped in dirty clothes, a small child, and Danny almost felt bad about how hard he hit him. Almost.

He brought Eddy down in one motion but kept him upright, popping the man's wrist at a sharp angle and his elbow back the other way, sending the fork high and flying. This time Eddy tried to cry out as he swallowed air after having the wind knocked out of him. He scrabbled against Danny, smacking at him, until Danny snapped off an open palm strike to Eddy's jaw that shut his mouth for good.

Eddy's eyes rolled up white and he collapsed into the grass, breathing shallowly. He'd wake up in ten minutes, or maybe an hour.

Danny was just shrugging the Colt Defender from the holster tucked in the small of his back when Dale and Amé appeared on foot from around the side of the trailer, their duty weapons drawn. Dale's eyes were big and as white as Eddy's had been moments before, pulled like magnets to the unconscious man at Danny's feet. Amé was scanning the cane, and Danny, too, checking him up and down, making sure he was okay. She still had on her sunglasses and it was impossible to read what she thought about the scene in front of her, but that was tough most of the time anyway.

She'd ditched her truck somewhere up front and the sirens were still going.

Dale was moving slow, too slow, and eyeing Eddy. "What the hell . . . ?"

Danny snapped his fingers twice at the other deputy to get his attention, to focus him, while he motioned at Amé to stay alert on the unseen river behind him. "He's all right, just get him cuffed up. He was bolting for the river but something spooked him, sent him right back into my arms."

Dale nodded, still unsure, but reaching for his cuffs. "Well, I'd ask him, but you righteously knocked his ass out . . ."

Amé stepped over Eddy and got up close to Danny, not taking her eyes off the cane or lowering her gun. "Any idea?"

Danny shrugged. "No, maybe nothing? Eddy seeing things?"

Now that she was out of Dale's earshot, Amé leaned in: "You okay?"

Danny made a face, embarrassed. "Yeah, he caught me by surprise. Hit me with a goddamn skillet."

"I figured," she said, trying to hide half a smile, there and gone again. "There's still egg in your hair." She reached up and brushed it away, her touch quick and light. If she let it linger, Danny couldn't tell. His hair had grown out in the last year—not too long, but regular, civilian length. It had been shaved down to nothing when they first met, and he didn't want her to ever see him like that again. He didn't ever want to be that person again.

"Now what?"

Danny nodded toward the path through the cane. "I'm going down there, and you're going to stay wide of me, off to my right." He looked around, pointed. "Work your way to that paloverde, see if I flush anything back toward you. Someone could have snuck out of the trailer while I was talking with Eddy."

"You mean while he was distracting you?"

"Yeah," Danny said through gritted teeth. "That."

She eyed his Colt, the small one he'd carried for this deal. It was easy to hide but it wasn't meant for something serious, and neither of them knew exactly how serious this was. "You want me to go back to the truck, get the rifle?"

"No, I'm good. Let's just get in there and get this over with."

"Bien, vamos a hacerlo."

He nodded, uncertain. He'd tried here and there to learn Spanish, not like Sheriff Cherry, who'd been studying seriously for months, and still only understood half the things she said.

But she tapped him once on the shoulder before moving off, sharing that half smile again. Their secret. It was a smile he'd grown used to since those days when she came to sit with him in the hospital after Jesse Earl; a smile he'd miss if he didn't see it at least once a day.

A smile that had kept him in the Big Bend, and would, for as long as she was here.

"*Ten cuidado*, Deputy Ford. Keep an eye out for skillets . . ."

DANNY MOVED INTO THE CANE.

The world turned different shades of green and gray around him, where the thumb-thick stalks blocked out the sun.

It was like peering through rough fingers held over your eyes.

It was tight, claustrophobic . . . submerged, but not like being inside Eddy's trailer. That had felt more like a coffin, the grave itself. Here, it was almost a world all its own, cut off from everything else. It had its own sights and sounds, somehow both muted and made loud and large at the same time. There was the buzz of insects and the heavy smell and whisper of the water itself. The quick-winged movement of mockingbirds and flycatchers going about their business, casting tightfisted shadows over everything and ignoring the man beneath them. It was hotter here near the mouth of the river, its breath causing him to sweat. It would have been ancient, primeval, if it weren't for the crushed tins of Spam, some discarded burlap, and a torn sneaker Danny could pick out half buried in the sand.

It was a blue Nike wrapped in electric tape. Men had been here, and recently.

Men moving back and forth from the river, across the Rio Grande.

What little wind there was then turned, shifting toward him, and he caught a new smell. Not the thick sourness of the river, but something else. Something worse. That dead and dying stink from Eddy's trailer, only tenfold. It stung his eyes and he knew immediately what it was. He'd smelled it before in Nuristan, after Wanat, after Rumnar. After a hundred other battles in places whose names he'd tried to forget. You never forgot the smell of a fresh corpse.

That's when he saw it through a fresh gap in the cane, right by the river.

It was faceup, staring into the sun. Muddy water was moving gently in and out of ugly, brutal cuts. Pooling in the open, breathless mouth, like the river itself was cleaning those wounds. Baptizing the man, or what was left of him.

That was the first of the bodies.

TWO

Although DEA Assistant Special Agent in Charge Joe Garrison couldn't see Ciudad Juárez from his window anymore, he knew it was there. In his old office down the hall he'd been able to look right through the thick smoked glass out over that Mexican city every day, and at night could count that unbelievable sprawl of lights that went on for miles and miles. It had been beautiful then, when night fell. *A mirage.* Close enough to touch though it was a whole world away. Although he couldn't blame one city or an entire country for all his problems, he wondered if staring at it the way he had for all these years was no different from being holed up in a muddy trench on the Western Front in World War I.

Juárez was now his personal Verdun or Gallipoli or Passchendaele.

Garrison had become something of a reluctant student of history over his long DEA career, coming to understand the brutal futility of trench warfare. The British had called the whole thing "lions led by donkeys": generals sending off their young soldiers to die in the Western Front.

Was that all he was now, a donkey? An ass? He'd never

wanted to promote from being a group supervisor, from leading agents in the trenches, but he wasn't given much of a choice. He'd been a marked man since that disaster down in Murfee a few years ago, an operation gone wrong that had killed Special Agent Darin Braccio and seriously wounded Darin's young partner, Morgan Emerson. Two of his best agents, and his friends. Although he'd never explicitly sanctioned their investigation in Murfee—Darin hadn't exactly been forthcoming about the true nature of it—he'd been their supervisor, so they were his responsibility and always would be, and he'd suffered through the agency's version of an internal affairs inquiry ever since. It had gone on and on and on, a long shadow darkening everything beneath it, just like the attack on Darin and Morgan. He'd never considered retiring—DEA's unspoken wish all along—figuring instead he'd be terminated. *Failure to effectively supervise.* But the agency had done worse: they'd promoted him instead.

Because of his friends back in D.C., and his long tenure on the border and intimate knowledge of the Mexican cartels operating on both sides of it, Garrison was deemed too valuable to lose. But when all was said and done, he was also too damaged to completely trust.

He'd fucked up, and people had died.

They'd let him keep his badge and gun, but they were never going to let him lead agents in the field again. They'd bridled him.

As they would say over in Juárez, he really was the damn *burro* now.

HE WAS STILL UNPACKING one of his boxes when Special Agent in Charge Don Chesney walked in. Chesney was only three years younger than Garrison but had aged better. The trenches hadn't been kind to the older agent, and he knew it; a lifetime of long surveillances and late nights were visible in his heavy midsection, the gray at his temples, the deep lines carved in his face. Chesney, however, was tall and still thin, his hair dark—perfectly cool and composed in an equally dark, perfect suit he'd had tailored while assigned to Chiang Mai. He'd reported to El Paso directly from headquarters well after the events in Murfee. He'd read about it, read about Garrison, but both were no more than a set of reports to him, thick file folders he'd glanced through a handful of times. He didn't know Garrison, and he sure as hell didn't know the border, either. The city across the river was just another report to him.

It wasn't that Garrison didn't like the man—he hadn't worked with him long enough yet to have an opinion one way or the other—but Chesney had a way of looking at him he didn't like. It was a mixture of sympathy and shame. Embarrassment. The look you reserved for your lonely drunk uncle, or a newly divorced friend who was talking and laughing and crying a bit too fast and loud at the bar, both situations that Garrison understood all too well. Chesney probably saw Garrison as a relic, an unpleasant reminder of all the things that could go wrong on the job or in life. Garrison figured Don Chesney was waiting him out, hoping he'd retire so he could bring someone else in, one of his own men. Someone he trusted. The decision to keep Garrison and promote him had been made above Chesney, and that still rubbed the new SAC raw. No doubt it got under his expensive tailored suit and his skin.

What his look said was: *Sooner or later, you'll make another mistake. You know it, and so do I.*

And that was the look in Chesney's eyes now, as he stood in Garrison's door.

"I was wondering if you were ever going to move up here," Chesney said, in a way that meant he'd never wondered about it at all. Even after getting promoted, Garrison had resisted relocating to the front office. In a way he couldn't explain, he'd been reluctant to let his view of Juárez go. They were old friends, old lovers, older enemies. He'd taken some time off and headed back east, made a thousand smaller excuses about changing offices even before that, and Chesney hadn't pushed him. Most of his duties were merely administrative anyway, overseeing budgets and intel and staffing. It was push-button stuff he could do from anywhere, including home. But if there was one place colder and emptier than his new office, it was there, and both men knew it.

"I'm sorry. I know I've been dragging my ass, but I'm here now." Garrison shrugged, as if he had been traveling for a long time in a place far, far away.

For a second it seemed that Chesney was going to come in and sit down, make some attempt at camaraderie that neither man wanted or felt, but he thought better of it and stayed in the doorway. "Well. I know you've been on leave and have a lot to catch up on." He made a vague gesture at Garrison's bare desk, at the bookshelf free and clear of anything personal: family photos, awards, mementos. "But I was hoping you'd take a look at some of the reporting about those students in Ojinaga. It's a mess down there, and that's an understatement."

Garrison had read about it on the plane back to Texas—a brutal attack on students from a tiny rural school called Librado Rivera in Ojinaga, Chihuahua, Mexico. Three students were confirmed dead, six injured, and nearly two dozen were still missing. *Vanished.* Less than a week old, the attack had already drawn international attention and outrage, and the government of Mexico was in full panic mode. Even the cartels, who'd always been eager and willing to take credit for every single beheading and atrocity, were wiping their hands of it. There was plenty of finger-pointing, leaving the border in turmoil. The Mex Feds, followed closely by worldwide media, had swarmed the Ojinaga area, and the government of Mexico had deployed specialized Mexican Marine units to strike known cartel strongholds in a series of brazen airborne raids. Publicized raids. Everyone was searching for answers, and a scapegoat. Drug and human trafficking on the Texas-Mexico border was a violent and bloody business, but also a very lucrative one, and right now, business was not good for anyone.

"I'll take a look today, draft something for you," Garrison said. The division's field agents and intel shop would already be canvassing their human and signal intelligence—HUMINT and SIGINT—to find their own answers. That meant talking to all their informants, and it wasn't lost on Garrison that the last time he'd been personally involved with cartel border violence, specifically in Ojinaga, it had all gone to hell with the disappearance and ultimate murder of the informant Rodolfo "Rudy" Reynosa, and the subsequent attack on Darin and Morgan.

Ojinaga was right across the river from Murfee, Texas.

Garrison ignored the mostly empty box he'd been sorting through and sat heavily in his new chair. He turned it to face Chesney. "Speaking of drafts, did you have a chance to read what I pulled together about that drug suppression unit operating in Terrell? The Tejas unit?"

Chesney nodded, smoothing out his tie. It looked as expensive as the suit. "I did, but I failed to see your point."

Garrison spread his hands on his desk. It still surprised him that his wedding band was no longer there, as if he were noticing it again for the first time. He wasn't. "Terrell County sheriff Chuy Machado set up the Tejas unit two years ago. It's made up mostly of deputies from his own department, a couple from neighboring Val Verde and Crockett, and a cop or two from Sanderson. Chuy's own son, Johnnie, leads the unit. Their seizure and arrest numbers are impressive."

"They're doing good work," Chesney agreed, still fixated on his tie.

"Don, *no one* is doing work that good. Not a handful of cops way out there in the middle of nowhere."

Chesney finally let his tie go. "Are you implying they're not good enough cops? I checked, and several of them have been through our very own narcotics training classes, right here in the division. Whatever they're doing is exactly what your agents taught them, with equipment we paid for."

"No, what I'm suggesting is maybe a few of them are, in fact, *bad* cops. Straight-up corrupt. The numbers don't add up. Nothing about that unit adds up, and I think . . ."

Chesney held up a hand, stopping him. "Joe, you've been on this border a long time. We all know your history. I get it, this interest, *obsession*, you have with corrupt law enforcement. You lived through it, and at some point in time, we *will* deal with something like it again. We always do. I'm just not sure that time is now."

You lived through it.

Chesney was right, Garrison had lived through the final, bloody days of former Big Bend County sheriff Stanford "Judge" Ross, and his chief deputy, Duane Dupree. He'd survived their reign of terror because he'd been safe and sound here in El Paso, in his office down the hall. Rudy Reynosa and Darin, on the front line down in Murfee, had not. Not even Morgan . . . not really. Not as she'd been.

Everything always came back to goddamn Murfee, Texas.

"You think I'm seeing ghosts?"

Chesney started to answer, but stopped. His eyes, for the second time, said enough.

And Garrison wasn't going to argue, not now. Darin Braccio was dead, but Garrison had seen that ghost a thousand times since. Every time he closed his eyes. He was the only thing haunting Garrison's empty house now.

Chesney continued, "Look, I've met Chuy Machado a

few times. He's colorful, but corrupt? I'm not convinced, not even close. Admittedly, I've never been introduced to that son of his, but nepotism isn't uncommon. Not in a small town, and not in Texas. What does your friend Sheriff Cherry say? I noticed from your own write-up that he doesn't have a deputy assigned to the unit."

That was true. Big Bend County bordered Terrell and was probably three, maybe four times as large, but Sheriff Chris Cherry—taking over from the deceased Stanford Ross—had never shared a deputy with the Tejas unit. Not that he had many to spare to begin with.

"Let's be clear, Chris Cherry is not exactly my friend," Garrison said. And although that was true, too, it was a hell of a lot more complicated than that. Three years' worth of complicated. "But it's curious that the two counties sit side by side and Terrell's seizure stats are easily double what Cherry is reporting from the Big Bend."

"You know as well as I do those numbers are always in flux. Holidays, our own surge operations, a handful of tea leaves the cartels are reading, or some plaza boss who's making a power grab. There are a thousand variables. This week they're pushing hard in one area and next week it's somewhere else. We can't predict that any better than the weather." Chesney checked his watch, and given the suit and tie, Garrison couldn't help wondering just how expensive it was, too. Chesney focused on him again. "Joe, it could just be someone's doing their job really well, and someone else isn't doing it well enough."

That was possible, too, and that was the real fear Garrison still couldn't quite let go of even three years later, long after the corrupt Stanford Ross had been gunned down in Murfee in his own living room. Fear that the corruption hadn't died with the former sheriff or his deputy, Dupree. That it was still running through the county down there like poisoned blood, soaked into the very soil of the place. Buried way down deep. *Bone deep.* Too deep for the young, inexperienced Sheriff Cherry to see, or something he was unwilling to look for.

That's why he and Chris Cherry could never quite be friends.

Chesney glanced at his watch again, and Garrison's audience was over. Chuy and Johnnie Machado and the Tejas unit were Chesney's problems now, if they were problems at all. And although the same should be true for Murfee and the Big Bend, Garrison didn't know how to escape that place. The shadow of everything that had happened there still hung over him. It chased him in his dreams, a horrible creature of black ash and bloody flame. Darin and Morgan had been set on fire, and although Darin was already dead by then, Morgan had burned alive for ten minutes on the banks of the Rio Grande. She'd tried to crawl into the water to put out her own flames.

"I'll review our Ojinaga intel today, and have something on your desk by Wednesday. I'll sit in on some of the informant debriefings myself."

"Your Spanish is that good?"

Garrison nodded. "I've lived here on the border a long time. It's gotten better."

But that's all he would commit to. He didn't want to admit that although he knew the region, the language, and the people as well as anyone working in the division, he still didn't know a damn thing at all.

"Joe, there's one more thing. I got a call from international ops. They want to send FAST out this way this month. Just one team. They're looking to do some environment training. HELO insertions, land nav, that sort of thing. They want it to be as close to the real thing as possible, and I guess that means our little corner of Texas."

As close to the real thing as possible. That meant Afghanistan. DEA's FAST program—foreign-deployed advisory and support teams—had been stood up to run counternarcotics and counterterrorism operations in the Afghanistan theater. It comprised a handful of elite squads—handpicked agents from all over the agency—that trained with Special Forces and rotated through the region and its war-torn provinces. FAST liked to say they used overwhelming firepower in an open-ended legal framework, and with the slow wind-down of U.S. operations over there, the teams were now being deployed in other countries as well. Some questioned the FAST mission statement, not convinced the risk was worth the reward, but Garrison couldn't deny the skill set of the agents involved. Agents who'd worked for him had been chosen for FAST, and they were always some of his best investigators.

They were the lions.

It wasn't lost on him that when they came looking for a place to approximate a blighted war zone, they came to the West Texas border.

"There are some very specific requirements. It needs to

be remote, somewhere people won't get all up in arms over guys in helicopters with guns. They're going to be working with explosives ordnance as well. I'll forward the specifics they sent me. I want you to handle that, okay?"

"No problem. It's done."

Chesney turned to leave. "You already have a place in mind that'll work?"

Garrison nodded. "Yeah, I think I have just the place."

AFTER CHESNEY LEFT, Garrison walked back through the building to his old office to get the last few things. A new group supervisor was taking over his place, some kid who was transferring in from Kentucky or Alabama or Georgia. Somewhere green. He wondered what that kid would think when he stared out at Ciudad Juárez for the first time through his window.

Garrison stood in what used to be his office, remembering the twelve years he'd worked in Texas, a decade of them in this very spot watching the afternoon sun burn shadows into Juárez's streets and alleys across the river, just as he was now. The city's poor *colonias* . . . Anáhuac and Chaveña and Anapra. Other places, even more infamous: Villas de Salvárcar, where, in 2010, fifteen young people were killed during a birthday party for an eighteen-year-old named Jesús Enríquez. Cartel *sicarios* attacked the house and the partygoers, carrying guns that were later alleged to have come from the U.S. in Operation Fast and Furious. And in 2001, Campo Algodonero, the "cotton field"—at the time nothing more than a vacant lot—where the bodies of eight young women were unearthed. It had become a symbol and memorial for the hundreds of women who'd disappeared in the city over the years. It was painted now with pink crosses bearing the names of the original eight women, and sat across the street from a mega-mall and a few streets away from the American consulate.

Finally, Cerro del Cristo Negro. Where the mutilated bodies of three other young women were found after a rainstorm. Allegedly the mother of one of the girls had recognized her daughter's hair exposed on the muddy hillside, and in the wake of the discovery, there were persistent rumors the girls had been killed as part of a satanic rite—the sort of rumors that had always swirled around the Nemesio cartel he'd been hunting for more than a decade.

The same cartel that had been at the heart of Darin and Morgan's investigation.

As Garrison watched, a dark helicopter circled once, twice, and then flew south deeper into Mexico, into parts of the country he'd never visited, had never seen. He'd been told it was truly beautiful over there, beyond Ciudad Juárez; beyond the city reflected over and over in his office window. But this was all he ever saw.

Maybe he'd had it wrong these last couple of years and it wasn't Juárez, or even Mexico, that was the real enemy. He'd only ever had two agents hurt while working on the border, and that had occurred on *this* side of the river. And they hadn't been attacked by faceless cartel *sicarios*, but most likely by a fellow law enforcement officer, Big Bend County Chief Deputy Duane Dupree—acting on the orders of Sheriff Ross—although that had never been conclusively proven.

That was because before Dupree could answer for what he'd done, someone had beheaded him, and then set his body and home on fire, the same way Darin and Morgan had been burned.

Someone who was still out there . . . *a creature of black ash and flame.*

Dupree's home had been far outside Murfee, in a remote corner of the Big Bend, as rugged and unknowable and violent as anywhere Garrison had ever visited.

Yeah, I think I have just the place . . .

It wasn't Ciudad Juárez, Chihuahua, Mexico, that Garrison truly hated.

It was goddamn Texas.

THREE

The goddamn sign was *still* crooked.

Sheriff Chris Cherry stood back and looked at it, hammer in hand, as a thick gust of Texas wind threatened to take his Stetson Brimstone. Deputy Marco Lucero was on the other side, staring into the middle distance past Big Bend Central High School, into a hard blue sky polished with low clouds, but Chris knew the young man was trying hard not to laugh.

He wasn't doing all that good of a job of it.

No matter how Chris tackled the sign, how he tapped down one side or the other, he couldn't get the damn thing straight. Based on his earlier remodeling efforts at the ranch house at the Far Six, both he and Mel knew he wasn't particularly good at anything involving tools, but this was ridiculous. It was just a hammer. *Just a goddamn sign*. But it was like the earth itself was refusing his efforts, pushing him away.

He should take that as some sort of hint.

Frustrated, he finally asked Marco, "What do you think?"

Now serious, his newest deputy cocked his head sideways, the only way to get the sign straight. "Almost there, sir." Marco scratched a freshly shaved chin, uncomfortable, obviously buying himself time to think up something polite to say. He gave up and pointed at the sign. "I think they got the spacing all wrong, though. Your name, I mean. To be honest, sir, it runs all together. Makes it hard to read."

Chris took a step back to get a fresh view of his crooked sign. He'd picked up the signs this morning from the printer and never looked at them too closely. He hadn't wanted to. In fact, he was embarrassed by them, embarrassed by the whole process.

But Marco was right. Mel had chosen the theme and the script for him, colorful and fancy lettering more suited for a movie poster or a carnival banner than a simple sign. It was printed brightly on both sides so that you'd see it coming and going, but it was also most definitely wrong.

RE-ELECT SHERIFF CHRISCHERRY

How many of these signs did he have? Forty, maybe fifty more, all cluttering the back of his Big Bend County truck. Bethel Turner's signs had started springing up all over the county weeks ago. The former Texas Ranger had hundreds of them, as bright and white and numerous as the flowering yucca you could see from the highway. Bethel had pulled them out of some very deep pockets, and they were everywhere now. For Chris to make his right, he'd have to throw them out and start all over again.

Or throw them out and say the hell with it. To make a real run at this election, he should have started weeks ago, too.

He yanked at the sign, pulling it out of the earth that didn't want it.

"Well, Marco, if the folks around here don't know my name by now, I guess I'm not winning this election anyway . . ."

MARCO SILENTLY HELPED HIM get the sign into his truck, unwilling to look Chris in the eye, probably wondering how much longer he'd be his boss. It was the same thing Chris wondered, now more than ever. Marco had been attending college at UTEP until a year ago, when his parents' house had been burned down on the orders of a violent member of the Aryan Brotherhood of Texas named John Wesley Earl. Eight houses went up in flames that night, and many more would have, if the Murfee Fire Department hadn't gotten a helping hand from a summer thunderstorm that had rolled through the area. The fires had only been a diversion, though, nothing more, for other crimes Earl and his sons Jesse and Bass were committing that night. But it was a costly one for Adalia and Jesús Lucero and their younger son, Emiliano—Marco's brother—who was a freshman at Big Bend Central.

The Lucero house was the second to burn.

Adalia worked long hours at the Dollar General, but made it home in time to cook a real meal every night, and Jesús picked up hours at the Comanche cattle auction and the Monument Ranch. They, along with Emiliano, were asleep when the blaze started, and were slow to react. Emiliano's tiny room was next to the kitchen, right where the flames first came through the wall, and he was up and running to the other side of the house to warn his parents when the combined explosions of a big sack of baking flour and two cans of Crisco cooking spray went off in front of him and knocked him off his feet.

His face and hair caught fire, so did his eyes, and although he survived, every doctor said he was never going to see the same again, making it hard—painful, in fact—for him to read. It was like there was a small sun constantly rising and setting in front of his face, the flames that had burned him forever trapped in his ruined eyes.

The fact that Chris later captured Earl, who was ultimately stabbed to death in his bed in the hospital unit of a federal penitentiary, was cold comfort for Emiliano's parents. Even less for Marco, who abandoned school and came back to Murfee to help them rebuild and care for his younger brother.

Marco had left Murfee wanting to be a doctor, but returned that morning after the fire, when the ashes were still black and wet and cooling and everyone could still smell the smoke hanging over the town. Something even the miraculous storm couldn't wash away fast enough.

Later that same day he walked into the department and asked what he needed to do to be a sheriff's deputy.

Chris had liked Marco from the start. He was bright, articulate, with a good head on his shoulders. Had a natural disposition for dealing with people, for disarming them. He'd be a good deputy if he kept at it, but would have made an even better doctor. He *should* have been a doctor. Chris hoped he could talk him into going back to school, where he truly belonged and where he could make a difference.

If any good could come out of him losing this reelection, it might be that.

After wrangling with the sign, Chris caught Marco staring back down the road again at the high school they'd both attended. Big Bend Central sprawled under the blue sky, with Archer-Ross stadium hulking behind it. Chris had played football in that stadium when it was still brand-new, remembering the smell of the freshly painted Raiders logo in the locker room and standing on the artificial turf in his bare feet right after it had been put down. He threw the first touchdown in that stadium, a thirty-yarder to Nat Bulger that Chris had lost in the brand-new Musco lights right after he let it go, never seeing it come down. He only knew what had happened after he heard the crowd yell, chanting his name.

His dad had been there, and Nat Bulger's dad, Matty, cheering as loud as anyone. And Sheriff Stanford Ross.

The last time Chris had actually been inside the stadium was the night of his high school graduation, a decade ago. Although he'd been able to return to Murfee, he couldn't bring himself to go back into that place.

It wasn't long after he came home that he'd discovered skeletal remains out on Matty Bulger's cow pastures, changing his whole life. It could be argued that the lives of everyone around him, everything he touched after, changed that day as well, including Murfee itself. Constantly preying on Chris's mind was the idea that the course of the years since had been forever fixed by that one forsaken moment when he'd knelt down to the exposed skull of DEA informant Rudy Reynosa.

"SHERIFF?" Marco asked, gently. His voice was caught in the wind, nearly taken away by it. Down here below the mountains, unprotected, the wind took a lot of things.

"Sorry," Chris said, closing the tailgate. "I was looking back there at our old school, like you were a moment ago, and at that damn stadium. It's hard to believe, but it seems even bigger to me now."

"Yes, sir. You know, I might start helping out with the boys' basketball team. I played varsity my last three years."

"Is the team any good?"

Marco smiled. "Nah, not so much. They can't be if they asked me to help coach." He leaned against Chris's truck for a moment, wandering his own memories. "You were a pretty good football player, though, right? I used to see all your pictures up in the hall by the front offices, all those awards in that glass case. A big-time quarterback." The deputy looked at Chris closely, like he was trying hard to imagine it. Chris had been much bigger then, weighed maybe fifty pounds more than he did now, but the Big Bend had weathered so much of him away. "They still say the team's never been as good since you graduated."

Chris laughed, shaking his head. "Well, that was a long time ago."

Marco shrugged. "I used to go to all the Friday night games. Trust me, the team did suck, for a long time." He pushed away from the truck with a grin, turning his back to his old school, taking another good long look at the signs stacked in the flatbed. "Are you worried about this?"

"You mean the signs? No, I can get those fixed. Probably get them turned around in a few days."

Marco hesitated. "No, I mean the whole election. I hear people talk . . ."

Chris stopped him, so his deputy wouldn't have to say things he didn't want to. "I do, too. Trust me, I'm fine. Bethel Turner's popular, and he's a good man. He's got lots of experience. Decades of it."

Chris didn't have to add: *Not like me.*

"But he's not you, Sheriff," Marco said. "He's not from Murfee, he didn't grow up here."

"Maybe that's a good thing. Does it matter?"

Marco thought on it. "To me it does, to other folks, too, I think. I guess we'll see." He kicked at the ground with a scuffed boot. He didn't look Chris in the eye. "You think you're going to lose, don't you?"

Chris tossed his hammer into the back with the signs and clapped his deputy on the shoulder, shaking him out of it. "Well, I think it's going to be damn close, and let's leave it at that."

Chris didn't want to tell him that losing might not be a bad thing at all.

THEY WERE ABOUT TO GET INTO CHRIS'S TRUCK when Marco asked him about the baby.

"How's the little one? Keeping you up at night?"

Chris laughed, thinking about his son: John Thomas, nicknamed Jack. The baby had been the center of his world for the past three months. Chris was just about to answer when he saw something over Marco's shoulder: a truck, approaching fast, using up both sides of the highway. Its blue and red wigwags flickering furiously, brighter than the morning sun.

Its emergency sirens would catch up soon.

"Well, he's keeping someone up at night, but it's not me . . ." He let the sentence go, as Marco turned to see what had stolen his attention. The deputy leaned forward, squinting, and asked, "Who is that? Dale, Till?"

At this angle, head-on, Chris couldn't tell which of his deputies it was, either. He realized that all this time standing outside his truck messing with the sign, he and Marco had been ignoring the truck radio, and both his handheld and his cell phone were still in the center console where he'd left them. Someone must have been trying to raise him, and when they couldn't, Miss Maisie had sent out a posse to track him down. She knew he was out here on Route 72 by the school.

It was supposed to have taken only a few minutes.

"What's going on?" Marco asked.

Please not the baby . . . not Mel.

The first wave of the sirens finally reached them, a long echoing wail that Chris hated. He'd hated it for as long as he'd been deputy and then sheriff, and it was one of many things he wouldn't miss when Bethel Turner won the election.

He wouldn't miss it at all.

"Trouble, I guess," Chris said, taking a long breath and opening his door to get his phone, to check his messages. "Looks like trouble."

Because that's what that wail meant.

And it always was.

FOUR

The whole house smelled like dog and baby.

Melissa Bristow could remember when she'd first come to Murfee and how she thought the whole place smelled like cows and shit. She'd hated that smell, hated the town, but that was then—a lifetime ago—and this was now.

A lifetime. That had never been truer since John Thomas "Jack" Cherry had been born.

"John" because she and Chris both liked the name.

"Thomas" for Chris's dad.

And "Jack" just because it fit the baby perfectly.

Everything about him was perfect. The way his gentle skin and wispy hair smelled, and most of all, his pure breath on her face. Like nothing else in the world.

Out here at the Far Six in the wilds of the Big Bend, there were no cows—not anymore—though Ben Harper had once encouraged her and Chris to get some, since a ranch wasn't much of a ranch without them. But with the windows wide open to the morning, there was still the receding sounds of night: the wind-whisper of mesquite and creosote (which had a unique smell all its own after a good hard rain) and breeze-blown ocotillo. The creak of the old rocking chair out on the porch they'd brought from Chris's childhood house, and the breathing of the baby held tight in her arms.

There was Rocky the dog panting and staring up at her, trying to get a good look at Jack as he slept.

Rocky had come in from chasing shadows around the caliche, and smelled of heat and the desert. He always did after a few minutes outside, reminding her of the leather seats in her daddy's old Pontiac after they heated up in the sun—feral, raw, and real. That car, a green or gray Bonneville if she remembered it right, had also often smelled of oil and whiskey: oil beneath her daddy's fingernails from the Permian Basin rigs he worked outside Midland, and whiskey that he liked to drink one fist after another on Friday nights (and pretty much the rest of the weekend, too).

She wondered what he'd think about her and her baby, if he were around to see them both.

Rocky nosed against her knee, his almond-shaped eyes dark, curious. When Jack shifted in her arms, those eyes followed his every tiny movement. Each night, the dog slept as close to them all as he could, relentlessly patrolling the house at any sound. His thick fur was a pure, startling white—the color bred so Hungarian shepherds could distinguish the dog from wolves—and he was Mel's constant shadow. Ben had been worried about her being this far out here alone, so he'd given her the dog for protection, and Rocky had grown big in the months since the older man's passing. The dog would get much bigger before he was done. She missed Ben more than she ever wanted Chris to know, but moments like this, with Rocky watching over her and Jack, it was like the former chief deputy had never left them.

What would he think if he could see them all now, still making a go of it at the Far Six? In the Big Bend?

She bent close to Jack, listening to his heart, breathing him in. She could never do this enough and he amazed her. The idea that she and Chris had somehow created this tiny life, this infinite spark, now the brightest thing in the whole world. She loved Chris in a way that she never knew was possible to love another, but in so many ways it paled compared to what she felt for the baby in her arms; to the great light he gave off that she felt burning on her face when he breathed, and in the heat in her hands every time she held him.

She'd heard stories about the lengths mothers would go to in order to protect their children, and she understood them all now. She'd once held a gun in her hands for Chris—aimed it steady at a man who'd wanted to kill him—and would have pulled the trigger if she'd had to. She would have done that for him, for them both, without a second thought or regret.

She'd pull a thousand triggers for Jack.

No . . . there was nothing Mel wouldn't do to keep safe the baby they'd created together.

SHE LAID JACK DOWN in the bassinet next to their bed, still messy and unmade from the morning, and searched for her phone. She wanted to call Chris and find out how the signs had turned out. He was supposed to pick them up and start putting them around town, and she'd written down for him a list of places she thought would be good. Places where they'd be easily seen, but then again, pretty much everything was easily seen out in the Big Bend and around Murfee itself. Sometimes you could go miles in any direction with only the farthest horizon bounded by mountains. Bethel Turner had been at it for a couple of weeks—his signs were everywhere— and he'd bought out not one but two billboards on I-67 and I-90. Vianey Ruiz had called Mel and said she saw one out on Texas 118 as well. But Chris had been slow to follow suit. In fact, he'd dragged his feet throughout this whole reelection. He'd always blown hot and cold about being the Big Bend County sheriff—a position that had been thrust on him at a time when he didn't feel he had a choice—and that was even truer now that he did have one. Ben Harper's and Buck Emmett's deaths at the hands of the Earls still haunted him, but Jack's birth had affected him just as powerfully. Chris had never been easy to read, had a natural tendency to melancholy and brooding that could overwhelm him, and they'd both dealt with some of the worst of it in the weeks running up to this reelection. So much so that he'd left most of the planning and what fund-raising he'd agreed to do in her hands, and he hadn't even started thinking about the debate that was scheduled at Big Bend Central—a debate that was now a week away. He wouldn't say it exactly, but it was as if he *wanted* to lose. She'd lived through a mood like this with him once before, after he was injured at Baylor and the broken promise of a foot-ball career had brought him limping back home to

Murfee, bringing her along with him. Although they'd both resented being here at first, that was then, and this was now.

And *now* was a whole hell of a lot different. For Chris, for her, and for their new baby.

She didn't know what Chris thought he'd do or where they'd go if they left Murfee . . . if he wasn't the sheriff anymore. Focus on his writing, maybe, although she never knew if he was writing a bunch of short stories or one longer one—something like a whole book. He never talked about it much, other than to say that one day he hoped he might publish something. Writing was his dream though, a dream that had stayed with him through high school and college and his return to the Big Bend.

At least the burden of being the sheriff hadn't killed that.

But without much apology, the only life he'd offered her was the one that she'd gone on to make with him here: working at Earlys, that crappy old bar in town, and Rocky the dog at her feet and Jack the baby in her arms and all of them together in this rickety house at the edge of the Big Bend. At the end of the whole damn world.

It was all she had. It was *their* life, and she now damn sure didn't want another.

And if this was their life, that meant accepting all its ghosts, too. It meant Chris understanding he was never going to completely escape the dark, heavy presence of the man he'd replaced—Sheriff Stanford Ross—or the specters of Ben's and Buck's deaths, which had occurred long after Ross was gone. It was like her daddy's old gray or green Bonneville again—growing up, that damn car had been as much her home as anywhere. Her daddy had driven them all over Texas in it, from Odessa to Galveston, chasing work and fleeing his own demons and ghosts, and yet he was never able to outrace any of them. He couldn't. You couldn't. They were already there waiting for you wherever you ended up, because you carried them with you. *They were part of you.* The best you could do was make your peace with them, with yourself, and get on with your life.

Find a place you could call home, protect it, and let them share it with you.

The Far Six Ranch was her home now. It was the only home Jack had ever known, and she was going to watch her boy grow up here, if she had any say in it.

Maybe that was part of being a mother, too. Not only a fierce protectiveness for your child, but a desire . . . *a need* . . . to have a true place to call home.

For the both of you.

She found her phone and bounced it in her hand before dialing Chris. She looked out the window to the sky and scrub around her, a new sun burning the world alive. It was a view like no place else in the world, and she thought she could see forever from here. Chris had once nearly died right outside that window—shot on the orders of Sheriff Ross—and knowing that had admittedly scared her for a long time . . . all that emptiness and all the possibilities so easily lost within it, stretching endlessly into the unknowable future; the remnants of different lives and different choices left behind. But now she couldn't imagine any other view, any other choice, any other life.

When she'd aimed her own gun that night at Sheriff Ross, ready and willing to kill him for what he'd done to Chris, she'd been protecting all their future choices . . . and the later promise of this view.

Forever was fine, and she wasn't afraid of it anymore.

Rocky was then leaning against her leg, as if he could see out the same window, enjoying the view with her. She could feel the dog's heart beating through his fur. It was strong, steady, constant. Mel bent over and kissed Jack between his closed eyes. He stirred once, safe, just knowing she was there.

It was enough for her.

FIVE

There were five bodies.

Four young men, and the last a teenage boy.

It would be a few days before they could determine exactly how long they had been in the river, and maybe they never would, but it had been long enough. *Demasiado largo.* Too long. America Reynosa had listened closely as Doc Hanson explained to Sheriff Cherry about body temperature and river pH and maceration: where the dead men's skin had absorbed . . . *drank* . . . the river itself. That process had turned their skin milky and opaque so it hung on their bodies in rolls, like a second set of loose-fitting clothes. At least one of them had also been gotten at by a predator, but whether that had been before or after ending up in the water was an open question. Most of them were savaged in some way or another, their faces ruined, except for the boy's. His face was fine, unmarked. His young features were clear and clean; only for that strangely colorless but somehow still pale skin.

It was like he was only sleeping, and someone, maybe his mama, had just brushed wet hair out of his closed eyes.

SHE'D HELPED DALE HOLT bring four telescoping light stands down to the river's edge, where, once night started to fall, they could run them off the department's portable generators. There were also two more farther back up in the yard. Sheriff Cherry had called in a full Department of Public Safety forensic team, but until they arrived, she and Dale Holt and Marco Lucero were responsible for the crime scene that ran from the front of Eddy Rabbit's trailer all the way down to the water's edge. Two months ago, the sheriff had sent her to a weeklong DPS course about homicide investigations and homicide crime scenes. She'd stayed in Austin for the classes, and Danny had come with her the first weekend to show her around, since he'd spent time in the city before. They'd had a good time, but the main draw had been the course itself. She wanted to attend more, to learn as much as she could, although it was far different being in the middle of her own real crime scene rather than reading about one in a classroom. She couldn't help wishing Ben Harper was here with her, helping her know what to do or not do. The last time she'd stood over a dead body this way he'd been at her side, but that had been just one, not five.

Not a young boy.

THE SHERIFF WAS WALKING TOWARD HER, finishing up a phone call. Danny and another deputy, Till Greer, had transported Eddy Rabbit back to Murfee, where they were processing him. The sheriff had stationed his last deputy, Tommy Milford, in his department truck out on Farm Road 170, near the Fort Leaton historic site and at the outer edge of the canyon, ready to help lead the DPS team down to the trailer, which was difficult to find if you didn't know the area. But Dale and Marco were still standing by the water's edge, drawn to the bodies, returning there again and again as if they couldn't stay away. Dale had been a deputy as long as she had (which wasn't saying much), so those weren't the first dead men either of them had seen, but this was all new for Marco. Nothing prepared you for it, not really. Not five raggedy things that were once people floating in shallow, dirty water.

Fat-bodied *moscas* turning in circles above them.

To take Marco's mind off it, she'd had him help her draw maps of the scene, record measurements, and shoot video and still pictures inside the trailer—it's what Ben would have done—although they'd stopped short at searching the trailer itself. The sheriff had decided to wait for the DPS techs to do that. There was no hurry. The bodies weren't going anywhere soon, so neither was America.

It was going to be a long day and a longer night, which was why she'd set up the lights. In a few more hours, once the shadows grew thick as the sun set, she'd turn them on, and she couldn't help wondering what the bodies would look like under their harsh, unforgiving glow.

Would that pale dead boy appear even whiter, even less real?

Or only more?

"YOU KNOW, Dale doesn't like it when you and Marco talk only in Spanish to each other. He thinks you're talking about him," the sheriff said, stopping next to her. He was looking down toward the giant cane and the salt cedar.

"*Lo sé*. And we are. It wouldn't hurt him to learn a few words."

"Yeah, but he's got as much chance of learning Spanish as I do of building a new wing on my house." America couldn't help smiling. The sheriff's struggles with home repairs and renovations had become legendary in the county. "Anyway, just give it a rest, okay? You two will make him paranoid, and the last thing I need is another paranoid man with a gun." He made a vague motion at the canyon around them. "I have plenty of those in this county already."

"*Sí*. I'll try not to talk in my native language anymore."

He looked at her sideways, shaking off a smile of his own. "Don't pull that oppressed minority bullshit with me, Amé. I personally think it's great that you're a smartass in not one but two languages." He grew serious again, turning away from the river. The bodies were downwind, but he could still smell them, like she could. She'd probably still smell them tomorrow and the day after. "I didn't have much of a chance to talk to Danny. Was he okay?"

"He was fine. Ashamed that Eddy Rabbit caught him with that skillet, but he's okay."

"I hate to admit it, but I forgot you all were going to be out here this morning. You know, with the baby, this damn election . . ."

She shrugged. "*No es un problema*. We had it taken care of. We had no idea about *this*. Any of this." She added, "I don't think Eddy did, either, *honestamente*."

Sheriff Cherry nodded. "Danny suggested the same thing before he transported him. Had the feeling that Eddy was just as surprised, just as scared, as anyone."

She agreed. "After the autopsies, I'll still show some pictures of these men to Charity, Eddy's *novia*. Maybe she'll recognize them. Maybe this wasn't the first time they were here."

"But definitely the last. A hard way to end," the sheriff said, now looking past the river, farther south and east to the Chisos Mountains, where they carved the horizon. "I sometimes wonder why our remote corner of Texas is the last thing so many people see. I don't understand that. It seems wrong to me. Seems like it should be too safe, too removed . . . hell, too beautiful, for all this ugliness."

America shrugged again. She'd gotten used to the sheriff and his ideas, *sus esperanzas*—his hopes. She admired him and the way he tried to hold on to them, for himself and his *novia* and his new *bebé*, maybe for her, too. For all his deputies, although he knew better, like she did. Ben Harper had admired that in him, too, even as he'd warned the sheriff right up until the day he died that there was the world the sheriff wanted to believe in, and the world as it truly was—*el mundo real*. Ben had made her promise that she'd never let either of them forget that.

"This place can be beautiful, but it's no different than anywhere else."

"I know," he conceded, without much strength, as if agreeing with her made it all true. He was still watching the mountains, like he was searching for something better in the shadows and sun there.

"El mundo es peligroso," she said. The world is dangerous. "You can die badly anywhere."

SHE WAS ABOUT TO WALK DOWN to the river to check
on Marco and Dale when the sheriff held her back. He
still had his phone in his hand.

"I was just on a call with Joe Garrison, that DEA
agent out of El Paso," he said.

She thought he'd been checking on Melissa and the
bebé, or Danny back in Murfee. She wasn't sure what it
meant that he was talking to the DEA so soon.

"He's heard about this?" she asked, shaking her head.
"Or did you call to tell him?" The sheriff's long-standing
relationship with the DEA agent was difficult, hard to
explain, and the sheriff had admitted to her before that
she and her *familia* were the reason, though her own
relationship with them was just as difficult and just as
hard to explain. Rodolfo, her *hermano*, had been both a
member of the Nemesio cartel and a federal informant,
and either truth alone would have been enough for
Agent Garrison to distrust her. Worse, Rodolfo's involvement with Nemesio and former Sheriff Ross and Duane
Dupree had ended not only with his own death, but with
the death of one of Agent Garrison's agents, and Garrison could never forgive or forget that. And he either
couldn't or wouldn't let the sheriff forget that, or that
one of America's *tíos*—her mama's own *hermano*, a man
she knew only as Fox Uno—still had ties to Nemesio.

That meant by birth, by blood—*por la sangre*—
America did as well. And to the agent, that meant she

probably had plenty of blood on her own hands, too, even if she now wore a badge.

On this, Agent Garrison wasn't so wrong.

"No, he didn't know about this," the sheriff said. "I mean, he does now, but I didn't call him. You know me better than that. He reached out to me about something else, although he didn't get into it on the phone. He's coming out here, and no matter what's on his mind, he'll no doubt circle back to what's going on over there." The sheriff pointed with his phone south, over the river. "You've read the same stuff I have. It's a mess right now. All those students that were attacked? It's like it was before, Amé, and those bodies in the water mean that craziness and violence over there is only spreading. It always does, right? It's like a sickness, or a goddamn fire. Burning its way to our backyard again."

It's like it was before . . . like the way it was with Rodolfo and with Garrison's agents. With Sheriff Ross and that *pendejo*, Dupree.

The boy *sicario*, Máximo, who Fox Uno sent to Murfee—to her—from his *rancho* across the river.

Two silver *pistolas*—unwanted gifts, terrible promises—for her and her *hermano*.

And finally, Caleb Ross—Sheriff Ross's son—who'd loved her once, but fled Murfee's secrets after the sheriff's death.

These were all *her* secrets, and Sheriff Cherry knew most of them; all but *la pistola* she kept hidden in her apartment. She had never asked the sheriff to carry them for her, but he would, and he would never reveal them to Agent Garrison. That was the sort of man he was.

"Do you think he's coming here to talk about me?"

The sheriff turned to face her. "Probably. That's usually the way it is. *Él no te quiere.* And he doesn't know you the way I do." He tried a smile.

"You've been practicing," she said.

The sheriff held on to the smile, like it was the most important thing in the world, holding on to it just for her. Wanting her to believe that he didn't care about Garrison and his concerns and never would. "Yeah, I have. You know, if I win reelection, I think I should be able to speak the language. Mel looked up the percentage of households here that speak Spanish daily. More than half this county is Hispanic. I hope they're voters." He didn't say it as if he was convinced. "And even if I don't win, at least I'll know what you and Marco have been saying about *me* all this time."

"I saw the signs in the back of your truck."

"Yeah." He laughed. "They didn't turn out quite right. Not the way I thought they would."

"*¿Qué vas a hacer?*" she asked, testing the Spanish she knew he'd been practicing.

He looked toward the invisible river, hidden by the cane and salt cedar. You could only tell where the bodies were by the yellow tape she'd put out and the sunlight gleaming on the light stands. "Well, I'm going to burn them I guess, and then decide how to start over."

They stood silent together, listening to the wind move. The handheld radio on the sheriff's belt crackled, breaking the silence, coming to sudden life. It was Tommy Milford relaying that he'd heard from DPS. They were still a couple of hours away, but Doc Hanson, the county's ME, had just passed him on his way to the trailer.

Finally, she said, "I don't know anything about this, or what's going on over the river. Not then and not now."

The sheriff nodded, putting a gentle hand on her shoulder. "I know, Amé, I've always known that. You don't have to say it, and I wasn't going to ask. I just wanted you to know he's coming."

"*Bueno*," she said. "So he really doesn't like me?"

"I'd say it's more a matter of him not quite trusting you." And the way the sheriff said it, he almost made it sound like there was a difference. "But I do. I trust you with my life, and *you* know that. Honestly, he probably doesn't trust any of us out here, including me. There's not a hell of a lot I can do to change his mind, so I don't try. Not that hard, anyway." He looked like he was going to say more, but instead he nodded to himself, and started walking back around to the front of the trailer, to meet Doc Hanson.

Before he rounded the corner, he turned back to her one more time.

"But whatever reason has got him coming out here tomorrow must really be bothering him. No matter what he thinks about you, or me, he truly hates this place."

SIX

CHAYO & NEVA

Neva would never be pretty again, but she was still beautiful.

For one whole day, Chayo cradled her face, talking in her ear. She cried most of that time, from both pain and fear.

He held her tight and her heart beat fast against him, fluttering like one of the small swallows that circled the fields at Librado Rivera.

She cried even more when he went to stitch her smile back together.

She couldn't speak, but she didn't have to. Her eyes said everything.

Neither of them knew if she'd ever smile again.

THEY HAD RUN, Chayo using his body to protect her, but a bullet had caught her across the face anyway.

It ricocheted off a light pole first, probably saving her life. But it still carved an ugly, ragged path from the corner of her mouth to her left ear, spinning her around and knocking her off her feet. Another bullet struck the same light pole, tossing tiny sparks, and even as Chayo waited for a third and final bullet to take him, he picked Neva up to carry her the rest of the way through the night . . . onward toward dawn.

Her blood soaked his shirt, hot and thick against his skin. It was precious and he wanted to save it all.

By then, other *normalistas* were running, too. His friends. All the boys he knew. There were more sounds of gunfire, of screaming. Dogs barking. The deep rumble of truck engines.

He called for help, kicked on doors.

But he never stopped, and never looked back.

MORE THAN A DOZEN BLOCKS AWAY an older couple took them in. They lived above their small candy store, Dulcería La Bonita, and Neva bled all over their tile floor. All the candy wrappers beneath the glass were impossibly bright, but none as bright as Neva's blood. The old woman, Carmelita, wiped it all up with an apron, while her husband, the even older Amador—who reminded Chayo of Naranja—pulled the metal shutters over the storefront windows.

They all carried Neva upstairs in darkness, in silence.

So it had only been by candlelight that Chayo had finally gotten a look at her face.

THE STITCHES WERE FRESH so she still couldn't talk, but they could watch Carmelita and Amador's tiny television.

For three days, they did.

They saw the pictures from the morning after, the

bodies and the blood still on the street, the piles of clothes and broken glass.

The rocks that some of the fleeing *normalistas* had thrown, and that others had used to mark where bullet casings littered the ground.

One report said that one hundred shell casings had been found. Another claimed it was more than two hundred.

Six *normalistas* had been admitted to the hospital, three more were dead. The rest were missing.

In the day right after the attack, some people claimed they'd seen the surviving students herded together and hooded, driven away in municipal trucks.

A day later, no one admitted to seeing anything.

One *periódico* claimed it had been shown a text from one of the *normalistas* who had disappeared:

HELP ME NOW I AM DYING

AMADOR SAID THE ATTACK was the work of the mayor and his wife, who'd always been associated with the narcos. The mayor had started off as a simple street vendor, selling watches from the United States, and his wife had won a small local beauty pageant, years ago. They were royalty in Ojinaga now, owning several stores there and a second *casa* in Lomas de Chapultepec, in Mexico City. Carmelita was less sure, but to Chayo it made no difference who'd attacked the buses, or why.

None of that would return Castel or his other friends.

None of that would give Neva back her smile.

———————

FOUR DAYS AFTER THE ATTACK, a picture appeared online first, and then was picked up by all the news.

It was everywhere, inescapable.

It showed a boy on a pile of garbage, half buried in mud. His clothes were pulled up, torn off in some places, and deep cigarette burns tattooed his chest and stomach. There were purple bruises around his throat, and his hands and feet had been severed.

There was a tennis shoe soaked in blood sitting empty and upright by an outstretched, handless arm.

His face had been peeled off, removed. His *ojos* had been taken as well, scooped out, and his ears were gone.

He'd been tortured and mutilated and thrown in a trash heap on the outskirts of Ojinaga.

He was faceless, nameless.

But he had the distinctive shaved head of a *normalista* from the Escuela Normal Rural Librado Rivera.

IN THE HOURS AND DAYS immediately following the attack, a few of the *normalistas* who'd survived came out of hiding, and it seemed that everyone in the world was still looking for the others. But after that picture, no one else returned.

The final number of students who'd disappeared was nineteen.

But not all who survived came out of hiding. Not Chayo. He recognized the tortured boy in the photograph, the tennis shoes and the ruined clothes.

He didn't need the missing face to know it was Batista.

SHE COULDN'T SPEAK, but she didn't have to.

Neva wasn't crying anymore, but lay still and silent on the small bed Carmelita had made up for her. The old woman brought tortillas for him and soup and water for her, but Neva wanted none of it.

She just stared into the darkness, seeing and unseeing, and let Chayo hold her.

Amador moved their one tiny TV in for them to watch, alone, but Chayo only searched for American shows, like the ones Neva had talked about before. They lay there together in the TV's faint glow, let it flicker over them like the light of faraway stars, and he whispered to her for hours. Stories about growing up in Blanco and fishing with his papa, and the smell of blood from a newly birthed calf; how it was always his job to help the animal stand on its spindly legs, and the sound of its first live breaths against his chest.

Eating fresh *zarca*, pulling it apart with his fingers beneath a midday sun, and the way the juice stained his fingers for days.

Drinking from a well his uncle had dug, how the water from it was always so cold and came from a deep part of the earth that no one had ever seen. He had believed there was something magical about it and maybe there was.

Smelling the stew his mama would make from *xoconostle* peels that was sweet and sour and burned all the way down his throat.

When Neva had first walked up to the bus—smiling, laughing—he'd thought to himself that he'd carry her all the way to Chihuahua City and back, to be with her. And although he'd carried her through the streets to safety, until his arms and his legs and his heart had nearly given out, he understood now that he still hadn't carried her far enough.

He had many, many more miles to go.

All the while he was telling her stories, he was also watching the TV; all those bright and beautiful images of another world, another place. Somewhere safe, where she'd always wanted to be.

He left their darkened room long enough to talk to Amador, to explain what he wanted to do, and ask Amador if he could help him. There were a few things he needed, and although he'd already asked too much of the couple, and probably put them both in danger, there was no one else.

There was no other way.

Amador sat silent for a long, long time, before finally nodding.

When he told Carmelita what Chayo was planning, the old woman started to cry.

CHAYO HELD NEVA'S HAND in his own and told her one final story.

About a boy and a beautiful girl and a long, hard journey. But the girl didn't have to worry, the boy would carry her the whole way if he had to.

Neva couldn't speak, but she didn't have to, either.

Her eyes said everything, and Chayo understood.

SEVEN

America was exhausted, mentally and physically, but she couldn't leave the bodies behind, so she accompanied them up to the Hancock Hill Medical Center.

She'd imagined how hard it was for Marco Lucero to see his first corpses floating in the river, but even she wasn't prepared to see them spread out on those metal tables in neat, cold rows in the morgue, their wounds stark and ugly and bloodless.

As awful as they had appeared in the water, they looked barely real now.

She stood at the swinging doors a long time, unsure if she could go in.

"There's no reason for you to stay for this," Texas DPS crime scene technician Ron Delaney said, standing too close to her. Ron had taught one of her classes in Austin, and they'd both been surprised to find each other again on the banks of the Rio Grande in the Big Bend. After Doc Hanson had officially signed off on the bodies, it had been left to CST Delaney to coordinate the evidence collection and recovery of them on scene, and he'd gone out of his way to allow America to watch him work, carefully explaining in clipped sentences everything he did. He was a tall man, with thinning hair and an unfortu-

nate mustache, and other than the obvious habit of trying to hide his thick silver wedding ring, she liked him.
He'd been gentle with the dead, *paciente* was the word
that came to America's mind—almost reverent—as the
hours had worn on and they'd had to work in the mud
under the hot glow of the light stands. He never sped up
or took a long break, giving each one his full attention.

Danny had been there, too, for a while, helping her and
Delaney and the other technicians. He didn't have the
same interest in forensics that she did, but he'd wanted to
be there with her all the same. Then he got called out again
to a fight at Mancha's, a place she knew all too well, and he
and Till Greer had ended up wrangling three drunks, two
broken car windows, and one stabbing. Other than the
occasional text message, she hadn't seen him since.

It had been a hard twenty-four hours for both of them.

"Look, I don't think your ME is in any hurry, to be
honest. I know there's another pathologist on the way to
help with this, but they're not going to get started on the
postmortem for another couple of hours." Delaney
turned the ring on his finger—it was a lot harder to hide
when it wasn't covered by the blue nitrile gloves they'd
both worn at the scene—and checked his watch. It was
gold-colored and big, with green digital numbers, and
she could read the time: 5:00 a.m. She had been out at
Eddy Rabbit's trailer all night. "So, you know, you
should go home, too, get some sleep. I can call you if it's
anything important," Ron said, a little too hopefully.

"No, it's fine. I think I'll wait here. I couldn't sleep
now anyway."

"Are you sure about that?"

"*Sí.*"

Delaney turned his ring again, then gave up on it. He was covered in the same dry river mud as she was, and was just as tired. The lights in the morgue were far too bright, too demanding. He squinted beneath them, looking at her. "You've never attended one of these postmortems?"

"No. But I think I should. At least once. I think it's important, and I don't even know why."

He smiled, thin, barely there. He rubbed at some mud on his shirt as if he could make it go away, only making it worse. "Because you want answers. You want to understand. But even with all the tests and exams, they never *say* anything, you know?" He motioned at the bodies. "Not anything that matters. It's impossible to ever understand how they end up here, how they end up this way. I've done this for ten years, and I never have. Trust me, *once* will be enough."

"I hope so," she said, trying not to stare at the pale, smooth face of the young boy who now, for some reason, reminded her of Caleb Ross.

But she hadn't seen Caleb in five years. She had no idea what he looked like now, how he might have changed.

Ron looked away, embarrassed. "Hey, look, I'm sorry about this . . . I'm worn-out. Five bodies at one time, it's a lot to take in. That was a tough scene." Then he added, "But you know, they're all tough in their own way."

"No, it's fine. It really is. *Entiendo.*"

Ron stared down at his boots, still embarrassed. "Well, since I can't offer you any answers, how about some coffee down in the cafeteria?" He tried a smile, still awkward, but at least genuine. "We got some time to kill . . . if you know what I mean." He watched her, waiting for her to laugh. "Yeah, that's an old CST joke. Gallows humor. Most folks find it funny. Kills 'em every time."

America smiled back, letting him know that it was all okay. "Sure, that sounds good."

THE PATHOLOGIST STARTED with a complete external examination of each body, talking quickly into the hanging microphone above his head, noting the old scars and faded tattoos and the variety of damage that had been inflicted on the dead: bullet wounds, sharp vertical slashes attributed to a heavy-edged weapon—something like a machete or large knife—and then the work of the weather and the river and the predators that prowled its banks.

Pictures were taken, a camera clicking away.

The internal exam started with a Y-shaped incision at the shoulders, meeting at the sternum and working down to the pubic bone. Mottled skin was pulled back and separated to reveal glossy ribs and a distended stomach. The entire whiteness of the rib cage was removed to get to the neck and chest organs, which were taken out and weighed and examined.

Trachea. Thyroid gland. Parathyroid glands. Esophagus. Lungs. Thoracic aorta.

Heart. *Corazón.*

Each heart looked far too small to have beat within the body that held it, and tidal blood washed down the tables, disappearing into metal drains.

The blood was red and then black in the cold air.

Bullets and metal fragments were pulled into the light, washed with water, and set aside, gleaming in the hard, unforgiving light.

After that, the abdominal muscles were dissected and separated: intestines, liver, gallbladder, kidney, reproductive organs.

When these things were cut free they appeared colorless, faded, and discarded beneath the overhead lights, as each body was turned inside out and put on display.

Finally, the pathologist moved to the scalp, cutting it away from the skull and pulling it forward.

When the young boy's face was removed, America had to turn away, run from the room, realizing then that she'd been wrong—he didn't look so much like Caleb anymore, but rather Rodolfo, as she remembered him from when she was a little girl.

Ron Delaney, though, had been right all along. *This* boy, naked and exposed and carved open, was never going to say anything again.

And seeing it all once was enough.

DELANEY CAUGHT UP WITH HER OUTSIDE, standing in the parking lot. She hadn't smoked in a long time, but thought she could use a cigarette now.

"Hey, it's okay. It's hard. It still is for me." This time, Delaney kept a respectful distance. "You won't see a full report for another few days, but it's pretty obvious what happened. Someone shot and stabbed those men and dumped their bodies in the river. At least two someones, maybe more, although there's no way we'll know until we get ballistics and all that. We didn't recover any shell casings last night where we found the bodies, but I think it's worth a second look. No guns in the trailer, either, but that doesn't mean anything. Those fibers we recovered from their clothes might match the burlap in the kitchen, we'll see. Then there are those radios . . . My guess is they were muling drugs across the river, and somehow crossed the wrong people."

"I'll need the photographs of the faces. To see if Eddy Rabbit's girlfriend recognizes them, or he does."

"I'll make sure you get those." Delaney hesitated. "And if you want my official opinion about the report, or want to talk about the results or anything, just call me." He fished around in his wallet and found a card, gave it to her. As she read it, he raised his hands. "Promise, all business. The state prints those things out. I don't get a chance to use them too often. No one ever seems to want them. Not many repeat customers." Another one of his bad jokes.

"*Gracias.* I do appreciate your help."

"No problemo . . . and that's the only Spanish I know."

"That's not even real Spanish," she said, but did so with a smile. She was beginning to appreciate Delaney's quiet competence and horrible sense of humor. He'd called it "gallows humor," and although she didn't know the English phrase, she understood well enough. Delaney's attitude reminded her—painfully—of Ben Harper. She would never ask, but she wondered about Delaney's wife, or if he had children. What were they doing on a sunny morning like this?

He took a deep breath, like he was clearing his head of his own thoughts. Maybe he'd been reading hers from a moment before, because he reached into his coat pocket and took out a crumpled pack of Marlboros and a blue plastic lighter. He lit one, offering it to her first, but after a long pause she shook her head.

"I knew you were smart," he said, drawing hard and then blowing smoke skyward. "These things will kill you."

He studied the end of the cigarette, watching it burn. "I saw you really looking at the one decedent, the boy. Like I said, it doesn't get any easier, you know? I kind of thought it would, but it doesn't. Particularly when you see a kid laid out like that. He was what, seventeen, eighteen? He was probably following an older brother or dad or uncle, trying to be a man. What a damn waste."

Just like Rodolfo, she thought.

He drew hard again on the cigarette. "It's not supposed to, I guess. When it does, it'll be time for me to find a new line of work."

"Not supposed to what?" she asked, putting his card away, and reaching over and taking the cigarette from his fingers. It helped keep her hand steady as she put it to her lips.

Delaney looked up into the sky, his hands now in his pockets, watching their shared smoke chase itself and fade into nothing. "Get any easier, Deputy Reynosa. It never gets easier at all."

EIGHT

Garrison arrived late in the afternoon, having driven all the way down from El Paso. He'd gotten lost twice, and Chris was standing on his porch waiting for him, drinking his second beer, when he finally pulled down the long gravel drive. Chris had been reluctant to invite Garrison out to the Far Six—it had already been a long forty-eight hours, and he'd always hoped to keep his work and home separate, even after realizing no such separation could exist—but Mel had agreed it was better than anywhere in town, or worse, the department. Chris's deputies, Tommy Milford more than the others, liked to talk shop with anyone who'd pull up a stool at Earlys or the Hamilton (except for Amé, who hardly talked to anyone). The agent's presence in Murfee would fuel even more stories than those already being shopped around since the discovery on the river yesterday, though Chris had made no official announcement about it, and had asked the local media to hold it close for another day or so.

Chris wasn't ready to answer official questions from the *Daily* about Garrison or Eddy Rabbit or anything else.

He didn't have any answers.

It had been about a year since he'd last seen Garrison in person, when they'd met in that cemetery in El Paso and he'd talked to the agent about the Earls. Garrison hadn't looked great then, and getting out of his dust-covered car, Chris hated to see that he looked worse now. He'd picked up more weight and his hair had gotten grayer. He'd grown a beard, and it hugged his face in a salt-and-pepper shadow. He was carrying a folder and wore tan slacks and a collared shirt with the sleeves rolled up, but no coat and tie, and his duty weapon was settled on his hip in a scuffed paddle holster. Everything about him looked heavier—those clothes, that gun—as if he were carrying a great burden. He even came up the porch steps slowly, stopping to take in the view, shaking his head.

"Jesus, you're way out here." He got to the top of the steps and extended a hand, and Chris was glad to find that at least his grip was still strong. *Determined.* "Is this where you found Rudy Ray . . . Rodolfo?"

Chris finished the last of his beer and set the bottle on the porch rail. "No, that was over there, near Indian Bluffs." He pointed east to a mesa purpled by the late-afternoon sunlight, a shadow of a shadow. "This is where Duane Dupree and I met that plane."

"The plane . . . you mean where you were shot?" Garrison said. "Damn near killed?"

"Yeah, damn near that."

Garrison looked back and forth across the scrub, taking it all in. He scanned it as if he were searching for something: something hidden, something he'd forgotten. An explanation, maybe, although Chris knew there wasn't one out there. "It all looks the same to me, Chris. I don't know how you keep from getting lost out here."

Chris nodded. "Sometimes, I don't either. Let me get you a beer, and you can meet Melissa and Jack."

MEL HAD INSISTED ON DINNER, so she was putting together a salad and working on some black beans when Chris brought Garrison in. Chris was going to grill steaks to serve over the beans, along with a homemade chimichurri sauce Mel had picked up from Vianey Ruiz. Barely three months after giving birth to Jack, Mel still had the beautiful, tired . . . exhausted . . . look of a new mother, but she'd insisted on playing the good host, even to a man she wasn't sure she liked. She had seen Garrison maybe once at the hospital after Chris's shooting, but that was several years ago, and they'd never spoken. All she knew about him was whatever Chris had said, and since Chris's own opinion had waxed and waned, he had been reluctant to have her go out of her way. But she greeted Garrison warmly, without a hint of reservation. She took his folder and replaced it with a cold Rahr, and said that Jack was still asleep, but would be up soon. She told Chris to get the steaks on the grill, and that whatever they needed to talk about could be done just as well, and probably better, on a full stomach.

Garrison smiled, agreed, and took a long drink of his beer, as Rocky sat on the floor at Mel's feet and looked up at everyone.

CHRIS DID THE STEAKS MEDIUM-RARE, the way everyone wanted, and they sat in the kitchen and ate them with the windows open so they could watch the sun roll lower and smell the creosote and the sweet acacia. Mel finished first and brought Jack in and showed him off, and as Chris held his son, Garrison said he looked big and might grow up to be a football player, like his dad. Mel asked if Garrison had children of his own— carefully avoiding the question of whether he was married, something Chris didn't know—and Garrison said that he had two daughters, Angie and Megan. Angie was a freshman at Juniata in Pennsylvania who hoped to be a doctor someday, and Megan was a senior in high school, also back east. She was a field hockey player, and pretty damn good.

He admitted he didn't get to see enough of her games, but she sent him plenty of videos. He hoped maybe she'd consider University of Texas at Austin, or maybe Chris and Mel's alma mater, Baylor, but so far none of the schools she was interested in were this far west.

Garrison then asked for another beer, and Mel went to get him one.

After dinner, Mel stayed inside with Jack, and Garrison and Chris went out to the front porch, where they'd started. Chris brought out an ice-choked bucket of Rahrs, and Garrison brought his folder, still unopened, and settled into a chair, as Chris fished out a beer for each of them. Mel had told Garrison there was room enough for him to spend the night, but the agent had insisted he had a room back in Valentine. That was a long drive, but he had meetings all the next day, and it wasn't as long as going all the way back to El Paso.

Chris got the impression that Garrison had slipped

out of El Paso quickly to come see him, maybe without telling anyone that he was coming to Murfee.

It also wasn't lost on Chris that Darin Braccio's and Morgan Emerson's burned bodies had been recovered outside Valentine.

THE TWO MEN DRANK their beers silently.

The sun wasn't yet down, and long shadows were still gathered on the ground where cenizo and Texas mountain laurel ran into the distance. Over time Chris had learned to pick out the tall spikes of spice lily, the dark brown of chocolate flowers, and even the trumpet shape of sacred datura—jimsonweed—that opened its flowers only at night for hawk moths. Chris had spent nights watching Rocky chase the hand-sized moths drawn to its pale white flowers under the glow of the house's security lights.

As with his Spanish lessons, Chris had made it a point to learn about this place. He wasn't sure he'd ever *know* it, truly understand it, but for as long as he was here, he had to try.

"It's quiet here. I don't know if that would drive me crazy or not," Garrison said. "But I can see the beauty."

"It takes some getting used to," Chris conceded.

"And have you? Gotten used to it?"

"I don't know. Some days . . ." Chris shrugged. "It's weird. I think Mel has taken to it faster than I have, more than I ever would have guessed. She despised Murfee so much when we first got here, and now . . ."

"She seems like a good woman." Garrison laughed. "Tough."

"Better than I deserve," Chris said.

Garrison raised his beer, a lonely toast. "Well, Sheriff, on that we can agree. I'm glad you said it so I didn't have to."

GARRISON TOLD CHRIS about DEA's FAST program, and how they were looking for a place to get some specialized training done. It'd be a week, tops, and Garrison was hoping they could use the outskirts of Murfee, and Chris agreed—he had no problem with that. Better, he could talk to Terry Macrae over at Tres Rios and see about them setting up shop there. Macrae might let them use some of his currently empty bunkhouses, so they wouldn't have to stay in town at all. It would be ranch-hand living—rough—but Chris imagined it had to be better than whatever accommodations they'd gotten used to in Afghanistan. Chris had talked to Danny a few times about his military tours over there, and had a hard time picturing anyone investigating, well, *anything*, in a place like that.

When he asked Garrison what an agent could truly accomplish in a war zone, Garrison said he didn't know, either.

"HOW'S DANNY FORD DOING? Has he made the successful transition to small-town deputy?" Garrison asked.

"He's fine. I wasn't sure about it at first, but after everything that happened with the Earls, he wasn't going to leave Murfee anyway, so at least some good came out of him staying. He felt responsible for Ben Harper's death, I think."

"I went to Harper's funeral," Garrison said.

"I didn't see you there," Chris said, legitimately surprised.

"No, I didn't want to intrude. You were there with your other deputies, and with Melissa. It wasn't my place, but I wanted to be there."

"I appreciate that. I never got a chance to go to Darin Braccio's memorial. Sheriff Ross did, on behalf of the department." Chris spun a beer bottle in his hands. "Anyway, if Danny was responsible for Ben's death, then I guess I was, too. But I don't think that was exactly all of it, even if he didn't say it then, or now. Danny was always going to stick around because of America."

Garrison paused, then: "Are they a thing?"

"Well, that's hard to say. They spend time together, I guess, but they don't talk about it, and I don't ask. On duty, they're all business, and that's what matters."

Garrison stood, searching for another beer in the ice. He leaned against the porch rail, with stars just turning on in the east; one at a time, a rising glow coloring the horizon. "Speaking of business, what do you think of Chuy Machado?"

"The sheriff over in Terrell? Nothing. We talk every now and then."

"Do you ever talk about his Tejas unit?"

"I know about it. It's another one of those task forces you Feds are so fond of. He offered a spot to one of my deputies. I turned him down."

"Why?"

"Because I'm not in the drug interdiction and investigation business. Particularly not in another county. You know that. That's what you do."

"C'mon, Chris, that's not exactly true. You know that better than anyone."

Chris set his empty beer down. He was done drinking for the night. If Garrison had come to the Far Six to talk about Chuy Machado, or Chris's stance on drug trafficking in the Big Bend, it had been a long drive for a very short conversation. "What I do know is that I have a handful of deputies who have enough to do just keeping *this* county policed, all ten thousand acres of it. I'm not going to waste one by shipping him off to chase drug smugglers an entire county away." What Chris wanted to say was that he wasn't going to *risk* one of them, not for that. "If we catch them here, we handle it."

"Sheriff Machado's Tejas unit has been catching a lot of them lately."

"And we're not?"

Garrison raised his hands. "Put the guns away, Chris. I'm just curious what Chuy Machado is up to. Specifically, his son Johnnie, who runs the unit."

Chris paused, trying to read Garrison's face in the retreating light. "Is this where you tell me you've been hearing things again? That you think this is like our situation with Sheriff Ross?"

Garrison hesitated, and Chris knew that both of them could agree that no situation, that *no one*, was exactly like the former sheriff. Garrison shrugged. "Possibly. I don't know . . ."

"Sounds to me like Chuy's deputies are doing their

job, and doing it well, if that's what you think the job should be."

Garrison tapped his bottle against the porch's railing, a sound that sent faint echoes across the scrub. "Would you consider putting Danny in bed with them for a while?"

"Why?"

"You told me what he did with the Earls, then all that undercover work he did before that for DPS. He's a natural, and . . ."

"And I'm not asking him to do that again. Not like that, not ever. I'm not helping you run any sort of operation, undercover or otherwise, against another sheriff. I told you I'm out of that business, for good."

"You can say that, Chris, and tell yourself you believe it, but that doesn't make it true. It can't be true. Look at what you found floating in your river yesterday morning."

"And look at how your last operation down here turned out. How's Morgan Emerson doing?" In the gloom, Chris could see Garrison's jaw clench, hard, and the sudden darker cast to eyes that were only focused on him. It was a horrible, shitty thing to say. "I didn't mean that. That was over the line, way over the line, and I'm sorry."

"No, you said it *exactly* because you meant it. I get it, I do, and that's the one thing you are damn right about. It didn't turn out well for anyone. What a goddamn mess." Garrison pointed his beer bottle at Chris. "And we're never going to escape it, you and I . . . *ever*. I don't know how, and I'm not sure I even want to anymore. It defines us. There is no 'us' without it." Garrison paused, took a breath. "But to answer your question, Morgan's doing okay. She's still back home, with family. It's where she should be."

Chris let a long silence settle, let the sparks between them blow out before he said something to flare them again. He wanted to rewind the conversation a few minutes . . . a few years. "Anyway, there's already history between Johnnie Machado and Danny. They had some sort of run-in at one point, up in Crockett. I don't know the details. Danny's had run-ins with all sorts of people. He's got one damn gear, full-speed ahead, whether people get out of his way or not. I can ask him about it if you want, but I won't have him tangling with this Tejas unit."

"Forget it, I'll let it go. But that wasn't the only reason I wanted to talk to you."

Chris sighed, and then despite what he'd decided only moments ago, got himself the last beer out of the bucket. He opened it and steeled himself with a long drink.

"Yeah, I didn't think so. I didn't think so at all . . ."

NINE

Danny watched her sleep.

The slow, rhythmic rise and fall of her chest.

Her gently closed eyes.

It seemed like right now, sleeping was the only time she was ever truly peaceful, relaxed.

Dreaming?

There was always far too much going on behind those eyes when they were open.

And he had no idea what was going on behind them when they were closed, either.

DANNY GOT UP QUIETLY from the couch, so as to not wake Amé, and went to get himself a beer out of her fridge. She'd finally come in a while ago, muddy and exhausted from the nearly forty-eight hours straight she'd been awake and working. He hadn't seen her at all during the day, since she'd been at the autopsies at Hancock Hill and he'd been dealing with Eddy's initial appearance and the drunken altercation at Mancha's.

There was still plenty more work to be done at Eddy's trailer, but at least the bodies were gone, and the rest of it could take its time.

There was no hurry. Eddy wasn't going anywhere for a while, and those five dead men would keep. After a long, hot shower, before drifting off to sleep, Amé had said they'd start getting the forensic returns soon. Maybe sooner than expected, since one of the DPS techs who'd come out to the canyon was the same one who'd taught a class at that training in Austin. His name had been Ron, Don, something like that, and he'd clearly remembered Amé. That didn't surprise Danny, since she was pretty damn memorable, after all.

Before getting called back to town to deal with that clusterfuck at Mancha's, Danny had been at the trailer long enough to watch Ron or Don follow Amé all around. Danny had recognized that look, the way he watched her. The way he asked questions he knew the answers to just to hear her talk. Danny knew all about that, too.

Been there, done that. He just hoped that with all his fumbling around, Ron or Don actually got some real work done, more than what he'd discovered with the radios, though Danny had to give him credit for that. The issue with the radios was going to be a long conversation with Eddy and his court-appointed lawyer, Santino Paez. A very long conversation.

Danny wondered if Ron or Don found the time to ask her out when they were pulling the bodies out of the river.

Danny put the cool beer against his forehead, caught a glance of his shirtless torso in the small apartment's even smaller window. They weren't visible in the ghostly image reflected in the glass, but the wounds he'd received out at the Murfee Lights were still there: pale crosses on his skin. Wounds he got the night Ben Harper had died, and he and Amé had carried his body out of the desert.

In the moments before he was killed, Ben had given Amé his old Saint Michael pendant—Michael was the patron saint of cops—and she still wore it, every day. He never saw her without it. Danny had his scars from that night, and she had that necklace.

That was probably the heart of it . . . Ben's death. The deputy had been Amé's friend, her mentor, and it was his murder that had drawn her and Danny together. Ben had been killed by that piece of shit Jesse Earl way out by the Murfee Lights—trying to save Danny's life—and during Danny and Amé's long walk back to town together carrying his body, they had talked. Or Danny had talked, sharing secrets with her he hadn't spoken out loud for years. She'd listened, never judging, and somehow, out of all those horrible hours, they'd discovered something about each other. *They'd found each other out there.* But it also meant a part of their relationship might always stay in that place, far beyond the Murfee Lights.

Now they lived this weird, shadow life. A constant twilight, like it had been that night in the desert. Amé had taken up Ben's old apartment, and Danny found himself spending more time here than anywhere else. They saw each other first thing most mornings, and the last thing at night, and on many of those nights, one of them would fall asleep within a hand's reach of the other on her couch. Close, but not touching. It was a joke that everyone thought they were together, when they themselves couldn't say one way or another, or explain exactly what they did mean to each other.

They were inseparable, and somehow still separate.

But Danny was fine with that, just like he was fine spending all his free time with her in Ben's apartment above Modelle Greer's garage—although enough months had passed that it was properly Amé's place now. There was nowhere else he'd rather be, and no one else he'd rather be with. He wasn't wasting his time, because the only hours that mattered were the ones he shared with her.

Hours like those at the Lights.

A TRUCK SLID BY OUTSIDE, lights leading the way, as Danny turned his back to his reflection, to where Amé lay curled on the couch. Her gun was unholstered on the table in front of her, always within reach, whether he stayed the night or not. That was something Ben had taught her, or something she'd learned in her past. That past, before Danny had come to Murfee, before Ben and the Earls, was another thing she didn't talk about. He knew about her brother's murder, and the rumors that Sheriff Cherry—when he was a brand-new deputy himself—had implicated the former sheriff and his then chief deputy, Duane Dupree, in that killing, but no one had all the details. Just whispers and local Murfee gossip, some of it bitter, since there were still plenty of people in the county who fondly remembered Sheriff Ross and wished he was still alive.

Danny guessed they'd all learn just how many in the upcoming election.

Amé moved, turned a bit, started to reach out a hand

to where Danny had been sitting. Her dark hair had grown out over the last few months, like his own, and when it was like it was now, a beautiful mess against her flushed skin, he always wanted to reach out and brush it away.

To touch her, just so he could see her eyes.

All those half smiles of hers, all those secrets she didn't share. All the conversations they never had. He'd always thought he had this compass inside him pointing in only one direction, but whenever she was around, it went absolutely haywire. He lost all sense of direction, but he wasn't lost. . . . All directions pointed only toward her.

She was a mystery, but he wanted to believe that because of her, he'd solved one or two of his own.

Danny slid back down next to her, gently, cradling the beer so it wouldn't spill. He wasn't going to sleep, though, still troubled by the sudden fear that had gripped him in Eddy's trailer yesterday. It wouldn't let him go, and when he'd closed his eyes earlier, he'd had a brief, vivid dream of Afghanistan . . . the first real one in years. He didn't want to sleep if he had to relive any of that.

He was fine just sitting here, letting her sleep for them both.

And maybe Amé was dreaming for them both, too.

Her fingers reached out, searching, touching his leg, as if making sure he was still there.

Making sure he was real.

Just for a moment, and then they were gone.

TEN

I was back east when that attack happened in Ojinaga, so it's taken me some time to catch up with the situation. My boss put me in charge of managing our intel collection, and we're actually making progress," Garrison said. "Even getting direct reporting from the Mexican government itself, which is highly unusual. They're embarrassed, the whole thing is a worldwide humiliation. They know we're sitting over here listening to their side of the border, and they want our help."

"You're talking about all those students in that attack?" Chris said, taking another mouthful of his fresh beer. "What are you hearing?"

Garrison leaned in. "Okay, you remember how just before Sheriff Ross died, the border was in turmoil, right? Two cartels, Nemesio and the Serrano Brothers—Los Hermanos Serrano—fighting over control of the smuggling routes through Chihuahua and the Ojinaga corridor. This happens all the time. We saw it in Juárez, Nuevo Laredo, you name it. There's a truce for a while, an agreement, and then someone breaks it or tries to strong-arm the other and all hell breaks loose. Ross probably got caught in the crossfire of something like that. We always suspected Ross was working for Nemesio, mainly because of the Rudy Reynosa connection, but who knows? Ross may have been working with *both* cartels, or cheating them both. Personally, I think he got greedy, and it got him killed."

"Whatever Ross was into also got Rodolfo Reynosa killed."

"True. And Rudy was definitely working for Nemesio."

"And you."

Garrison nodded. "Fair enough. Look, we'll never know exactly what happened back then, but the dynamic today is the same. It's always the same. Bad guys over there fighting for control of their assets *here*." He pointed at the scrub around them. "This is where they make all the money, Chris."

"Fine, makes sense. But this is all ancient history."

"Not that ancient."

Chris shook his head, conceding the point. "And what does any of this have to do with killing students, kids?"

"That little war between the Serrano Brothers and Nemesio never really ended. It's been going on, all along, below the surface. Guerrilla warfare. New battlegrounds, new tactics. The prevailing wisdom is that one of those cartels *purposely* ordered that attack to draw a forceful response from the Mexican government. It was a setup, something so horrible even the politicians couldn't ignore it. No one could. No different from the bodies they leave stacked in the streets or the big banners they hang from the bridges over there, what they call a *narcomanta*. The bus attack was a threat, another bloody message the cartels love to send each other and the Mexican government. Right now, the full strength of the Mexican federal law enforcement and military is sweeping through Chihuahua, looking for scalps. Message received, mission accomplished."

"So this was all done just to blame the other?"

"Three dead, six injured, nineteen vanished. All teenagers. It's all over the news. The whole world is watching. Someone will go down, and we believe Nemesio is set for the fall. They've held on to Ojinaga longer than anyone else, but now, finally, their grip is slipping. I've seen some reports that indicate the Serrano Brothers are all over this area now. The bus attack may be the final push."

"And by 'this area,' you mean right here, the Big Bend."

"Exactly. There are purges and reprisals going on all along the river now. Another bloodbath. Like Juárez, like 2009. You found five dead bodies yesterday, you may find ten tomorrow. Just another *narcomanta*, Chris. A message. A warning." Garrison closed his eyes like he was tired, going to sleep. But he opened them again and kept going. "Everyone talks about the U.S. War on Drugs, but if there is a war, it's right over our shoulders, right over the border, where the cartels are waging this never-ending battle against each other. Like those bodies that washed up yesterday, like those students from a week ago. Those are the real casualties." Garrison paused and stood. He put his hands on the wooden porch rail, looking southward. "You told me one of those men you found looked young, right?"

"We don't have the ages yet, but yes, one of them looked like a kid, no older than those students, I guess."

"Both Nemesio and the Serrano Brothers have been using younger and younger drug mules for the last year or so because they know our federal legal system won't prosecute minors. They just get kicked back across the border, ready to be used again. That's the sort of people we're dealing with. The sort who exploit kids on purpose, and kill them by mistake."

"Okay, I get it. But what's the real point? Why are you here now?"

Garrison sat down again, moved closer. "One of the highest-ranking members of Nemesio is a man we know only as Fox Uno."

Chris hid a grim look behind his beer bottle. Took a long drink. "You know, I've heard the name."

"Everyone has. He's a legend around here, on both sides of the border. He and his brother learned the business from all the old-time narcos, Shorty Lopez, La Vibora, and Pablo Acosta Villarreal, known as El Zorro de Ojinaga—the Ojinaga Fox. Pablo Acosta, along with Fox Uno's brother, was gunned down in 1987 in a cross-border raid by the FBI and Mex Feds. Fox Uno picked up the pieces and started his own cartel with Acosta's surviving men, calling it Nemesio, allegedly in honor of the brother who died. We think Fox Uno also took his nickname as some sort of tribute to Acosta, but who knows where these guys get their cartoon names from. Anyway, he's since become kind of a Godfather figure along the border. For three decades, nothing has happened in Ojinaga without his blessing. However, he's been on shaky ground for a while now. He's old, maybe sick, not quite as sharp as he used to be, and he's got several lieutenants and allegedly a son eager and ready to take over. Plus, he's been locked in this bloody, never-ending struggle with the Serrano Brothers, who've been successfully encroaching on

Nemesio smuggling routes in Ojinaga and the Big Bend. Our informants suggest this whole attack on the students was aimed directly at Fox Uno, to put him on the run and take him off the board once and for all."

"Is it working?"

"That we don't know. Time will tell. He's a cagey son of a bitch, a survivor like a fucking cockroach. He's lived a long time in a business with a notoriously short life span." Garrison stopped, counting the gathering shadows. "Chris, why do you think Darin and Morgan were so interested in Rudy Reynosa?"

"He had information about Duane Dupree and Ross, about corruption here in the Big Bend . . ."

"Sure, it was easy for Rudy Ray to snitch on Dupree and Ross because they were all working for Nemesio, for Fox Uno. But it was more than that. They believed Rudy Reynosa was related to Fox Uno."

Chris understood then why Garrison was giving him this history lesson about the Big Bend, about the cartels, and why he'd driven all the way down here to deliver it face-to-face. "Right . . . and this is where we circle back to America. You always start and end there, do you know that? This is nothing new."

"Rudy Ray was snitching not only to get free of Nemesio, but to help his sister, too. *Deputy Reynosa*. He was very clear about that. Why do you think that was?"

"A brother worrying about his sister? That's not suspicious. *At all*. And it's certainly not a goddamn crime." Chris took a deep breath. Amé had confided in him all about her brother and her family, and Garrison's suspicions were right—Fox Uno was America and Rudy's uncle. She'd even told him about a boy named Máximo from Ojinaga, a Nemesio *sicario*, who she'd arranged would kill Dupree—the man who murdered her brother and buried him in a field; the predator, *monster*, who sexually terrorized her for more than a year after that.

Fox Uno had sent Máximo to save his niece and avenge his nephew.

So Chris knew all about her history, a hell of a lot more than Garrison ever would. He also knew Amé and believed in her as much as Garrison believed in his agents.

"This is different this time, Chris, it really is. I wanted to warn you. In the wake of that attack, we've moved assets and priorities. The Mexican government is granting us some access we didn't have before. Remember I mentioned purges, reprisals? Men who've worked for Nemesio for years, men we consider high-value targets, are suddenly clamoring to get over that border to the U.S. to buy themselves a few more days of breathing. They'd rather take their chances with us, with the same American justice system they fucking despise, than stay on the ground in Mexico. They're trying to trade what they know for their safety and that of their families, just like Rudy Ray. And we're going to listen . . . to whatever they have to say."

"And now you're afraid you're going to hear something about Amé." Chris laughed, the final piece slipping into place. "Not just her, though. It all ties together, right? *My* reluctance to track down drug smugglers, the fact that my 'numbers' are lower than Chuy Machado's, whatever the hell that means. Fox Uno's long connection with the Big Bend. You always talk about how this is 'my area,' but you don't mean that at all, and never have. He owns it all, and maybe that means he owns me, too. Like Fox Uno, I just picked up the pieces from Sheriff Ross. Started all over again."

"I didn't say that."

"Damn it, you didn't have to." Chris stood. "You drove a long way to insult me to my face. I hope you enjoyed dinner, because I think we're done here."

Garrison stood as well, giving Chris some room. Stars were now high above their heads and the new night was between them, going darker by the moment. "If I hear something about Deputy Reynosa, about Murfee or the Big Bend, I'm coming to you first, Chris. I think I owe you that much. Hell, I know I do. I'm only asking the same of you. If anything happens out here, anything at all, you let me know first, too. I don't want either of us to be surprised."

"This is for my benefit?"

"If you have to look at it that way, yes. You're not going to believe this, but I don't want to be right. I don't want Deputy Reynosa to get hurt. I don't want *you* to get hurt. This place has cost both of us too much fucking blood."

"True, but it's not the Big Bend, not these mountains or the river or the land itself. It's just *people* with blood on their hands. Always. Goddamn people. Ross and the Earls and this Fox Uno. And us too, with our badges and guns. Maybe us most of all."

Garrison pointed at the folder he'd left by his chair. "That's the real reason I drove out here. It's everything we have on Fox Uno. Everything meaningful, anyway. If he is who we think he is, then that information is also about Deputy Reynosa's family. I'd be fired for giving that to you, since some of it's DIA, NSA, and CIA classified intel. All the alphabet agencies. Hell, I'm not even supposed to have some of it, but I thought you should. Read it, burn it, whatever."

"You hope it'll change my mind."

"I hope it'll open your eyes." Garrison reached in his pocket for his car keys. "My personal cell phone is written in there, too. I'm not the enemy, Chris, and I never have been."

"The last time you gave me a folder like that, it held a dozen photos of men I'd shot. Men I'd killed, right here at the Far Six. I was in the hospital and it was the first time we'd ever met in person, before I was sheriff. I might not have the office much longer. Maybe you should have waited for the next guy."

Garrison hesitated, looking at the keys in his hand. "When I was driving in I saw the signs for Bethel Turner. He's putting on a full-court press, huh? Facebook page, lots of media stuff."

"Yes, he is. He's outspending me, what, three to one, at least? I've got some support from some of the ranchers, they've been generous . . . and . . . well, it is what it is. We have a debate next week, sponsored by *The Murfee Daily*, the Big Bend County Junior College Criminal Justice Student Association, and something called the Big Bend Crime Watch Group. We're holding the debate here, at my old high school. You should come back for that. It'll be fun."

"I take it this so-called crime watch group is not your biggest fan?"

"I took over for a man who was revered in the Big Bend under bloody circumstances that remain, at best, suspicious. In the past year, a decent chunk of Murfee burned down and two of my deputies were killed on my watch. I'd say there are some legitimate concerns."

Chris gathered up the bucket with melting ice and empty beer bottles. It was still cold and heavy in his hand. "Hell, would you vote for me?"

Garrison didn't respond, his long silence answer enough. As much as the agent angered him, Garrison was right. They'd always be bound together by what had happened with Sheriff Ross. It gave their relationship fierce, sharp edges, making it at times nearly impossible to hold, but neither was ready or willing to let it go.

Garrison finally said, "Chris, you have done some good here. No matter what happens with the election, try to remember that. And try to take care of that family of yours. Melissa and Jack are beautiful. Even if the Big Bend doesn't need you, they do. They always will."

Garrison extended a hand, and after an uncertain pause, Chris reached out and shook it. He didn't agree with him, but he did respect him. "I appreciate that. I do. And I'll try. Speaking of family, you said that you were back east? Were you visiting your daughters, maybe catching one of those field hockey games?"

Garrison shook his head as he stepped off the porch. Chris thought that, if it was possible, he'd aged even more since he'd come up to them only a few hours earlier. Garrison paused at the bottom, tossing his keys up and down. His expression was a map without any landmarks, featureless. Barren.

"No, I wasn't. I was visiting Morgan Emerson. That's all."

ELEVEN

Danny was afraid he'd been dreaming again, as he woke up fast to a small sound.

Something soft, secretive, coming from the front door.

Fortunately, Amé was already awake, her gun in her hand.

THE DREAM HAD BEEN FULL of dead men.

You never forgot the smell of a fresh corpse.

Each one had been chanting Danny's name in Ashkun, and he was back in that small village of Rumnar, in Nuristan Province.

"Nuristan" meant Land of the Enlightened.

Each of the dead wore a pakul hat and their skeletal hands had reached for him, pulling him down, their rotted bodies draped with crawling, buzzing flies.

They were dead because Danny had killed them, killed them all.

They'd dragged him back into the bloody earth with them where he belonged, and dirt had filled his eyes and his mouth . . .

———

AMÉ MADE A MOTION to him in the darkened apartment, indicating she was going to step out wide, near the window by the door. Danny found his holstered Colt on the end table next to the couch and drew it quietly, down by his leg. He wasn't sure how long he'd been out, falling asleep upright next to Amé on the couch, but the last thing he remembered clearly was standing in the tiny kitchen, drinking a beer and looking out the window.

His reflection.

Truck lights.

That had been at least an hour ago, maybe more.

The apartment sat above Modelle Greer's detached garage, the house itself tucked away in Murfee's version of a historic neighborhood, not too far off Main Street. It was a neighborhood of wooden houses, watered yards, and small trees: sweet acacia, Emory oak, piñon pine. If Danny's and Amé's trucks weren't parked out under that big juniper that shaded one side of the garage, someone might not even know there was an apartment here.

It was out of the way for a reason.

Amé crouched down low, moving toward the window. She was in her jeans and a dark tank top, barefoot. Danny was in his jeans, but shirtless. The tiny apartment was always hot even with the Arctic King AC unit in the bedroom window running on high. It just never quite reached the front room, and tonight was no different. He didn't have time to search for his shirt, though he felt naked, exposed, but did grab at an extra magazine from

his holster belt on the ground and saw across the shadowed space between them that Amé had two spare mags
tucked in the back of her jeans.

Trapped in that apartment, he snapped back to that
moment in Eddy Rabbit's trailer, how he'd felt trapped
there, too. Buried down in a small space, like a hole in
the ground . . . like a coffin.

The dream was full of dead men.

Goddamn, he'd been dreaming again of Afghanistan.
He'd tried so hard not to fall asleep . . .

He was already sweating a river and it had nothing to
do with the shitty AC. He swore he heard flies where
there weren't any, almost brushed a phantom one away.

It was the second time in two days that the old fear
had grabbed him. He needed to find a way to get free,
and get his shit together.

Fast.

Then his left eye fizzed, static coiling through and
around him—a great gray wave higher than his head—
and it went out like a bad light.

HE STAYED UPRIGHT, THOUGH—on point—turning
sideways so he had the full benefit of his good right eye.
Amé was at the window, gun at high-ready—up by her
shoulder—using the muzzle to move the blinds aside a
fraction. Danny flanked the door opposite; he was on the
left, she was on the right, the door between them. They
moved with a certain silent understanding, as if they had
been doing this forever—as if an invisible string bound
them together. But he ended up with his bad eye toward

the wall—the kitchenette at his back—and the rest of the apartment behind him might as well have been the dark side of the moon. Worse, the door pulled open toward him, meaning Amé would be exposed to whatever was on the other side—she'd have to take the first shot.

For a second or two he would truly be blind, completely cut off from her by the arc of the swinging door, making not only his bad eye meaningless, but Danny himself useless. He could shoot through the door if he had to, stitch rounds through the cheap wood at a hard angle, but until he got around the other side and cleared the gap, Amé would be all on her own. The space was no bigger than his outstretched arms, and it would be quick—*no more than a fucking eye blink*—but it would be enough. There was no way to change their positions now, and she wouldn't let him anyway. She wasn't afraid of whatever was on the other side of the door. She wanted to face it first, she always did.

She looked over, raised her chin toward the door.

Ready.

The apartment was dark, but not impenetrable. There was a lamp in the back bedroom that leaked pale blue light into the front, and the window by the kitchen that Danny had been staring out earlier was also lit faintly by the uncertain glow of a faraway streetlamp.

A hint of a hint of light.

The crooked blinds by the front door bled their own radiance.

Amé was mainly wrapped in shadows, a single luminous halo around one eye. Light gleamed off her gun, the Saint Michael pendant at her throat.

Then there was that sound again . . . someone shuffling on the top step. *Breathing.* There was a small landing there and nothing more.

Barely enough for one person to stand.

Danny wanted to give it a second to see if that person
standing there knocked. Maybe it was one of the other
deputies, or Modelle Greer herself; maybe something
had woken the old woman up and she was scared . . . even
as Amé settled her weight on the leg curled beneath her
and took steady aim at the door's heart.

She and Danny could shoot holes into that door, the
same as someone outside could shoot through it.

Danny held up a fist over his gun hand's wrist, counting out three silent fingers one by one, and then reached
over and unlocked the door.

He pulled it open in one smooth motion and rolled
clear.

AMÉ CAME OUT OF HER CROUCH FAST, surprised,
holding up a hand to Danny and raising and decocking
her Colt with the other. Danny turned into the breach,
and saw—despite only one working eye—what had startled her. There wasn't a man there, but a *girl*, a very
young Hispanic girl, with long dark hair all twisted and
knotted by the wind.

Amé said "Shit" in English, and then something else
in Spanish that he didn't catch.

"What the fuck?" Danny said, getting to his feet and
aiming his gun away from the girl at the door.

It was everything he'd ever worried about in Nuristan;

the sort of dreams he'd had before, that he'd thought were over and done with but had returned. He'd pointed a loaded weapon into the face of a child.

Again.

"¿Quién eres, niña?" Amé asked, slipping her own gun behind her back into her jeans, out of sight, and kneeling to the girl's height. Danny had no idea how old she was. She was wearing dusty jeans and dirty tennis shoes and a T-shirt with some cartoon character on it, and then another unbuttoned flannel shirt over that. He'd seen a hundred little girls like her on the outskirts of Murfee.

Amé was still talking to her: *"Está bien, niña, no vamos a hacer daño. Nos asustaste, eso es todo. ¿No es gracioso?"*

Danny put his own gun into his jeans. The girl had to be lost, or someone had sent her specifically for Amé, someone who wanted a Spanish-speaking sheriff's deputy and didn't trust anyone else. It had happened before, but never at Amé's home.

Amé was just reaching out to touch the girl, to pull her through the door, when Danny's bad eye kicked back on. It flickered—once, twice—and he could finally see clearly.

A man.

Standing at the bottom of the steps far behind the girl, hidden near the trunk of the juniper by the long curved branches and the night itself.

Danny went for his gun again.

It was still warm to the touch from where he'd been holding it.

"Amé . . . hold up, there's someone else," Danny had time to say, pointing down the steps with his Colt. She looked over the girl's dark hair, hand resting on her small, narrow shoulder, and saw the man, too.

The man called up to them, *"No quiero hacerle daño."* But his hands were still down at his sides, lost in the blackness pooled around him.

"I don't understand what the fuck he just said, but do you know him?" Danny asked, keeping his gun steady, moving to put himself between the girl and Amé and the man who watched them both.

Amé stared down at him for a long time, but if she answered one way or another, Danny didn't hear her.

TWELVE

He switched the matchstick from one corner of his mouth to the other, side to side, relentlessly, watching the pumpjack do its thing. The windows were down on his unmarked Charger—a midnight-black 370-HP Hemi V-8 purchased with federal funds—letting in the night and a generous helping of West Texas grit, a fine dust that had already coated his dashboard. He could smell the metal skin and oily sweat beaded on the pumpjack, a thick stink like the thing itself was on fire. He was parked close enough that he could feel heat coming off it, could reach out and touch it.

He could also feel it in his gut every time it went up and down in long, rumbling strokes, pulling that black liquid out of the very earth. He'd lived in Terrell County his whole life, had seen these things scattered around forever, but they were still a mystery to him. He wasn't sure exactly how they did what they did, but that's one reason he'd become a deputy sheriff—so he'd never have to work out on the damn rigs.

Johnnie Machado, Johnnie Macho to his friends and family, glanced down the road. He had a good long eye down 349, a clean and empty line that ran as far as Dryden. It was dark out there, dark all the way, with a thick band of stars above him, but he didn't know shit about stars or constellations, either. He looked up only when he had to. Otherwise, Johnnie Macho was the sort of man who generally looked straight fucking ahead.

He checked his main phone, tried to make a bet on who'd text him first to bitch at him. Either Zamantha, his wife, or Rae, that nice piece of ass at El Diablo Norte he'd been tapping since June. Rae had gotten mouthy lately— needy—making more and more demands on him, but she wasn't the problem. The real problem was the goddamn bet he was trying to make with himself about the texting. Johnnie Macho couldn't avoid a good wager, any wager, on anything, anytime. He bet on the Cowboys and *fútbol*, on cock- and dogfighting. He bet on high school football games and would even throw money at a friendly dart game between his buddies or someone tossing a wadded-up ball of paper into a goddamn trash can. The thought of putting a little something on the line to make life interesting made his dick hard, and for the last three years he'd made steady use of his open line of credit at the book in Odessa. He was what they called a valued customer . . . VIP repeat business.

And more often than not lately, a goddamn loser.

He'd been on a ferociously bad streak for a year, so bad it boggled the fucking mind. It was like he was cursed. Like all the world's bad luck was piled up on his fucking head. He'd doubled down his way into a god- damn hole he couldn't see out of anymore, deeper than the pumpjack working right next to him. It was a light- less place in the center of the goddamn earth, but still not far enough away from the men he owed. Men who didn't care who his daddy was, or that he carried a badge and a gun, or that he was a goddamn *somebody* in this county. The sort of men who had no problem driving out from Odessa one night and filling in that hole he'd dug for himself with a ton of Terrell County dirt, if he didn't make at least some interest payments on what he owed. That's why Johnnie Macho never looked up much, because he damn well needed those eyes in the back of his head to see what was coming.

And that's why he was sitting out here on 349 in the dark, watching the road. He'd had to keep on making bets, spreading them around, so one bad hand could pay off the other, and tonight was one of those side wagers. It hadn't been placed with that tatted-up Crip bookie in Odessa who kept a sawed-off rifle with a plastic Coke bottle suppressor in the back of his 300M, but instead with those *indios* down south, even far more serious, if such a thing were possible. These side bets had paid off well, better than any card game or the goddamn Cowboys, but it was a goddamn hard way to live.

But he didn't have any other choice, either.

He'd bet his life on it.

FINALLY, THERE WERE LIGHTS. The sand-colored Malibu he'd been expecting, gliding down 349 right at the legal limit, not too fast, not too slow. He rolled the matchstick around his dry mouth some more and let the Chevy go past, waiting until it was only taillights—glowing red like the ends of a couple of cigarettes—before he threw the Charger into gear and hit his wigwags.

The night came alive, painted blue and red.

He smoothly chewed up the macadam and got right up on the Malibu's ass, which was signaling that it was pulling over. It slowed down in a spreading cloud of that West Texas dust and grit, all lit up hellish from Johnnie's emergency lights, and once it rolled to a stop, he sat behind it for a while, letting the driver and passenger think he was working on his Datalux TM110 tablet (more Fed money)—running their plates or whatever, although he didn't even have it turned on.

Instead, he was fiddling around with his phone. He guessed Zam was over at her fat sister Amada's with Johnnie Jr. and Antonio, watching that shitty reality TV show they liked, while Rae was still pulling a double at the club, working that round ass up and down in a way that defied all gravity, all logic. He figured he might have enough time after he wrapped this up to head over there for a few cold ones, maybe slip Rae a couple of fifties, just to shut her up. She'd been on him for some extra spending money for weeks, the same way Zam had been on him about Rae, although his wife didn't know the girl's name . . . *yet*. She'd just heard that Johnnie was keeping time with someone, and threatened to go to Johnnie's daddy over it, which was not an option. She didn't care so much about him picking up the occasional piece of ass, but didn't want him disrespecting her, whatever the hell the difference was. She took her role as the wife of Deputy Johnnie Machado seriously, and the daughter-in-law of Sheriff Chuy Machado even more seriously, because that's the one that got her all the free meals, movie tickets, and the comped weekly hair-and-nail session at Glamorous.

No goddamn way to live.

Johnnie shook his head and set the phone aside and got out of the Charger into the warm night.

HE APPROACHED THE MALIBU CAUTIOUSLY, just like he'd been taught, his body bladed away and his hand on his service weapon. He wasn't in uniform, but that didn't matter. He was going to dump these clothes in the bin behind Rae's club.

The Malibu's window was already rolled down and the driver, a young Hispanic male, was waiting for him. He could see the kid was trying to decide whether to speak in English or Spanish.

"Lo siento, yo no pensaba que iba a alta velocidad," the kid said. Sorry, I didn't know I was going that fast. *"Ni siquiera te vi allí"*—I didn't even see you there—he added, glancing to his passenger, who was a young female in thick, nerdy glasses. She was terrified, staring straight ahead, and might not have been half bad-looking without the glasses. They both looked like they went to UTEP or University of Texas Permian Basin. Johnnie smiled big, one of the good guys just doing his duty, letting them know it was no big deal at all.

"Oh, you weren't speeding, and you weren't supposed to see me hidden back there. Hell, I was betting on that," he said, still all smiles. If the kid was nervous, or even suspicious, and paying close attention to Johnnie's movements in case the whole thing was about to go bad, his eyes were focused on the wrong thing: Johnnie's hand hovering over his duty Glock.

Not the smaller throw-down Smith & Wesson that Johnnie had been hiding down low against his leg, pressed against his jeans.

The kid probably never even saw it.

Johnnie brought it up in one quick, smooth motion, firing eight rounds—seven plus one, until the slide locked back—right down into the open window, right into the kid's face, right through the girl's glasses. Thick, fresh blood fantailed all over the windshield, and the two of them bucked up and down and made some sort of awful noises or cries and grabbed for each other, before falling in an ugly pile and going very, very still.

It was a goddamn mess.

Johnnie took a long, deep breath, listening to the engine of the idling car and searching the stretch of road for other headlights, before tossing the tape-handled Smith & Wesson into the window with the bodies.

He stood for a moment longer, chewing the matchstick, looking at all the blood.

Usually on a deal like this, he had Ringo or Chavez or Roman or Ortiz with him—other members of the Tejas unit—and someone would start making a shitty joke right about now, but this one was all on him. It meant he didn't have to divvy up the take, of course, but it also meant he'd committed a double homicide and there was no one else to take the fall, to share the burden. It was a weird, lonely feeling, and a part of him wanted to get the fuck in the Charger and just drive away, not only from the cooling bodies in the car on the highway, or Zam and Rae, or even Terrell County (where he'd always be Chuy Machado's son, nothing more and nothing less), but from all of goddamn Texas. But that was foolish, betting himself he wouldn't get much farther than Houston before someone caught up to him. Either his daddy or those gangsters from Odessa, or the *indios* from Acuña.

Everyone owned a part of his ass nowadays, so all he could do was buy it back, one bloody piece at a time.

So he got that ass into motion, working it like Rae. He tore apart the Malibu's backseat—trying to steer clear of the blood—finding the four pounds of meth and one pound of heroin the *indios* had told him would be there. He had a bag in the Charger, and an area scouted out back near the scrub by the pumpjack, where he could dump the dope for a few days until he could come back for it. He also had a man in Del Rio who'd move it for him and cash it out in Dallas. After he got done stuffing the bundles into the bag on the Charger's hood, with a watchful eye down the road, he checked his main phone, where there were still no messages from either of those two bitches. But his *other* phone, the red one, was now blinking furiously in the Charger's center console.

That was the phone—paired up with a small handheld radio—that no one else knew about, not even the other guys on the unit. Because, let's be honest, there was a part of him that didn't quite trust those fuckers, either, at least not enough to turn his back on them. Sure, he was their leader, the one with the connections who'd started it all and brought them all in. He'd handpicked them and made the sweet deals they'd all benefited from. But he also knew that Roman was talking shit about him all the time now, and Ringo had been trying to set up his own things on the side. In some ways, every member of the Tejas unit was a gambler, just like him. They were all just betting on different things.

That blinking light meant Johnnie had a short message in Spanish, and about thirty minutes to return a call to the man who'd left it, a man whose name he didn't know. That man—who worked for the *indios* from Acuña, who answered to an even more important man they all called El Indio—wouldn't be calling him again about this shit out on the road, so it had to be something else. Something serious. Another piece of his ass. He shook his head and realized that he'd already lost his first bet of the night.

It wasn't either of his women who'd texted him first.

He was, in fact, the unluckiest goddamn son of a bitch he knew.

Deputy Johnnie Machado went to the trunk of the Charger and grabbed the can of gas he'd stowed there six hours earlier. He walked back toward the Malibu, shaking his head at his run of bad luck, wondering when the fuck it would finally turn.

When would it finally, mercifully end? It had to, right?

When he got to the Malibu, he popped the matchstick out of his mouth—finally time to put it to good use—as he poured gas over the car's hood.

PART TWO

NARCOMANTA

THIRTEEN

Eddy Lee Rabbit felt like hammered shit.

Eddy wasn't exactly sure what that meant: "hammered shit." But he'd grown up hearing it from his old man, and it seemed pretty damn appropriate right now.

Like . . . the way the lights were way too bright, drilling right into the soft parts of his skull. And how his court-appointed lawyer's teeth were too white, too big for his goddamn head. The same lawyer who was now sitting there doodling on some paper, instead of calling off these two attack-dog deputies. If Eddy didn't know better (and to be honest, he didn't), he would have thought his lawyer was in cahoots with them ("cahoots," another one of his old man's dumbass words). The three of them seemed determined to jump up and down on him until he admitted to some shit that he actually didn't do, or at least sure in the hell didn't remember.

Maybe that was the whole "hammered shit" thing.

Eddy was coming down from a three-day high (okay, maybe four), and every bit of his body felt it. His eyeballs were two fucking massive marbles in his head, so glassy he could throw sand off of them; his skin itched as if it had been pulled off by hand, turned inside out, and stapled back on that way. His teeth went up and down, up and down, like tiny knife points, so he kept his mouth open, drooling, trying not to cut himself. His hands were jitterbugging, but at least they'd taken off the handcuffs, which had been hot to the touch on his turned-all-the-way-around, fucked-up skin. And he was goddamn thirsty, like trapped-in-the-desert-for-four-days (okay, maybe five) thirsty, but was afraid the water would taste like his own blood, so instead he just sat there: mouth open, bug-eyed, tongue hanging out.

He looked like a panting dog.

On the table in front of him sat a small handheld radio wrapped in plastic. No one was saying anything about it, but it kinda looked familiar, although he wasn't sure.

The female deputy, the pretty Mexican girl, wasn't doing much talking about that radio or anything else. She stared past him, like she was a hundred miles away somewhere else.

That stare could set ants on fire, though. Like playing with a magnifying glass in the Texas heat, something Eddy had done as a kid.

He'd set a whole bunch of little grass fires that way.

The other deputy, the fucker who'd coldcocked him down in the cane, was pointing a finger at him and going on and on about how Eddy had nearly killed him with a skillet. Now, there was a real possibility that something like that had, in fact, happened, although Eddy couldn't remember it exactly. It might come to him later, though, unsummoned, while he was falling asleep or taking a piss, and then he'd be right back in that moment, reliving every second of it in too-bright colors. But Deputy What's-his-name was righteously angry right now, although Eddy got the sense that only part of what he was pissed about involved Eddy at all.

For all Eddy's faults, and they were legion, he'd had at one time a pretty good ability to read people, kinda a sixth sense. A Spidey sense (Eddy's favorite superhero, although that Bat-dude was kinda badass, too). It had served him well and had kept him (mostly) out of serious trouble. But after too many years on too many drugs, it now came and went like a shaky radio signal out on the edge of the desert. When it worked, it worked just fine. But when it didn't, Eddy was lost in the static, trapped between the AM stations his daddy had listened to while driving his truck. Then, it was like Eddy couldn't even read, much less recognize, his own damn handwriting.

Right now, Eddy was having one of those moments of clarity. There was something going on between those two deputies, some electric current running between them that had nothing to do with Eddy Lee Rabbit. They were both going through the motions, but they weren't happy about it, and they weren't focused on the situation at hand.

They weren't focused on him.

Maybe they were fuck buddies and had had a big fight, like he and Charity did all the time. Something like that.

Whatever it was, they had things on their mind that didn't involve totally hammering the shit out of Eddy, and that was totally fine with him.

"YOU TRIED TO OPEN my skull with a goddamn skillet, Eddy," the one deputy said. *Donnie? Danny?* Eddy

wasn't sure. "You're dealing with assault on a law enforcement officer, no matter what else. You got that?
With your record, you're fucked."

Eddy's attorney, Paez, waved that off with the pen
he'd been doodling with. "Eddy, despite Deputy Ford's
assertion, that's not actually a legal opinion." He pointed
his pen at the angry deputy. "And besides, my client
hasn't admitted to this alleged assault. Right now, it's
your word against Mr. Rabbit's . . ."

"Santino . . . please, please, don't pull that shit with
me . . ."

Before Donnie-Danny could get any further, the female deputy stepped in. "This isn't going to get us anywhere, Danny. Santino has agreed to let Eddy talk to us,
and he doesn't have to do that. Let's hear what Eddy has
to say." Something passed between Paez and the female
deputy that Eddy couldn't put his finger on, but it was
clear they had history and knew each other outside this
moment. In fact, it was like everyone in the room knew
each other but fucking Eddy. He'd woken up in the middle of a conversation that everyone was having about him
that he hadn't been invited to join.

Still, Eddy wanted to say his piece. He wanted them to
know he was sitting right here and not going quietly. "Yeah,
I don't remember any of that shit. Except for *you* trying to
rip my fucking head off. Cheap shot, motherfucker."

Danny started to stand and say something, maybe
even do something, but was stopped by another look
from the other deputy. Goddamn, she was a looker. Dark
hair, dark eyes. Cheeks high and sharp. But both deputies looked tired. Hell, they looked the way he felt. The

female deputy turned to Eddy, and although he thought . . . hoped . . . she was going to smile at him, let him know she was the reasonable one and things were okay between them, she didn't. Not at all.

For the first time, Eddy was truly scared.

"Eddy, my name is America Reynosa, and it's been a tough couple of days for all of us. Your attorney, Santino Paez, thought it would be a good idea that you talk to us, before things get out of hand. Before they get worse."

"Like I said, I don't remember hitting that son of a bitch over there. Maybe I did, maybe I didn't."

"This isn't about that," Deputy Reynosa said. "Not about hitting Deputy Ford. I wish that's all it was. But it's about the bodies, Eddy. The bodies." She reached down somewhere beside her, out of his line of sight, and brought up a folder. She opened it and slid it across the table to him, avoiding the radio wrapped in plastic.

There were pictures there, a bunch of them.

Of bodies, floating in the river.

Oh fuck me . . .

And then Eddy remembered . . . all of it.

"I DIDN'T HAVE ANYTHING to do with that, nothing," he said, putting his hands on the table to steady himself. There was dirt under his nails that looked like blood. He didn't touch the pictures, though.

"But they were there, Eddy. Out back, on your property," Deputy Ford said. He pointed at the photos. "Five of them. And we need an explanation, a reason. Right now, you're the only one we've got."

"Fuck that. Put me back in the clink for the drugs, or for hitting *you*. I'll cop to all that and more. *But that?* No fucking way. I'm not a killer."

"You almost killed *me* with a fucking skillet, Eddy."

"That was completely different. I was high, out of my mind."

Deputy Ford . . . Danny . . . took one of the pictures and turned it around to get a good look at it. Then he spun it back in Eddy's direction. "Maybe you were high when you did this? Maybe you can only be high to do this. You know, like out of your mind."

Eddy turned to his attorney, to Deputy Reynosa. Pleading. "I'm telling you, I know nothin' about this. I saw it and it scared the shit out of me, too."

Surprisingly it was Danny who nodded, softened first. "Okay, fair enough. I'm actually willing to buy that, Eddy. I saw you turn tail in the cane. I saw that look in your eyes when you ran up on me. You were surprised as anyone. Scared shitless, like you said. You weren't faking that."

"That's right, thank you. Goddamn right I wasn't. You see that, you know." Eddy made a gesture at the pictures, trying to push them away.

Danny nodded again. "I do, Eddy. I don't think you killed those men. Hell, one of them was barely that, just a kid. You didn't kill them, but I do think you know them. Or did."

Eddy opened his mouth, closed it again.

"I'm willing to forget that you tried to break my skull if you talk to me about these men. That boy. I don't want to put that on you. You help me and I'll help you."

Eddy looked away from the pictures. At his initial appearance before that prick Hildebrand, no one had said a goddamn word about a bunch of dead bodies floating in the river. "Charity know about this?"

"About the bodies? No, Eddy, she doesn't," Deputy Reynosa said, crossing her arms. "No one does, not yet. Not officially. But we can't keep it quiet much longer."

His attorney looked up, adding, "They only booked you on the assault on Deputy Ford, and the small amount of drugs in the trailer . . ."

Eddy cut him off. "That was personal-use shit. That was . . ."

Paez continued, as if Eddy hadn't opened his mouth. "They can, and will, make an argument that it was not, if they have to. It's leverage, Eddy. You sell drugs, that's what you do. They'll find fifty people who'll say that's *all* you do. As Deputy Ford pointed out, even without that, the assault itself is serious enough, given your prior record. They're still processing the scene with the murder victims. You haven't been charged with that. I saw an opportunity for you to help yourself before that happened. Your only opportunity. That's why we're all here."

"No, these two here saw an opportunity to fuck me," Eddy said, pointing at Danny and Deputy Reynosa. "And you're helping 'em. God knows why. You're supposed to be helping me."

Danny tapped the table, getting Eddy's attention. He leaned in close, right into Eddy's face. His voice was low, somehow incredibly loud at the same time. "The sheriff has held the newspapers off, but he won't be able to much longer. Whoever you've been working with is going to know. If Charity's been involved with them, she's going to know, too. Soon, everyone will. Then you're no good to us, and then maybe Charity's in danger. Someone's going to want some answers, and if they can't get to you, they sure in the hell will get to her."

Eddy slumped back in his chair. "I think I hurt her the other day . . . Charity, I mean. It wasn't her goddamn fault. I didn't mean to do it, you know? Shit just gets fuzzy, all jumbled up sometimes. Like my head's full of broken glass."

Danny looked right at him. "Yeah, I get that, Eddy, I do." And in that moment, Eddy believed him. Eddy could read him and knew it was true.

"But this has got to get clear, quick. If not for you, then for Charity. Don't hurt her again," Danny finished.

"I know, I know. So, look here, I'm telling you I'd remember something like that, all those people. But I don't know who the fuck they are, and I sure don't know who'd do that horrible shit to them. I don't hang with people like that. Sorry."

The room stayed silent, all eyes on Eddy.

"Goddamn," Eddy breathed, to no one but himself. His breath was a lit match in his mouth.

"Goddamn is right, Eddy," Danny agreed, and then, some silent signal passing between them, he turned to Deputy Reynosa, who reached down and pulled out a second folder. She opened it and took out a single picture. She held it up and then gave it to Eddy.

It was a picture of his kitchen, or what was left of it.

Before things had gotten too bad with the crank, he used to love to stand in that kitchen with the window open, facing the river. Listening to the sounds of the night and the water while drinking a cold beer, frying up some deer backstrap to mix in with some of that Patty Melt Hamburger Helper. He didn't know how long it had been since he'd done that. Maybe months, maybe years. He *knew* that kitchen, but it was like someone else's place now, even with the same old shit he recognized everywhere. Sometimes when he was using, it was like someone else had moved into his life, a real mean motherfucker pushing Eddy out of the way. Soon, there wouldn't be any room left for him at all.

He tried to focus on the picture, wasn't sure what he was supposed to be looking at, and then—another one of those moments of bright, hard clarity—he did.

He slid the picture back without a word, as Danny kept talking to him.

"Deputy Reynosa was taking photos of your place after our little altercation. Standard procedure. Evidence photos. All legal, with a search warrant and everything. You know what I'm talking about now, don't you, Eddy?"

Eddy bit his lip. There was some good cop–bad cop shit going on here, but he was suddenly, brutally, too tired to care. After five, okay, maybe six days of being awake—of being pulled taut like a goddamn wire—he was worn out. So goddamn tired.

He laid his head down on the table.

He wondered where Charity was, and when he'd see her again.

Paez put a hand on his arm. "Don't admit to something if there's nothing to admit to. But if there is, Eddy, now is the time. If not, then we're done here."

Eddy pulled his head up, it was like lifting a mountain. His sweat left a stain, and he wiped it away and then
pointed at the radio in the bag. The *evidence bag*, he now
saw clearly. It had red stickers on it and was sealed up
tight. "You took that out of my kitchen. It's the one in
the pictures."

But Deputy Reynosa shook her head, while it was
Danny's turn to sit back. "No, Eddy, that's the problem."
She picked up the bagged radio and handed it to Eddy.
Just like the photos, he didn't want to touch it, but this
time, he did. It was heavy, too heavy, like his head, and
there was some water staining the plastic, trapped inside.
Maybe a mouthful. He was so thirsty he wanted to cut
that bag open and take a good long drink. "That radio
in your hands was taken from the river mud beneath the
bodies we found. Just under the surface of the water. We
think one of the men was carrying it. It's *not* the one
from your kitchen, but it's the same. Identical."

"Now you see the problem, Eddy. *Your* problem,"
Danny said, softly. "What we've been trying to tell you
here." There was no anger there anymore, only disap-
pointment. "Now I'm going to get you a Coke or a coffee or a glass of water. Hell, I'll even get you a beer,
because I think *I'm* going to need one, too. Whatever
you want, because we're going to start this all over again.
We got all day."

Paez's hand left his arm, and although there were
three other people in the room, Eddy was alone.

"And tomorrow's a motherfucker," Eddy said, catching Danny's eye. Like when they'd shared that laugh outside his trailer, when Eddy had still been a free man.

"Yeah, it is, and for you, tomorrow's too fucking late."

Eddy Lee Rabbit put the radio back on the table and closed his eyes.

If he could sleep now, just lay his head down again for a few minutes, maybe he could think through this thing.

But instead, he opened his eyes and nodded yes.

FOURTEEN

═══

Chris was having trouble finding District Attorney Royal "Roy" Moody, which wasn't surprising. First, Royal didn't like him and pretty much avoided him whenever he could, and second, he had two offices: one in Murfee and another in Nathan. That was the burden of being the DA for Big Bend, Terrell, Jeff Davis, and a couple of other West Texas counties—almost sixteen thousand square miles. A lot of land and not enough of you to go around to cover it all. This morning Moody wasn't in either of his offices, but Chris finally tracked him down at the Whistle Stop Café in Nathan, enjoying breakfast with former Texas Ranger Bethel Turner. The two men looked up from their coffee when Chris walked in, and Bethel stood fast, his Stetson in his hand.

Bethel was in his fifties, and still looked every bit the Ranger. He was tall and broad-shouldered, with a touch of gray at his temples. His skin was permanently tanned, the way it darkened only for a West Texas native. In fact, standing there in his Wranglers and white shirt and Sam Browne belt and red tie with tiny silver Texas stars on it, he looked like the sort of actor you'd hire to play a Ranger in a movie. The only thing missing was the real silver-star badge. Chris remembered that Bethel may

have done some advertising for the Rangers a few years
ago, some sort of TV commercial or some poster. Chris
had nothing against Bethel, who was supposed to be decent enough, even if he was trying to take Chris's job.

Royal Moody, on the other hand, was a whole other
story. He was short, maybe five-foot-six, wearing his
usual blue chambray shirt, bolero tie, black vest, and a
dark blazer that was neither black nor blue but some
other color in between, the color of a fresh bruise. He
had his own Stetson Bent Tree straw hat on the table
next to a half-finished plate of sunny-side-up eggs and
ham. Chris had never warmed up to Royal—the feeling
was more than mutual—but he'd afforded him and the
office he held the respect he thought both were due, until recently. That's when it became clear that Royal was
not only going to back Bethel Turner in the coming election, but was actively helping fund the campaign against
Chris.

There were probably rules somewhere against an
elected official like Royal politicking while on the job, or
using the resources of his office to help a candidate, but
this was Texas, which made it politics as usual. You weren't
expected to whine about it or cry foul. If you wanted it
bad enough, you were expected to find a way to win.

"Sorry to interrupt breakfast, gentlemen," Chris said.
He nodded at Bethel. "Bethel, hope you're well. The
signs everywhere look great, by the way. I also like that
text message thing you've been putting out, 'It's OUR
Big Bend,' though some folks might take that as almost
racist, or at least not very welcoming. I could be wrong
about that. I hope I am."

Bethel shook his head, running a hand over his brush cut. "Sorry, Sheriff, it's just politics. You know."

"No, it's fine, Bethel. It really is. I'm not here about politics anyway. I'm here for Mr. Moody, for business. While being the sheriff is still my job."

Royal looked up from his coffee. "We'll catch up later, Bethel. I guess *the sheriff* and I have some stuff to attend to." Bethel stood awkwardly for a few more seconds, then turned his hat in his hands a few times and headed for the door.

Royal pointed his mug at the seat Bethel had vacated. "I assume you want to sit down? You know you could have called, made an appointment."

"I tried. You weren't answering. This won't take long, Royal, I promise." Chris slid into the booth opposite from the district attorney.

"You want some coffee?" Royal asked. "I'm buying."

CHRIS OPENED A COPY of *The Murfee Daily* he'd brought with him and handed it over to Royal, who took it without comment. He pulled bifocals out of his breast pocket and scanned the articles. He took his time, as if he hadn't already read the paper that morning. Chris knew he had copies shipped to both of his offices and probably his home, too.

"I take it you don't like the editorial?" he said, putting the paper aside. "If that's what you're here asking about, I had nothing to do with that." He took a slow sip of coffee before adding, "Although I can't say I honestly disagree with much of it."

"No, Royal, not the goddamn editorial. I don't care about that. It's the story across from it, about Eddy Rabbit and the bodies down on the river. The one continued from the front page, above the fold. I'd asked the paper to hold that story for another day or so."

"I don't work at the paper, Sheriff."

"Yes, but the facts they printed are very specific. Some of them sound like they came right out of Deputy Ford's complaint. They also mention the DPS forensics team, which was definitely not part of that complaint."

"Come now, Chris, no matter how large the Big Bend is, Murfee is still one-hundred-percent small town. Danny's complaint *was* sealed. The rest of that stuff probably came from your own deputies. Trust me, they all talk. How long did you think you were going to keep those five deaths a secret? And really, to what end?"

"Because I've got two of my people talking to Eddy Rabbit this morning. It's an active investigation, Royal."

Royal finished off his coffee and waved the waitress over for more, and as they waited for her to refill his mug, they sat in silence. One side of the Whistle Stop was floor-to-ceiling windows, looking east to the Amtrak line that ran down from El Paso and cut through the heart of the town. Morning sunlight washed through those windows, a heavy glow turning the inside of the café warm. Too warm for the old ceiling fans barely turning above them. After Royal watched the young Hispanic waitress walk away, he started again. "Pardon me if I don't put much stake in one of *your* investigations. Last time, we ended up with Murfee on fire and two dead deputies, not to mention that bloodbath down in

Killing. As a bonus, I got to have some serious conversations with one very pissed-off FBI agent about some warrants I gave you."

He was talking about the Earls again . . . and to a lesser extent, Ross, too. It all came back to that—always—and the fact that Chris was not, and never would be, Stanford Ross. Ross and Royal Moody had been good friends for a long time, but Chris often wondered just how much Moody knew about his friend. How much did anyone in Murfee ever truly know, or really want to know, about their former sheriff and all his secrets?

"Completely different, Royal, and you know that."

"It doesn't matter. Nothing's going to come of this. You're never going to pin those murders on Rabbit."

"I'm not trying to 'pin' them on him. I only want to know what he knows." Danny had called Chris first thing this morning to tell him he and Amé were on their way to meet with Eddy and his attorney, Paez. Danny had said something about some new information they'd come across, but didn't spell it out. It'd probably prove to be nothing, but Danny had wanted to press Eddy about it anyway. "What I hear you saying is you're not going to charge Eddy no matter what we learn. You don't give a damn about those five dead men. Bethel was right. This *is* politics. It's better if this case stays open. Another messy unsolved investigation, another obvious example of my incompetence."

"That's a serious accusation, Sheriff. One I don't appreciate. And those dead unfortunates represent just as much a political asset as a liability, *if* you can find their murderer . . . fast. Eddy's as good as anyone, right?

Maybe you're the one who's been doing the leaking? Didn't this morning's editorial refer to your 'haphazard notions of law enforcement and public accountability'?"

"You didn't have a hand in writing that?"

Royal blew over his hot coffee, but didn't answer.

"Here's the thing, Royal. We've worked together in the past, and you've always done what was needed for my office. I thought you believed in the law, above all else. Now it's all backward. I get that you never liked me much personally, but when did that become so *professional*?"

Royal set his mug down carefully. "Because I'm not sure you're good at *your* job, Sheriff. Maybe the job is too big for you, and you know what? That's okay. A man should be able to admit that, it's no failing. Since Ross died, there's been nothing but chaos in the Big Bend, and that's all been on *you*. Not every man can be Sheriff Ross."

Chris laughed and shook his head. "Thank God for that. What do you think it cost to buy all that peace and quiet?" Having Sheriff Ross's "peace" thrown in his face made Chris flash back to his talk with Garrison about Sheriff Machado over in Terrell County. *What was the price of Chuy and Johnnie Machado's success? And were they being paid with the same bloody money?*

Royal tapped his fingers on the table, making sure Chris got his point: one, two, three. "I knew the man. I know what he did for Murfee and the Big Bend. Everything he sacrificed."

"Sacrificed? You know only what he showed you. Don't think because two thousand people stood there at his funeral that he was a decent man, that he was loved and respected. Some of those people were there to make sure he was actually going in the ground."

"Like your deputy, Ms. Reynosa? Or that new boy, Marco Lucero?"

"Right. 'It's OUR Big Bend.' Isn't that the slogan? There are more Hispanics in this county than folks like you and me, Royal. You can't ignore them, and I believe most people don't want to. They're part of this community. That's not changing."

"Well, you better hope they vote. Each and every one of them. You should probably save all those arguments for the debate next week."

Chris took a long, slow breath. His fingers were white where he was gripping the chipped wood of the table. Garrison aside, he'd never discussed with anyone other than America and Mel all he knew about Ross, and that was only because they'd lived through it with him; Amé more than anyone else. Ben had carried his own suspicions about Chris's tortured relationship with his former boss, and understood how that experience continually shaped Chris's approach to the job, to his understanding of his duty and responsibilities that came with the badge he wore. But Chris had never breathed a bad word about Sheriff Ross to anyone else. There had never been a worthwhile reason to, no profit in it. His silence was less for his benefit than for Caleb's—the sheriff's son—or for all those who'd worked with the sheriff but had never been tainted by him. Now, sitting with Royal in this too-hot booth, Chris couldn't hold his tongue.

"You may think he was good for Murfee, for the Big Bend, but he wasn't fit to wear this goddamn badge."

Royal looked Chris straight in the eye, unblinking behind his bifocals. Gold rims burned with sunlight. "And neither are you. That's the heart of it, Sheriff Cherry. That's all this is about."

Chris was angry with himself and done sparring with Royal. "Okay, D.A. Moody, as long as we understand each other. As long as we're absolutely clear. But until the voters of this county turn me out, I have work to do. *My job.* I expect you to do yours." Chris stood, got ready to leave. "Besides, we both know it's too late to save my job anyway, right? One success isn't going to change that."

Royal looked him up and down, measuring him, running a hand through his thinning hair. He'd been a pretty good baseball player once, or so Chris had been told. It was hard to see that now. "Are you even trying that hard? To win this thing?"

"What do you think?"

Royal watched him for a few seconds more, then looked down at the *Daily* on the table in front of him, still open to the story about the bodies in Delcia Canyon. He stared at that longer, reading it again. "If you can make a credible case that Eddy Rabbit was involved with those deaths, I'll charge him."

"I appreciate that, Royal, I do. I'll do what I can. Hell, I'll do my best," Chris said, fishing for a twenty out of his pocket. He folded it and laid it across the open paper, across his own name in the editorial. "You can keep that. I'm done reading it. And breakfast is on me. For both you and Bethel."

FIFTEEN

E ddy Rabbit hadn't taken all day at all.

Once he'd started talking, he'd hardly taken any time at all. And since Sheriff Cherry wasn't back from Nathan yet to be briefed, that gave America the chance to head out to Chapel Mesa, where she and Ben used to spend hours together practicing her shooting. The scooped-out hollow they used for their makeshift range was already warm, holding on to the late-morning sun, and what little breeze there was barely moved the paper targets she'd set up in front of the berm. Fall was just around the corner, but you wouldn't know it by the way the quartz shined bright and hot along the mesa's flanks. Summer wasn't ready to let go.

It had been cooler a couple of mornings ago down in the shadows of Delcia Canyon, at least until they had found the bodies by the water.

America sighted down the Colt, wanting to keep her pattern tight, the way Ben had taught her. Ben had put new Wilson Combat grips on the weapon and had adjusted the trigger pull. He'd retooled the barrel and replaced the original sights with Trijicon Bright & Tough Night Sights. He'd made the weapon perfect for her, but in doing so, he'd made it *his* as well. She couldn't look at it, couldn't hold it, without thinking about him. She missed him more than she wanted to admit, more than she wanted anyone to know.

She lowered her gun, distracted for a moment by the spent brass sparkling on the ground. She and Ben had always policed up their brass after an afternoon of shooting, but always missed some. Even the kids who came out here at night to pick them up for scrap failed to find them all, and she always came across a few later—just like this—shining in the dirt. How many of those rounds had been Ben's? How many had he held and loaded?

¿Para ella?

She resighted on the target, the dark middle circle, roughly where the heart would be. Breathing slow, relaxing, feeling sweat bead across her forehead. Feeling the gun go heavy in her hand and somehow willing it to be light again. Making it a part of her, not gripping it too tight. *Don't hold it so goddamn tight*: that's what Ben had always told her.

The gun moved, alive, but she held it steady.

At this distance she could barely see the shot grouping, but had a sense there was a ragged hole in the target's heart.

The real reason she was out here didn't have much to do with target practice or with Ben Harper. It had to do with not going home yet, not restarting the argument with Danny they'd had all last night and then again this morning before they met with Santino Paez and Eddy Rabbit.

It had to do with the unanswered calls she'd made to her mama in Camargo.

It had to do with the old man and the young girl still there waiting for her, waiting to see what she'd do next.

She couldn't help wondering what the hell Ben would say to her about that now.

SHE WAS PICKING UP THE LAST of her brass when Danny walked up. He stood about ten feet away, watching her, with his Bullhide hat pulled low. He'd started wearing the vaquero hat like the other deputies, like Sheriff Ross, but still didn't seem comfortable in it. He was always taking it on and off, leaving it in his truck or on his desk. She'd find it all over her apartment, tossed aside. He held it as much as he wore it, but she appreciated as well as anyone that desire to fit in, to disappear in some ways and not call attention to yourself. That had been her once, a long time ago, but that girl had left Murfee and never returned. Danny's hat reminded her of the dark one her brother had sometimes worn when he was crossing over the river for a night at the bars in Ojinaga. He'd worn it low over his eyes to make him look older, tougher. Danny's shaded his face the same way now, so she couldn't see the angry expression that she knew was there.

"I figured you'd come out here, the way you blasted out after our talk with Eddy. I think you hurt Santino's feelings. He doesn't like dealing with me."

"He'll survive. Is Sheriff Cherry back yet from Nathan?"

"No, but he's on his way. He radioed in and wants to meet with us. He wants to follow up from that call I had with him this morning." Danny pulled off the hat for a moment, turned it around once and looked at it, before putting it back on his head. "You drove out here for nothing, Amé. Now you gotta turn around and go right back."

"And so do you," she said, walking over to put the brass bucket in the back of her truck. He trailed three steps behind her. "And it wasn't for nothing. I didn't ask you to follow me here. There was a reason for that."

If that stung him, he didn't show it. "Hell, if I waited for you to ask me to do much of anything, I'd still be sitting in that hospital alone." He walked up next to her and took the bucket out of her hand and set it on the ground between them. "I know you don't want to talk about this, but we're going to. We're going to talk about that man still sitting in your kitchen right now, not to mention that little girl."

"We already talked about it," she said. They both knew it was that man's sudden appearance that had kept them up all night, and prompted them to push on Eddy Rabbit so hard so early this morning. Neither of them had slept anyway.

"No, *I* talked, and you didn't say much of anything." Danny looked like he was going to put a hand on her arm, but stopped short. "Do you believe him? Those things he said last night?"

She took a step back. "You asked me that last night, again and again and again. My answer is no different. I do, and I don't know what choice I have."

"All because he talked about a gun?"

"No, because he talked about *the* gun, *la pistola*. The only one like it. No one else knows about it."

"Not even the sheriff?"

"No. *No él.*"

"And your brother used to own this fancy silver gun?" Danny was shaking his head, still confused.

"No, not exactly the same. It's different." She couldn't explain how she'd last seen her brother's gun in a hotel room outside Houston. It had been silver and pearl, etched with images of the Virgen de Guadalupe and Pancho Villa and Jesús Malverde; stamped also with several grinning *calaveras*. She'd left it with Máximo, when she foolishly thought it would be easy to walk away from her life in the Big Bend.

When she thought she would never see one like it again.

"This one is mine. It was sent to me. *By him.*"

Danny searched her eyes, and she didn't look away. She wanted him to see whatever was there. "All this time you've never mentioned it, never showed it to me? Not once?"

He wasn't hurt by her words a moment ago, but he was by this. He *wanted* to be hurt, but she wouldn't apologize. *Sí*, they'd spent the past year together, but the history tied to that *pistola* went beyond them. It went back much further than that, into a darkness that Danny couldn't see and that she didn't know how to show him. It was a hole as dark as the one her brother had been buried in.

Her gun wasn't the same as Rodolfo's; some of the same *calaveras*, but no Jesús Malverde or Virgen de Guadalupe. Instead, there was only one figure, clearly a woman, but skeletal and horrible. She was wrapped in a massive cloak, with her own tiny smiling skull, her hands holding a scythe and a globe.

Nuestra Señora de la Santa Muerte.

It was a skinless skull with no face, but America always believed it had been carved to look just like her.

"So what does it mean?" he asked. "This damn gun. Is it a message, a threat?"

"It means we know who we are, and the things we've done. All the things we're willing to do."

Danny stepped toward her again. "That's bullshit. This son of a bitch needs to know what *I'm* willing to do if he's here to hurt you."

"*Usted no entiende*. He's not here to hurt me, not now. I don't know what he wants, but you must trust me. You have no idea who he is, the things he's done."

"And you do?" Danny's breath was on her face, feathering her hair. They were close enough she could imagine his heart beating against hers, then remembered the bullet holes she'd put into that paper target's heart only moments before. He asked again: "What do you really know?"

But what could he really know about her? What could anyone truly know about someone else?

She let him stand close for few heartbeats longer anyway, wanting that, before backing away again. He let her go, bending down and picking up her heavy brass bucket and putting it in the back of her truck, as she opened her door to drive back to Murfee.

"*Sé que somos una familia,*" she told him, answering his question. "That man and I are family."

SIXTEEN

Chris was trying hard to listen as Danny and Amé recounted their interrogation of Eddy Rabbit. They were in Chris's office, but through his open door, and over their shoulders, he was distracted by two of his other deputies, Tommy Milford and Till Greer, talking. *Laughing*—beneath Ben Harper's and Buck Emmett's black-banded memorial pictures. Dale Holt was out serving a summons with Marco Lucero in tow. That was it: six—all the deputies he had now, to oversee thousands of square miles in the Big Bend.

"Sheriff?" Danny asked, turning to follow Chris's gaze out the door, as Till was still laughing out loud at whatever dumb story or joke Tommy was spinning. Chris had wanted his deputies to see those pictures of Ben and Buck whenever they walked out of the building as a reminder of what they risked each day, but now they passed those photos of their fallen friends—men they'd once known and laughed with, too—without a second thought or glance, as one day became the next day and then the day after. Until today was just another day. Maybe it had to be that way, so life could go on. Because life had to go on. But Chris still needed those photos, so he'd never forget those losses, never forget how these six men and women left behind were his responsibility, and the risks he asked them to take.

Yesterday. Today. Every day.

"I'm sorry, Danny," Chris said. "I got distracted by those two clowns out there. Why don't you grab the door and start again?"

"EDDY IS GOING TO BE A DEAD END," Danny said. "He told us what he knows, which isn't a whole lot. For about the last six months he's been renting out his trailer down in the canyon as kind of a way station for drug mules crossing the river there. They give him a heads-up on these Motorola radios, and he makes sure the way is clear when they cross. The dope is stored at his place until other men come and get it and drive it out of the Big Bend. He knows nicknames . . . Gato, Flaco, Chaca . . . stuff like that, but that's about it. His initial contact was a man named Apache. Eddy says he calls himself that because he works for some Mexican Indians or something, whatever that means. He's the guy who approached Eddy, got him all set up. They met once, maybe twice, right at the beginning, but pretty much everything since then has been done direct with the mules, and never the same group twice. They mostly use those radios we found because Apache doesn't believe they can be intercepted like cell phones."

"Can they?" Chris asked. He wasn't sure one way or the other. It was a question for Garrison, if he wanted to ask him.

Danny shrugged. "Not really my specialty. Apache

told Eddy they were encrypted. We used encrypted radio comms in the military all the time, so if that's the same thing, then he's probably right."

"What was Eddy's cut?"

"Fifteen hundred dollars a trip. Or they gave him half-pound quantities of meth. Eddy said at first it was mainly marijuana bales, but then it was meth or coke or heroin."

"How often?"

"Cada dos semanas," Amé said, finally stepping into the conversation.

"Probably whatever she said." Danny shrugged.

"Every two weeks?" Chris said, too loud. He'd given his grand speech to Garrison about not focusing on drug smuggling in the Big Bend, and he wasn't naive about what that meant, but still . . . *every two weeks?* No wonder Garrison had questions about what the hell Chris and his deputies were doing.

"Yeah," Danny said, "Take-Out's been busy. But the most recent run last week didn't go, no one reached out to him. Now we know why."

"The men in the river," Chris said.

"We showed him the pictures. He doesn't recognize them," Amé added. "But he didn't always meet the same men. He swears he never saw anyone as young as the boy. I don't know that I believe him . . ."

Danny picked up where she left off. "Eddy can give us shitty descriptions of the cars and trucks all day long, even the men driving them or wading across the river, but none of that gets us very far. Best we can do is keep the radios we recovered charged up and turned on, just in case someone does reach out for him. Or we try to force a face-to-face with Apache . . . I had Eddy walk me through every number in his cell phone, and I'll follow up with a subpoena on all of them, but I'm not holding my breath. I figure Eddy's got to have another phone or radio hidden away somewhere, but he swears he doesn't."

"Check with Charity. Get ahold of her phone, too," Chris said, thinking out loud. "Maybe she was the real connect with Apache. Probably not, but worth a look." Chris looked between his two deputies. "Where does that leave us?"

"It leaves us charging Eddy with the assault on me, or pulling together a decent historical case on all the dope he's admitted to helping cross over. A dry conspiracy, but with his priors, still enough to put him away forever, if that's what we want."

"But I get the feeling we don't want to do that?" Chris asked, uncertain. "I just had a difficult meeting with D.A. Moody, all but strong-arming him into charging Eddy with those bodies . . . if we could make the case."

Amé and Danny looked at each other, but it was Danny who spoke first. "We had to pull it out of him, but in the end, Eddy didn't lawyer up. He told us most of what he knows, and he did it without any sort of immunity agreement. What's more, I actually believe him. Not everything, not every word of it, but I *saw* him run out of that cane. He was scared shitless. Don't get me wrong, he's a grade-A fuck-up, and if his girlfriend wants to press charges on the beating he gave her, he deserves to sit his ass in jail for that alone. But the rest of it? I'm not ready to put that on him." Danny shrugged, let it drop.

"But those men aren't dead if Eddy Rabbit isn't involved. It's his trailer, Danny. He was part of the scheme. Legally, that is the conspiracy," Chris pressed.

"I know, but if it isn't Eddy, it's someone else. There's always someone else, always another Eddy Rabbit," Danny answered, echoing the same arguments Chris had made to both himself and Garrison. If he'd dealt with Eddy Rabbit earlier, those men in the river might not be dead, either. Chris always suspected what Eddy was up to—*not everything, not every word*—and could have made the case and locked him up two years ago. But Eddy had always been harmless, and Chris had wanted to believe he was doing better by him by leaving him alone.

Five dead men might think differently.

For the second time, Chris caught Danny looking over to Amé, as something passed between them they weren't ready to share. They were having another conversation right now . . . an argument . . . that didn't include him and didn't have much to do with Eddy Rabbit, either.

"I told Amé that I was meeting with Joe Garrison last night. He said there are problems all along this part of the border right now, all linked to the attack on those students in Ojinaga. Our murders could be part of that. That doesn't absolve Eddy, but . . ." *That sure as hell doesn't absolve me, either,* Chris thought. He turned to Amé. "What do you think?"

"*Sí, lo hago.* There's not much Eddy can do, or we can do."

"It'd be nice if there was a homicide in this goddamn county we could actually solve," Chris said, before immediately regretting it. It raised too many ghosts: not only the specter of Rodolfo Reynosa, but also Evelyn Ross, Sheriff Ross's third wife. Chris had long suspected the sheriff had murdered her, but her body had never been found, and most people in Murfee still believed she'd simply run off, maybe with another man. Chris believed she'd been buried on some hunting property Ross had owned—El Dorado—although he'd gone up there several times to search alone and never found anything.

It was tough when you didn't know exactly what to look for or have any idea what to do next. That was true now for Eddy Rabbit and the bodies in the river.

"What else did Garrison say?" Danny asked, followed by another of those looks at Amé.

"The usual cartel stuff, how they're all fighting each other over there. He also had some pointed questions about Chuy and Johnnie Machado and their Tejas unit in Terrell."

"Johnnie Macho is a piece of shit. He's like Eddy Rabbit with a badge, and probably not half as competent."

"Not according to Garrison. To hear him tell it, that Tejas unit is one of the most effective counter-drug task forces in the whole state. He wants to know why we aren't participating. Hell, he wants me to sign you up for it."

"Are you?" Danny asked.

"No, we have enough to do here. Besides, he has some legitimate concerns on how that task force operates. I'll let him figure that out on his own."

Amé was looking down at her hands. "Did he say anything about Nemesio? Is Nemesio responsible for what's happening in Ojinaga?"

Chris paused before answering, considering. She rarely, if ever, mentioned her brother's former cartel by name, and never so directly.

"He believes the attack on those students in Ojinaga was either ordered by Nemesio or made to look like it was. It's a power struggle between Nemesio and another cartel. Supposedly this Fox Uno, the leader of Nemesio, is at the center of it. We're lucky enough to have our own front-row seats here in the Big Bend. Our five dead are likely just more nameless victims, and Eddy, a not-so-innocent bystander. Garrison thinks Fox Uno's days are numbered." Chris had stayed up for a while going through the folder Garrison had left him. It had been a tough, dispiriting read, and he'd learned more than he ever wanted to about Fox Uno. "He's on the run or may already be dead."

Amé stood up, leaning against the closed office door, as if she wanted to make sure none of the other deputies walked in. She looked again like that teenage girl Chris had first met wrapped in a hooded sweatshirt outside Mancha's, her face hidden by sunglasses and cigarette smoke. Unsure, unsteady, but not necessarily afraid. "Agent Garrison is wrong," she finally said.

"What do you mean?" Chris asked.

"Fox Uno isn't dead, Sheriff," Danny quickly added. "And he definitely isn't in Ojinaga."

"That's because that man, my uncle, *está aquí* . . . in Murfee," Amé finished.

Danny folded his arms, looking up at Amé with an expression Chris couldn't read: worry, anger, relief. A tired mix of all three. This was what Danny had been waiting for since they'd walked in, the reason for all their shared glances. *Danny knew.* He'd known all along. He'd only been holding out for Amé to say it first.

"That's why we had to talk to Eddy first thing this morning," Danny admitted. "We needed to find out if he knew anything about Fox Uno, or could at least tie the man who showed up on Amé's porch last night claiming to be him to the bodies we discovered. We don't think so. Not now, not directly. My hunch is Eddy and Apache are actually working on behalf of this *other* cartel, these mysterious Indians he went on about. Eddy's just too far down the totem pole to know."

None of them smiled at Danny's grim humor. "You're both telling me Fox Uno's here, now, in Murfee?" Chris asked, incredulous.

"He calls himself Juan Abrego," Amé said.

Danny slumped in his seat. "Whoever the fuck he is, he didn't come alone, and they're both sitting in her apartment right now."

SEVENTEEN

Juan Abrego watched Zita sleep on the girl America's couch.

Su sobrina. His niece.

America—a name he did not like—had made sure Zita was comfortable before she'd left. She'd talked to her and helped her wash after days on the move. He had tried to imagine some resemblance in the two girls, something in their eyes or the way they moved; a turn of a head . . . some link between himself and them. Between himself and America. There was nothing, and it was foolish to think there would be. But America had treated Zita as her *hermanita* all the same. Smiling at her, saying over and over again, *Tu eres muy, muy bonita . . . una princesa.*

That had been a distraction, so Zita would not notice the other man, the one America had called Danny, holding a gun on them the whole time.

THEY TRIED TO KILL HIM IN MANUEL BENA-VIDES, a place he knew better as San Carlos.

Shorty Lopez had once owned a great *rancho* there, La Hacienda Oriental, and Juan Abrego could still remember the parties, nights filled with the soft light of lanterns and torches, the smell of smoke and horses and perfume and *mota*. That was all gone now, like Shorty himself. After he and some others ambushed Shorty on the orders of La Vibora they'd taken to wearing pieces of Shorty's broken skull on gold chains and had done so for many years. La Vibora had made the chains for them as a reminder not only of the high price of loyalty, true loyalty, but more important, the true cost of betrayal.

It was a lesson he had taken to heart.

JUAN ABREGO HAD BEEN IN THE SECOND VEHICLE, a van, with Gualterio in front and two more cars behind (all *americano*, stolen from this side of the river), when they ambushed him.

They came in a fleet of black SUVs, like a flock of *cuervos*, and he did not know if they were Los Hermanos Serrano, or Secretaría de Marina, or *federales*, or all three. They drove out of the shadows of an old barn, churning up dust as they came, and the first SUV's windows were down so that Juan Abrego could see sunlight winking on and off the barrel of a gun—many guns— like pesos flipped end over end in the air. Those guns spat fire, and glass shattered and two of the tires blew out in the car behind him. It lifted up, up, and then rolled over and over along the packed earth of the road, throwing gravel and broken glass high into the air where it seemed to hang forever. The car behind tried to swerve away, but clipped the rear of the rolling car before it came to a stop, setting it spinning again like *una tapa*.

One of the other dark SUVs, and there were so many Juan Abrego lost count, pulled alongside the wrecked vehicle and men in even darker clothes got out and approached it in a crouch, leading with more gunfire. Someone tried to crawl out of the twisted metal and a line of bullets stitched his body, making him jerk and shake.

Juan Abrego grabbed Zita and pulled her close to him as heavy rounds punched into his van. Bulletproof plates had been welded onto the frame, making it heavy and slow, and his driver—a young man Juan Abrego did not know—fought the wheel and talked on a handheld radio at the same time. Over the screams of Luisa, who'd squeezed flat into the floorboards at his feet, Gualterio was calmly giving the remaining cars in their caravan instructions.

Over the open radio channel, there was the echo of more gunfire.

Metal on metal and men yelling.

The man in the front passenger seat of the van had foolishly rolled down the window, firing his AK-47 out of it, so that the spent shells—a sound like wooden *castañuelas*—clattered back into his lap and on the dashboard and all over Juan Abrego and Luisa and Zita. Juan Abrego reached out and pulled two of them out of Zita's hair, still hot to the touch, and kissed her and told her it was okay. Then the man with the AK-47 was shot through the mouth and the temple, one right after the other—sudden, harsh sunlight appearing above his right eye—and he fell completely apart in the seat around them and sprayed them all with his hot, pumping *sangre*.

Crazy with fear, Luisa screamed louder, raised up, and

tried to crawl out of the open window of the moving van, and a bullet caressed her throat. She reached for it, surprised, as her *sangre* spouted into her face and her eyes rolled back in her skull.

The driver tossed his radio aside, pushing the van to its limits. They'd left the road and were driving downward through scrub, through ocotillo and yucca. They were bouncing up and down, the whole world shuddering, and what Juan Abrego had thought were bullets punching the sides and belly of the van were instead harmless rocks, churned up by the spinning wheels.

The driver, his expensive sunglasses crooked on his head and his face red from the *sangre* of the two fresh bodies in the car, called back to Juan Abrego.

"*Padrino*, I can buy you a few minutes, nothing more than that, so you and the girl can run, run . . ."

Juan Abrego had a small leather bag with him, the same bag he'd always carried for a moment like this. His son Martino had bought the bag for him in Los Angeles, or maybe San Diego. It was Gucci, expensive, and he rarely opened it. It had a few documents, a thick wad of both *americano* money and pesos, three cell phones, and a silver-plated Ruger. It would be easy enough to take the Ruger and shoot Zita and then himself, save them both from whatever horrors awaited them if they were caught alive . . .

Or he could run.

Zita huddled against him, crying. There was *sangre* in her hair, on the hands he held her tight with. His hands, again. He looked back to his driver, this man he did not know, who was no different from any of the men who'd surrounded him for years. Young, his thick mustache crimson. Sweat and blood plastering his wavy hair to his head. He truly looked like a little boy playing grown-up. He was scared. Shaking all over, but still he kept driving.

"What is your name?"

The driver did not turn, staring instead through the dust and sunlight that rose in front of them like a wall. "I am Abrahán Sierra. My family, my wife and my own daughter, are in Parral. Remember them, please, and this thing I do now."

"I knew a Sierra once, long ago. I knew many men."

"Please, *padrino*, they live in Parral. Parral." He spat at the shattered windshield, adding, "Here . . . I can stop for a moment here . . . but no more than that." He waved with a shaking hand. "This is a low place, sheltered. Follow the arroyo and they may not see you. I'll drive back toward them, try to lead them away."

Juan Abrego pulled Zita toward him, too roughly, and told her to get ready. "I will remember them, Abrahán. Parral. Your wife and daughter. *La familia Sierra.*"

The driver turned to him as the van shuddered to a halt, desert dust roiling through the open window. It coated them, choked them. There was the stink of *sangre* and heated metal. Somewhere, not far away, the sound of more gunfire and engines revving.

"You are very brave, Abrahán Sierra," Juan Abrego said. "You are going to die now."

The driver laughed. "I am very, very foolish." Then: "They promised me so many things, but I was dead anyway. I see that now."

Then the boy named Abrahán Sierra jumped out and pulled open the van's back door, dented and scarred with bullet holes, and took the crying Zita out of Juan Abrego's arms and carried her out into the light and dust.

JUAN ABREGO WAS NO ONE.

But the man called Fox Uno still had friends, all throughout Manuel Benavides, even though the *sicarios* and *contrabandistas* of Los Hermanos Serrano crawled everywhere, like *hormigas.*

So Juan Abrego was left behind, one piece at a time.

He left his bulletproof vest in the desert about two miles from the van, the last time he saw Abrahán Sierra.

He left behind two gold rings and a Patek Philippe watch in Escobillas de Abajo, and those things bought him and Zita food and some used clothes. They also bought them time, and that was almost priceless.

He left behind most of his pesos in Nuevo Lajitas, and that bought them another two nights' rest and a ride to the crossing.

He left behind one of the three cell phones, crushed beneath his boot under a mesquite near the river. He wanted to believe Gualterio was still alive, but it was unclear how many of their men had been compromised. Everyone was on the run—dead or dying or captured.

Maybe not everyone.

They promised me so many things, but I was dead anyway . . .

And then before he and Zita crossed over the river

near Santa Elena in their borrowed clothes, he left behind the silver-plated Ruger.

He tossed it in the water and watched it sink.

NOW THERE WAS NOTHING to be done except to
watch Zita sleep, and wait for his *sobrina* to come home
and decide what to do with them. She might decide to
send the one she called Danny, alone, with his gun. Or
more *policía*. Or Las Tres Letras, the DEA. Did his *sobrina* believe him, trust him? Could she?

Could he trust her?

He still had his two remaining cellular phones, secure
for a handful more days, because if they weren't, he was
dead already, as he would be if he tried to return now to
Ojinaga. America and the one named Danny had eyed
them all morning, expecting one or the other to ring at any
moment—to give them answers, to help them decide
whether he was telling the truth for her *familia*—although
only he knew those phones would never ring on their own,
and whatever answers and secrets were on the other end
could never satisfy them. There were no answers . . . no
easy way to describe his life and the man he was.

Yo soy la Muerte, mi amigo . . .

Those phones were his only way to reach back into
Ojinaga to find out who still lived, who did not. Who he
could trust, and who would still call him *padrino* . . . El
Patrón. They were his lifeline to Gualterio, even Martino,
if he thought he could risk that. His *sobrina* would soon
decide to take them from him, as the one named Danny
would have already done, had she not stopped him.

Por el momento, she still believed Juan Abrego. It was easy not to lie when one didn't know the truth.

His money and valuables and the fake documents still in his Gucci bag had been enough to get him this far, but like the phones, they would not serve him much longer. He would never leave here with them, and worse, he was *enfermo*, dying. What was the point of running if there was nowhere go?

How long did he truly have to decide who he could trust?

Or who had betrayed him?

Gualterio? His own son, Martino?

Fox Uno had not been ready to die outside Santa Elena, and Juan Abrego was not ready to die here, either, in this place.

Juan Abrego reached into his boot and pulled out one of the small plastic-wrapped slips of black plastic he had hidden there. It was no bigger than his thumbnail.

He popped open the back of one of the phones and slipped it in, like Martino had once shown him. He wondered if his son remembered that now.

In another week, if he could survive that long, he needed to be someone and somewhere else.

It reminded him how he had not been able to hold back a laugh when he and Zita finally waded through the sluggish current of the river, moments after throwing the Ruger into it: stinking water no deeper than his ankles. Warm on his bare skin, like a woman's touch. But there had been no one there to question their false papers . . . *su nombre* . . . anyway.

Just *la luna* above, shining like *plata*, like the gun he had tossed away.

Zita had asked: *Why are you laughing, Papa?* And he had hugged her and whispered: *Because the world is such a funny place, little one.*

And that is why he had laughed: at the foolishness of it all.

All these men, all these years, hunting for Fox Uno . . . *para él* . . . across México, but there had been no one at all to watch when the most wanted and feared cartel leader in history crossed the border for the first time into Los Estados Unidos.

No one to watch, or remember, what appeared to be a young *nieta* holding her *viejo abuelo*'s weakened hand against the slight current of the mighty Río Bravo.

EIGHTEEN

M y uncle is at my apartment now, along with a girl
he claims is his daughter. They crossed over the
border earlier. How long ago, I don't know," Amé
said.

"How long has it been since you've seen him?" Chris
asked. "In person?"

"*¿Tal vez nunca?* When I was too young to remember?"

"So he really could be anyone at all?"

"Well, except for the gun," Danny added. "Except for
that."

Amé nodded, reluctantly. "Rodolfo had a silver gun,
a gift from Nemesio, from my uncle. I also received such a
gun. It arrived in a package at my front door. This was a
year ago, right after Ben died. There was no note, *nada*.
I never showed it to anyone or talked about it, but I knew
who sent it. The man in my apartment described it."

"You never told me that, Amé," Chris said.

"I know. I never told Danny, either, or anyone." She
stopped, didn't add anything else. If Chris thought she
was going to apologize for it, she didn't.

Danny stood again. He'd been up and down as they'd
been talking about what happened last night, rising and
falling in rhythm with the story. "I searched him. He had

some money and a Mexican passport and license, both probably fake. Neither are in the name Juan Abrego, which is what he called himself to us. He's got a B-2 visa visitor stamp in the passport, although he says he's never been to the U.S. He also has two phones, one a regular Telcel, the other something called a Blackphone. I looked it up, it's some super-high-tech phone, hard to hack or trace, but you can fucking buy it on Amazon. For what it's worth, neither of his numbers were in Eddy's phone, which was another thing I checked this morning, and another reason why we went to see him."

"These phones are how he's talking to his people in Mexico?"

"Whatever people he has left," Danny answered. "He claims he needs time to get him and the girl out of Texas, probably out of the U.S. altogether. He says he can get someone to meet him here and bring him new passports, money, whatever. Just a few days, and then he's gone."

"But what about Amé's family . . . ?" Chris added. Chris didn't know much about Amé's mother—Margarita—who used to work at the Supreme Clean in Murfee. He remembered picking up Sheriff Ross's uniform shirts from her. But she and Amé's father had moved back to Mexico a few years ago, after they'd identified their son's body in the desert, and although his deputy talked to her mother once or twice a month, he didn't think she'd seen her in a long time. Margarita was always trying to get Amé to come south to stay with them, but she wouldn't cross the river, at least as far he knew.

Danny nodded. "Yeah, there is that."

Amé completed the thought for them: "He has to

make calls each day to his men across the river. If I don't help him, if he can't get out of Texas, or if he doesn't make those calls on time, my mama will be killed."

THEY ALL SAT SILENT for a long time after that, watching the sun move outside Chris's office windows. The lemon trees the city council had planted long ago all along Main Street were trying hard to cast thin, barely-there shadows. The trees had never quite taken hold, no matter how much care they'd been given. He'd stood under them once, afraid to lean against them for support, after he'd talked with Sheriff Ross about the skeleton he'd recovered from Indian Bluffs. The skeleton they all later learned was Amé's brother.

"It's bullshit," Danny finally said. "He's bluffing, both about who he is, and what he's doing here." He turned to Amé. "And this threat about your family? These mysterious phone calls? It's crazy, I don't buy any of it."

"Maybe," Chris conceded, "but it tracks somewhat with what Garrison told me. Think about it—if Fox Uno is on the run, what better place to hide than here? The one place no one is looking for him, or would ever expect him to be." Chris penciled an empty circle on a piece of paper in front of him. It was a copy of an election filing form, something he'd forgotten to fill out until Mel had done it for him. He looked up at Amé. "Do you really think he'd let your mother, his own sister, die over there?"

But it was a question Chris hardly needed to ask. He'd read Garrison's file—all the things Fox Uno had allegedly done. The tortures and beheadings and bombings.

In 2010, some sort of suitcase bomb he'd meant for a rival had killed three small children. A couple of years later, he ordered the killing of three Catholic priests, who were strangled with their vestments. Those were only a few of the murders that had attracted attention, but how many more had not?

Amé agreed with a shrug, a small, desperate gesture. "I know I cannot reach my mama. I cannot reach anyone. If he is the man I know he is, then yes."

"*If* he's really in charge of anything at all anymore," Danny countered. "If he's running for his life, who's left to call? Who can he trust? Everyone he knows, everyone related to him, is probably already dead anyway." Danny stopped, realizing he was talking about the rest of Amé's family, but then pushed angrily ahead anyway; Chris could feel the heat of it. "He's buying time with money he doesn't have. Whoever he is, he came over the river in some shitty clothes he stole off someone's laundry line, dragging that poor girl with him. Maybe she's his daughter, or granddaughter, maybe not. It doesn't matter. He used that girl as a shield, just like he's now trying to use Amé."

Chris said, "I could call Garrison right now. He's always talking about his people listening to stuff down here, like they have satellites spinning above us all the time. Hell, they probably do. Maybe he's finally heard something about Fox Uno slipping over the border?"

Amé nodded, although Chris wasn't sure she was agreeing with him. "He'll ask questions. He'll want answers."

"And you'll tell him the truth. You've got nothing to

be afraid of. We explain what we have, *who* we think we have. He'll be down here before nightfall. Then we turn this man over to him and see how it plays out."

"¿*Y la chica?* What happens to her?" Amé asked.

Chris and Danny both stayed silent.

"I don't know, Amé," Chris finally admitted. "We're all just guessing here."

"We're guessing about *mi familia*. What if we were guessing about Ms. Bristow, or your son?"

Chris drew a second empty circle, close but not touching the other, then tossed the pencil down. "Are you seriously asking me to let him stay here in Murfee? To go along with this?"

Amé crossed and uncrossed her arms. "*No lo sé.* But if it's only a few days . . . and there's a chance it can save my mama . . ."

"When's the last time you spoke to her?"

"Two weeks ago. My mama is in Camargo, my papa is . . . is not. He works outside the city and returns home now and then. Fox Uno says he can do nothing for him anyway. He may already be lost to me."

Chris picked up the hesitation, but it didn't matter to him what Amé's father did over the river. Like so many, he did whatever he had to in order to survive. He hoped the man was doing that now.

"You tried to reach out to her last night, this morning?"

"*Sí, nada.* And I have no way to talk to my papa." She looked at her hands, like she was holding her anger, all her desperation, there. "I have no way to know what's going on over there. But . . . if it's just a few days . . ."

"Then what?" Chris asked. "This man is gone for

good? If you do this, do you really think he's out of your life forever? Is that what you really believe?"

"Eso es lo que dice," Amé said.

Danny looked back and forth between them. "Look, I know I don't understand much Spanish, but I know enough that I can't believe you two are actually considering this." Danny leaned so close to Amé that Chris thought he was going to grab her hand, but he didn't. "Listen to me, I'll even accept for the moment that he's your uncle, and that he's this big-time cartel figure. So let's look at what he's done, who he's hurt. *Your own brother*, for starters. If you truly believe him . . . if you believe all the things he's done and the things he's saying now . . . then you have to acknowledge that maybe, just maybe, he's been setting you up for this from the beginning. He's playing you. For fuck's sake, he's threatening to let his own sister die if you don't help him. He's *killing* her if he doesn't make one fucking phone call, and he's holding you hostage at the same time. There's no way this ends well for anyone. It can't."

"Before I decide anything, I'll have to talk to him," Chris said.

Danny turned back to him. "Sheriff, *please* listen to me. Listen to yourself. Go down there and arrest this son of a bitch and be done with it. I nearly shot him last night—please don't make me regret that I didn't."

"I hear you, Danny. Don't think for a minute I don't know how goddamn serious this is, for all of us. This man tried to have me killed, too." Chris stopped, not sure what else to say, how to explain and summarize the last four years of his life . . . and Amé's. Maybe if it wasn't

Amé they were talking about, he would feel differently, which didn't make him feel any better about it at all. Maybe then he would go down there and haul this man in and let the chips fall where they may.

What if we were guessing about Ms. Bristow, or your son?

Chris knew there shouldn't be two sets of rules, one for those he loved and another for those he didn't—he and Mel had had that exact talk when the Earls were holed up after Ben's death—but this was different. He couldn't help remembering Amé as that girl outside Mancha's, the one with the sunglasses and cigarettes—the one he'd promised to protect, save—and thinking how little he'd actually done.

He'd waited too long to deal with Sheriff Ross, and people had died. He'd waited too long to deal with John Wesley Earl, and people had died. Both times, he'd done what he'd thought was the right thing, only to have other people pay for that with their lives.

He'd made those choices and had to live with them.

And if he chose the right thing here again—and the only choice that made any real sense at all was to put handcuffs on this man calling himself Fox Uno and let Garrison deal with him—then it seemed likely more people would die. For the third time, on his watch.

If Chris believed the man in Amé's apartment was who he was claiming to be.

Was it about believing that man . . . or Amé?

Because if Chris chose wrong and helped his young deputy harbor an international fugitive and murderer, he had to wonder what that said about him.

Maybe it said he wasn't fit to be the sheriff after all.

And in the end, he'd have to live with that choice, too.

Chris turned all his attention to Amé. "Would you have told me about this if Danny hadn't been there, too, last night? You never said a word about the gun. For God's sake, Amé, I thought we were past all that."

She didn't shake his stare. "*Sí*, I would have told you about Fox Uno. No matter what he had said or promised, I would not decide this without you. It affects too many. *Todos nosotros.*"

Was it about believing that man . . . or Amé?

"That makes me feel better, I guess," Chris said, although it didn't, not at all. He stood up anyway, though, slow, and got ready to leave.

"What are we doing?" Danny asked, serious. He looked ready to block the office door with his body, if Amé wasn't already standing in front of it.

Chris said, "Well, I guess I'm going to formally introduce myself to Amé's uncle."

G etting across the river wasn't the problem.

It was surviving the other side.

Surviving the sun and the rocks and the crushing emptiness. It was easy to get turned around and lost there, to die from the heat and thirst in that unfamiliar place before you ever found what you were looking for.

That's why most who crossed bought maps, hand-drawn things that tried to make sense of that tangle of canyons and arroyos and roads. Endless trails that had been worn smooth and glassy by centuries of callused feet; places where water and shade could be found, dug-outs and holes where you could lay up and hide from the *camisetas verdes*, the *americano* Border Patrol in their green shirts. Most of these maps were also marked with tiny *calaveras*, faded ink warnings marking those smuggling paths controlled by *los narcos*. They would kill you if they found you there, and leave your body to rot as a warning to others.

As would the *bajadores*, thieves and murderers who preyed on anyone they could catch.

Maps were expensive, but guides—*los coyotes*—cost even more. For a handsome fee, they promised you safe passage not only over the river, but to the cities on the other side: Houston and Dallas and Chicago and New York. Places that meant nothing to Chayo, places so far away they might have been *la luna*. He'd heard all about the men and women and children who'd hiked through the desert only to find themselves crushed into small airless cars and vans, driven to houses where they waited for days or sometimes weeks to be moved on. Sometimes more money would be demanded of their families, and sometimes a woman or child was taken away in the middle of the night anyway, never to be seen again.

Like Chayo's fellow *normalistas*.

Chayo understood that he and Neva could not be found, could not be caught. Not now. As far as anyone knew, they were already dead. They'd been taken away in the middle of the night, and everything they might know about their attackers, the men in the police cars and uniforms, had disappeared with them. It would be worse for them and, more important, their families, if they were caught now. They had to get across the border.

Chayo had no money for a map or for *los coyotes*.

He would have to be both.

ON AMADOR'S COMPUTER, the old one he kept in the candy store, Chayo was able to search up a map of the area around Barranco Azul and Tabaloapa. It wasn't much, and it didn't show him the truly safe trails or passages, or anything important at all, but it gave some direction, some shape, to his plan. He wrote down a list of towns within a few days of the river on the *americano* side: Presidio, Terlingua, Redford, Nathan, Dryden . . .

He didn't think he could get Neva all the way to Houston or Dallas, places she'd talked about before, but she and Batista had *familia* over the river . . . somewhere . . . and if he could get her that far, it was a start. If they traveled at night to escape the day's brutal heat, if he read the shadows and stars as he'd done since he was a little boy on his papa's farm, *if* . . . well, there were a thousand ifs, but only this one choice. This one chance. Amador had tracked down some of the things he'd asked for: oranges and plastic water jugs and rope and muslin cloths to tie around their shoes and their faces; a small knife, some aloe cream and bandages and needle and thread. Also a small hemp pack for each of them, where Carmelita had hidden some tightly rolled tortillas and a handful of chamoy candy, and Chayo had smiled at that . . . almost cried.

He didn't know if any of it was enough, but it was all they had.

Later, he handed Neva his list of American towns and a pencil, told her to circle the one where her *familia* lived. She studied it for a long time, her wounded mouth and the stitches across her face trembling, tears at the tight corners of her eyes. At night when she slept, clenching her teeth in her sleep, her wounds wept, too; bloody tears all their own, and every morning Chayo wiped them away with his shirt. He did it again now, as she finally leaned forward and added another town to his list.

He watched over her shoulder. Like those other places, it didn't mean anything to him. He may have heard its name once or twice, but he knew nothing about it other than it was where Neva wanted to go, and that was all that mattered.

He studied it, said it out loud, committing it to memory.

Murfee.

Then he took the paper and tore it into small pieces, tossed them on the candle Carmelita had lit for them, and went to pack their bags.

TWENTY

D anny bought the girl Zita an ice cream and sat with
her at one of the small tables beneath an umbrella
in front of the store. He and Amé came here every
now and then, and she always ordered the same thing: a
single-scoop strawberry cone. She liked it well enough,
but said it wasn't as good as the *paletas* of her youth. She
claimed that Vic Ortiz, who worked at the jail, had man-
aged a small *paletería* many years before, and made a
point of stocking her favorite, *mango con chili*. Amé said
he used to drive over to Ojinaga once or twice a week to
buy the *paletas* for his store, bringing them back in cardboard boxes packed with ice. It was hard to imagine the
dark-eyed and quiet Vic—forever drinking one of his
cups of strong black coffee and reading the paper in the
jail office—selling popsicles to kids, but she swore it was
true. It was harder still to imagine Amé herself as that
little girl, like Zita.

Zita had ordered a strawberry cone, too, and Danny
didn't know what to make of that, if anything at all.

Across the street, the sheriff and Amé and the man
claiming to be her uncle walked beneath a row of lemon
trees, their images reflected over and over again in the
windows of the stores that lined Main Street. They were

out in the open, casual, and the uncle in his faded chinos and flannel shirt and straw hat looked no different from any of the other older Mexicans who lived and worked around Murfee or the Big Bend. He could be Vic Ortiz or Javy Cruz or anyone at all, and maybe that was the point. If the old man was worried about being seen, he didn't show it. He moved slow, though, with a slight limp, and Danny wondered how and when he'd gotten that injury—a consequence of the life he'd lived and the things he'd done. The sheriff suffered the same damaged walk, not only from his old football injury, but from the shooting at the Far Six that had nearly killed him. Now he was walking beside the very man who may have ordered it.

At this distance, they could be mirror images of each other—more hazy reflections lost in the windows around them.

Danny shook his head, turning back to the girl next to him.

"Do you like it? The ice cream?" He raised his own uneaten vanilla cone, struggling for the word for "ice cream" he'd heard Amé use before. "Um, *helado. Helado*?"

Zita smiled, nodded, but didn't answer. She didn't understand any more English than he did Spanish, which he supposed made them perfect companions right now.

Neither of them really knew what the hell was going on.

TWENTY-ONE

The face meant nothing to Chris.

He'd never seen it on any wanted posters or in any High-Intensity Drug Trafficking Area—HIDTA—intel reports, or the occasional bulletin he got from the El Paso Intelligence Center. The folder Garrison had given him didn't include any recent pictures, either; only grainy photos many years old. This man could have been anyone.

Or no one.

Still, Chris had imagined he'd be more like Sheriff Ross. It was as if he'd expected the man to have some dark aura, some twinned shadow . . . *something*. Something ominous. While the former sheriff had always appeared to bend the very light around him—bend everything around him so that he was always the center of it—this man wasn't like that. His hands had a slight shake and his voice was quiet and he moved slowly, carefully. Maybe it was an act, maybe it wasn't—Chris hadn't decided yet—but he wasn't intimidating or threatening, at least not in any overt way. He was calm, deferential. If Chris didn't know better, he'd say Fox Uno—if that's who he was—had the demeanor and pallor of a very sick man, something Chris had experienced firsthand when his own mother had passed from cancer. For months, she'd carried her body in the same careful way, as though afraid that if she moved too fast or tried to do too much, she might wake the disease. Anger it.

The only thing this man did share with Ross was the eyes, a certain sharpened hardness in them you saw only when you caught them at the right angle and in the right light, when he thought you weren't looking. He didn't try to hide those eyes behind sunglasses, and his thin hat did nothing to shield them. But as they stepped in and out of the shadows and sun along Main Street's sidewalk, he never blinked—not once—even as the hot light hit those eyes again and again. It lit them up, made them shine like steel, like sunlight on a rifle muzzle, and that was enough to remind Chris just how dangerous this man could be.

"You tried to have me killed," Chris said. It wasn't a question, simply a statement. As true as the sun rising and setting.

The old man disagreed. "I did not. That was your Sheriff Ross, I think."

His English was heavily accented and little used, but it was passable.

"You expect me to believe that?"

"It does not matter what you or I believe. That is all done now. It is the past. Like your sheriff." Fox Uno stopped, hands behind him, looking into a store window. It was Murfee's only bookstore, new and used with some rare collectibles, and Chris had spent hours there with his father as a kid. Most of the books in the display now looked dusty, showing cracked leather spines. There was a handful of faded and well-thumbed paperbacks piled together, and Chris could read the cover of one of them, a reprint of *The Light of Western Stars* by Zane Grey. "But if you must know, he tried to steal from both of us, Señor Cherry."

"And you also expect me . . . *us*"—Chris glanced over to Amé, who so far had stood rigid and mostly quiet at Fox Uno's other shoulder—"to believe you had nothing to do with that bus attack in Ojinaga?"

"I did not. But again, what does it matter? Here, now?"

"It matters because you're running from what's happening over there, and God knows what other past crimes. I *should* be arresting you, here and now, and ending all this."

"Yet you do not. I have committed no crimes here, Señor Cherry. If I am not the man I say I am, then I've done nothing wrong. If I am, what can you prove?"

"There are others . . ." Chris started, but stopped when Fox Uno raised a callused hand.

"*Ah, sí, Las Tres Letras.* What you call the DEA?" Fox Uno said the letters slowly, disdainfully. "Once they decide who I am, it will not matter anymore."

Chris shook his head. "You come here, threaten my deputy, demand her help . . ."

"I did not threaten. I did not demand. I explained to her the way things *are*, the way they must be. She understands this. You do not. You cannot. *Es la familia.*"

Chris let his voice rise, leaning in close so others on the street wouldn't hear him. "Don't fucking talk to me about family. We're her family. You? You're just a sick old man who showed up one night claiming to be someone that mattered."

Fox Uno turned and said something to Amé in Spanish, something far too fast for Chris to catch. Fox Uno fixed Chris with those hard eyes of his, eyes that could will away the sunlight, but he was smiling. "I was wrong then, perhaps you do understand. You will do this for her, for me, because she is *familia. Somos todos familia.*"

Fox Uno started to walk again, turning his back to the bookstore. "I need only a few days. Men *will* come, with money, new documents. Important things I had to leave behind in my haste, now that I cannot return to México. I will make a call every day until they are here. That call will keep her *madre, mi hermana,* hidden and safe, because as long as I live, men must still fear me. They must obey me. But if I cannot make this call, if I disappear . . ." Fox Uno didn't finish the thought, and didn't have to. "When Zita and I are gone, you will never see us again."

"As long as you're alive, that means others might come for you, too. Someone will be hunting you, right?" Chris asked.

Before Fox Uno could answer, Amé finally spoke up. "The girl, Zita, too? She will leave with you?"

"Por supuesto, ella es mi hija." Fox Uno smiled at Amé. "You can come with us, if you wish."

Amé nodded. "Then let me take you wherever you need to go, both of you. Tell your men I will bring you to them," she said. "No one has to come here."

"Not happening, *ever*," Chris said, crossing in front of Fox Uno and putting a hand on the old man's chest, stopping him, feeling his heartbeat. It was slow and steady, unconcerned. *Human.* Chris used to think Sheriff Ross didn't have a heartbeat at all. "I'm not letting her do that. If you try to leave the Big Bend with her, I'll have marked units parked at every highway, farm road, and cattle path. Everyone I know with a badge and a gun for three states." Chris stared Fox Uno down. "There have to be other people here who can help you, hide you. Someone else who can give you whatever the hell you need. You've never had any trouble conducting business on this side of the border before."

"*Esto es verdad.* But this is not, as you say, before. This is now. *No sé en quién confiar, sin duda usted entiende.*" I do not know whom to trust. You certainly understand that.

"I do . . . yet you've somehow decided you can trust us. Me and Amé?" Chris said it all in Spanish. It wasn't perfect, but it was close enough.

Fox Uno smiled again. "I thought you might know the language. You are very clever, Señor Cherry. *Pero no*, I trust only *her.*" He pointed at Amé. "She has never failed me."

When Fox Uno said that, Amé's eyes flashed with anger. Chris wasn't sure what the old man meant, but he didn't like the sound of it, and neither did she.

"Don't suggest I've ever helped you," she said in Spanish, spitting the words at his feet.

They stood that way for what felt like a long time, sharp points of a triangle, each staring at the other.

Chris asked, "What do you know about five bodies we discovered on the river? Young men, basically kids. Drug mules. You show up a day after we found them. That's a hell of a coincidence, right? Do you understand that word in English? Are you going to tell me you had nothing to do with that?"

Fox Uno shrugged. "Who can say? There's much violence on the river now. These men may have worked for me or not. Again, it does not matter." The old man stared at Chris with eyes as hard and sharp as knife edges, flashing as Amé's had done only moments before. *"Yo soy la Muerte."*

"Right, Fox Uno, the great and terrible. We know all about you. But pull back the curtain, and what are you really? What's left of you now?" Chris gestured at the street, at people passing them without a second glance. "Here, in my town, you're nothing at all. Don't dare threaten me. Not here."

Fox Uno said nothing.

Chris tapped Fox Uno on the chest. "If we do this, you really are gone for good. And you'll put an end to this bloody little war of yours in the Big Bend, on both sides of the river. You're done with Amé and Murfee, do you hear me? *Forever.* If you come here again or try to talk to her or contact her in any way, you're not going to have to worry about running anymore. I swear to you, I will kill you myself."

For emphasis, and to be sure he was clear, Chris said it again in Spanish: *"Te mataré."*

Fox Uno laughed. "Then that will make us both murderers, *¿si?* We are not so different, you and I." And for a second time, he said something in Spanish way too fast and low to Amé, before stepping past Chris to start across the street, to where Zita and Danny were sitting watching them. He left Chris's hand hanging in the air, pushing back against nothing.

As the old man moved carefully across the sunlit street, Chris let him go. Instead, he turned back to Amé. "What did he say?"

She hesitated before answering. "He said he likes you, but you sound like Sheriff Ross. He knows now why the sheriff wanted you dead."

Then she also crossed the street, to where Fox Uno, Danny, and Zita were waiting with ice cream.

TWENTY-TWO

S he smelled smoke sometimes.

Maybe it was because she used to be a smoker—unfiltered Camels—although she gave that up when she learned she was pregnant with Jack. But that smell was still there for her and always would be: in her clothes, in her skin . . . in her memories.

Like growing up around the oil fields with her daddy. The heavy and sooty sky above the rigs, the whole world gray and black, and his own skin, too.

Like the night Murfee burned and Buck Emmett died, where she'd stood outside Earlys and caught that first bit of flame on the wind. It had made her search the night, staring into the dark, trying to find it.

A warning.

Or maybe it was the Big Bend itself.

Maybe in all the desert and scrub and unbounded emptiness, there was always something burning out there, somewhere.

MEL WAS THINKING ABOUT SMOKE as Chris finished telling her about the old man and the girl.

She'd been nursing Jack when Chris came in—a feeling

of closeness or completeness that as a woman she had no words to describe, that a man would never truly understand anyway—and the baby was asleep now. She had the bedroom window cracked open and Jack cradled soft and quiet in her arms, and all she could think about was smoke.

There on the wind, blowing through the window. Faint and then gone again. A campfire somewhere far off.

She prayed that's all it was.

"Tell me how I'm supposed to feel about this, Chris. Tell me and I'll do my best to convince you that's how I really feel."

Chris stood in the door of their bedroom, arms crossed. He hadn't yet come to sit next to her and Jack on the bed.

"You think I'm wrong."

She admired how he still wanted to make everything a question of right and wrong, as if there was ever a way to do that so neat and clean. Ben had never believed that, and the two men had always argued about it. Sheriff Ross had definitely not believed that, and it nearly cost Chris his life. Yet here he was again, trying to make the case, even if it meant being on the wrong side of it this time.

That's what she thought.

"It's foolish. It's dangerous. This man's a threat to Amé and this town. He's a threat to you, to your career . . ."

"Hell, babe, I might not have a career much longer."

"Don't use that as an excuse. You're still the sheriff now. And if you're doing this because you truly believe he's the man he says he is, let that sink in. Remind yourself what that has to mean."

Chris stayed silent, struggling. He had thought about it, and the weight of it was crushing him.

"But you're going to do this anyway . . ."

"I'm still deciding," he said.

"That's bullshit, Sheriff Cherry. Every day that goes by and he's still here means it's already been decided. What are you going to do, let him stay with Amé? Have Danny help her keep an eye on him?" Chris's expression told her that's exactly what he'd intended to do. "People will talk, Chris. Someone will find out." She held Jack tighter. "Someone could come for him, the way they came for you."

Chris bent down and rubbed Rocky's ears. The dog had moved from his spot on the floor to stand next to Chris, as if sensing their tension. "No one here knows who he is. Not yet, anyway. He's an old man. And with that young girl . . ."

"Don't be foolish. He's *not* just any old man, and that poor girl, whoever she is, needs to be out of the middle of this."

Chris started again, quieter. "So I turn him over to Garrison and the DEA, what then? What if they can't prove he's really Fox Uno? I have no idea what happens to him, but I have a damn good idea of what happens to Amé's family."

"Yes, if he's telling the truth. And that's a big if. Seems to me that if he's here looking for help, he can barely take care of himself."

"Danny said about the same thing. But if I believe he's Fox Uno, I've got to believe all of it, everything he says. The threats, the risks. Otherwise, I am a fool. Besides, it's not just what I believe, it's what Amé believes."

"She's not the sheriff, Chris, you are."

"Okay, so this isn't about being the sheriff, it's about . . ."

She stopped him. "Friends, family, loyalty. *I get it*. And if that's how you need to look at it, then maybe you can also convince yourself there's no right or wrong answer, either, only what you need to do. That's what Ben would say . . . That's what you want to hear."

"Yeah, I know. Damn, I wish Ben were here." Chris shrugged. "Sure doesn't make me feel any better about it, though."

Mel tried a smile for him. "And that's good. That's the way it's supposed to be. And that's why I want to believe that whatever you decide, in the end, it was the right thing all along. The only thing."

Chris closed his eyes. "But I could still talk to Garrison. There is that. It's hard to imagine, but in a lot of ways, since Ben's death, Garrison is one of the few friends I have, if I can even use that word. He's not one of my deputies, he doesn't work for me, I'm not responsible for him . . ." Chris stopped, started again, his eyes now open. "Since coming back to Murfee, I've known him longer than anyone else. With Ben gone, he may know more about me than anyone else, other than you."

"He knows what you went through, Chris. Just like you know about him. Maybe it's not a friendship, but whatever it is, I think it's strong enough you can call him about this."

"Garrison said you were too good for me." Chris moved close, leaned down and kissed her, then Jack. And she would have sworn that as he bent over them, his passage had stirred unseen smoke that had drifted in through the open window. It made her want to get up and shut it, to keep them safe inside. But instead, she grabbed him, kissed back hard, wishing with everything she had that the three of them could stay just like this for a long, long time. Forever.

"Listen to the man, and don't ever forget it."

THEY REMAINED THAT WAY, silent for a while, until Chris pulled away. She knew he'd made his decision. "It's just a few days," he said, as much to himself as to her. "A few damn days, and then he's gone. We can handle that, right?"

Mel didn't answer him. She couldn't. After allowing herself to convince him that she wasn't half mad with worry and fear, she couldn't say what was really on the tip of her tongue.

God, I hope you're right.

TWENTY-THREE

Later that night, after Fox Uno and Zita were asleep, Danny joined Amé on her tiny apartment landing, where she stood smoking a cigarette. She'd been there an hour, maybe more, leaning against the unpainted wooden railing and watching her smoke rise through the settling dark into the spreading arms of the juniper that flanked the garage. There was barely room for them both, and the night was only made warmer by her cigarette in the small space at the top of the stairs, where they'd found Zita what felt like years before.

"I didn't know you smoked," he said, standing close enough to breathe the smoke right along with her, to feel the heated tip of the Marlboro on his skin.

"I used to, when I was younger. Far too much."

"When your brother was still alive. When you knew Caleb Ross, right? Sheriff Ross's son."

She flicked ash. "It's not important. It was a long time ago."

"No, Amé, it wasn't. It wasn't that long ago at all." He wanted to tell her that Jesse Earl, who'd given him his damaged eye, or Afghanistan, where'd he been trapped in all those small villages (and maybe still was), wasn't all that long ago, either. Not even the murder of his father on a highway in Sweetwater more than twenty years earlier was all that far away. Scars like that, inside or out, were always still there. Still fresh. All Danny had to do was close his eyes. And if that was true for him, then he had to believe that was true for Amé, too, no matter how she tried to pretend otherwise.

Danny would never fully understand the relationship between America and Sheriff Cherry. Never know all the facts and details, but it didn't matter. They bore too many of the same scars. It wasn't just that their shared past wasn't distant enough for clarity or perspective, it was that they were still far too close to help each other see.

"You know the sheriff is doing this for you, right? Not for your mother, or the rest of your family, or that girl in there. Not because it makes sense or because it's even close to being right. But for you. He'll go to the ends of the earth to protect you."

Amé studied the fire at the end of her cigarette. "What do you want me to say to that?"

"He's the goddamn *sheriff*, Amé. You're asking him to break the law. It's not who he is. This goes against everything he believes in."

"He would not be the first sheriff in this town to break the law, or decide that the law is only what he believes it to be." But she said it without conviction, and they both knew it. "I did not *ask* him for anything, Danny. I told him what was going on, and if I had not done that, you would have. You gave me no choice."

"Yes," Danny conceded.

"I promised him once before I would not keep secrets. I had to tell him."

"Like you told him about your mysterious gun? That's a little too convenient." But Danny raised his hands, surrendering the point. "I already told you what I think, so you tell me how this ends."

"*No lo sé*. No more than you do. What would you have me do?"

"We call Agent Garrison. Tonight, now. We do it together, and then this will all be over before the sheriff commits to anything one way or another. Before it goes too far. We take back this thing we put in his hands."

"That *I* put there." Amé watched him through her smoke, before looking away. "Do you know what my papa does, since he returned to México?"

"No, you've never told me. Like a lot of things, I guess." Danny hated himself for saying it, but if it angered Amé, she didn't show it. She continued to look away.

"He tends marijuana fields in a place called Búfalo, far outside Camargo. Fields owned by Fox Uno or those who work for him. My papa would never tell me this, but my mama did. She is ashamed, but he needs the work. I send them money, but it's never enough. Tell me, how do I explain that to Agent Garrison?"

"Fuck him, you don't have to. That's not your fault, not your responsibility . . . no more than Rodolfo ever was. What you're doing now sure in the hell won't bring Rodolfo back, and it's not going to keep your mother or your father safe."

Danny reached out and took Amé's chin in his hand, turning her face toward him. "They're dead, Amé, don't you understand that? Your mother, your father. Everyone associated with that man in there is already dead, or soon will be."

"How do you know that?"

"Because I think that man is on the losing side of a war, and I know a goddamn lot about wars."

"Then what about the girl, Zita?"

"I don't know. We'll figure that out. There are places . . ."

"That girl in there is *me*, Danny. She could be me."

Danny shook his head. "No, that's too simple, too easy. Don't use her to justify what you're doing, the way Fox Uno used her to help him get here."

She pulled away, crushing out her nearly spent cigarette on the railing. She dropped it into the gravel below them, and pulled another from a pack in her jeans. She was frustrated and furious with him, way beyond angry.

"Did you also have those hidden away with this gun I've never seen?" he asked.

She held the cigarette, didn't light it. She broke it in half and tossed it away.

"Why are you saying these things? Why? What are *you* going to do, Danny? *Dime*."

There was so little space between them already, but he moved to her. Closer. Closer. He first put a hand on her shoulder and then both of his arms all the way around her and she didn't stop him. He could feel she wanted to but didn't. He wasn't sure how long she would let this last.

"Because, like our good sheriff, I'm going to do whatever you want me to, whatever I have to do, so you're never hurt again. I thought you knew that. Goddammit, I'll do anything. I'll go all the way to the end of the world."

TWENTY-FOUR

I n St. Louis in 1999, in the backseat of a Pontiac Grand Am, with light gray snow blowing in through a rolled-down window, Joe Garrison was shot once in the chest with a .38 revolver.

It wasn't something he talked about anymore, and many of the agents who'd worked with him through the years had never asked about it, not directly, although they'd all heard some version of it from someone else. To Garrison, it was old history, so long ago it was a thing that might as well have happened to someone else. He was lucky he was wearing his soft vest that day (usually he didn't), beneath a Carhartt jacket and a flannel shirt that Karen had bought him the Christmas before, and although it hurt like nothing he'd ever felt before or since—like Mark McGwire hitting him in the chest with a Rawlings Big Stick swinging for the left-field wall—and the back-face signature of the blast had left him bruised and tender for three straight months and sometimes doubled over coughing up blood, the truth of it was he still walked away. *Alive.* Someone even pulled the flattened slug out of his vest, and he carried it around for some years in a small plastic case that had once held Angie's baby teeth for the tooth fairy.

Just a reminder . . . a totem or lucky rabbit's foot.

He talked even less, though, about the man who didn't walk away that day, the one he shot and killed in the backseat as they struggled over that .38. Garrison fought that gun out of Junior Worrell's hands, and in all the chaos—ears ringing and blood on the window and a smoky haze choking and blinding him—he worked it up under Worrell's chin and pulled the trigger, or Worrell did—one shooting investigation by the St. Louis Police and two months of trauma counseling never decided the issue—blowing the top of that man's head all over the inside of the car. Garrison had watched Worrell's face explode right in front of him; crawling out of that Pontiac with Worrell's blood still thick in his eyes and his mouth . . . *swallowing it.*

And really, what was there to say about that?

How the hell did you explain that to anyone?

In the end, it was just one of those dumb undercover deals gone bad, the sort of thing you pray never happens, but that occasionally—horribly—does. Garrison had been applauded as a hero for a few months, but struggled with it for quite a while longer. There were the nightmares and drinking and that one lost weekend in D.C., but time passed and he got over it and the nightmares finally started to dim like an old light. Karen forgave him for the things he'd said and done, and life had moved on.

But after Darin and Morgan were shot, some of those old nightmares came flooding back—that old light turned on again, twice as bright. This time around, he was the one trapped in the Tahoe with Morgan Emerson, and it was Worrell—not Duane Dupree—shooting them in a field outside Murfee, then setting them on fire on the riverbank.

Garrison struggling to get out of that burning car, dragging Morgan with him, his mouth full of blood again. Not Worrell's, not even his own, but Morgan's.

Her blood . . . and the thick ashes from her burning skin, choking him . . .

How the hell could he explain that to anyone?

So he didn't. Not to a counselor or to Karen or the other agents he worked with.

He never talked about it, and instead spent months trying not to sleep at all.

HE SAT IN HIS EMPTY KITCHEN, looking through the hazy window at the even emptier pool. After Karen and the girls had left, it had slowly gone down—dried up—day after day. Taking care of the house and the pool had always been Karen's job, and he wasn't sure who to call anymore. The last time he'd looked down into it he'd seen little more than floating bugs and branches. Some ugly, wayward feathers; a thick detritus of El Paso dust hiding the Pebble Tec bottom. It was a hazard, and he should probably just fill the damn thing in with concrete. He wasn't likely to ever swim in it again, and neither were the girls. The last time they'd used it they'd been celebrating Megan's birthday—her last birthday in Texas—and Karen had strung up dozens of paper lanterns around the deck, glowing green and red and blue above the clear water. It had been beautiful, and he'd had three Coronas and two pieces of cake and then he and

Karen had made love by that lantern light filtering in through their bedroom windows.

That was three weeks, maybe a month, before Darin and Morgan were shot in Murfee.

It was about six months after that when Karen and the girls left for good.

IT WASN'T THAT Karen couldn't forgive him for the drinking and the anger again; it was the goddamn silence she couldn't take the second time around. Day after day of him not saying anything at all, at least not to her. She'd begged him to get help, made the appointments for him, but when he ignored them—when he called her all those names after those long nights of drinking and had raised his hand like he was going to hit her (although he never would)—she'd packed up the girls and pretty much everything else and moved back east.

He came home after six hours of finally talking to OPR investigators to find the house empty, to find it pretty much the way it was now—some furniture odds and ends and things like a rake or a broom out in the garage; an old Ikea bookshelf without books. Their unmade bed that still smelled like her body wash and shampoo and a couple of pillows. There wasn't even a note, because Karen had finally run out of things to say, too.

He didn't blame her, and they still shared a phone call every couple of weeks. Gone, but not forgotten.

Those calls were halting, though, filled with lots of stops and starts. A silence as thick as static, a dead radio station, since neither of them knew what or how much to say, or if there was anything left to say at all.

HE SWALLOWED A MOUTHFUL OF BOURBON, turning away from the kitchen window and the pool beyond it, back to the files he'd brought home with him. It was against policy to take sensitive documents out of the office, like he'd done for Sheriff Cherry, but he was long past the point of caring about that. In some ways, surviving that shooting in St. Louis in 1999, and surviving the investigation of Darin and Morgan's shooting, had made Garrison almost bulletproof. What could they do to him that hadn't already been done?

What could he lose that hadn't already been lost?

The files in front of him contained the most current intel on Fox Uno, and they were as barren as his empty house. Garrison had given Chris everything they had about Fox Uno's past, but this was what they had about him *today* . . . all the fall-out from the Librado Rivera attack. The elusive Fox Uno had all but disappeared, even with everyone from the U.S. intelligence and law enforcement community and the Mexican government to every rival cartel in northern Mexico hunting for him.

Fox Uno had become more of a ghost, if that was possible.

Some of the intel indicated he may have died in a recent shooting in Chihuahua, but there was no clear confirmation of that and zero reliable, firsthand sourcing. Just a dozen conflicting reports, and no body. Other intelligence suggested that Fox Uno's right-hand thug, Oso Ocho, had taken over daily operations, or that Fox Uno's mysterious son, another ghost called Tiburón, was now running what remained of Nemesio. One brief suggested that Tiburón may have joined forces with Fox Uno's biggest rival, the Serrano Brothers, but to Garrison that hardly made sense. The Serranos had wanted Fox Uno dead forever. They'd taken plenty of Nemesio smuggling routes and plazas. They didn't want pieces of the kingdom, or a mere handshake with the prince. They wanted the whole crown, and the head wearing it.

A big net had been thrown out for the old cartel leader, but so far it had come up empty. Garrison had to think it was only a matter of time, although things would get a lot bloodier until then.

That was the conclusion he planned to put in his report to Chesney. He suspected the SAC wouldn't ask too much beyond that, but in the quiet of his own kitchen, he couldn't help wondering where in the hell the old son of a bitch had gone. Few people understood how hard it could be to find one man in the world—even when most of the world was looking for him—but with Fox Uno, you really didn't need to look *all* over the world, only the northern states of Mexico. Chihuahua, Coahuila, maybe Nuevo León. Those were Fox Uno's traditional strongholds and he'd never been known to move out of them.

It was still a hell of a lot of territory, but not impossible. Not the whole world.

But . . . Fox Uno did have one other traditional stronghold—right here in Texas, in the Big Bend.

Was it possible he'd try to slip over the border? No,

but it wasn't unheard of, either. Back in 2008, DEA's McAllen office arrested a high-ranking member of the Gulf cartel buying a watermelon in a local H-E-B supermarket. An agent just happened to be in the store at the same time and recognized Carlos Landín Martínez from the agency's long-running investigation. It was pure luck, a joke, but it had happened.

Garrison had to ask himself: Could it happen again?

Not the same way. This wasn't like Landín Martínez—DEA didn't have a great photo of Fox Uno, and nothing current, so no one would recognize him wandering the street. Unless that person was Deputy America Reynosa, who Garrison was convinced knew a hell of a lot more about her alleged uncle than she'd ever admit to Chris Cherry or anyone else.

Could it happen again?

Even if the possibility existed, Chris's unwillingness to help, and Garrison's refusal to run any more unilateral operations in the Big Bend, meant it was a dead end. It was such a remote chance anyway, it probably wasn't worth raising in his report to Chesney. But for the sake of completeness—he was still a goddamn investigator, after all—he'd put it in. One sentence, no more.

After his talk with Chesney about Sheriff Machado's Tejas unit, his SAC already thought he was jumping at every shadow . . . seeing goddamn ghosts everywhere.

What the hell was one more?

GARRISON SWEPT THE REPORTS back into his briefcase and poured himself another shot of bourbon, three fingers of Garrison Brothers, no relation. It was an old joke, one Darin would always laugh over when they were sharing a bottle after work. Darin used to come over all the time after his own divorce to grill out or watch a game or have a few drinks. Anything so he wouldn't have to go back to his own empty apartment.

The house was quiet, as it was all the time now. No TV, no stereo. He'd always loved mellow classic rock, and although the girls used to make fun of him for knowing all those old songs by heart, he sang them on surveillance all the time—an audience of one, sitting in his car alone. He was even caught on an open mic once, and Darin wouldn't let his boss live it down—he bought a fake plastic microphone that mysteriously appeared and disappeared around Garrison's office for nearly two years. He had no idea where it was now, packed away after Darin's death, but the memory still made him smile.

Karen had left the kitchen radio behind for him, but just like with the TV, he hadn't turned it on since she'd left, and he wasn't going to start now.

When he'd visited Chris Cherry out at his house on the Far Six, he'd told the young sheriff he wasn't sure he could ever get used to all the stillness and silence out there, but that had been a lie.

Garrison had gotten used to it just fine.

TWENTY-FIVE

T he deputy was taking Eddy home, back to his trailer in the canyon. Charity was still pretty pissed at him and had refused to do it (and his spic lawyer, Paez, had said it probably wasn't all that good an idea anyway), and that's when Eddy realized he didn't have anyone else to call. Sure, when he was holding some shit, he was everyone's friend, but when he was in some deep shit, those "friends"—a loose collection of fuck-ups like himself—mysteriously up and disappeared, like cockroaches scurrying from the light. Truth was, without Charity around, Eddy had no one, and other than his trailer, had nowhere else to go, which was how he now found himself being given a lift home by the deputy he'd attacked.

After Eddy spilled his guts, Danny Ford had declined to push the assault charge from their little run-in—just like he promised—and Paez seemed to think the sheriff's department wasn't planning to put the five bodies floating in the river on him, either, so for the moment, he was both free *and* sober.

The world was a goddamn funny place.

Funnier still to think that, right now, this Danny Ford might be the closest thing Eddy had to a friend in the whole world.

"Them bodies ain't there no more, right? They're all gone?" Eddy asked.

Danny nodded, keeping an eye on the road for the turnoff to Eddy's place. It was still early, with a mix of sun and shadows spread across the road. The sky was blue, though, the blue of no clouds and no rain. Of emptiness. "They're all gone, Eddy."

"You believe in ghosts?" Eddy said, chewing a fingernail.

"What are you getting at?"

Eddy shrugged. "You know, like when I'm using, like on a three- or four-day bender, I see all sorts of shit. Crazy shit that ain't there. But I'm never quite sure, right? I get all spooky, yelling at empty rooms." Eddy tapped his fingers on the dash. "Now that my head is kinda clear, I hope I don't see any *real* ghosts. You know, pissed-off spirits of those dead wetbacks or something. I've seen movies about shit like that."

Danny smiled. "Those are just movies, Eddy. They aren't real, either."

"Yeah, that's what I figured. That's what everyone says. That's what everyone in those movies says, too, right until something horrible grabs their fat asses and drags 'em away . . ."

Danny laughed, but it was a serious laugh. "Do ghosts out here have some reason to be angry with you?"

Eddy slid deep in his seat, not wanting to get Danny all spun up and asking a bunch of questions again. "Naw, it's nothing like that. I already told you everything I know."

"Then you should be fine, Eddy. Nothing to worry about." Danny slowed down and made the turn onto crushed quartz and dirt—an opening cut into some low, twisted trees and ocotillo. "Welcome home . . ."

AS DANNY PULLED UP TO THE TRAILER, Eddy could see the yellow police tape, just like in the movies. It was strung around the front door, another long piece fluttering on some of the rebar out in the yard, near that big Admiral fridge. Eddy couldn't remember how most of that junk in the grass had gotten there, or where it had come from. It was stuff that might have been important once, that maybe he thought he could resell or make something useful out of, but nothing had ever come out of it. It had all gone to shit, rusting away. Like his goddamn life. That police tape had come loose from somewhere else around the trailer and was now waving around like a bright flag. Like NASCAR. It reminded Eddy of those weird balloon men bouncing around in front of car dealerships.

Even when he was sober those things freaked him out.

Danny stopped in the grass, but left the truck idling. He rolled down the window to let some air in, turning to Eddy, who couldn't take his eyes off that winding police tape.

A yellow flag in NASCAR meant *caution*.

"Charity is still up at the family crisis center, so don't go there. Don't even look that direction. If she wants to see you, she'll come back. But if I get word you're up there messing with her, not only am I going to knock the shit out of you again, I'm booking you on that assault charge, got it?"

"Yeah, we're good."

Danny seemed even more distracted than when he and Deputy Reynosa had questioned Eddy. But he reached around to the backseat and pulled up a heavy brown bag that he put in Eddy's lap.

"That's some of the stuff we took out of the trailer. Wallet, phone, things like that. You signed for it all back in lockup, but you can check it now if you want. It's all there."

"Naw, I don't need to do that."

"If someone tries to call you, this Apache or anyone else, or if someone tries to find you out here . . . threaten you . . . whatever. You call me."

"Okay."

The deputy pointed at the bag. "There's some other stuff in there. Bologna, bread. Maybe potato chips. A carton of eggs." Danny smiled at that, and Eddy did, too, remembering those damn eggs. And the skillet. "My number is written on the inside of that carton, tucked away. You need it, that's where it is."

Eddy held on to the bag, thinking for a minute he might cry. He didn't know why, couldn't explain it, but the fact that Danny had gone to any kind of trouble hit him hard, right in the chest, harder even than the beating Danny had given him down by the giant cane. Maybe he was only doing it because he wanted Eddy's help with his investigation or whatever, but it was the first time anyone had wanted anything worthwhile from Eddy Lee Rabbit in a long damn time.

"You know, I used to run track," Eddy said. "One season, when I was like a sophomore. I was skinny . . . I mean, not like now, but healthy . . . fast. So goddamn fast. I set a state record. Some black dude beat it a couple years later, but for a while there, I was the fastest man in the state. Look it up, it's got to be in some book somewhere. It's true, bet my life. Hard to believe, right? I wasn't always like this."

"I know, Eddy." Danny stared out through the open window. "So why'd you give it up?"

"Shit, man, I just hated sprintin' around that track. Runnin' in a goddamn circle and never gettin' anywhere."

"Makes sense. But you know, you could start again." Danny waved out the window, at the scrub and the canyon walls. "Out here, you're not running in a circle. Hell, you could run near forever. Straight on, just keep going."

Eddy thought about that. "Brother, I wouldn't even know where to begin."

Danny smiled. "It's easy enough. Just put one foot in front of the other." Now both Danny and Eddy watched the yellow tape dance around the trailer. "Look, I can't help you stay clean, Eddy, but you have to try. If you don't, what you're doing now will straight-up kill you. Or it'll get you killed."

"I know. I understand. I appreciate this." Eddy held up the bag.

"Then don't let it go to waste."

Eddy opened the door and slid out, still holding the bag tight. "You guys better not have fucked up all my shit in there. I'm particular about how I keep my things."

Danny really laughed this time. "Yeah, we could all see that. Good luck, Eddy. Remember, one foot in front of the other . . . and steer clear of those ghosts . . ."

Eddy stepped back so Danny could pull away, and knew that the deputy wasn't talking about ghosts at all . . .

EDDY WAITED UNTIL DANNY WAS LONG GONE, and then put the bag on the trailer steps—he still hadn't gone inside yet—and circled back out into the yard.

He avoided the yellow tape twisting and turning on the rebar, giving it a wide berth.

Caution, motherfucker, caution.

But here he was all the same.

He couldn't remember where most of this junk had come from, except the old Admiral fridge. He'd grown up with it, but it had sat out here in the grass for years, getting rained on and occasionally dusted with snow. A knot of snakes had taken up in it once that Eddy had to burn out with some gasoline, and he put a couple of bullet holes in it one spring, goofing around. It was originally white, but now all discolored, like a tooth gone bad. Like Eddy's own teeth. It even smelled bad, like it was still giving off the stink of spoiled food.

Memories. Ghosts.

But when he opened it, the door pulled back smooth, because he'd kept the hinges well oiled. And although the inside was dirty and filled with debris, it was all stuff he had carefully arranged there: paint cans and glass bottles and oil filters. He knelt to the bottom of the fridge, where he'd hollowed out a hole into the soil beneath it that he'd covered with some wood and greasy aluminum foil, and reached inside.

He found it easy: a Glad freezer bag still heavy with a quarter pound of meth, still all glassy and yellow—big, chunky shards—as well as the plastic-wrapped phone hidden underneath it that Injun fucker Apache had given him.

He thought it was funny: the freezer bag in the old broken fridge.

He'd been keeping his stash out here for a year or more, afraid someone might try to rob him. Even Charity didn't know it was out here, and she pretty much knew everything about him, but to be honest, when she was using, he didn't trust her much, either.

He unwrapped the phone and flipped it on, and while he waited for it to power on, he stood and stared at that clear bag a long time, as the shadows around him grew even longer.

His hand was trembling.

I can't help you stay clean . . . but you have to try . . . If you don't, what you're doing now will straight-up kill you. Or it'll get you killed.

He'd come to this moment again and again; a hundred, hell, maybe a thousand times in his life. His thoughts were as clear as that freezer bag itself. He could see straight, think straight, and it felt good. Like the old Eddy. The sun was warm and nice, and the wind was moving over him like Charity's fingers on his skin, and Deputy Danny Ford had been damn decent to him, when he had no reason to be. This was a good day. The sort of day Eddy Rabbit could hold on to and remember—the first of many—if he just didn't fuck it all up.

If he just took the whole bag and tossed it into the river and never looked back.

One foot in front of the other . . . and then he could be running again.

But he continued to stand there . . . way too long . . . trapped in place, turning the bag this way and that in the sun. The meth inside glowed with its own yellow light.

Like the police tape, waving like a flag.

Caution.

He was still holding the bag, staring into it, mesmerized, when the phone from Apache started to buzz.

TWENTY-SIX

Z ita needed new clothes.

Even after a couple of good, hot showers, and America trimming away the gnarls in her long, dark hair with some desk scissors, the fact remained that Zita only had the one shirt and jeans, and the girl was embarrassed by them. They weren't hers and they didn't fit right. Now that her initial fear had passed—a fear that had awoken the girl crying, screaming, in the middle of the night—Zita was animated, eager to talk. She was fascinated by everything in her new country. She was *una pequeña urraca*, as America's mama would say—a little magpie—with a quick mouth and quicker fingers. America had found the girl's tiny collection of stolen hair ties, gum, a *TV Guide*, a tiny black chess piece, and even a 9mm bullet—things she must have found in the couch cushions. Ben had played chess, and that lost piece, like the bullet, had been hidden in the apartment since his death. She turned it over and over in her hand for a long time before putting it back with Zita's other treasures.

The bullet, however, she slipped into her own pocket.

Fox Uno was sitting at the tiny table in her kitchen, eating the eggs and tortillas she had made, when she told him she was taking Zita out.

If he had any thoughts about not letting Zita leave with her, he didn't share them. He kissed the girl on the forehead and told her to behave.

America wanted to tell herself she was taking the girl shopping because it was the right thing to do, but she'd be lying.

There was another, more serious reason.

She wanted to get Zita alone and see what she would tell her about Fox Uno and their life across the river.

THERE WERE A COUPLE of clothing shops in Murfee, right on Main Street—expensive vintage and specialty shops, and a newer Target over in Nathan—but America didn't go to any of those. Instead, she drove to the west side of Murfee, over the train tracks, to the place some people still called Beantown. It was where she had grown up, and where she had lived in the same tiny house before the fires. There were several businesses here that only the town's Hispanics frequented: Mancha's bodega, a restaurant tacked onto the back of a trailer that served traditional Chihuahuan and Sonoran food, and a sprawling ranch house filled with the sort of Mexican products one would find over the river in Ojinaga. The ranch house also sold clothes, most of them secondhand but some new, which had been bought cheap at the Walmart in Midland and then driven down to Murfee for resale. When she'd been no older than Zita, America had gotten most of her clothes from the place that everyone simply called La Tienda, so she knew it well, but was surprised how out of place she felt now, walking down its dark, cramped aisles, showing Zita one thing or another. Although the girl was polite, it was clear she was used to much nicer things.

On the drive, and now in the store, Zita talked endlessly about all the fancier stores and places she'd been: Mexico City and Guadalajara and Monterrey. All about her brother Martino, who she did not like much because he fought with her papa, and someone called Gualterio, who she did. Also a woman called Luisa, who she'd loved very much, and who America understood was now dead, because whenever Zita said her name, she started to cry—small, hot tears that she fiercely wiped away. She talked about riding horses and having tall men with guns always bring her pieces of her favorite chocolate cake and sitting on Papa's knee and riding in big black cars with windows thick and dark as smoke.

She talked about how when she slept there were always two or three of those men with guns in her room. Sometimes they slipped her gum and candy and small toys, and once when she couldn't sleep, one of them with a thick beard had sung her old songs in a beautiful voice, but then he was gone the next morning and never returned.

She said that her papa was an important man and everyone loved him and was afraid of him, too, and she once saw him walk across a green field with a bloody knife that he'd tried to hide from her, and how another time he hugged her and smelled like gasoline and smoke and fire.

She remembered a burning building, once.

She did not know her mama, but was told by everyone

she'd been beautiful and had won many awards because she was so pretty.

She described a big accident on the road and men yelling and gunshots and how scared she was when Luisa was slumped over, covered in blood.

She told a story about standing on a hotel balcony on a beach, watching the blue ocean roll and roll and roll.

She talked about sleeping in a barn and walking across the hot desert.

She once saw a fat lizard and it ran from her. She then saw a scorpion fighting another scorpion, until her papa had stepped on them both with his boot.

She asked if she was ever going home again, or if this place was her home now.

Zita talked about so many different places and people—story after story, out of time and out of sequence, like she was quickly flipping through the pages of an immense *libro*—but she never mentioned America's mama or papa or other uncles.

Even when America asked about them by name, Zita did not know them. She wondered out loud if they were friends of her papa's she had never met. He had many, many important friends she did not know.

As they walked around the poorly lit store, America realized all eyes were on her and the girl; all ears were straining to hear Zita's singsong stories. Even the owner of La Tienda, an old woman with gray hair who'd known America forever, followed them around, pretending badly not to listen.

America walked them out without buying anything.

———————

WINDOWS DOWN, warm sunlight heating the seats between them, America drove them back all the way across town to Main Street. To a place called Cowboy Rose, the most expensive specialty clothing store in Murfee. America had never been in the place, but she walked Zita straight inside as if she'd shopped there a hundred times. It smelled like leather and denim and perfume, and America told the girl to pick out whatever she wanted.

As much as she wanted.

Then she followed around behind her, holding out her arms and letting the girl fill them with fancy T-shirts and jeans and skirts and long dresses. As Zita chatted on and on in her lilting Spanish—about singing men with guns and bloody knives and faraway oceans and scorpions and people who were now dead—America took comfort in knowing that no one else in the store understood a word of what she was saying.

TWENTY-SEVEN

When Danny came in from Delcia Canyon, Amé and Zita were gone.

But Fox Uno was sitting at the tiny table in the kitchenette, his phones in front of him. He'd either completed or was about to begin another one of his mysterious calls, but this did not stop Danny from sitting across from him.

"Where is Amé?" Danny asked.

"She is gone, with Zita." If Fox Uno knew more than that, he wasn't inclined to say it.

Danny unholstered his Colt and put it on the table in front of him, between them. "Good, it's finally just you and me. I've wanted to have this talk since you showed up." He pointed at the phones lined up on the table. "Tell me, who do you really call on those things?"

Fox Uno sat back, ignoring the gun between them, regarding Danny with cool eyes. Danny first thought the old man was going to get up and walk away, but he didn't. Instead: "It does not matter to you, but I speak to very old friends. Still loyal, or so I believe."

"Loyal, like a dog? You tell them to bark, they bark? Bite, they bite?"

Fox Uno smiled without teeth. "Not so different than you, I think."

Danny picked up one of the phones, it didn't matter to him which one, and turned it over and over in his hand. It was the Blackphone. It was still warm from where Fox Uno had been holding it. "Everyone thinks dogs are naturally loyal, but I'm not so sure. There was a private I knew in the army, named Newberry. He grew up in Georgia and had himself a shepherd mutt he called Norris, short for Chuck Norris." Danny could tell by Fox Uno's stony expression that he didn't get the reference, but he pushed forward. "Even as a puppy, Norris the dog didn't want or need a master. True to his name, he was tough, the real alpha male. Didn't like to be leashed or crated. Newberry loved that mutt, treated it as well as he could, but as he got bigger, he got tougher to control. Baring his teeth at everyone, chasing neighbor kids around. Newberry got married real young, had a baby, and that damn dog would stalk the newborn. Newberry would find it lurking by the crib, guess he didn't like the competition. Sometimes Newberry woke up with Norris in his room at night, growling over him. Newberry was more loyal to that dog than it ever was to him."

Fox Uno allowed a thin smile. "What happened to the *perro*?"

"The dog? I don't know. I never got to hear the end of the story. Newberry put it down, I guess. That's what you're forced to do with any animal like that." Danny tossed the phone back across the table to Fox Uno, who caught it with two hands. "See, Newberry died on patrol in the Nuristan Province in Afghanistan, right outside a small village, Rumnar. He was twenty years old, and we'd already survived a bad ambush together at a place called Wanat, but on September 10, 2009, he stepped on a roadside IED and got blown to pieces. I was right there next to him, but I was too late. Hell, it could have been me. We're walking along and he's telling me all about his wife and daughter and that damn dog of his, and then he's gone." Danny made a vague motion with his hand, and with Fox Uno's own hands occupied holding the phone, Danny then picked up the gun from the table. He sighted down the barrel, aiming at a space in the air between them. "That whole time, I didn't know I was talking to a dead man."

Danny leaned forward. "There's no one over there taking your damn calls, because they're already dead, just like Newberry. And all that loyalty you're going on about? That's gone, too. There's not a goddamn thing you can do for Amé and her family, because if there was, you wouldn't be hiding behind her here in Murfee. Let's face it, you never thought in a million years you'd end up *here*, like this. I know that, and she's going to know that soon enough, too. The only question is, what the hell are we going to do with you then?" Danny decocked the Colt and dropped the mag, ejecting the chambered round. He caught it with one hand and set it upright on the table. He reholstered his gun and stood to leave.

Fox Uno laughed, then took both phones and put them in his pockets. He also picked up the round and bounced it in his hand, smiling. "We will see, *diputado. Me gustas.* I would have wanted you to work for me, as you say, over there. And I think over there is not so very far away."

He stood, too, no longer smiling. He reached over and grabbed Danny's hand, surprisingly strong, and put the round in his palm and folded his fingers over it. He held Danny's hand tight as he talked, letting go only when he was done. "Always remember that I have talked to many, many dead men, too."

TWENTY-EIGHT

I t took a surprisingly long time to cut all the way
through a man's neck.

It looked to be very, very bloody.

Although Martino Abrego Cabrera had been called
Tiburón since he was fifteen years old, he'd never actually
seen a man hurt in such a way in person, and he had
never participated in such an act himself.

It wasn't that he was particularly troubled by the sight
of blood (he wasn't), or sympathetic to the begging and
screaming (it was distasteful, but unmoving), it was that
he appreciated keeping a clinical—*safe*—distance from
the unpleasant work itself. It was one of many differences
between Martino and his father, Fox Uno, and even
Gualterio, Oso Ocho . . . both of whom stubbornly held
on to the past. The old ways . . . *las viejas formas*. Whereas
Fox Uno didn't mind getting his hands bloody, figuratively or literally, and in fact relished it—believing it the
true source of his strength—Martino knew that only exposed you to unnecessary risks and unforeseen consequences. He had done a year of an MBA program at San
Diego State University and thought about everything in
terms of risk assessment and minimization. In so many

ways, he'd studied hard for this moment, preparing himself to lead his father's business into the future.

That did not mean, however, that some of the old ways were still not useful.

HE CONTINUED WATCHING THE VIDEO that had been sent to him through a secure, end-to-end encrypted e-mail, via Protonmail, whose servers were in Switzerland, a country he had visited when he was nineteen. That was another difference between Martino and his father: the older man had long refused to leave the country of his birth, the mountains and forests and dirt-poor farms and towns in Chihuahua and Durango and Coahuila de Zaragoza. He'd always considered them his strongholds, places where he was safe, untouchable. Fox Uno had bought the loyalty of the people in those places and believed they would protect him, and to some extent, he'd been right for a long, long time.

Too long.

Martino, however, had learned that the real world was much, much larger than Chihuahua, and that what could be bought once often had to be paid for again and again, or had to be taken by force. That brought him back to the young man in the video—Abrahán Sierra—who'd survived the attack in Manuel Benavides. Abrahán had been offered more than ten thousand dollars U.S. to drive Martino's father into that ambush, but had balked at the last moment. Perhaps it had been an instinct for self-preservation, or some measure of that loyalty Fox

Uno had always relied on, but in the end the driver had helped the old man escape, and although Martino's men and those of the Serrano Brothers had been turning that shithole upside down for days—using both money and threats to flush him out—his father, and Gualterio, too, had all but disappeared.

Fox Uno had last been seen with Zita, on foot, running into the badlands around Manuel Benavides.

Running . . . very much alive, and very much trying to hold on to what remained of Nemesio. The attack on the *normalistas* had been the first part of Martino's plan, and although it had done enough to unseat his father, the ambush in Manuel Benavides was meant to finish the job. It had not.

His father still had access to those old methods of his, scattered networks of runners and mules and *sicarios* and *compadres*. Enough of them still loyal, and alive, to carry out his threats and orders from wherever he'd hidden himself.

For a very desperate man, all alone and on the run, Fox Uno was proving to be surprisingly cagey and resourceful. But Martino didn't know if his father could even begin to comprehend just how alone he truly was.

The question was not how long and how far he could realistically run, but *where?* That question had been put to Martino several times by Diego Serrano in the last two days, more forcefully each time. Martino had started to form an idea, but not one that he was ready to share yet with Diego, who might decide to take matters into his own hands. Diego was sniffing around, sending his own men out to find Martino's father, and that was unacceptable. It was true that everyone involved wanted, *needed*, Fox Uno dead, but Martino couldn't risk letting the Serrano Brothers and their *sicarios* claim that prize.

When Fox Uno finally fell, all those men Martino had promised and negotiated with, including Los Hermanos Serrano, needed to know that this one thing was done on *his* order, by his hand, even if his finger wasn't on the trigger.

This was his contribution, his legacy, to the hostile takeover he had orchestrated. If he had any hope of retaining his position in the aftermath, of surviving, he could not fail in this.

Martino had learned about corporate takeovers in business school, as well as rebranding: changing the identity or corporate image of a business in the minds of investors, stakeholders, and even competitors. Nemesio, through the long, bloody years, had finally outlived its usefulness. It had been irreversibly weakened by its battles with the Serrano Brothers and had lost its influence and protection with those in power in Mexico City. Those powerful men needed peace between the cartels, at least for a while, because they also had been weakened by the bloodshed and publicity. They could no longer explain or justify Nemesio's continued existence, and Martino had grown to understand that the only way for any of them to survive was to tear out the old and start again new.

Rebrand.

Martino had brokered a deal with the Serrano Brothers and those powerful men in Mexico City to destroy the very thing his father had built. He'd successfully staged the bus attack, an admittedly clumsy and hastily put-together affair that had not come without costs. In fact, he'd been scrambling ever since, the wheels now in motion turning faster than he'd anticipated or planned. But he always knew he had to first undermine Fox Uno's support network—put a target on the man's back before cutting off his head—and the opportunity in Ojinaga had been too good to let pass, despite the chaos afterward. Only his father, a former *normalista* himself, would ever appreciate and understand the attack's true significance.

It had been an unfortunately emotional decision, though, and Martino didn't have the luxury of such decisions anymore. Before the bus attack, he'd already begun the slow and systematic removal of many of those men most loyal to his father, those who could not be bought. He'd also made numerous changes to Nemesio's operations and finances, some his father knew about, most he never would learn of, all in preparation for the right moment; all designed to demonstrate to the men in Mexico City his competency and usefulness. But the moment came too soon, before he was fully prepared, and the single most valuable thing he'd planned to offer to guarantee his own safety, his ascendancy in whatever came after, had been his father's head.

The one thing he figuratively, and literally, did not have.

And the head of the man in the video, Abrahán Sierra, would not be enough.

If that butcher Diego Serrano had said it once, he'd said it a thousand times: Martino should have been at

Manuel Benavides. Should have handled it personally. It all sounded so much like his father, yet it went against every instinct Martino had tried to cultivate. He'd wanted to avoid unnecessary exposure, the unexamined risk.

The emotion.

He believed then, and now, he could still get it done his way.

He wanted to start his leadership of the Nueva Generación—the name he'd chosen for the entity set to rise in Nemesio's place—as a businessman. Professional, not personal. He planned to run it as the twenty-first-century multinational corporation it truly was, or could be, and not as a thuggish cartel mired in the history of the brutal men who'd made their fortunes as ignorant border smugglers.

Martino had heard his father's stories, knew the names of all the dead men he revered who'd created the very caricatures of the narcos with their gold and silver guns and jeweled belt buckles. Martino would still broker the necessary deals, as he had with the Serranos, and he'd still pay the bribes to Mexico City, even more expensive than those from before. But he also planned to establish new plazas and smuggling routes, push NG's influence and sales beyond the United States to the lucrative markets in Europe, something his father had avoided. He was going to increase domestic heroin and methamphetamine production, replacing the marijuana plantations with poppy fields and working directly with Chinese distributors for precursor chemicals. He had so many ideas to modernize and update and streamline. *Vertical integration.* Martino's NG would be borderless. His father had long refused to look much beyond the mountains of his youth, a myopic worldview that might have made him rich, but over time had also made him weak and vulnerable. Rotten from the inside, unwilling to change or adapt. Predictable, at least until now.

Because his father was *not* in Manuel Benavides, or likely anywhere else in Chihuahua. Worse, perhaps not even in Mexico.

Martino was prepared to accept the fact he hadn't given his father enough credit, or had not paid close enough attention to what he'd been doing, tucked away on his ranches. Perhaps he'd been preparing for this moment, too, just as Martino had. But what Martino had not been prepared to do was search the whole wide world for him. He'd never planned for that contingency, never believing Fox Uno would have the chance to run so far.

Martino had staked his new business on that.

In fact, he'd staked everything on it, including his life.

IN THE VIDEO, Abrahán Sierra's head finally came off in a torrent of blood, overflowing the bucket and the tarp on the floor. The man also pissed and shit himself. He'd said nothing useful, nothing more than what they already knew, and in the end, he'd only talked about his family in Parral, who would have to suffer similar fates. The two hooded men in the video, laughing in their enthusiasm, castrated Abrahán and shoved his penis and balls in his mouth, cracking his jaw in the process. His eyes were still open, looking right into the camera the whole time, and it was a disturbing image—those eyes nothing more than incredibly dark, empty holes, unblinking, accusing. One could get lost in them if stared at too long. The head would be found tomorrow on a street in Ojinaga, beneath a *narcomanta* claiming that Fox Uno had killed him for his disloyalty, and the grainy video itself would be released on the internet, where it would spin in an ever-widening circle for days, reaching every corner of the world.

To wherever Fox Uno was hiding.

If there was any advantage to Martino not having been at Manuel Benavides, it was that his father did not yet know the extent of his betrayal. There was still the very real chance his father might reach out to him, seek his help, so Martino had to do everything in his power to keep that possibility alive. It was his best chance of finding him, maybe his only chance now, much better than turning over every rock. If he tried to talk to his father directly—too soon—after everything that had happened, El Patrón would get rightfully suspicious, but if Martino could just stay patient, hold on until every other avenue of escape was closed off, Fox Uno might run right into his waiting arms.

If Martino was patient enough . . . if he had enough time.

Of course, it was his impatience that had put him in this predicament. He'd grown frustrated at his father's slights and thousand small insults, tired of waiting for the old man to either die or hand over Nemesio. And he'd worried, too, that he might choose Gualterio over him—another loose end he'd eventually have to tie off. Fortunately, Martino had listened to enough of his father's old narco stories to know that violent succession was commonplace, almost encouraged. It was a rite of passage, and Martino had decided his time had come.

If anything, it was past due.

Now he just needed a little more time.

Martino was done with Abrahán Sierra's video. He deleted the file, although the laptop itself would be destroyed in under an hour, only to be replaced by another. When that one arrived, he was going to take a few moments to review some lengthy e-mails from some new associates in Spain and Romania.

Martino only wanted to be a businessman, but it was a damn bloody business.

TWENTY-NINE

CHAYO & NEVA

Amador drove them away from Ojinaga hidden in the trunk of his car.

The *federales* were still manning checkpoints all around the city and the surrounding roads. The news said they were there to maintain the peace, to keep the narcos from shooting one another and to protect the citizens. But Amador told Chayo that people were whispering how they were really there looking for any last survivors . . . eyewitnesses.

Amador had a friend who had seen black-clad men calling themselves *federales* at the Hospital Integral de Ojinaga. They had searched every room, grim-faced, and had refused to answer questions.

They had shown badges that had meant nothing.

Similar stories came in from Unidad Médica Familiar No. 54 and Hospital General de Guadalupe y Calvo. As the days went by, although few expected anyone to find the nineteen missing students alive, some hoped there were no survivors at all.

Before they left, Carmelita had hugged Chayo tight, and then turned her attention to Neva. She brushed the girl's hair and kissed her and held her hands, said something to her that Chayo could not hear. Neva had smiled, as best she could, and kissed the old woman back.

After that, they'd crawled together into the trunk lined with old blankets, and it was Carmelita who shut it over them.

THERE WAS A MOMENT WHEN, trapped in that light-less, almost airless space, Chayo thought they were caught. He was holding Neva close, their nest of blankets protecting them from the worst of the bounces and turns, when the car shuddered to a stop. There were voices—rough, commanding—but he couldn't pick out one from another or the words they were saying. He and Neva were slicked with sweat, sliding against each other, close enough he could taste the salt on her skin and hair.

She trembled in his arms as a bright light played against the car. That cool, pale light crept through the cracks and the open spaces as if it was searching for them, too.

A hand, maybe a hand, or the heavier butt of a gun, struck the trunk. It was as loud as thunder. It rolled and echoed over them, and they were trapped in a storm that would never end.

More words were said.

Someone laughed.

That light swung back and forth, back and forth, and then it winked out. A great eye closing.

Then the car was moving again. Slowly, but moving all the same. It wheezed and shrugged its way over gravel and dust, and Chayo realized the salt he was tasting was not just Neva's sweat, but her tears as well.

———————

LATER, AMADOR WOULD TELL THEM that he'd explained to the men with the guns blocking the road that he was going to see his sister in Atascaderos. That she was ill and he was the last family she had left.

He'd given them a huge bag of candy and they'd been happy and let him go.

Calaveras de azúcar.

Sugar skulls.

THE SKY WAS FULL OF STARS when they finally crawled from Amador's trunk—hot, feverish, ready for air. Chayo helped Neva stand, and she stared above them as if she'd never seen all that faraway brilliance before.

They were wrapped in darkness, their eyes adjusting to the night around them.

There was barely a slice of the moon high above the trees. All the light, what there was of it, came from the stars.

Chayo thanked the old man, although there was no true way to thank him. There were no words, not enough of them, what Amador had risked for the two of them: a boy with dirt underneath his fingernails and a girl with a broken smile. Amador was at a loss for words, too.

He might have wanted to tell them to get back in the trunk so he could drive them back to the city, but after clutching his veined and gnarled hands together— embarrassed—he settled for hugging them both and then getting inside his car alone.

He waited for a few minutes to see if they changed their minds, and Chayo stood aside, letting Neva decide for them both.

When she didn't move, Chayo waved at Amador to go on, as Neva continued to watch the stars.

AMADOR HAD DRIVEN SOUTH away from Ojinaga, dropping Chayo and Neva off in the Parque Nacional Cañón de Santa Elena. From there, Chayo planned on hiking them back north again, through the wilds of the park, crossing the river somewhere east near the U.S. border at Lajitas, before finally curving west toward Murfee. This kept them moving through state and national parks, away from towns and ranches, and hopefully, clear of the most heavily used smuggling areas.

But it would be rugged, and in truth, he just didn't know.

Watching the trees and the darkness circling them, he had to admit he had no idea what they would find.

He adjusted Neva's pack for her—he'd secured it with some extra rope so it would ride high on her shoulders and not put so much pressure on her back. Then he checked his own heavy bag, and the water he was carrying. The two jugs were cool to the touch and heavy now, but as they gulped each precious mouthful they'd need to stay alive, those jugs would lighten and lighten until they weighed next to nothing at all.

Lighter than air.

Chayo could only pray that by the time they'd run out of water, they'd be near this place: *Murfee*.

Something flapped in a nearby tree, taking flight into the night. It made no sound, uttered no call, and other than the whispered movement of feathers beating against the wind, it might not have existed.

They needed to go.

He took Neva's hand for what seemed to be the thousandth time since that night on the bus, and followed that graceful sound of wings . . .

THIRTY

Johnnie Macho was willing to bet that Roman was fucking Rae.

He'd known Roman since high school, when Roman had weighed about a buck ten soaking wet, with scraggly hair way too long, always in his eyes. He'd looked like a goddamn scarecrow. A nerdy scarecrow. Other than an old hooker they'd fucked together in Dryden (at least Roman had paid for her), Johnnie knew for a fact that Roman hadn't gotten laid as a teenager. He'd spent most of his time jerking off to his daddy's titty magazines. He'd been a stutterer, too, getting all tongue-tied when he was nervous. He couldn't look a girl in the eye back then, and barely could now. But lifting a few weights (popping a few 'roids), having that rat's-nest hair shaved down to a fine, sleek stubble, and carrying a silver shield and gun on your hip did wonders for your social standing.

Johnnie figured Roman owed him, owed him big, since he was the one who'd brought him on to the sheriff's department and gotten him into the Tejas unit. Come to think of it, he'd turned him into a man, and frankly, fucking Johnnie's girlfriend behind his back was a shitty way to pay him back for all that kindness.

That was all about to change.

Roman was about to get another chance to settle up with his old friend Johnnie.

THE CLUB WAS PAINTED bright blue and red, all the harsh lights making Johnnie's head hurt, and the music was too goddamn loud.

The music was *bright*, too, if there was such a thing.

But tonight, loud was good, since if any of these fuckers were wearing a wire, that jungle bunny music drowned out most of what Johnnie was saying.

They were sitting at their usual table in the back of El Diablo Norte. Johnnie, as well as Roman, Chavez, Ortiz, and Ringo—the bloody heart of the Tejas unit. Johnnie had bought all the drinks, so the others knew they were there to talk *real*, not police, business. But their guns and badges were visible here (like they always were), shining just as bright in the lights that were sharp enough to cut glass. Everyone knew who they were and how they "owned" this place, like they owned most of Terrell County, so no one would ever say a word to them no matter how drunk they got, or if they waved their guns at some piece of shit who pissed them off. It bothered Johnnie, though, that Roman kept stealing glances up at the stage, where Rae was again defying gravity with that ass of hers. Johnnie could swear he even saw her smile at that cocksucker, which meant he was going to have to slap it right off that bitch's face later.

All he could do now was chew his matchstick harder and take a long drink of the warm Pacífico he didn't want.

If he didn't drink with them, the others would notice. They'd know he was nervous, as sure as they could smell it on him, and when you're surrounded by wild fucking dogs—and Johnnie was, all the time now, on all fucking sides—the last thing you wanted to do was show any damn fear.

So he drank his Pacífico and tried not to choke on it, as the others debated the thing he'd said. The thing he'd told them they were going to have to do.

While Rae up there on her pole turned and turned, like she was about to spin away into all those lights above them and disappear. And to Johnnie, who hadn't slept much the past three days, that didn't seem like a bad idea at all.

IT WAS CHAVEZ who said no first. He was the oldest, older than Johnnie. He was a big man, always had been, and had worked for Johnnie's father as a deputy for more than twenty years. He was one of the first Johnnie brought on to the unit, known all around the area for the catch dogs he bred for bull and boar baiting and for the dogfighting rings he ran on the side, and sometimes Johnnie could look at Chavez's weathered face, into his deep-set black eyes, and see more dog than man there. Like he'd slowly changed into one of those bully breeds he kept caged and chained in his barn.

Surrounded by wild fucking dogs . . .

If Chavez said no, the others would follow his lead. Johnnie needed to straighten this out fast.

Johnnie set his beer aside, leaning forward. "See, I'm

not really asking, okay? This isn't a goddamn negotiation."

Chavez crossed his thick arms, revealing a faded blue tattoo of a pit bull running up his forearm. "And this isn't like the other things, Juanito." Chavez was the only one who could get away with calling him that. Sometimes he used it as a term of affection, like a kindly uncle. This wasn't one of those times.

Ortiz spoke up. "Yeah, I agree with Chavez. I really don't like the sound of this thing at all." Ortiz was the newest member, his hair still a high and tight crew cut like a goddamn road trooper. He'd just gotten married, too, and was always checking his phone and texting his wife, who was waiting up for him.

Johnnie pointed to the phone in Ortiz's hand. "When you walk the fuck out of here and get into that nice department ride you're driving, where the fuck you gonna go?"

Ortiz glanced at the others, still unsure of himself. He'd always be unsure of himself. "Home, Johnnie. Just home, you know that."

"Right . . . *home*. Not to that fucking shitty double-wide you grew up in, but a nice two-story. Garage. Pool. That *muy bonito* house you bought that new wife of yours. How the fuck do you think you bought that home?"

Ringo raised his hand for another beer (that motherfucker would drink up a storm on someone else's tab). "You know, I fucked that new wife of yours a couple of times last year, before you all got together. Trust me, she ain't worth that house you bought her." Everyone laughed—everyone always laughed when Ringo told a joke or a story—even when it was a story they'd heard a thousand times and that Ringo never, ever got tired of bringing up. He enjoyed rubbing salt into Ortiz. If there was any man on the unit Johnnie thought he could trust, it was Ringo. He was slim, good-looking—dark hair and dark eyes and dark skin—and there probably wasn't a girl in the county he hadn't fucked one time or another. He was also a stone-cold killer in expensive snakeskin boots (he loved those damn boots), and so far, he was the only one of the unit who hadn't blinked at what Johnnie had told them they were going to do.

"It doesn't matter whether she was worth it or not," Johnnie said, trying to steer them back to the thing that mattered, the *only* thing that mattered right now. "You couldn't have afforded that place without *my* help, without me bringing you into this." He sat back in his chair, taking them all in with a glance. "All of you. Every fucking thing you have is 'cause of me."

Chavez finished his beer and set it carefully on the table. The dog jumped on his forearm. "Watch it, Juanito. We've all earned what's come to us . . ."

"No." Johnnie stopped him. "This thing here, now, is how you earn it. This is the final bill for the house and the trips and the fucking cars and the money you all have hidden beneath your mattresses."

Roman finally spoke up, sliding his eyes away from Rae's tits, but still not quite looking at Johnnie. "It somehow doesn't seem right, Johnnie. Not fair . . ."

Not right, not fair, like fucking my girlfriend behind my back? That's what Johnnie wanted to say, but he choked it back.

"There is no 'right.' No one cares what you think is

fair. I don't, and trust me, *they* don't. We're going to do this thing. If we say no, these fuckin' Indians will scalp us. We all might as well go ahead and set fire to the lives we have. The expensive lives we bought with *their* money, like Ortiz's goddamn house." He could have added *because if you don't, they will*, but there was no need. They understood, even if they didn't want to. They might be wishing right now they'd never met Johnnie Macho or joined the Tejas unit—hell, they might be wishing they'd never become deputies—but they had to see the sense of what he was saying.

They'd escorted drug loads and protected murderers.

They'd stolen drugs from rival cartels.

They'd ripped off other drug crews and submitted sham dope as evidence—taped packages Ringo had made in his kitchen with cement mix—and then resold the real dope on their own.

They'd sent messages in blood.

They'd killed and buried out in the desert.

And they couldn't just take all that back now, like they couldn't just give back all the shit they'd bought and hoarded, either. If they even thought it, Ortiz's ugly new house might suddenly burn down with his wife inside, taped to a dining room chair.

Chavez wanted to argue anyway.

"Let me talk to them, Juanito. I can explain things. We're untouchable here, but outside Terrell . . ."

"Now you want to explain things, like I didn't already?" Johnnie pulled out the special red phone from his pocket, the one they had given him. He never did this, never showed it around in public, but he was desper-

ate and this was his last play. He put it on the table between them, and the red and blue club lights spun on it,
reminding Johnnie of the police lights hidden in the
grille of his Charger. "Then you go right ahead and call
them. You tell them whatever the fuck you want
to . . . tell 'em how we're not doing *this* thing or *that*
thing. But you be sure to tell 'em your name, so they
know exactly who the fuck they're talking to."

The phone sat on the table like a live snake, no one
eager to grab it.

Ringo only smiled and turned his attention to a
dancer on a far stage.

Ortiz's face went pale, which was almost impossible to
do under the lights, but he wouldn't look at the phone,
pretending it didn't exist.

Roman never looked away from Rae's sweat-slicked
body, just nodded.

Finally, Chavez moved his empty beer bottle aside,
and for a moment, it looked like he was going to reach
for the phone. But then he, too, pulled back.

Johnnie let it sit there a few beats longer, before sliding it off the beer-slicked table.

"You guys shouldn't feel so bad about this. We're still
going to get paid. Hell, Ortiz, you'll even be able to buy
that wife a new car to put into your new garage."

HE ORDERED ANOTHER ROUND of beers for everyone except himself.

He kept talking fast, while he still had them under his
thumb.

"It's a nobody, a no one. No one is going to care. We clip him and we're done." Johnnie had heard the word "clip" on one of Zam's TV shows and used it all the time now.

"Someone cares plenty, otherwise they wouldn't be asking us to do this. And it's not Terrell, Juanito. We're going to have to travel," Chavez said, but not as forcefully as he'd complained before.

"Fuck," Ringo said, shrugging. "We're only driving up the road. It's just Murfee."

"Right," Johnnie added. "*Just* Murfee. And hell, we're cops. We got every reason to be wherever we want to be."

"Tell that to that Sheriff Cherry over there. Or to that deputy, Danny what's-his-name," Chavez said. "He's a prick. You have history with him, right?"

Johnnie nodded. "We had a dustup, but it was nothing. He didn't like something I said about some girl."

"Let me get him in my sights," Ringo said, faking a gun with his fingers and pointing it right between Johnnie's eyes. "I fucking owe him, too."

"Okay, I got it. We all got it," Johnnie said. "But we're not going to see Danny Fuck-off or any of the rest of 'em. We're in and out before anyone knows we're there." But Johnnie honestly didn't know how things were going to play out, had no fucking idea at all.

"You're going to get it all squared away, right?" Ortiz asked, looking back and forth at everyone across the table. He asked it as if Johnnie could give him a sort of guarantee, as if he could promise that it would rain tomorrow.

Fuck it, fine.

"Right as rain."

"What do you know about the . . . mark?" Roman asked. Since Rae had finished her set, his attention was now fully back on the table.

"Like I said, he's a nothing, a nobody," Johnnie lied, although the others had to know that wasn't exactly true. Their mark had to be *somebody*, for all the effort. "He crossed our Indian friends or fucked up and failed 'em, and now they just want him taken care of. They can't get any of their own shooters across the border right now to do it, so it's gotta be us. *If* he's even hidin' out on this side."

"What about your daddy?" Roman asked, leaning back in his chair, somehow flexing his arms at the same time. All those pills he'd popped had turned him into one big son of a bitch, and Johnnie wondered if he chewed up some Viagra, too, before throwing it to Rae all night when Johnnie was home playing husband to Zam and daddy to Johnnie Jr. and Antonio. Johnnie also couldn't help wondering if Roman fucked Rae in that amazing ass, and the thought made his head hurt.

The veins popped in Roman's neck, and he wasn't stuttering so much anymore. He sure was fucking talkative now that Rae was off the stage.

Johnnie always thought Chavez would be the first to cross him, but maybe he had it wrong. Maybe some good pussy and a few Chinese pills were going to make Roman the brave one.

It was right then that Johnnie decided, before all was said and done, he might just have to kill Roman, too.

We're all killers now.

"I'll handle that. Don't worry about it. He doesn't know what he doesn't know."

"And you're sure this 'nobody' is really there in Murfee?" Roman stared right at him, muscles still flexed. They ignored gravity like Rae's ass.

How the fuck does he do that?

Since when did he ever look *anyone* in the eye?

Johnnie shrugged, told the truth. "They're not sure. I'm not sure . . . not yet. But I will be." The Indians, those *indios* from Acuña Johnnie answered to, really didn't seem to know if the man they were looking for was in Murfee or not; they were just guessing, and it was up to him to find out for sure. Although he had been running dope for them out of the Big Bend for the past few months, the *indios* didn't have a lot of other eyes or ears in the area— mostly just Johnnie, and Johnnie had his own guy. In a year, maybe two, they'd own all of West Texas, and probably have a dozen shooters and spies on speed dial, but not now. Now, some sort of final shakeout was going on down south between the *indios* and their rivals, and the man they wanted dead was at the heart of it.

That's all that mattered to Johnnie.

Johnnie stood, tossing a couple of hundreds on the table. He had no idea what the bill was, but it was nowhere near the amount of money he'd thrown down. Money he didn't really have, for drinks he couldn't really afford.

Like he couldn't afford to let the other men around the table fuck this up for him.

He stared Roman back down, letting him know he was going backstage to visit Rae right now, reminding him who was in fucking charge. Roman and the others didn't need to know everything he knew—it was better they didn't—but they needed to know enough to stay in line and remember that Johnnie Macho was always on top of things.

Making the right calls, placing the big bets, righteously handling his business.

He spat his chewed-up matchstick onto the floor. "I got someone in Murfee. When the time comes, he's gonna help us out."

THIRTY-ONE

D eputy Marco Lucero liked her tattoos.

Okay, it was more than that.

He liked the way she laughed when she laughed, which wasn't as often as she should. He liked her purple eyeshadow, and the way she chewed the end of her straw when she was drinking a Coke, and the way she kept her long hair in a braid that draped over one bare shoulder. When she worked at Earlys she usually wore a tank top and dark jeans, and it was that thin-strapped top that best showed off those tattoos on her left arm, running all the way to the smooth hollows of her throat. A few more peeked out around the curves of her small breasts, and he imagined—too often—what they might be. All he could ever see was a smudge of dusky color; a flower, a sun, a dragon. He had no real idea. But when he was bored sitting at his desk listening to Till Greer tell his unfunny jokes, or was in his truck, running the radar gun on U.S. 90—the only gun he'd ever drawn since joining the department—he kept coming back to Vianey Ruiz's tattoos. They told a story, just like all the tattoos Danny Ford had, and it was a story that Marco desperately wanted to know.

To get to know. Vianey had to know that, too. She was

a bit older than him, probably flirting with everyone since it was part of the job description of working in a bar, but when he came into Earlys and sat down, she always made a point of setting them both up with a cold Coke (lots of ice for him) and ordering him some wings or whatever was on special, and then spent a good part of Marco's time in the bar leaning over the old wood and chatting him up.

Again, it was probably part of the job description. But sometimes, *sometimes*, he imagined she was standing there waiting for him to say something more. It was the way she looked at him over the rim of her glass, over that chewed end of her straw stained with her lipstick. It was a look they both held for a few seconds too long, just before it became uncomfortable and one of them would have to say something to fill that silence. Just before she was always called away to serve someone else.

That look would stay with him for hours . . . for days.

Like those tattoos and their stories.

OF COURSE, they already shared a story together, although they never talked about it. Her former boyfriend, a man named Billy Bravo, had been killed by Jesse Earl, and it was the Earls—Jesse and his father, John Wesley, and some others—who'd started the fires that cost Marco's brother, Emiliano, most of his eyesight. It's what had brought Marco home again and to the Big Bend County Sheriff's Department, and to Earlys on those nights like this one when he wasn't helping Emil.

One thing leading to another . . . to another . . . on

and on. You never knew the start of something important—often never realized its importance at all—until it was over; until you had the benefit of hindsight, although sight of any kind was something Emil Lucero was never going to have again.

Like Marco's decision to drop out of UTEP and come back home and join the department. Had that been a good thing, or foolishly shortsighted? Had he derailed his college career—his dreams of becoming a doctor—to become a second-rate deputy? And if Sheriff Cherry lost the upcoming election (which Marco was pretty sure was going to happen), what future was there for him in the department?

What future was there, really, for him here in Murfee?

That's what he imagined passed between them when he and Vianey shared those too-long looks.

She was simply waiting for him to tell her: *Let's get the hell out of here.*

TONIGHT, EARLYS WAS BUSY, so although he'd finally worked up the courage to at least suggest to Vianey they catch a movie or something (he didn't know what something else would be), she hadn't been able to spend much time at his end of the bar. But as she popped open a beer or poured another whiskey, she did make a point to turn his way and flash a quick smile. There were plenty of people in Earlys, but few he recognized, and that had been true since he'd returned home. Murfee was changing, finally. Slowly but surely. There were still those old families who'd always been here and always would be, but there were newer faces who'd come to settle and start lives. There were more Hispanics in Earlys than ever, and that was due to Sheriff Cherry. In years past they would have all stayed on the other side of town at Mancha's, or headed down to Terlingua or Presidio, but now they felt comfortable coming into a place like Earlys because the sheriff had made them feel welcome. Not only this shitty old bar, but all over Murfee. That's why it was a shame he was going to lose the election; he'd been good for the Big Bend, even if some folks didn't see that.

Even if some were damn shortsighted.

Marco wasn't surprised at all that he didn't know the dark-haired young man on the stool next to him. He wasn't Hispanic, though, and hadn't said anything to anyone else since he'd sat down. He'd ordered a beer, still sitting mostly untouched in front of him, the foam falling in place, and he was looking around Earlys like he recognized it, like from a picture he'd once seen; trying to figure out how it might have changed. He had a few days of stubble and slim hands without any rings. Not even a watch. He was wearing a black leather jacket that was too warm for the weather, and definitely too warm for inside the bar.

He looked at Marco's deputy badge pinned to his belt and raised his still-full beer to him.

"Have you been a deputy long?" he asked, setting the beer back down without taking a drink.

"Awhile," Marco said, curious. The man had a soft voice, too soft for the loud bar, and he had to lean forward to hear it.

"You know Sheriff Cherry?"

Marco laughed. "Sure, we see each other every now and then." He turned on his stool to face the man better. "And you are . . . ?"

"A reporter, covering the election. Out of Austin."

"Huh. I can't imagine anyone in Austin, or anyone outside the Big Bend, caring about who our sheriff is. It's all just small-town politics." Marco glanced past the man to Vianey, who was intent on some limes she was cutting.

The man moved his beer mug around, chasing water circles on the wood. "You'd be surprised."

"Yeah, I guess I would be."

"How many deputies do you have in the department? The articles I read don't quite match. You cover plenty of rough ground out here."

Marco gave the man a closer look. There was nothing threatening or intimidating about him at all, but the question troubled him all the same. He laughed again to lighten the curt answer he was going to give: "Enough."

The young man smiled, neither angry or irritated. "That's fair. Look, I don't suppose you'd be willing to give me an interview? Off the record. You know, a color piece, what it's like to live and work here . . . to work for Sheriff Cherry." He took stock of what Marco was drinking. "I'll buy you another Coke and whiskey."

Marco shook his head. "Just Coke. And an interview? Not on your life."

The man pressed on. "Okay, there's a young female deputy in the department, too, right? Hispanic? In a town like this, that's a whole story in and of itself. I read about the trouble that occurred down here last year with some bikers, some sort of Aryans or skinheads. It was a big deal for a few days, and she was right in the middle of it. Do you think I'd be able to talk to her?"

Marco paused, buying time with a long sip of the just Coke. "If you want to interview anyone in the department, you're going to have to clear that with the sheriff. I'm sure you understand."

The man put a folded twenty on the bar for the beer he didn't drink, and for the Coke he didn't buy Marco. He smiled, unfazed. "I do. I'm only trying to do my job. I'm sure you understand that, too."

"I do. So I guess that leaves us understanding each other pretty well. You're here to cover the debate tomorrow night, right?"

The young man stood to leave. He was thin, and the thick leather coat did little to give him any bulk.

"Sure, that's it," he answered as he shook Marco's hand, then headed for the door. "Be safe, Deputy."

But for reasons he couldn't put a finger on, Marco didn't think that was it at all.

IT BUGGED HIM FOR THE NEXT HOUR, even after Vianey brought him another Coke.

She tried to talk to him, but he was distracted, and soon she had to go back to the other customers, leaving him alone.

Marco wasn't going to ask her out tonight anyway. It was a missed chance, but he hoped there would be others.

He was bothered by the young man in his leather coat and his questions. Questions about the sheriff and, more important, about America Reynosa, although he'd never once said her name. Marco couldn't shake the idea that the whole conversation was about her and had been all along, and not about anyone or anything else.

He didn't think the man from Austin cared about the election.

He'd heard the other deputies talking, and some folks around town. In the last couple of days, America had been seen in the company of an old man and a young girl. Probably just relatives or friends, although no one knew exactly which. Come to think of it, Danny had been seen with them, too. It wasn't a secret, exactly; the sort of thing people might notice and comment on, maybe consider strange, but never think of asking directly about. It just wasn't how things were done in Murfee. For a place that did such a poor job of hiding its secrets, most folks did an admirable job of keeping their mouths shut.

Now you had America being seen with two strangers, and another stranger suddenly appearing in Earlys, asking about her.

All that was strange.

Marco would never consider raising it with America, either. Honestly, he got nervous around her, but that didn't mean he couldn't mention it to Danny. In fact, it was the sort of thing he absolutely should tell Danny, who could then decide what to do about it.

One thing leading to another . . . leading to another . . . on and on. You never knew the start of something important—often never realized its importance at all—until it was over.

But maybe, just sometimes, you did.

THIRTY-TWO

A merica woke Fox Uno with a gun pointed between his eyes.

He was sleeping on the couch, Zita nearby on a pallet on the floor. The sheets were cartoon characters she had picked up, and the pillow was a big yellow thing, like a sun. Danny, too, was there—back in her bedroom—all wound up in a sleeping bag he'd been issued in the army. He had one gun, maybe two, slipped down into the sleeping bag with him. The last couple of nights he'd fought to stay awake, before finally, angrily, succumbing. He talked in his sleep, words and names she didn't know, hands moving on their own, flying toward his face as if he were startled and about to wake from whatever dreams were troubling him. But he never did. He rose each morning confused, with circles under his eyes, unrested.

It wasn't just Fox Uno troubling him, but he wouldn't talk about it, and since he refused to leave her alone in her apartment at night with Fox Uno and the girl, it was a tight, uncomfortable fit for everyone.

It had been hard getting up and moving through the bedroom and stepping quietly over Danny, and then Zita, to get to her uncle.

He sat up without a sound when she touched the

gun's muzzle to the weathered skin between his eyes, and if he recognized the gun—with its grinning silver *calaveras* and Nuestra Señora de la Santa Muerte—he didn't show it. He blinked and said nothing. She forced him to get up and grab his precious phones, and then she guided him silently out the door.

It was still dark outside, but the sun would likely be up by the time they got to where they were going.

SHE DROVE OUT OF MURFEE with the gun across her lap pointed at Fox Uno's stomach. She'd accepted that's who he was now, so there was no need to think of him as Juan Abrego or anyone else—as anything other than what he was. If he was concerned that she was going to kill him, he didn't beg for his life. Instead, he ignored her, letting it play out, watching the darkened world roll by.

She angled them south of town, toward Texas 118, out past Chapel Mesa, along the line of the Del Norte and Christmas Mountains; within sight of Nine Point Mesa, then in the direction of Terlingua and Study Butte. She kept going, eyes searching for the ranch road. To her left, hidden behind the mountains, the sun was still rising, and the sky there was slowly softening . . . lightening. A memory of a thousand other dawns. She had her window down but the cool morning air did nothing for her. Her skin was beaded with sweat, her hand steady on the gun.

She finally found the turnoff she was looking for, a switchback to the darkened west, and it was like driving down a long, shadowed tunnel—toward a place the sun was still a long way from reaching.

She had been out here many times after Sheriff Cherry had shown it to her.

She could find it with her eyes closed. A shallow hole, a blemish on the earth. It was part of her, a hole dug right into her heart.

A hole like a grave.

She finally pulled the truck over but didn't get out, not yet. They still had some walking to do. She smelled the creosote, the desert itself. It was sour and arid, and behind her the stars were giving way to a sun she still couldn't see.

She motioned at Fox Uno with the gun. Held it up high. "Get out," she said in English. She wasn't going to give him the courtesy of speaking Spanish.

It didn't matter, he knew exactly what she meant.

He opened the door and stood, stretching.

Then they both started walking.

THIRTY-THREE

About twenty-file miles away from America and Fox Uno, Chris rose, too, with the dawn.

His son was asleep, curled up close to Mel, tiny hands by his face. Chris remembered those long, waiting months of her pregnancy.

His hands gently following the taut curve of her belly, the immenseness of what it contained, what it meant for them both.

That impossible heat of her, from the bright flame of the thing growing inside her.

And, here, now: John Thomas Cherry.

They'd remade the world when they'd brought their son into it, and Chris had to believe, had to hope, they'd remade it for the better.

Jack was all the endless possibilities of better things.

A better world.

CHRIS TOOK HIS COFFEE and sat in the kitchen, with Rocky watching him from the floor. He had his papers spread out in front of him: the new story he was working on (he was always working on a story), and Garrison's folder and some notes—finally—for tonight's debate. He needed to think about it seriously, or at least for Mel's sake seriously pretend that he was thinking about it, but he was afraid there was nothing he could say about his time as sheriff that anyone would truly understand.

Instead, his thoughts kept returning to Murfee's bookstore on Main Street; all those old, dusty books in the window, safe behind glass. The store he and Fox Uno had stood and talked in front of, owned by Homer Delahunt, a friend of Chris's dad. Homer was well into his seventies, and everyone could see it was getting harder and harder for him to keep it up. He'd talked to a few folks about selling the place, but so far, there hadn't been any takers.

Chris had called him, ran a few questions by him, just curious.

He made the call to Homer after deciding, again, not to call Garrison. He'd thought a hundred times about calling the agent, but each time he had put his phone away and hadn't followed through, until it got easier not to think about it at all.

While talking to Homer, he noticed that some of the new reelection signs Mel had put up for him had been taken down, or had disappeared.

Maybe they had fallen and blown away.

HE FOCUSED ON THE BLANK PAPER in front of him, trying to make a list of the things he'd accomplished.

He could point to visible improvements around the jail and around the department itself. He'd implemented new policies and practices that had brought the Big Bend

County Sheriff's Department in line with modern and, Chris hoped, more ethical policing. He'd trained and equipped his deputies better, hiring good people to be those deputies: America, Danny, and the new kid, Marco.

He'd expanded the department's outreach to the Hispanic community.

These were all things he was proud of, but were they enough?

Did they matter?

Though he liked to argue with himself that he was nothing like Sheriff Stanford Ross, for most folks . . . the Royal Moodys of the world . . . that wasn't a winning argument. Hell, that wasn't even exactly true, not anymore.

Maybe he and Mel had remade the world by having Jack, but Chris wasn't convinced he'd made the Big Bend one damn bit safer by being its sheriff.

A lot of blood had been spilled on his watch—far too much—and in that way, Chris and Sheriff Ross weren't that goddamn different at all.

Chris wadded up the blank paper into a tight ball and tossed it against the far wall. Rocky chased it down, brought it back, and dropped it at his feet.

The dog sure had Mel's personality.

He roughed up Rocky's fur, then went back to the bedroom to watch his son sleep some more.

THIRTY-FOUR

S he had Fox Uno walk several steps in front of her, the gun trained on the small of his back.

It was slow going, the old man taking his time. It was his age, or his limp, or a way to buy himself a few extra minutes to think. It didn't matter. America would walk all day if she had to.

For this, she had all the time in the world.

THE SKY TURNED PEARL behind them.

America thought she saw a coyote skulking away, avoiding the light.

She definitely spied a great *búho*, hairy tufts rising high above its head and its yellow eyes regarding them as it flew past in a long graceful arc. It was bigger than any she'd ever seen, the wide space beneath its wings and across its chest far paler than the ruddy feathers across the rest of it.

It flew so softly, so gently, it made her think of snow falling.

They walked through a herd of cows, which moved aside at their approach. They stank—thick and unavoidable— and it reminded her of Duane Dupree driving her out to the Comanche cattle auction with his windows down.

The cherry glow of another one of his endless cigarettes, his eyes all over her.

Fox Uno stumbled, fell, but she didn't make a move to help him. He struggled, his pants and hands muddy or covered in cow shit, but he finally stood again.

She didn't have to tell him to keep moving.

The sky went whiter and whiter with the day's dawn.

Then they were there.

IT LOOKED NO DIFFERENT from any other part of Matty Bulger's ranch, Indian Bluffs. It was indistinguishable from the rest of the rolling scrub and the stubbled Bahia grass and a random scattering of twisted mesquite. Maybe there was a fence line from long ago that Dupree had remembered, or a crushed gravel path or road that America could not see, but she'd never know why the former chief deputy had chosen this spot to kill and bury her brother.

Where Sheriff Cherry had dug Rodolfo out of the earth.

Fox Uno wasn't standing on the exact spot, but close enough. He sensed it, too, or at least understood the importance of the place where she had brought him. He knew what happened in empty places like this, far from seeing eyes. He breathed hard and, with the rising sun flaring in his eyes, finally shielded them with a hand as he turned in place, unsteady, taking it all in.

"You will not shoot me here," he said in Spanish, shrugging. "You have thought about it. You have dreamed about it. But you will not do this thing. Not today, and not here."

She raised the gun higher. She wanted to talk only in English, but was now afraid the thoughts, the words, wouldn't come fast enough, and she wanted to make sure he understood her perfectly. "My brother died here. Your nephew. He died because of you."

Fox Uno looked at his hands, raised them, showing her his palms. "He was a liar, a thief. He was weak. His fate was in his hands, not mine. I did not kill Rodolfo."

"Then why send Máximo to avenge him? Why care at all?"

"The men who did this thing to him were liars and thieves as well. They stole from *me*. Rodolfo's life was not theirs to take. They had not earned that right." He paused, staring right into the rising sun. "I sent Máximo *for you*. You do not remember this, but I saw you once as a baby. A tiny thing, fists clenched. Angry and so strong then, refusing to cry. You were . . ."

"Don't do that. Don't pretend you know me. You know nothing about me."

"This is where you are wrong. I know you all too well, *mija*."

Mija was a term of affection, a nickname for a daughter. She'd heard Fox Uno use it with Zita. America's own papa had used it with her. "Do not call me that. I am not your daughter."

"Are you not? Look at what you have become. You should meet my son, Martino. He would admire you, and fear you. You have strength that he does not, that Rodolfo did not have." He waved at the gun, dismissing it, and then bent down and grabbed a handful of earth, crumbling it in his hands. He looked through it as if he was seeking something. "If you take my life today, you, at least, have earned that right." He tossed the dirt into the wind.

"You ruined Rodolfo's life. My life. No one here trusts me, *because of you*. Because of all the things you've done. Because of what you are. Everything you say is a lie."

"Because of what *we* are, and not everything is a lie, *mija*. The truth can be as dangerous or deadly as that gun you hold. I have only wanted to protect you . . ."

She laughed, bitter. "The way you've protected Zita? Running, begging for help? Begging for your lives?"

Fox Uno considered before answering, gathering and searching for more dirt. "You care for the girl."

"I'm not going to let you protect her anymore, if that's what you mean." It wasn't a threat, simply a fact. "Look at you. Old and feeble, standing in a cow field covered in shit."

America took a few steps forward. The silver gun was heavy in her hand, but she kept it steady. The first month after she'd found it on her doorstep, she'd slept with one hand on it. In many ways, she'd been holding it forever. "You planned for this all along, didn't you? You were always going to run here, *to me*, when everything you've done finally caught up to you."

Fox Uno stared into the dark muzzle of the silver gun, unblinking. He tossed the last bit of dirt away. "What do we do now? What have you decided to do with me, *mija*?"

She stepped closer, right next to him. She put the gun underneath his chin, and although it wasn't necessary, she pulled back the hammer, a sound that echoed over the scrub. Fox Uno looked skyward, his features pinched from the barrel of the gun pressed hard into the soft skin of his throat, before he slowly leveled his gaze at her again.

The sun was high enough now that they were both bathed in its light, but his face remained shadowed by her own.

She screwed the gun into his skin, making sure he felt every inch of the metal. Hoping he could smell it, almost taste it. "When I left that gun you gave Rodolfo with Máximo, I thought I'd never see one like it again. I used to wonder why you would send me this horrible thing. What was the purpose? What was the message? But when you showed up on the very same doorstep where I found it, I knew. I understood there are some choices that are already made for us. We've both been planning for this day." She pressed harder, pushing his head farther back so he was staring straight up into the sun. "I have a mama, a papa. Do you understand me? Are you listening to me? Really listening? I told you once, and now, after this, I will not say it again. Do not dare call me your *mija*. You haven't earned that right."

She gave the gun one more twist. "If you do, I'll blow your brains all over this field. And then, maybe someday, someone else will dig you up. Like they did my brother."

She reached into his pocket with her free hand and pulled out the phones she'd made him bring. She tossed them on the ground at his feet.

"The truth is dangerous. Now we're going to find out if you've been telling me the truth at all."

THIRTY-FIVE

This time he knew he was dreaming.

Everything is dark.

PV2 John Newberry whispers in Danny's ear as Danny tries to hold the boy's stomach together. It keeps slipping away from him. It is hot in his hands, steaming. Not that it matters, the IED made from an old M795 155mm U.S. artillery shell (he knows this only because it's a dream) blew Newberry's legs twenty-five yards across a dirt road.

Then he is in a hut in Nuristan or he is in Eddy Rabbit's trailer or he is in both at the same time, and he is having trouble breathing.

There are a thousand pounds of darkness sitting on his chest.

A bullet comes through the wall: a single Soviet 7.62x39mm round (again, he only knows this because it is a dream), leaving a band of furious light in its wake. It is like water in the desert: bright, unexpected, necessary.

Now a second round . . . this one close enough he can feel its passage on his skin. Heating the air next to his cheek, making his bad eye blink.

Someone is screaming.

Someone is calling his name.

How is something a choice when it isn't a choice at all?

He grips his own gun tighter and aims it under his own chin.

The hut and the trailer and the grave or whatever are crisscrossed with blinding light—a hundred bullets.

Desert sun here and now and half a world away.

A hundred crosses.

Now, IN THE DREAM, *the entire hut or trailer is filled with light and noise, a war's worth of bullets seeking him out and punching through the walls that Danny knows aren't walls at all.*

They are cloth. Just cloth, and nothing more.

And then the girl's hands are on him . . .

AND THEN THE GIRL'S HANDS were on him . . . *Zita.* Waking him up, as Danny kicked free of the hot sleeping bag with his Colt in one hand and a Glock in the other. His bad eye was buzzing, coming into focus, and he pointed them both at her and she screamed, backing away, talking rapidly in Spanish.

Danny crawled to his feet and checked the bed to find it was empty.

Amé was gone.

Early-morning sun was coming in through the blinds of the bedroom window, filling the room with new light.

The inside of the hut and the trailer and the grave or whatever is crisscrossed with blinding light.

Desert sun here and now and half a world away.

Danny stepped into the next room and saw the rumpled pallet, and knew that Fox Uno was gone, too.

Zita had retreated to the kitchenette, as far away from him as she could get. Hiding behind the table, peeking around it, her hands up. Crying.

Jesus, it was the second time he'd aimed a gun at the girl.

"It's okay, it's okay. I'm so sorry." He held up the guns, dropped their mags and ejected the chambered rounds, and set them both on the coffee table far away from him so she could see.

He had done almost the same thing with Fox Uno.

Now he kept his empty hands raised, where they could both see they were shaking.

Zita's crying had begun to trail off, but she hadn't moved any closer to him.

She was talking, asking him questions, he guessed, but he had no idea what she was saying.

"No, no, it's all okay. It's fine. I don't know where they are, but I'm sure they'll be back soon."

He tried to think of what little Spanish he knew, something—anything—to calm the terrified girl down.

"Helado," he finally said. "I'm so sorry, Zita. *Helado. Helado."*

He knelt—like he'd knelt beside PV2 Newberry in his dream—and held out his hands to her, steadier now. She watched him closely for several long, heartbreaking minutes, and then—slowly—came out from behind the kitchen table and ran into his arms.

Helado.

Goddamn ice cream.

That was the best he could do.

————

HE GOT ZITA SETTLED DOWN in front of a Mexican cartoon on the TV. He put his Bullhide hat on her head, and she seemed to like that.

Amé and Fox Uno had slipped out earlier, before first light, and he had no idea where they'd gone.

He tried calling and texting Amé several times without success, until he found the note she'd written on the bathroom glass.

It said simply: *Dime*.

The only other word in Spanish she knew he could figure out: *Tell me*.

He didn't have to know the language to understand what she meant. She'd asked him the same thing the other night in front of the apartment, with his arms tight around her.

He went back and forth on calling Sheriff Cherry, but what was there to say? What was there to do now, except give Amé the time to get whatever answers she thought she needed from Fox Uno—however she had to get them.

Tell me.

HE WAS STILL SITTING NEXT TO ZITA watching cartoons, an arm loosely around her steadying the Bullhide hat that was too big for her, when his phone finally buzzed.

He grabbed at it.

An incoming text, but not Amé.

It was Marco Lucero.

THIRTY-SIX

Make the call," she said. "I want to hear my mama on the other end of that phone."

A few minutes before, Fox Uno had knelt and picked up both phones, and was now holding one in each hand. "It does not work that way. There is a schedule, certain numbers at certain times . . ."

"I know. Secret words and names, like Rana and Araña and Diablo. Little boys playing silly games. But when I dialed Rodolfo's phone all those years ago, someone *did* answer, and you sent me Máximo. I thought it was magic, the stupid dreams of a stupid girl. But it wasn't magic and it wasn't a game. It was just you. And I'm no longer so stupid. *Make the call.*"

She'd already had Fox Uno unlock the phones and hold them up to her, scrolling through the call logs and the contact lists. In the sunlight they'd been hard to read, but it was clear enough both were empty. Either he'd been deleting them or there had never been anything there to begin with.

America knew better. There *was* someone else out there, somewhere.

She only had to force Fox Uno to call them.

"How is it that you think I have survived so long?"

"You're not going to live through this morning if I don't hear my mama or someone who knows where she is on the other end of one of those phones."

Fox Uno shrugged, a futile gesture. "This is not the way. If you do this thing, you will kill her. You might kill us all."

"*Me?* Men kill on *your* orders. Hundreds have lived and died on nothing more than your word, and now you have nothing to say to save yourself?"

"Yes, I killed men. But I bought and sold more, too, many to count. Important men, untouchable, far more dangerous than me. I have survived so long only because I trusted so few of them."

"Don't you dare fucking talk to me about trust."

"Listen to me," Fox Uno said, almost calling her *mija* again, before catching himself. "Understand, these men will not let me be found alive. They cannot afford to let me live, not with the things I know. All their names, all their secrets. Yes, I am a murderer, a thousand times over, but it's not the dead I will answer to."

"You can't protect my mama. You can't save yourself. You're weak, scared. Like the sheriff said, you are *nothing*." A few moments before, she'd stepped back from him so he could pick the phones up off the ground, but she was still close enough that when she pointed the gun at his face—now—it touched his skin. "Just empty threats and emptier promises."

He nodded, and it was clear to her that he was done arguing, defending himself. He held up a phone, the one in his right hand. The Blackphone.

"I am many, many things, but I am not a liar . . ."

He began pressing buttons from memory, but she stopped him with a sharp push of the gun against his chin.

"No," she said. "The other one."

He shook his head, and kept pushing buttons. "I will make this call, but no one will answer. A phone somewhere I do not know will ring, and a man I do not know will hear that ring, once, and know to go buy five phones from one of ten different stores. He will ride a bike, and pay for those phones in cash. If he does not do this thing, or if he takes longer than an hour, another man I do not know will kill the daughter, or mother, or father of the man on the bike." Fox Uno shrugged. "This I do not know, either. The man on the bike will take this phone to another, who will drive it to a third, maybe a fourth. Eventually, it will end up in the hands of a man who, if he is not dead, too, will open all the brand-new phone packages. He will choose one and . . ." Fox Uno trailed off, then started again. "If all is well, he will call me."

He then held out the phone in his left hand to her, the Mexican Telcel. When she had seen it that first night, it had reminded her of the phone her brother had once carried. The same one she used to summon Máximo. "When this one rings, answer it. Do not speak first. Someone on the other end will say a word. It will be one of three words. Each one is a color. White . . . red . . . green." He smiled, those were the colors of the Mexican flag. "If you hear the first word, stop the call and wait five minutes and there will be a second call. If you hear the second word, stop the call immediately and toss the phone into the desert. It is useless to us. If you hear the third, then . . . we are fine." Without asking her if it was okay, he slowly folded his legs and sat down in the dust. He took the Telcel and tossed it at her feet.

She remained standing, looking at the gun in her hand, and the phone down by her boots. "How long do we wait?"

He picked at a piece of grass, then another. "As long as it takes." He studied her. "This is how it starts. One thing, then another, always one more thing. You are part of this now. There is an old, old saying: 'One nail drives out another.'"

She relented and sat cross-legged from him. "Unless I ask you something, I want you to stay quiet."

But he kept talking. "It has been a long walk. I will lie here in the sun and wait with you, Señora de la Santa Muerte. We will learn together whether I have told the truth."

He stretched out in the dirt and covered his eyes with his arms.

"But we know in our hearts that neither of us are liars."

AMERICA WAITED MORE THAN AN HOUR, the sun tracking higher above them, and watched the old man sleep and snore on the ground a few feet away from her.

A white-haired old man in his borrowed clothes, muddy and stained in cow shit. He *could* be her papa, come in after a long day of working the cattle ranches around Murfee, or the giant marijuana fields in Chihuahua owned by her uncle.

For a few moments, she was eighteen years old again . . . holding Rodolfo's phone.

Holding Rodolfo's gun.

Now her own.

Señora de la Santa Muerte.

THE PHONE RANG.

Fox Uno stirred when it did, rising up on his elbows. Faster than she'd imagined, so maybe he'd never been sleeping at all. He watched her closely, but said nothing.

He was just as curious as she was about what would happen when she answered it.

One nail drives another . . . *Un clavo saca a otro clavo* . . .

She finally put it to her ear, waited, and heard a single word.

She blinked once, twice, holding her breath.

"Mama?" she asked the following silence, and waited for a reply.

THIRTY-SEVEN

M el couldn't remember the last time Chris had worn a suit.

She'd bought him this one in Midland and had to drag him there to have it tailored. It was charcoal—a shade or two darker than that—and it fit well, but he said he looked like an undertaker in it. Despite the fancy bloodred tie she'd chosen.

The suit, and the tie, had cost too much money. They both knew it, but she'd done it anyway.

She focused on straightening the gold pin in his lapel, a small Big Bend County Sheriff's Department star. Sheriff Ross had always worn one, and Chris had found boxes of them in the man's desk. They were some of the only things Chris kept around after Ross's funeral, and he'd let the deputies wear them or give them out at schools.

He always refused, but she put this one in now.

It shined sharply, from where she'd polished it bright on her hem, matching the one she had pinned to her dress.

Till Greer had already poked his head in to report he'd seen Bethel Turner heading over to the school in a charcoal-gray suit of his own, and a new Stetson the color of morning fog.

Chris had his Stetson Brimstone on the desk, the same one he'd owned since he'd taken over as sheriff, but he wasn't committed to wearing it. Yet.

The debate was only thirty minutes away, and they were in Chris's office, where he was reluctantly letting her fuss over him. She was brushing off his shoulders with her hand, brushing his neatly cut hair out of his eyes. She'd made him shave back at the house, and it had left his face raw, exposed. She counted them both lucky he hadn't nicked himself, leaving bloody spots on ruddy skin roughened by the Big Bend's wind and the sun. As she was about to get into the shower, she'd caught him staring at himself in the mirror with a last bit of Barbasol on his chin, and tried to read his thoughts: that he looked way too young, way too thin, too frail. That he was pretending and playing dress-up, wearing a grown-up's suit and another man's badge and gun. Worst of all, that he didn't even like the man he was looking at. To break those darker thoughts, she'd pulled him right into the shower with her and wrapped her arms around him and run hot water over them, hot enough to make them both gasp.

Only for her to gasp again, and again, when he entered her and breathed her name into her wet hair.

Later, getting dressed, he still hadn't wanted to look at himself too long in their bedroom mirror, and driving over to the sheriff's department, he'd tried not to catch his reflection in the truck's windows.

All those damn, dark thoughts of his, and a few of her own that she needed to rid herself of.

Yesterday, when he was out of the house, she'd come

across his papers in the kitchen, decided to glance through them quickly and see for herself the notes he'd made for the debate. Instead, she found the folder Joe Garrison had left. She had sat at their table for an hour and read far too much of it, all of Fox Uno's horrors, and it had been far too hard to think about much else since then.

It had been a long damn drive for them both.

MEL FINALLY STOPPED AND STOOD BACK to take him in, all at once, as Jack—wrapped up in his car seat—watched them both with his big eyes. Vianey Ruiz had offered to watch the baby for the night, but Mel wanted him with her. She didn't feel comfortable yet with anyone other than herself or Chris watching over their son.

"Jesus, babe, this is ridiculous. I look and feel ridiculous," he complained.

"No, you look handsome. Professional. Serious."

He held out his arms. "I look like the Grim Reaper."

She laughed. "I'd still vote for you."

"Well, there we go. One solid vote. Maybe I won't lose this thing in a complete landslide."

She crossed her arms and leaned against his desk. "You're not going to lose, Sheriff Cherry. I have a good feeling about this."

"I have all sorts of feelings, none of them good. Do you know I've never run for anything? Not student council president, nothing. I didn't even run for this office the first time around. They handed it to me."

She moved closer, took his smooth face in her hands.

"Chris, they gave it to you because you were the only man worthy of it. You're going to be fine tonight. It's just like taking the football field. No one who's ever come out of this shitty little town has ever thrown a football like you. *No one*." And that was true. She'd watched him launch those balls heavenward at Baylor, then again out in the yard of his parents' house in Murfee. The night he was shot, he'd thrown those balls so high they were probably still up there, never to come down. "And no one . . . *no one* . . . has ever cared as much about this shitty little town, and the people in it, as you do."

She added, "And if they don't see that, fuck 'em."

He laughed. "Lady, you do have a mouth on you. Does your boyfriend know you talk like that?"

"My boyfriend has never complained about my mouth . . . *ever* . . ."

Chris was still smiling, ready to say something else smart, when the grin died on his face. He was suddenly serious again, glancing over her shoulder. She turned around and followed his stare to see Danny, America, and the newest deputy, Marco Lucero, standing outside his office, waiting.

"Are they here to drive you over?" she asked, already knowing the answer.

"No, it's got to be something else."

"Do you want me to stay?" But she knew the answer to that, too. She could read their faces . . . their thoughts . . . the way she had read Chris's earlier. Whatever they wanted to say to him was serious and couldn't wait. It had nothing to do with the debate, and probably everything to do with Fox Uno, that monster she'd read about. She didn't want Chris more distracted than he already was, not now, but it was futile to be angry about it. There was nothing she could do anyway.

He was still the Big Bend County sheriff, and this debate—important or not—wouldn't change that, at least not for today.

Not until they counted the votes.

He shook his head. "Go on now with Jack. Get a good seat, up front, with Javy Cruz or Vianey. Right where I can see you. I'll find out what's going on, and then I'll get one of them to bring me over."

She put a hand on his chest, right near the gold lapel pin. She tapped it with a finger. "Goddammit, don't be late, Chris."

He worked up a smile, and kissed her cheek, before bending down to kiss Jack on the top of his head.

"Babe, don't worry. You can't be late to your own hanging."

THIRTY-EIGHT

The last time he had been inside this gym, people were cheering for him.

It was a pep rally, the last one of Chris's senior year. An away game against Ozona, and after everyone left the gym whooping and hollering, they drove in a long convoy of school buses and pickup trucks with all their carefully rendered homemade signs jammed into windshields (not so different, he figured, from his reelection signs now scattered around town), and under the lights of that other school, he went on to throw three touchdowns. One of them, a forty-yarder that Nat Bulger caught one-handed in the back of the end zone, sweetly toe-tapping the chalk sideline. Chris could still remember the smell of the fresh-cut grass, the way the warm Texas sky got so easily lost behind the glow of the sodium lights, an infinite night. The salty smell of popcorn and the sour tang of diesel fuel and the whisper-gentle murmur of the crowd between plays. Even the slickness of sweat running down his arms and into his eyes, although he was somehow still able to see everything *so clearly*—the stitches on the ball spinning in the air, escaping his hand.

His dad, calling out his name.

The whole world laid out in front of him.

He had been heavier then, more solid. He didn't want to use the word "stronger," though, because he wasn't sure that was fair, not even to himself. He wanted to believe that everything he had been through in the intervening years—Ross, the Earls—had made him strong enough, but all those days had taken their toll, too, and in all his time on the football field, playing in front of all those people beneath the bright lights, he'd never felt so exposed.

Not the way he did now in this gym.

Where he was now weightless, insubstantial.

Like everyone could see right through him.

HE WAS SWEATING THROUGH HIS NEW SUIT, ruining it, and had been for the last hour.

It had started right after he wrapped up his talk with Amé and the others in his office—after they told him what had happened between Fox Uno and Amé in the desert, and the stranger Marco had met at Earlys who'd been asking about her. It only got worse after he shook hands with Bethel Turner and took his chair to the right of the microphone, and the debate had gotten under way. A table had been set up in front of the chairs, right on the Big Bend Central logo on the center of the gym's floor, and the moderators were there: Clancy Monroe from *The Murfee Daily*; Dave Wilcher, who owned the Monument Ranch; and Marion Dunham, assistant principal at Big Bend Central. They'd been taking turns asking questions, and he and Bethel had been taking turns walking over and standing at the microphone, giving their answers. It was a constant process of getting up and down, followed by a few awkward steps, that Chris imagined had been designed only to draw more attention to the limp in his leg. To torture him. Bethel had, in fact, dispensed with that bit of theater altogether. Instead of sitting in his seat, he had hitched one leg up on it, which had a way of making him look taller. Although Bethel wasn't necessarily a short man to begin with—and Chris was over six feet—it still made Chris feel like the former Ranger was towering over him. It was a bit of theater in its own way, and it did a good job of showing off the custom boots Bethel had bought at Heritage Boot Company in Austin—a variation of their Badland in Black—which even Chris had to admit looked damn sharp.

Awkward. Sweating and uncomfortable, that's how Chris felt, and that was a good word for it. The whole debate felt that way, as if the town itself didn't know what to do or think. There hadn't been a "real" election, a real choice, in Big Bend County for decades, and it showed.

It wasn't that it was going that bad. It just wasn't going all that good. His opening statement had been shaky enough—again, awkward, like his labored steps to the microphone—and it amazed him that for someone who found it easy enough to write a thousand words, he could have so much trouble spitting out a few hundred.

The problem was, Chris couldn't concentrate. Not on his prepared statement, or the questions that had followed, and not on the circled faces he could barely see on the risers around the gym—most of Murfee, many of whom had watched him out on the fields or in this very gym, all those years past. Mel had been forced to step out when Jack had woken up crying, and despite all the people he knew, he was now alone in her absence.

After all he'd been through, after everything those he'd cared about had suffered, this silly debate and whatever might happen after it was no more important than all those high school games he'd played, or that last pep rally before the Ozona game, which most people here had long forgotten. All those things that had once mattered to him—to Murfee—had been just more empty moments, ephemeral and fleeting.

Impossible to hold on to.

Escaping his hand, like every touchdown ball he'd ever thrown.

BETHEL LOOKED THE PART—tall in his suit and his Stetson. He was easily twenty years older than Chris, and the gray at his temple (just enough, not too much) gave him a certain seriousness. He cleanly answered questions about community policing and use of force and protecting ranches from the influx of illegals across the river. He talked tough about *enforcing the laws*, and getting more federal funding for the jail and hiring more deputies and getting them better training and strengthening Big Bend County's relationship with other counties as well as the Texas Department of Public Safety.

All things Chris had been doing.

And in a subtle reference to the fires of a year ago, he emphasized that because Murfee didn't have its own city police—the county sheriff's department had always filled that role—one of his priorities would be "Murfee First." He planned on focusing on the safety of the town, something that had been ignored for far too long.

Murfee First. It's OUR Big Bend. Bethel's case could be made with a couple of easy slogans, and backed up by a lifetime of law enforcement work—he'd been a constable before being a ranger—they made for a damn compelling argument. Chris had plenty to say, too, and good work of his own to defend, but would never escape the specter of the deaths and fiery violence that had occurred on his watch, or the lack of experience that many felt had helped ignite it.

Chris wasn't sure how many of the debate questions Royal Moody helped write, but plenty of them took direct aim at Chris again and again—how Chris was simply unqualified to carry a badge and a gun, an inescapable fact that had compromised everyone's safety. On his watch, Murfee and the Big Bend had been all but overrun by illegals and white supremacists and drug runners and murderers, most of whom Chris had failed to anticipate or deal with, if not outright aided and abetted by his incompetence.

It wasn't necessarily his fault, but Chris was simply too young, too naive, too unseasoned, and as the debate rolled on, Bethel—who claimed to have helped capture the notorious serial killer Tommy Lynn Sells outside Del Rio—only had to nod sagely. Sorrowfully. He was the veteran lawman the Big Bend needed to ride out of retirement and set things straight again.

When Royal finally gave Chris a question about ISIS—goddamn ISIS, some vision of turbaned terrorists sneaking through the desert—he'd had enough.

He clutched the microphone on its tall, silver stand, wiping sweat off his forehead with his sleeve. He scanned the audience, searching out a familiar, maybe even friendly, face.

He settled on Dave Wilcher, one of the moderators. Dave was in his late sixties, and although he wasn't tall, he was strong. The muscles were corded in his neck as he worked a wad of long-cut tucked between his cheek and gums, and his arms stuck out thickly from the rolled-up sleeves of his chambray shirt.

Chris took a deep breath. "Dave, how long has your family owned the Monument?"

Dave looked left and right, uncertain that Chris was addressing him, although he was the only person who owned a ranch called the Monument in West Texas, and it ran right alongside the Rio Grande. "That land's been in my family for about a hundred and fifty years. Hell, you know that, Sheriff."

"Exactly. One hundred and fifty years. Now, how often in all that time have you ever seen a terrorist crossing that river, sneaking over your pastures?"

Dave laughed, shook his head. "Well, now, I can't say I've ever seen one, exactly." Then he added, "Don't reckon I will, either. But if I do, I'm damn ready."

A small ripple of laughter ran through the gym. Most of the men had guns openly displayed on their hips.

"I'm sure, so if Mr. Turner here wants to spend his time hunting for terrorists, I think we can all agree he's going to be looking for a long time, and he better find them before most of you folks do." Another roll of laughter, louder, and Chris pressed on. "Now, how many times have you asked me to come out and deal with some illegals on your land?"

Dave paused, uncomfortable, so Chris answered for him. "It's okay, Dave, I'm not trying to put you on the spot. You're a good man, we all know that, so I'm just going to go ahead and tell everyone here that the answer is *never*. In all my time with the department, you've never fretted about that. You see it the way I do. The way most of us do. We're talking about mostly good men themselves, sometimes even women and kids, looking for work. A better life. And we can all understand that."

Chris looked down at the microphone. "Fact is, Dave, last time you called me up, it wasn't about terrorists or illegals or anything like that at all. It was about your daughter, Tammy. She'd gotten all worked up about that boyfriend of hers, Carl Rider, and hightailed it up to Monahans in that nice new F-150 of yours, the pearl-colored one you'd just bought from Sandy Dean. You asked me if I could bring her home."

Everyone knew about Dave's legendary battles with his redheaded nineteen-year-old daughter. She'd been dating the much older Carl Rider, who worked seasonally at the Comanche. Everyone also knew Carl still had a wife and three kids in Odessa. It was a natural fact of living in a small town that all your problems were always on display, and Dave himself had been particularly vocal about this problem to anyone who would share a beer with him at Earlys.

Dave looked over his shoulder at someone in the

crowd, maybe his wife, Margaret Ann. "Yes, yes, that's right, Sheriff. Actually, you *and* Ms. Reynosa. Deputy Reynosa."

"And we got that new truck back without a scratch on it, didn't we?" Chris asked, adding, "Of course, we got Tammy back all right, too. Not a scratch on her, either." The laughter was loud this time, clear and honest, and now Bethel Turner wasn't nodding. Instead, he looked uncomfortable.

Chris pulled the microphone off the stand and took a step forward, toward the bleachers. "That land of yours at the Monument is as pretty as there is around here. Tammy was born right out there, like you were. Constance Merrill did the midwifing. My daddy knew both you and your daddy, Malcolm, although I never had the pleasure. But my daddy always told me that Malcolm believed if you're born a Wilcher, the first and last thing you were ever going to see is that land. It's your birthright, the land your family has lived and died on, laughed and loved and cried and bled on, for more than a hundred years."

Chris wasn't sure at what point Mel had walked back in, or how much she had heard, but she was now standing by the propped door out into the parking lot, holding Jack in her arms. That large exit sign glowed above her and shadowed her face.

"To be honest, I don't have any stories about terrorists, but I have a hundred stories like that one about Dave's truck and his daughter. I have a story like that for almost every one of you in here, the things my deputies and I do every day. The little things, which maybe don't seem like much, but to me, make all the difference in the world. It's what makes Murfee and the Big Bend the only place I want to raise my son. That, and land like the Monument. All those beautiful views that are ours to keep, that are like no place else in this whole damn world."

Chris turned to look straight at Bethel. "Bethel Turner was a fine Ranger, and he'll make a good sheriff. He's a serious man, experienced. There's no doubt about it. There's plenty I don't know about this job, including how to keep you all safe all the time. I can't . . . won't . . . promise that, and if he can, then he'll get my vote, too.

"But I do know this town." Chris pointed the microphone into the dark. "I know *you*. Your sons and daughters, the way many of you have known me my whole life. And I know the Big Bend, this land we all love. The Far Six is *my* Monument, and I nearly died out there trying to defend it . . . to defend *us*. The same way my deputies do every day. None of us will ever buy the safety and security of the Big Bend with another man's blood." Chris glanced at where Royal Moody and some of the others were sitting. "I've proved that. I've already bled plenty enough for it."

He stopped, looked down at the microphone in his hand, at his ravaged body. "I've enjoyed being your sheriff. It's been an honor, the greatest honor of my life. But I think I've already talked too much tonight, so that's pretty much all I have to say."

He turned and held out the microphone to Bethel, who looked as if he wanted to do anything but grab it, but he finally stepped off his chair and did. Chris shook Bethel's hand, and turned back to the silent gym.

The last time he had been inside this gym, people were cheering for him.

He looked over to where his deputies were sitting—Tommy and Dale and Till and Marco and Danny and America. He nodded at them and smiled.

His dad, calling out his name.

Then he looked for Mel again, standing beneath the exit sign. The Big Bend night was out there, just on the other side of the door, and its breeze was moving her hair.

The whole world laid out in front of him.

He walked toward her, past the assembled town and all the people he knew, and out into the night.

artino was sitting on the whitewashed balcony in his room at Las Hadas in Manzanillo, a resort once made famous by an actress in an American movie, an actress like his mother. It was primarily Canadians who flocked here now, to the brown-speckled sand and the blue ocean and the green sweep of the mango and palm trees all the way to the water's edge.

The resort got its name, which meant "the fairies," from mariners who saw sparkling lights illuminating the ocean at night—a chemical by-product of phosphorus in the waves, but entrancing all the same. Magical. Martino had seen it before, too, on his other visits here.

Martino did not know much about his mother, but understood that she had been born near here, in Comala. She'd been an actress, successful in only small parts in telenovelas like *María Mercedes*, before she'd somehow caught the eye of Fox Uno. She had circled in his orbit for a while, but not long after Martino was born, she was gone. He'd been raised by a woman he only called Abuela, a much older version of Luisa, the woman who had looked after Zita (and like Luisa, Abuela was now gone). Martino knew only a little more about Zita's mother, a onetime beauty pageant winner in Nuestra

Belleza Nuevo León, who was killed along with three of his father's men in a shoot-out with soldiers at a checkpoint on a dirty road outside Saucillo. She came out of her truck firing first, eight rounds from a 9mm pistol, before she was shot at least twenty-seven times, including twice in the face that had made her a pageant winner. The truck was later found to contain three AR-15 assault rifles, a dozen more 9mm handguns, more than eight hundred rounds of ammunition, and eighty-five thousand dollars.

Martino had seen the pictures of her body in a newspaper when he was barely sixteen years old.

He had not chosen this life. It had chosen him.

Actresses and beauty pageant winners. Martino had bedded both, and men as well, preferring the latter, since those he could not impregnate. He found them in small towns like Comala and put them up in a hotel like this one for a week, and gave them more money than they had ever seen in their lives. He then returned them to their towns again with all the clothes or watches or jewelry he had bought them and a thick envelope with even more money—enough for the inevitable six brothers and sisters and sick grandparents. He didn't love them, didn't care for them all that much. They simply fulfilled a need, like drinking cold water on a hot day, and he wanted nothing to tie him to them or nothing to remember them by.

He never wanted to see them again.

He never wanted to look at a bloody picture of them in the newspaper.

He wanted no threat of heirs, no sons or daughters of his own, who might ever tear him down.

He sipped a chilled glass of Louis Roederer, the setting sun turning the sea a thousand different colors; the colors of the legions of brightly hued fish that swam below. From his room he could see the towering cruise ships, as well as ugly gray navy ships that he couldn't name, since Manzanillo was also the base for the Fuerza Naval del Pacífico. He wondered how many of the marines chasing his father had stared out over the same water, watched these same sunsets. His father had never come here, had never seen this place. It was possible he'd never seen the ocean with his own eyes.

What was he looking at now?

Where are you, Father?

He was still lost in thought when Xavier came up out of the darkened suite behind him, a room lit only by the lights of three laptop computers and six charging phones. Xavier was twenty-one or twenty-two, looked even younger shirtless. His skin was smooth, flawless. He was wearing silk shorts and his hair was still a bird's nest from the bed.

He had one of Martino's phones in his hand.

"It has been insistent," he said, handing the still-buzzing phone to Martino, who exchanged the glass of champagne for it.

"Go inside, Xavier, get ready. We have reservations soon. There is a suit for you in the closet, the white one. With the red shirt. Choose no other."

If Xavier had a complaint, he did not voice it. He finished Martino's glass of champagne and disappeared

308 || J. TODD SCOTT

back into the room. He wanted to be a singer but had a horrible voice, although he had many, many other talents. He was from Poncitlán or Jamay, Martino could not remember which, and it did not matter; Xavier had traveled several times to the United States, which at least had made for more interesting conversations.

Martino checked the phone, scrolling through a series of messages via WhatsApp.

He read them, read them again, and almost laughed out loud.

THREE DAYS BACK HIS MEN had finally tracked down Gualterio, holed up in Saucillo of all places.

They took him without incident. He became cooperative, though, only after they tortured Gualterio's favorite nephew, Juan Daniel, who'd been traveling with him. They did it in front of him, with pliers and a hammer, making him watch it all. Trusting the fat pig after what Martino had done at Manuel Benavides was an impossibility; long as he lived, he would be a significant threat. He had his share of loyalists, too, and had made contingency plans of his own throughout the years. Martino suspected that if he hadn't moved against his father with the Serranos' help, Gualterio would have eventually done it on his own.

He *was* a pig, and a pig always wanted the whole trough to itself.

But if there was anyone his father trusted more than Martino, anyone who knew most of Fox Uno's secrets and his little hiding places and war chests, it was Gualterio.

Trusting him was impossible, but keeping him alive a little while longer had been necessary.

Just as it had been necessary after the mess at Manuel Benavides to leave others of Fox Uno's people untouched and in place, a safety net designed to snare his father whenever he decided to move.

A move that had finally, mercifully, come yesterday morning.

In the end, Martino was not all that surprised his father had turned to Gualterio, not him. The only real surprise was this girl's involvement—America. Allegedly his *prima*. He knew of her, knew that Fox Uno had always favored her for reasons of his own, but never imagined her involvement in this thing. It was a shame now he would never have the chance to meet her. He would like to have known what she thought of her uncle, and of him.

It also reminded him just how much he had already underestimated his father and how that had nearly cost him everything.

Not anymore, never again.

Martino stood to take one last look at the ocean.

Outside his suite door were twelve armed guards, and two on each floor down to the lobby. In the lobby were six more, mixed in with the crowd, including two federal police officers. This was the last safe place he'd be for a while. Tonight, he needed to be on a plane back to the heat and dust of Ojinaga to oversee the arrangements Gualterio had made with his father and this girl, America. If it all went well, Fox Uno would be dead in seventy-two hours, as would that fat pig Gualterio, and *that* was something Martino would gladly do with his own hands.

Like Diego Serrano had said, he had to personally get involved. He simply could not fail again.

Xavier reappeared in his red shirt and the Giorgio Armani suit, holding two fresh glasses of champagne. He looked like a young American executive, perfectly complementing Martino's own slim Brioni suit in amarena red, and his expensive Lucchese boots, cut out of black elephant leather with a stitch pattern reworked as a skull, something you could only see if you got close enough to them and stared hard.

The boots were called Terlingua, and they'd been handmade in Texas. It was this silly coincidence that had made Martino laugh out loud as he read the WhatsApp messages on his phone.

Martino took the offered glass of champagne from Xavier, who did look amazing in the clothes he'd bought him. It was a shame that he had to leave, but staring at the other man, and thinking of his *prima*, had given him an idea. "Xavier, I'm afraid I'm not going to be able to go to dinner as we'd planned, but I do have a question." Martino sipped the champagne, which had somehow gone warm and lifeless. It was bitter, no longer sweet.

Martino poured the rest over the balcony.

"Your passport and visa are current, correct?"

PART THREE

===

TEJAS

FORTY

CHAYO & NEVA

Their most constant companions were *murciélagos*.

They had first appeared at dusk, when Chayo and Neva were starting to stir from wherever they had hidden for the day. As much as Chayo had hoped they could travel only at night by the glow of the moon and the stars, it was proving too risky—too easy to fall down a ravine, or simply lose their way when the sky was made unreadable by a thick smear of clouds. He had never been afraid of the night before—not of the animals that moved or hunted in the dark—but after Neva tripped and tumbled face-first into a shallow, rock-lined arroyo, he was all too aware of the dangers hidden there.

They had to travel with the true light of the sun.

Now the *murciélagos* were fading pencil marks in the sky at dawn when they awoke. Thousands of them turning in tight circles, calling to each other, catching the last few bugs. They were a tattered cloud visible for miles, their wings the sounds of thick hands rubbing together.

He and Neva watched them rise and fall and spin and disappear. There was some magic purpose or message in their movements, and they followed in their wake, moving slowly over the broken ground. The *murciélagos* nested in the cooler hollows and caves along the river, high up on the canyon walls, so instead of using the stars, Chayo traced the sounds of their fading wings.

Those pencil marks in the sky sketched out a path for them to follow, pointing the way.

A path they soon discovered others had followed as well.

THEY FIRST FOUND A RED BACKPACK, torn and weathered. There was a string of several numbers written in black ink inside. Maybe a phone number, someone to call if the pack or the person wearing it was lost . . . or found.

They saw a sole-less tennis shoe, just one, hanging upside down on a branch.

They stepped around other shoes handmade out of dirty carpet and rope.

They moved past discarded shirts and bandannas.

They walked among a constellation of empty plastic water bottles and shopping bags and tin cans.

Once, Neva grabbed at Chayo, pointing at something dark and feral moving away from them beneath a knot of trees. They could smell its fur, thick and pungent, and they both held their breath as Chayo wondered if it could be *un lobo* or perhaps a jaguar. But it proved to be little more than shadowed movement, a rustle of dry leaves and a bending of grass, before it was gone. Whatever it was, it left them alone, and they did the same.

Chayo let them move slow, with many rests to help Neva, who had never hiked over such rough ground or for so long. Sometimes when they stopped, she folded into his arms and he could feel her body trembling with exhaustion.

One time she kissed him, and fell asleep standing that way, held up only by his arms, her dry lips still touching his.

As they silently walked, despite the trash and things they found, it was easy for Chayo to imagine they were the only people left in the whole world. Everything had been made only for them, and they were seeing it for the first time. Nothing existed until they arrived, and it would all disappear after they left. Each labored step created the very ground under their feet. If they chose one way, it created a new world, and if they chose differently, it made another.

If they stopped moving, there would be nothing at all.

Chayo finally decided that wasn't so far from the truth.

AT LEAST NEVA'S WOUND was looking better, not so red and angry.

It was a jagged line running from the corner of her mouth to just short of her ear. Many of the stitches had pulled loose without it getting worse, and it didn't bleed so much. It was still difficult for her to chew, forcing her to slip strips of tortilla and water past her barely open lips, and she was frustrated at all the things she wanted to say, but whenever she tried to speak, Chayo put a hand to those lips and shook his head to stop her.

Or he kissed her, and that worked just as well.

THEY SLEPT UNDER SKIES that flickered orange and red and white. Lightning, far away and high above the clouds. Afterward, the air around them was scorched and their skin was electric to the touch, but there was never any rain, no push of a wind, and if there was thunder, they could not hear it.

There was no storm at all.

Only a silent sky, playing tricks on their eyes.

BY LATE AFTERNOON OF THE FOURTH DAY, they found themselves crouched on a rise above the river.

It was thirty feet across, with a pebbled sliver of shore on their side—like a gnarled fingernail—and rising grass and thick brush on the other. The water was dark, not brown or black, but deepest green, and it moved with a slight current. Up, down. Up, down. The river was breathing, and its breath was foul. Even high above it, they could smell that it was as thick and pungent as the unseen animal they had crossed.

Ripples rolled out across its surface, dimpling the green skin, before disappearing again as if they'd never appeared at all.

It didn't look deep, but Chayo wouldn't know for sure until they waded into it.

They had made it to the Río Bravo. Los Estados Unidos was on the other side.

Chayo did not know what he'd expected—gleaming towers, green fields, streets of perfect houses as he'd seen on TV. He'd never given it much thought, focusing only on getting here, and although he was from a small village and had not traveled to many places, he'd never been foolish enough to think there could be a real difference in a place only thirty feet away.

Still, he had expected . . . *more* . . . and it worried him
that grass and rocks and canyon walls visible across the
water looked no different from any of those they had
walked through. *Exactamente el mismo.* He tried hard to
find differences, staring closely, getting more desperate,
and when he could find none—not a sign or a chain-link
fence—he became scared that he'd brought them to the
wrong river. He'd set them on the wrong path, and the
real Río Bravo was still miles, or another one of those
imagined worlds, away.

Neva was making ready to slide down the rise, toward
the water, but it was Chayo who suddenly couldn't,
wouldn't, move.

He was convinced now that even if it was the Río
Bravo, they'd be unable to pass it. Someone or something would keep them out; some monstrous, invisible
hand would push them away.

He sat like that for several moments, with Neva staring
at him curiously, waiting. He caught sight of a bird, a large
one—possibly *un halcón*—appearing above and behind
them, gliding in a long, dropping arc. It was the gray of
smoke, with a banded black and white tail, unlike any he
had ever seen. It flew over them and he could feel its
shadow on his skin as it passed overhead. It rose, dipped,
turned on one of its powerful wings, and crossed over the
river into a long row of mesquites on the other side.

It disappeared like the ripples on the river itself.

It had made it look so easy, effortless.

It reminded him that it was time to fly.

Para volar.

That's what he'd told himself the night of the attack,

and that's what they'd been doing every day since. Now that they had made it this far, he could not be afraid of the sky.

HE JOINED HER ON THE SANDY BANK, searching in his pocket for a peso, and although they needed every bit of money they had, he tossed it into the barely moving river. It was an old ritual from Blanco, his home, meant to satisfy whatever spirits or *fantasmas* might lurk in the water. He didn't know that he believed it, but it couldn't hurt. They needed all the help they could get.

The coin dropped out of sight.

He took her hand and they both stepped into the water . . . deeper, deeper. It was surprisingly cold, rising to their waists and then chests, and he wrapped an arm around her as the bottom dropped suddenly away from their feet and then he was kicking them across, helping keep her head above the stinking water. Beneath the surface, the water moved faster than he'd imagined, and as the weight of their nearly empty packs pulled on him, filling with water, he felt for a heart-stopping moment like they were suspended above an impossibly deep hole, eager to suck their heavy bodies down. But just as quickly, his feet were touching the sandy bottom again and he'd regained his footing. They splashed out of the river on the other side beneath the very same sun they'd left behind them, and stumbled together into the high, green grass, and it was over.

Neva smiled, a true smile, and hugged him. There were bits of leaves and grass in her wet hair, and a smear of mud on her hands and face and she smelled like the water, but he couldn't love her any more than he did or imagine anyone more beautiful.

He looked at the ground at his feet and realized he was farther away from his home than he'd ever been, and understood for the first time that he'd never return. He was finally, truly, a whole new world away.

His heart was both joyous and hurting, and he held Neva close so she wouldn't see his tears and wouldn't feel his own trembling.

He let them sit in the shadows of the high grass as their clothes dried in the hot air, and then he helped her up and told her it was time to go. They had to keep going, always going, because although they'd crossed the river, they hadn't gotten anywhere at all.

Not anywhere truly safe.

And as before, they soon discovered others had come their way.

They found the same discarded bottles, shoes, clothes.

A rotted book.

A bicycle wheel.

Even an old rifle, an ancient thing, leaning against a mesquite. Chayo knew nothing about guns, but took it anyway, using a strip of his shirt to hold it together.

They found a thousand forgotten things, seemingly cast up and left behind by the river itself, instead of by those who'd crossed it.

Neva found a doll with a melted face. It looked as if it had been set on fire or had burned in the sun.

It was only two hours after they'd crossed the river into the United States, when the men found them.

===

FORTY-ONE

Are you out of your mind?" Mel asked him, loud enough to get Rocky up off the kitchen floor. The dog barked once, joining her, as if he was mad, too.

So far, this conversation hadn't gone well at all.

Chris set aside his coffee mug and folded his arms, leaning against the counter. Mel was sitting at the table with Jack in his booster, and like last night in the high school gym, everyone—Mel, Jack, Rocky the dog—was staring at him.

He hadn't slept much. He hadn't started this conversation last night because he knew it might get ugly, but given how he'd tossed and turned anyway, troubled by vague, gray dreams—as heavy and ominous as stacked clouds threatening rain—he should have bitten the bullet and talked to Mel then. The new day had done nothing to make it any easier. He turned and looked for a moment out the window, where real rain clouds loomed over the Far Six. They towered like the mesas themselves, striated in white and gray and as solid and immutable as granite, mirroring the ground below. The storm they heralded might blow over, or it might not.

Not like the storm in his kitchen, which was only gathering strength.

He turned back to Mel, who hadn't moved, still waiting for his answer. She was wearing one of his old Baylor T-shirts, and it was too big for her, as it was for him. It was hard to remember himself at that size. He'd changed so much outwardly since college, but in so many ways, Mel looked the same. Beautiful, even when she was mad.

"I don't think you understand," he tried, before she cut him off again.

"Really? Let me explain what I understand . . . what I can't believe I just heard you say." Mel was leaning over Jack, who was sitting upright in the Fisher-Price booster Amé had bought for them. Jack was still too young for solids, but Mel liked to prop him up in it when they had breakfast together.

"You want me to pack up our son and *leave*, so you can open our house to Amé and this man that you're convinced is a lifelong murderer. A man, I might add, you once thought tried to have you killed, Chris, right *here*, right outside those windows. Now you're telling me he has to stay in our home?"

He tried to slow her down. "Danny's convinced someone's in Murfee looking for her, or for Fox Uno. Probably both. And he's convinced me they're not safe in town anymore. We need a place to wait out the arrangements Fox Uno's made for Amé's mother."

"Oh right, I'm sorry, I didn't mention the *other* part of this that doesn't make any damn sense." She fixed him with a hard stare. "This man, who's on the run from the law on both sides of the border, not to mention who knows how many other killers like him, is now miraculously going to spirit Amé's mother, *here*, with a phone call? That's convenient, isn't it? You said he was only go-ing to stay in Murfee a few days, but this is a lot more than that, a hell of a lot more. Too much. *This is our home.* Why doesn't he make a goddamn call for himself and get the fuck out of our lives?"

"Babe, that's what he's trying to do. That's what we're all trying to do. But it's different now . . . Amé spoke to someone . . ."

"Her actual mother?"

"No, someone else," Chris admitted, reluctantly. "A man who works for Fox Uno. He's called Oso Ocho . . . Gualterio."

A man Chris had read about in Garrison's folder. A man who, with one phone call, had made his young dep-uty believe in all the things Fox Uno had told her and, more important, the one thing he was promising now: that within seventy-two hours he could get her mother safe to Murfee, bringing along with her whatever money and new identities Fox Uno and Zita needed.

"Mel, I can't ignore this stranger that Marco Lucero told Danny about, either. He was right there in Earlys, where *you* work, too. He claimed to be a reporter from Austin covering the debate, but Marco didn't see him there. Danny made some calls, there was no news cover-age out of Austin."

"Oh, finally, the debate. I figured you had forgotten all about that. I don't suppose this decision about Fox Uno and Amé has anything to do with your performance last night? I didn't say anything about it then because it was clear you didn't want to talk, but we're going to talk about it now. You walked out, Chris."

"I'm not winning, we both know that."

"No, we don't know that. Are you justifying this insane plan of yours because you think you're not going to be the sheriff anymore? There were plenty of people in that gym who believe in you and trust you and need you, too, more than just America Reynosa. What about them?"

"Amé needs me *now*, today. I need to see this thing through. I don't know what else to do."

"No, you don't *want* to do anything else. You've convinced yourself you owe her, or you're punishing yourself for some past mistake you won't let go. You're not seeing another way because you won't look for one, but you know who really gets punished? Me, and your son. We're the ones that get to stand by to see what happens. We're the ones that'll be praying you don't nearly die out here a second goddamn time. This isn't what I agreed to."

"It's not? *When?* Are you only upset because it's hitting so close to home?" Chris said.

"Don't you dare fucking say that. That's not fair, not with everything we've been through together. At least be honest with me, even if you can't be with yourself. You owe *me* that." Mel folded her arms, holding herself tight. "Chris, I read the folder that Joe Garrison brought you. I'm sorry, I didn't mean to, but I did. I only wanted to see if you'd done any work for the debate. It doesn't make it right, but I know now all about Fox Uno and his goddamn people. I saw all those horrible pictures . . ."

Chris wanted to be angry with her, but she was right; he owed her the truth. "I just want to get this over with. To do that, I first need to get Amé and Fox Uno out of town, away from prying eyes. Murfee will be safer, and I can keep them safer out here."

"Until something goes wrong, then there won't be a way to save any of you. You want to hide them out here exactly because you know how goddamn risky this is." She collected Jack out of his booster seat, and he kicked and struggled, started to cry. "He's killed women and children, Chris. Don't talk to me about America. *That's* the man you're trying to help."

The room was electric, Mel's fury almost visible in the air. It had been years since she'd been this mad at him, since their first year in Murfee, when Chris had been consumed by Rodolfo Reynosa's murder. Mel had always had a matchstick temper, but Chris had almost forgotten what it was like to feel that raw, red heat again. He'd fallen in love with her partly because of that fiery streak— the way it fueled her, sometimes burned him. It was a small price to pay.

"What do you want me to do?"

She tried to quiet Jack. "I *want* to trust you on this, Chris, I really do. Until now, I have. But . . . but I think you really should call Joe Garrison. Today. Now."

Chris shook his head, tired and frustrated. His whole tiny family was in the kitchen, but they were on one side of the table, and he was on the other. They were together, but he might as well have been alone.

He thought about all the times he'd almost done exactly what she wanted and called Garrison, but it was too late for that. He'd spent five years trying to protect the Big Bend as its sheriff; now he was going to spend these last days protecting and helping Amé.

"I'm sorry. I don't think I can do that. I already told them to come. They'll be here before noon. Seventy-two hours, that's all I need from you."

She blinked, once, twice. "I guess I need to pack our things then. And before you ask, I don't want your help."

She looked at Chris hard again, over the top of Jack's head. She had their son held tight to her body and her eyes still flashed, her fury still smoldering.

"You know what's funny? I keep thinking about that speech you gave before you walked out last night. You were up there talking to Dave Wilcher, but I knew you were really talking to everyone sitting in that gym, pretty much the whole damn town. And I saw how they responded to you, Chris, the way they looked at you. It was like you were on the football field again, playing in front of a big crowd. You may want to tell yourself you were throwing away your badge, but you weren't. You were throwing *to win* . . . one final, fourth-quarter touchdown. You sure didn't sound like a man who was ready to quit or wanted to lose . . . a man who doesn't give a damn anymore about being the sheriff in this county, no matter what you're telling yourself now. And I've never, ever been prouder."

Mel walked to the kitchen door, with Jack still whining, and Rocky trailing behind her. "You better be goddamn sure about what you're doing, because win or lose, I'm afraid you're going to have a lot of explaining to do."

FORTY-TWO

America watched Danny put his sleeping bag in his
truck.

Not the department's truck, but his own: a dark
'91 Ford Bronco with tan trim and a tan camper shell
that she'd gone with him to buy at Sandy Dean Auto.
Sandy had bought it from Billy Glaspy, who owned the
Three Forks Ranch. He'd used it for years to run around
the acreage and hunt, and had lifted the tires and made
a bunch of other small modifications that America didn't
fully understand. Danny had needed something of his
own to drive after his motorcycle was destroyed by Jesse
Earl, and he'd been happy to find the Bronco at a decent
price, even though it was scratched and dented and
weathered—like a lot of things around Murfee. He'd
told her the truck reminded him of his dad, who'd owned
one like it when he was a kid.

She knew why he was refusing to use his deputy truck,
like he was refusing to wear his uniform shirt or his
badge. Instead, he was in jeans and a faded black long-
sleeve T-shirt from a band she did not know.

Nothing they were doing was about being the law
anymore.

HE WOULDN'T TAKE NO FOR AN ANSWER, and refused to let her and Fox Uno and Zita go out to Sheriff
Cherry's house alone.

Just like he'd stayed with them in her apartment, he
wasn't going to let them stay out there without him, although the sheriff himself hadn't agreed to that yet.
Danny had told her to get together whatever things she
wanted and he'd drive them all over to the Far Six.
They'd argued about it, but not much. If she didn't let
him go now, he'd show up out there anyway, and the
sheriff would have no more luck turning him away than
she'd had. He was frustrated, angry, not only because she'd
disappeared with Fox Uno, but because he'd been wrong
about him all along. He'd been so convinced that Fox
Uno was lying, he still didn't want to believe the voice
she'd heard on the phone. The voice Fox Uno had introduced to her as Oso Ocho . . .

Gualterio . . . the same Gualterio Zita had talked
about.

But in a way, Danny had been right all along, too:
when she'd spoken to Gualterio, it had become clear just
how little her uncle had revealed to him or anyone in
Nemesio about where he was or his next moves. Fox Uno
really had been hiding, biding his time, working out who
he could still trust or who had already betrayed him, and
his own uncertainty and fear gave her some real hope.

Because if he truly wasn't in control of Nemesio anymore, he had to risk himself and make a deal with *some-*

one to help him get what he wanted, and now that someone also had to deal with her.

I get it. Secret words and names, like Rana and Araña and Diablo. Little boys playing silly games. But when I picked up Rodolfo's phone and dialed it all those years ago, someone did answer . . .

Someone just like this Gualterio. Fox Uno might never have made that call on his own until she'd dragged him off into the desert with a gun to his head, but it had worked once before with the *sicario* Máximo, and she was willing to risk Fox Uno's life and hers that it would work again.

She had no better idea than he did about who would show up, or what would happen when they did, but if they brought her mama along with them to get to him, she didn't give a damn.

DANNY SAID, "I'll go up and get the rest of your stuff, then I'll drive you guys out there. Once you're settled, I'm going to head back into town. I have a few things I need to take care of, and I'll get back out to the Far Six later tonight or first thing in the morning. You guys should be fine for the one night."

She wanted to ask him what he needed to take care of, but he was in no mood to share; no more than she'd shared with him her plan to take Fox Uno out to the desert. But it was more than that, like he'd come to some decision on his own, something serious he'd been turning over since her call with Gualterio. Whatever it was had been weighing on him, still was, but it was clear he

didn't want to talk about it with her. For all their closeness of the last few months, she'd opened a cut that
would take a while to heal, if it ever truly did.

"We'll be fine. Gualterio only knows that we're here
in Texas, somewhere near Murfee. He won't know exactly where until my mama is safely over the border."

Danny shook his head. "I think it's insane to use the
word 'safe' to describe any of this." His face was shadowed by the juniper they were standing under, his eyes
hollowed by a lack of sleep. She wanted to take him by
the hand and walk him upstairs and put him back to bed,
wondering when he—or any of them—would get a good
night's sleep again.

"*Lo sé*, but I have to try. I can't explain . . ."

"That's just it, Amé, even though I don't understand,
I'm the last person you have to explain it to. But maybe
someday you will have to explain it to Melissa, and the
sheriff's baby son."

"I didn't ask for this."

"No, no, you didn't. But here we are, all the same.
That's how it works, and you were the one who first reminded me of that after I'd lost my way with the Earls."

While they were talking, Zita appeared at the top of
the stairs, framed by the apartment's open door. She was
wearing one of the new dresses America had bought her,
pink and white, and her hair was down around her shoulders. She was watching them, tentative.

"You don't have to do this," she said, smiling up at
Zita, but talking to Danny. "I don't want you to do
this." As she said it, she meant it as much as she'd ever
meant anything, but not for any of the reasons he prob-

ably imagined. She'd been more than willing to risk Fox Uno's life and her own, but not Danny's.

Not like this, not for this.

But as Danny just said, here they were, all the same.

He smiled. Sad, resigned. A smile only faintly mirroring her own. "I know, but I won't let you do this on your own. There's nowhere else I *can* be." He waved at Zita, and she waved back, as Fox Uno appeared next to her, one hand on her shoulder. Danny's smile faded, and he turned away from them both.

"Time to go. Let's get this over with."

FORTY-THREE

They showed up in the morning, not long after dawn, in two separate cars.

The first was a gunmetal-gray Suburban with tinted windows, big tires, and an even bigger engine. Eddy could hear it rumbling outside his trailer as it practically rolled right up to his front door—damn near through it—its big hood nudging the wooden steps. It sat there idling as the second vehicle pulled alongside it: a black Charger with equally dark windows. Now, *that* was a damn beautiful car, and Eddy knew by its own deep-throated hum it was a Hemi, big sucker, fast enough to escape gravity if it had to. That black Charger drank the morning light, and if a car could look mean, that one sure did, like it'd whip your ass and steal your money and fuck your girlfriend.

Eddy didn't want to go out and meet his visitors and possibly get shot in the face, so he watched them from behind his blinds, turning over his options. He didn't recognize the four men getting out of the Suburban, but he knew the type: nice jeans, boots, baseball hats, rolled-up shirtsleeves revealing taut arms, a few tattoos here and there. They had mostly short haircuts, and they were all pulling identical black bags out of the Suburban.

Heavy black bags. Like body bags, like these jokers were headed off to war.

Soldiers.

Or more likely, cops.

He did recognize the lone man who got out of the Charger. Eddy had seen him only a couple of times in person, once here at the trailer, the other times at a shitty bar in Rosenfeld where neither of them would be known. At those two meetings, he hadn't driven that Charger, but it was the same guy.

Same haircut, same sunglasses. Same goddamn matchstick in his mouth.

Apache.

It had never occurred to him that Apache—the cold-blooded motherfucker who'd hired Eddy to meet his drug mules crossing the river—might be a cop. He'd always assumed he was just another cartel guy, a real narco, which was bad enough.

But if he was an honest-to-god, badge-carrying cop, that was infinitely worse.

THEY MADE THEMSELVES AT HOME, dumping their bags and checking every nook and cranny of his trailer. They told him to sit the fuck down in his ratty chair, not move an inch, and the one called Ortiz—slimmer than the others, with a high and tight crew cut—kept a gun trained on him. Eddy could practically smell the piss on this one, figuring he was the newest, or youngest. The guy didn't want to look at him, not at all, and that worried Eddy even more—like if Eddy coughed, the guy might freak out and shoot him by accident. So he sat quietly with his hands in his lap, as if he'd been called to the principal's office. That got Eddy thinking about how he'd never finished high school, and maybe if he had, his life could have been different.

Who the fuck am I kidding? It was freeing in a way— goddamn liberating—to know that no matter what choices he'd made, he was always going to end up truly fucked.

The others talked among themselves, and he quickly picked up their names: the old, grizzled dude was Chavez. The big motherfucker was Roman, big enough to unscrew your head with his bare hands. The quiet one with the fancy snakeskin boots was Ringo, and if Eddy had money to bet, he'd take the odds that Ringo had a knife slipped down in those pretty boots. He had dangerous eyes, like eyes you'd see on a shark or something. Not like the pussy, Ortiz, who looked like he wanted to cry.

After they all got done tearing through his shit and turning things over, they started to unpack their own bags.

Big-ass guns Eddy didn't recognize. Bulletproof vests. Handheld radios and knives and helmets and all sorts of other police-looking stuff. He could make out the bare Velcro strips on their vests that once held the patches or badges of whatever unit or department they worked for. These sons of bitches *were* cops, every one of them, but they weren't here for official business. Eddy figured it had to be about those weird messages Apache had sent him, and it probably ended with him dead and floating in the river behind his trailer like those damn wetbacks.

That's why they didn't give a shit if he saw their faces or knew their real names.

Eddy Rabbit was well and truly fucked.

APACHE WALKED HIM OUT BACK behind the trailer, while the others pulled the Suburban and the Charger near the salt cedar and giant cane, hiding them from the dirt road leading up to the front of the house. The rest of them sat around drinking beers they'd brought, while Apache nudged him on down toward the water itself, where Eddy had seen the bodies. The path was all trampled down and easy to follow, first from where all the mules with their backpacks had walked back and forth to the riverbank over the last few months, and then where he and Danny had chased each other. Eddy figured other people had walked there recently, too, when they'd finally pulled those dead wetbacks out of the water.

Apache offered him a beer, a warm Budweiser, and Eddy took it. He knew Apache's real name now: Johnnie, or Johnnie Macho. He'd heard the others use both, and he was the real ringleader of this circus.

Charity used to wear a ratty old T-shirt all the time: *This is my circus. These are my monkeys.* Looking at Johnnie or Apache or whatever the hell he wanted to call himself over the top of the warm Bud, hearing the other men who were now lounging around his property loudly cracking jokes and laughing, that seemed about right.

"Nice to see you again, Eddy," Johnnie said, sizing him up with a long stare.

"Look, if you're here about that shit that went down,

I didn't say nothin'. Not a goddamn thing," Eddy said. "See, it all started with my girl, Charity. She was shootin' off her goddamn mouth and—"

Johnnie stopped him with a slap across the face. Slapping him like Eddy was his bitch. "No, Eddy, it's not about that. I don't give a shit about those dead mules. They were a fucking business expense, a write-off." Johnnie took the unfinished beer from Eddy's hand and tossed it into the water. Eddy had only gotten two deep swallows. "But you've been slow answering my messages."

Eddy rubbed his jaw, although the slap hadn't hurt much at all. "It's not like that. I did answer 'em. You wanted to know if I'd seen some old Mexican in Murfee, and I told you that's all Murfee is full up of." Eddy waved at the river and the trailer. "Look at where the fuck I live. Do you think I'm just running into folks on the street out here?"

Johnnie laughed. "You're being funny, I get it. But here's the thing, our friends, these fucking Indians *we both* work for, don't have a goddamn sense of humor. Not like me. Hell, I like a good joke. But they want this old man found, Eddy, like *yesterday*, and they're more convinced than ever he's here in the Big Bend, in Murfee. Possibly shacked up with a female deputy named America Reynosa. You know her?"

Eddy gave his own best bullshit grin, bracing to get slapped again. "I think I saw her when I got arrested, but you know, we didn't really socialize. I've heard about her, from around, but that's it."

Johnnie chewed his matchstick. "You heard about her? 'From around'? What the hell does that even mean?"

336 II J. TODD SCOTT

"Exactly. Exactly what I said. As you can imagine, since I got pinched, my dance card's been a bit light." Eddy figured he was going to get slapped around some more if he kept talking Johnnie around in circles, but fuck it. He pressed ahead. "You know, if you want, we can just take a drive up there to Murfee together and look for this old guy."

"*No . . .* no. You're a known felon, and I don't need my face plastered around town, not with you." Johnnie watched the water. "This old man probably is hiding in plain sight. I can see how parking his ass in the center of town, with a cop, makes a righteous kind of sense given the sort of people who want to get their hands on him. No, we're just gonna hang out here with you for a few days until we figure out exactly where he is and what he's up to. We gotta wait for a good moment to make our move, and trust me when I say our friends are hard at work finding that moment. Or making one happen."

"You just gonna grab this guy? Then what?" Eddy thought about all the bags, the guns, spread across his trailer.

"That shit doesn't concern you, amigo. Be glad we're looking for *him*, and not you. It's a good thing you didn't run off after fucking up and getting arrested. I smoothed that over for you, but let's be honest: we're still gonna have a talk about it. Fortunately, it's going to be a much different conversation than it could have been. Understand?"

"Yeah, I got it."

"So, your dance card just got filled up, Eddy. You're going to be *my* eyes and ears, maybe my fucking tour guide, if I gotta find my way around this place. Jesus, don't you people put signs up anywhere?"

"It's the Big Bend. It's supposed to be easy to get lost," Eddy said, shrugging, turning his attention to the river, too. It was flat and still.

"Last time I saw you, Eddy, pardon my saying, but you looked like death warmed over. You're looking a mite better now. You finally off that shit?"

"They had me locked up for a few days. It kinda flushed my system, and I was all out of stuff anyway. They took everything." But that wasn't true. He'd had his bag in the Admiral fridge, packed heavy with his stash, and he'd held on to it for two days, practically sleeping with it, before tossing it into the river they were now both staring at.

He'd kept Apache's—Johnnie's—phone, though. That's what he should have thrown in the goddamn river.

"You don't have any on you, do you? A little bump?" Eddy asked. "I sure could use it."

Johnnie took his matchstick out and stared at the end of it, before slipping it back into his mouth. "Fuck no, I don't do that shit. It fucks with your brain, Eddy, fucks it up good." He tapped Eddy on the side of the head with a sharp finger, hard, and Eddy resisted the urge to pull back. "It's gonna be fine, though. Once this is all over, it's back to the usual. Even better. I think this old man is the competition, Eddy, and once he's out of business, our friends are gonna have a goddamn monopoly around here. In fact, you'll be the only store in town, practically one-stop shopping. Isn't that what they used to call you? Fast Food, Take-Out, something squirrelly like that?"

338 | J. TODD SCOTT

"Nah," Eddy said, "not so much anymore. That ain't me."

Johnnie flicked his match into the water and made another appear from somewhere, clenching it between his teeth. "Then smile, Eddy, you practically just got promoted to manager."

I SMOOTHED THAT OVER FOR YOU, but let's be honest: we're still gonna have a talk about it.

Fortunately, it's going to be a much different conversation than it could have been . . .

Later, when they tied Eddy to his chair—Ringo checking to make sure the restraints they'd made from his bedsheets were tight—Eddy wondered just how much worse that *different* conversation would have gone . . .

JOHNNIE ASKED THE QUESTIONS, and the others— except for Ortiz—took turns hitting him. Mostly in the stomach, and ribs, although the big one—Roman— cocked him good in the face. It rocked his head back and he spit a mouthful of blood, maybe a tooth. It was like he'd been in a bad car accident, and now he really was wishing he had taken that meth—all of it—because he'd still be flying high above his body, and it would almost be like someone else, someone he didn't even know, was getting the shit beat out of him.

That motherfucker probably deserved it, not Eddy.

Johnnie asked him about this old man he didn't know and the wetback girl deputy. He asked him what he told the cops after he got arrested, and what Charity might have told them, and what happened to their Motorola radios and his cell phone, and Johnnie had Eddy unlock it so the fucker could search through it. Johnnie also looked through the cell he'd given him, the one Eddy had hidden with the meth, to make sure there weren't any other calls to or from it. Eddy wasn't sure he was giving the right or wrong answers, because there didn't seem to be much connection between what he said and the punches he got, so whenever the opportunity presented itself, he basically lied through his teeth . . . through all the blood in his mouth.

It was freeing in a way—goddamn liberating—to know that no matter what choices he'd made, he was always going to end up truly fucked.

Particularly when it came to any questions about the deputies, about the Mex girl, America, or even Danny, who Johnnie seemed to know personally and not much like.

Eddy didn't tell them jack shit about Deputy Danny Ford.

HE DIDN'T KNOW how long they had him tied to that chair, but when they were done, and Johnnie brought him another Bud to drink or put against his darkening bruises, it had gotten good and cold sitting in his minifridge . . .

"I didn't want to do that," Johnnie said, as Eddy clutched the beer. He held on to it like it was a goddamn rope, and he was drowning. "See, I didn't enjoy it, not at all, not like some of those other fuckers in there." Johnnie hooked a thumb behind him into the trailer. Johnnie and Eddy were standing behind it outside in the grass, or rather Johnnie was standing, drinking his own beer. Eddy instead was hunched over, every muscle, even his fucking eyes, hurting. Like he'd taken a bath in sand and salt. He'd tried to stand up straight, but when dark blood had leaked out of his goddamn pecker, he decided it was best he just kinda stay down low.

The others were still inside; through the pain, Eddy could hear them laughing and cutting up again, probably about him.

"There's a good lesson here, though. Don't ever fuck with those boys of mine. *Ever.* They're nervous now, amped up about being here. They get up a head of steam like that again? Who knows what might happen. For me, this is all business, all professional. They take this shit way more personal. They get off on it."

As fucked up as Eddy was, he still picked out some uncertainty in Johnnie's voice . . . something weak and unsteady and unsure. That old Spidey sense of his was tuning right through the static and pain to a clear station—it always worked a helluva lot better when his brain wasn't burning like a forest fire—where he could hear the frustrated sound of a small dog that had grabbed hold of the bumper of a big car, like that Dodge Charger hidden down in the salt cedar, and now had no idea what the fuck to do with it.

Even as Johnnie stared down at him in the grass, Eddy knew Johnnie was seeing a future where he was the one all bloody and busted up, if those laughing fuckers inside slipped their own leashes and decided they weren't taking orders from him anymore. Maybe, if things here didn't go quite as planned, Johnnie himself might end up tied to some fucking chair, getting his clock cleaned.

Eddy was trapped out here with them, but so was Johnnie. Roman and Ringo and the rest may have been cops once (or still liked to think they were), but *none* of this shit was official or professional. This wasn't god-damn police business, no matter what Johnnie said. They were sneaking around the Big Bend, and they didn't want to be found out if they could help it.

Yep, his beer-drinking buddy Johnnie, good old Apache, was way off the reservation now.

"I'm going to do my best to keep those psychopaths off you, Eddy. You just gotta do what I say. Don't fuck around, don't ever fuck around. I'll keep an eye out for you, but you gotta keep an eye out for me, too. We'll get through this shit together, amigo."

Eddy knew they were probably going to kill him. That shit had been decided long before they'd showed up at his door, but that didn't mean he had to make it easy for them.

Sure, Johnnie called the shots *today*, but who knew what tomorrow would bring?

He smiled up at Johnnie, and spit both beer and blood into the grass. "We're good, amigo, we're good. All good."

And tomorrow was a motherfucker.

arrison didn't know a damn thing about helicopters. Frankly, he didn't know how they stayed airborne. It was a physical impossibility to him, an act as amazing as any Catholic miracle, which was what he needed now, because he had eight FAST members cooling their heels at Fort Bliss with their DEA chopper grounded, suffering from mysterious "engine problems." He'd made calls, trying to beg or borrow one from the base, but since Bliss was home to an armored division and various artillery brigades, they had plenty of tanks sitting around, just not many free birds. And the bird he needed had to be suited to the kinds of exfil exercises the team wanted to conduct, so the other DEA Air Wing assets he could get his hands on wouldn't work. The team was already two days late getting out to the ranch owned by Terry Macrae that Chris Cherry had helped arrange, and it looked like it could be as many as two more even if the repairs went without a hitch. Garrison hated imposing on the old rancher, but he seemed honored to host the team, no matter when they showed up.

The whole thing made Garrison feel more like some sort of party planner rather than a real agent, and now that he was an ASAC, he never felt much like a real agent anymore anyway. His badge and gun were just props since he spent most of his time in meetings or briefings or signing off on travel vouchers and funding documents or reading other people's reports.

Reports like the daily write-up the intel unit was still giving him about Fox Uno and Nemesio, the ongoing hunt for the cartel leader. Garrison had submitted the brief Chesney had requested, and Chesney hadn't asked him any more about it, so the issue was apparently dead as far as the SAC was concerned. But Garrison insisted on getting fresh intel reports anyway, making a point of looking through them. He told himself he was being thorough, but he was really just pretending that he could still do worthwhile agent work.

And this morning, while pretending, one of those reports had jumped out at him.

Or at least one word had . . .

Tejas.

IT WASN'T MUCH.

A single word picked out of the air: a thirty-second radio transmission between two members of the Serrano Brothers cartel. *Not* Nemesio, but intriguing all the same. Mexican traffickers sometimes used the word to talk about the border generally—the old northern Mexican state of Tejas—but it had more specific roots in the Native American history of the state itself. In this case, it could have been a direct reference to Diego Serrano, the older of the two brothers, who was often called El Indio due to his ruddier skin and features. It was a title he wore proudly, allegedly bragging about his supposed ancestral ties to the original Aztecs or Mayans or whatever the hell it was. But neither Diego nor Axel Serrano, the younger brother, had finished eighth grade, so although they claimed they were *indios*, Garrison guessed they had no more knowledge about their ancient ancestry or the more recent history of Coahuila y Tejas than he had about fixing a broken helicopter.

It was possible, though, that the radio intercept crew had overheard two Serrano plaza bosses talking about Chuy and Johnnie Machado's Tejas unit, and that would make unfortunate sense. The Serrano Brothers had been moving across Texas for at least five years now, murdering or bribing their way along the border. Diego had started in the Rio Grande Valley, working west, while Axel—in Nogales, Arizona—had expanded eastward, with the siblings planning to meet in the middle. It was a giant hangman's noose, an awful snake eating its tail. They'd successfully seized the most important smuggling and plaza routes along the way, carving out huge chunks of territory by buying off or killing Nemesio loyalists, and fatally choking out the rival cartel in the process. For the last eighteen months, the Ojinaga corridor, including the Big Bend, had been Nemesio's last, best stronghold, and that wasn't saying much.

Ojinaga *was* the knot in the noose, the middle of the snake.

Had the Tejas unit been helping the Serrano Brothers tighten that noose, stealing or harrying Nemesio drug loads? That could account for all their seizures . . . all those alleged successes. Over the past year, they easily could have been using their badges to "legally" steal Nemesio drug loads, turning around and then selling them on behalf of the Serrano Brothers. Local rip crews in El Paso did the same thing all the time. Why buy the dope and incur the risk and expense of smuggling it over the border, when you could just steal it from someone who already had?

It was an effective business model, but a goddamn vicious one. Missing drug loads bred distrust and reprisals. You ended up with a lot of people disappearing, whole families wiped out.

Bodies dug out of makeshift graves.

Garrison had all but given up convincing Chesney that the Terrell task force was worth a hard look, but maybe it was at least worth another discussion. And if that one word alone—"Tejas"—hadn't caught his eye, another term in that intercept would have: *el viejo*, the old man. Again, that could be a reference to Diego Serrano—another honorific, the way some had called Fox Uno "El Patrón"—but Diego was barely in his thirties, and his brother, Axel, only a year or two younger, so that didn't fit. When Garrison had pressed his intel folks, they'd admitted they had no idea who *el viejo* was, and wouldn't hazard a guess based on the limited context. All they did have was a handful of garbled words across thirty seconds of static, a coded conversation buried in white noise. Trying to make sense out of that was like putting together a thousand-piece puzzle without any idea of what the final picture was supposed to be.

Every piece might as well have been a shade of black or gray, nearly indistinguishable.

Garrison had two pieces: Tejas . . . and the old man.

But it had only taken a couple of similar puzzle pieces to spur Darin to take a hard look at the heart of Murfee, searching for Rodolfo Reynosa and evidence against the corrupt Sheriff Ross. Darin just hadn't survived long enough to see the finished picture.

A few nights ago, Garrison had dismissed the idea of Fox Uno crossing the border, but maybe the Serrano Brothers hadn't. Maybe they were looking for him *here*, and they had more than enough motivation to find him and finish the job they'd started in Ojinaga. Even if the Serranos, or Tiburón, Fox Uno's son, had successfully orchestrated his ouster from Nemesio, he'd always be a threat if he was alive. If he ever fell into the hands of the U.S. government and agreed to cooperate—highly unlikely, but a risk impossible for them to ignore—he was a walking, talking Rosetta Stone. There was no end to what he could reveal about how all the current cartels recruited and negotiated among themselves, how they were organized and communicated to their trafficking cells in the tight United States.

Who they bribed, and who protected them in Mexico.

You truly would have a goddamn snake eating its tail, choking on itself.

If Fox Uno talked, he could do more with a few words to single-handedly disrupt Mexican narco-trafficking than a hundred federal arrests or a thousand seized dope loads.

A few words, a few puzzle pieces was all Garrison had.

But that had been enough for Darin.

LATER, AFTER CHECKING ONCE MORE with intel to see if anything else had come in, Garrison returned to his nearly empty office and shut the door.

He'd pulled teletype intelligence traffic from all the DEA offices across Arizona and California. If Fox Uno had slipped over the border, he was going to need help on this side. A lot of help. Unfortunately, Garrison had a suspicion where he'd go looking for that help, but he wanted to check everywhere to be sure.

He wanted to be thorough.

He undid his tie and took the typed transcript of the radio intercept and laid it in front of him, along with all the other intel briefs and teletypes he had, including the half-assed report he had written for Chesney. He made a couple of notes to himself, so he'd say everything just the way he wanted to, then he picked up his secure phone.

He needed to make two calls.

The first was back to Washington, D.C. Technically, he was going over Chesney's head, way over, but he'd deal with the fallout of that later. Garrison still had friends back there in those other "alphabet" agencies, and he wanted to see about calling in a favor or two. Hoping to get another pair of eyes or ears focused down on his problem.

To find a few more puzzle pieces.

Then, after that, he'd make the second call—on his personal cell phone.

And that one was going to be to Sheriff Cherry.

FORTY-FIVE

The plan was for Javy Cruz to pick Mel up before America and the rest of them invaded her house.

Chris had arranged for her to stay out at Javy's place, about eight miles east of the Far Six; close enough for Chris to get to her if he needed to, but just as remote. But Javy was running late, and then Chris got stuck on a sudden call from Joe Garrison—a call that now had him pacing back and forth across their bedroom.

That was how Mel ended up opening her door to Fox Uno.

THEY WERE ALL OUT THERE ON HER PORCH: America, Danny, the young girl Zita all done up in a dress, and last, Fox Uno. They'd come in Danny's Bronco, dragging with them an odd assortment of bags, even a sleeping bag. The girl was shy, half hidden behind Danny and Amé, but Fox Uno stared at Mel without concern or embarrassment. He had the same weathered look as Javy Cruz—thinning white hair pushed back high on his head in a near pompadour, deep crow's-feet at the corners of his eyes, a thick turkey wattle. But those eyes of his were clear, calculating. It was like the eyes weren't as old as the rest of him, or somehow—and this was worse—far, far older. They sort of reminded her of her daddy's eyes midway through a solid night of drinking, only without the bloodshot.

Given all the things Mel now knew about Fox Uno, she couldn't help wondering how many people had looked in those eyes as their final act on earth.

"You all come in now, make yourself at home," she said, keeping her voice steady, composed. She pointed down at the sleeping bag. "I think we have enough beds and pull-outs for everyone. I don't think you'll need that."

No one moved, and Danny wouldn't even look at her. Amé did, but it was impossible to guess what she was thinking.

Mel tried again, this time forcing a smile she didn't feel. She couldn't take her eyes off the girl, Zita. Why on earth had they brought her here? *Had they all lost their minds?* "C'mon, let's get you inside. I'm grabbing a few more things for Jack, and then we'll be clearing out of here. The house is yours."

Finally, Danny tried something: "Thank you, ma'am, we're—"

She stopped him. "It's okay, Deputy Ford. Just fine. Just give me back my house the way you found it, unless you want to do some cleaning or fix that leaky faucet in the kitchen. That would be great."

She held the door wide for them, and went to get Chris.

FORTY-SIX

A bout once a month, Chris would drive out to the place Sheriff Ross had called El Dorado.

The land was still owned by Caleb Ross, as far as Chris knew, although the boy had sold off the house in town he'd shared with his father. Chris figured Caleb held on to El Dorado for the same reason he drove out to walk its paths—it was now a memorial to Evelyn Ross.

They both believed the woman was out there, some-where.

If she was, El Dorado had stubbornly refused to give up its secrets. *Her secrets.* More than five years had passed since her disappearance, and no one truly knew what had happened to her. In the end, for all the crimes Sheriff Ross had seemed ready to justify or accept responsibility for, he'd never admitted to killing Evelyn. It was a thing Chris had never understood, that had never made any sense. The *not knowing*, the *never knowing*. And how often did Caleb—far away and safe in Virginia—think of that place anymore? How often did he still dream of his mother buried beneath the scrub, lost forever beneath the oak brush and red oak, in the shadows of the moun-tain peaks? In its own way, it was a beautiful thought—it was truly a beautiful place—but still cold comfort. If her spirit was all that remained to haunt the land, then she wandered alone through its empty vales and creek bottoms and uncaring rocks and swaying timeless trees tipped by sunlight.

Except for Chris's occasional visits, Evelyn Ross had all of El Dorado to herself.

Although his bad leg wasn't much good for hiking, he always tried to give it a couple of hours, marking each new path with chalk, small signs he could read on the spruce, fir, and aspen: a map of where he was going and where he'd been. It was futile, but also important; a sense of duty that he forever owed victims, like Evelyn Ross. Like all those who'd been hurt or lost or forgotten since he'd taken up the badge, including America Reynosa, who despite all her strength and success was still a victim. A victim of Fox Uno and men like him—Dupree, Ross—who'd always cast long, inescapable shadows in her life.

He kept coming back again and again and again to that young girl who'd stood outside Mancha's and asked for his help. Who, now years later, was still in desperate need of it, even if she didn't believe that anymore.

Was it just about her, though, or also that young deputy he'd once been? A boy both foolish and serious enough to make a girl promises as large and immovable as the mountains that surrounded El Dorado and the Big Bend.

Impossible to scale . . . impossible to keep.

But that boy, that deputy, had made them all the same: *I'm going to do everything I can.*

GARRISON TOLD CHRIS what he'd learned, and what he was now starting to suspect.

Unlike his visit out to the Far Six, he didn't circle around it or make any effort to be delicate or diplomatic. He came right out and asked Chris if he'd been lying to him.

"Has Fox Uno tried to reach out to Deputy Reynosa?"

Chris shut the bedroom door and sat down on the bed and closed his eyes. "No, no, he hasn't."

"I'm not screwing around, Chris. I mean it. This idea that he might have slipped over the border isn't quite as crazy as we all might have thought. We're going to have to look at it."

"You mean, *you're* going to have to look at it."

"Fine. Yes, me. Please, Chris, hear me out. These are not people to fuck with. Fox Uno is ten times the monster Ross was. There is nothing he is not capable of. If he somehow made it to Murfee, someone will come for him, the way they came for you. And remember, Chris, you were no one then, a rookie deputy in a pissant town no one had heard of or cared about. Look at what they did to you, and then imagine what they'll be prepared to do to get to him. Imagine what he'll be prepared to do to save himself. It doesn't matter if it's the Serrano Brothers or Nemesio or someone else. They will finish what they started down in Ojinaga . . . what Ross and the Earls started. They will burn you and your entire town to the ground if they think you're in the way." Garrison took a deep breath, gathering himself. "Chris, it doesn't matter what's happened up to this point between us. I don't give a damn about any of that. But I can't help you if you lie to me now. So I'm going to ask you one more time, is Fox Uno in the Big Bend with America?"

Chris opened his eyes and stared at a photo of Mel and Jack on the nightstand. She was holding their son and sitting in his mother's rocking chair. He'd taken the picture three days after Jack was born, his first day home.

In the picture, there was sunlight falling on them, lens flare like a halo. Mel was smiling down at Jack, and her hair had been caught by a touch of the wind, hiding her eyes.

Through the thin bedroom door, he could hear Amé and the rest of them entering the house.

"No," he said at last, getting up off the bed.

"Would she tell you if he was?" Garrison asked, his voice edged, sharp.

"Yes, she would." At least that wasn't a lie.

Garrison breathed into the phone again. "Then I guess the real question is, would *you* tell me?"

But Garrison hung up, without waiting for an answer.

Neither of them had anything more to say.

FORTY-SEVEN

C hris had just finished up his call with Garrison when Mel came into their bedroom to find three guns laid out on their bed.

The first was the twelve-gauge Remington Versa Max shotgun they got last Christmas to keep permanently around the house. It was still new; Chris had barely had the chance to put many rounds through it, and Mel had not shot it at all. It was a big gun, with a twenty-six-inch barrel, and it looked even bigger propped up on their pillows.

The second was the Browning A5 Mel had bought for Chris, the one she'd had cut down and modified to make it easier for him to carry right after he'd been shot. He'd recovered well enough that he could use the full-size Remington, but still carried the A5 with him whenever he was on duty. She'd had the barrel and stock engraved and etched with the mountains and sun of the Big Bend, an expense she was still paying off, but the gun was beautiful, if you could say that about such a thing.

Chris had shot John Wesley Earl with the A5. He hadn't died, not then, but had only been paralyzed from the waist down. He was murdered, while under federal protection at a prison hospital, by a suspected member of the Aryan Brotherhood of Texas.

The last was Chris's first gun, his duty pistol: his Colt M1911. Colt had been the preferred weapon of the Big Bend Sheriff's Department since Chris first put on the badge, but he'd given his deputies the latitude to carry whatever make and model of handgun they preferred. He was carrying the Colt when he nearly died here at the Far Six; he'd killed three men—*sicarios*—with it. Still, it was unnerving to see the Colt naked and exposed like this, since it was normally tucked away in his holster. He hadn't drawn it in her presence in years.

"This is supposed to make me feel better?" she asked, staring at the guns on their bed and shutting the door behind her. She'd tied Rocky up out back so he wouldn't go crazy with the house full of strangers, and Jack was still asleep in his nursery.

Everyone else was standing in her kitchen.

Chris looked up, guilty. "I want you to take something with you when you go to Javy's."

"Chris, that's foolish and it's a lie. Javy's probably got three times as many guns. He's an actual hunter. You got those out for *you*."

Chris ignored her. "Amé's here?"

"Yes, they're all here, including Danny, all waiting for you. But you're trying to avoid telling me what Joe Garrison said. Why did he call, Chris? You don't hear from him for months at a time, and now he's visiting and calling twice in a week? He knows, doesn't he?"

"He suspects, I guess. He's an investigator, so he's investigating."

"But you still didn't tell him, did you?"

Chris didn't say anything for several seconds, looking down at the guns on the bed—*their* bed, where they'd planned their future and made love and slept together with Jack. She knew he was wondering if his decision now was one of those moments they both would regret; if it was a splinter that would work its way under the skin of their marriage. If it was something they'd always feel there, raw, just under the surface.

She didn't know, and neither did he. He turned back to her. "Let's get you and Jack packed up and out of here. I think I finally hear Javy's truck pulling up the drive."

BUT MEL WASN'T READY to get pushed out the door of her own home.

She had a few more things she wanted to do and say.

First, she went back into the living room, Chris trailing behind her, and pinned down Amé and Danny, ignoring Fox Uno, who was looking at some of the leftover election yard signs stacked in a pile and the mountain view beyond the windows.

"I told myself I was going to hold my tongue, but I'm not. Not in my own house. I know I can't stop any of this, but I won't let you put that girl in harm's way. She's not staying here. She's coming with me."

Chris tried to put a hand on her shoulder. "Mel, she's Fox Uno's daughter. We can't—"

Mel shook him off. "We're not having a discussion. If

she stays, Jack and I stay. Otherwise, after you've done whatever insane thing you're doing here, we'll bring her back or meet you wherever you want. Once it's safe, and only then."

Danny spoke up. "She doesn't speak much English."

"Javy can translate. We'll be fine."

"Mel, don't do this, please," Chris said. "Just let me handle this."

"I am letting you handle it. But listen to me, loud and clear, I'm taking care of that girl, because the rest of you aren't thinking straight. I'm not sure you're thinking at all." Mel next wheeled on Amé and Fox Uno. "You tell that murdering son of a bitch over there his daughter is coming with me."

Fox Uno had forgotten the view outside the window and was now returning Mel's glare, a slight smile on his face.

"He speaks English well enough," Amé said. "I think he understood you."

"Good, then I don't have to say it twice."

Of all of them, Danny looked the most ashamed. He had taken off his hat when he came into the house, and had been clutching it nervously in his hands, turning it round and round. He now propped it on Zita's head. "Ma'am, she really likes ice cream, strawberry. I'll get her things." He added, "I'm sorry about this. I hope you know that."

She did, and she believed him. "Good, Danny, thank you. Javy will be knocking on the door any second. I'll make sure we pick up some for her."

Finally, she brought her attention back around to America. "Now I'm going to get my son. Deputy Reynosa, do you think you can come back here and help me for a second?"

THEY'D KNOWN EACH OTHER almost as long as Chris had known her, but Mel had never had many conversations with Amé, and none of them alone. There was a time when a younger Mel would have been furiously jealous of the beautiful girl and Chris's relationship with her, but that time was past, and Mel wanted to believe that younger version of her had passed on as well, or at least had grown up some. She would never understand the closeness between Chris and Amé, the protectiveness he felt for her, but she'd never been threatened by it.

Until now.

Amé stood in the doorway of Jack's darkened nursery with her arms crossed, as Mel started to fill a diaper bag for Jack.

"Can I have one of your cigarettes?" Mel asked.

Amé looked over to where Jack lay asleep in his crib.

"No, don't worry, I'm not going to light it up here. I haven't smoked since I knew I was pregnant. Chris would kill me if he thought I'd started up again, but I think I'm going to need one when I'm at Javy's."

Amé reached in her back pocket and pulled out a soft pack, and handed it over to her. "I was supposed to quit, too, a while ago. How did you know?"

"The smoke," Mel said, as she took the pack and shook out a couple of cigarettes and slipped them in Jack's bag. "I smelled it on your clothes." She pulled the baby up out of his crib. He hardly made a sound and didn't wake up.

"Do you think you want kids someday?" Mel asked, as she added a few more diapers, hiding the cigarettes beneath them. As she juggled Jack and the bag one-handed, America came over and started to help.

"*No lo sé*. I've never thought about it."

Mel knew that was a lie. Every girl thought about it at least once, one way or the other, and there was no right or wrong answer. There didn't even have to be a final answer. Mel had been convinced for years that she didn't want to be a mother, until all of a sudden she did. It was a lightning strike. It took the right time, the right place, the right love.

"It changes things, Amé, it truly does. In ways I can't describe. I've heard it said you don't realize how much you can love someone until it happens. And I'm not just talking about the baby." She kissed Jack's head, and then turned and gave him to Amé, who slowly, reluctantly, took him. It was obvious the girl had never held a baby before, and Mel helped settle her arms around him. It reminded Mel of how awkward Chris had been the first time.

"He loves you, do you understand that?" Mel asked, but Amé didn't say anything, didn't know who she was talking about or how to respond. "Chris. And Danny, too. He's so obvious about it you can't walk into a room with him and not trip over it. They're both standing out there in my living room because they love you, each in their own way. That's the reason, the *only* reason. I know that, and so do you."

America looked down at the baby in her arms, her hair falling into her face, but still didn't say anything. Mel hadn't realized just how young the girl truly was until now. She'd seen so much, been through so much, and still . . .

Mel saw in her the same girl who'd followed her own daddy to Galveston and Midland, bouncing around the Permian Basin. A girl who'd made a hard life in the shadows of trailers and shitty motels, beneath the constant fire and smoke of the oil rigs. A girl who'd somehow made it through to something better.

She saw herself.

"That means *you're* the only one who can put an end to this. No one else is going to change their minds, except you. Love is that powerful, that goddamn strong, and you don't even have to be a mother to know that. It's like a gun, and just as dangerous. I think that's something women like us learn early, in a way a man never does. I hope to God you know what you're doing here, because those men out there won't stop unless you do." She let Amé hold Jack a bit longer, while she went to get something out of her purse. She'd grabbed it earlier, and although she'd contemplated using it herself a dozen times, she couldn't do that to Chris.

They'd have to find a way to work that splinter out on their own.

But Amé still could, and Mel hoped she would.

She folded the small paper into an even smaller square and tucked it carefully inside the cigarette pack she'd been holding on to. Then she pressed the pack into Amé's hand as she took Jack from her.

"Hold on to those cigarettes. I think you're going to need one yourself."

America looked at the pack, before slipping it into her back pocket. "He's beautiful, your son."

Mel smiled and gathered up her bag. It was time to go.

"Thank you. I think he's going to grow up to look just like his daddy."

FORTY-EIGHT

CHAYO & NEVA

The men had quietly slipped in behind them, moving up from the river as they had, and caught them two hours after they crossed over.

Chayo heard something, wheeling around in time to bring the ancient rifle up as if it were loaded. It was awkward in his hands, like it would fall apart if he shook it or gripped it too hard, but it held together, for now. And at least it kept his hands steady, as he aimed it at the two men who'd appeared out of the scrub.

The first was tall, all right angles. He looked like one of the *espantapájaros* Chayo had seen on the farms in Blanco—an ugly thing made of straw and wood and newspapers and bits and pieces of other old things.

But this man wasn't made of newspaper, his bare arms covered in ink, *tatuajes*. Because of the sweat beaded on the man's skin, reflecting the flattened sun, Chayo couldn't tell exactly what the *tatuajes* were supposed to be. Most of them were scrawled in blue or black, giving him a sooty appearance, as if he were permanently dusted in ashes. He wore a sleeveless shirt that hung down far past his waist; his thinning hair was covered by a bandanna, and big sunglasses wrapped around his wasted skull.

There was a machete in his waistband.

The other was shorter, but just as thin. He had a Delfines del Carmen baseball cap, with its purple dolphin and green C, and sunglasses similar to his companion's, but his were mirrored, so Chayo could see himself and Neva reflected. This man had a red bandanna twisted around his neck, and an open-necked shirt revealing two rosaries—one metal, one wood—dangling against his chest.

He had a gun, a large black one, aimed at Chayo.

Coyotes.

Or worse.

Neva took a half step behind Chayo, as Tatuaje stared at her from behind his darkened glasses, breathing hard.

Baseball grinned, showing two silver teeth and many blackened ones. "It's okay, my friends, no problem here. We don't want trouble. Maybe just talk, then we all go on our way." He spoke in Spanish and licked his lips between every couple of words, glancing back and forth between Chayo and Neva. In the mirrors of his sunglasses, their image wavered back and forth. Appearing, disappearing. "We can help you. We can guide you. We've done this many times. It's dangerous here without true friends. Bandits, Border Patrol, snakes."

Chayo shook his head. "No."

Tatuaje took a step closer, his hand stroking the length of the naked machete at his waist. He laughed at something and nothing at all.

Baseball sighed, looking at the ground at their feet. "You do not understand. Walking here is like breaking into a man's home. It is a beautiful home, filled with pretty things. All that you see is owned by this man, so you must knock to enter. You must be invited, or you must pay for the privilege, and you do not look like you have much money." He turned slowly to Neva. "But there are other ways to pay." He waved the gun up and down her body. "We are the ones who guard the house for this man, for Fox Uno. Are you here to take Fox Uno's pretty things?"

"I do not know what you're talking about. We have nothing," Chayo said. These men were not simple *coyotes*; either they were real narcos like they said, working for this Fox Uno that Chayo had heard of, that everyone in Ojinaga had heard of, or they were even worse: *bajadores*, those who preyed on both human and drug smugglers—stealing their drugs, taking the money the immigrants had saved for years to start their new lives, assaulting the women. Both had backpacks and canteens, they were unwashed and unkempt. Chayo could smell them, and they had been in the desert for a while. They probably had a camp on each side of the river.

They were right; they were the ones who guarded the house.

Tatuaje spoke up, laughing and smiling wider. "There's always something . . ."

"He is right," Baseball agreed, scratching his nose with the gun's barrel. "It is simple. We are not bad men. We will give you food, some water, and point you the safest way to go. For this we will take ten minutes with your girl. She is ugly, but she will do. Ten minutes for the rest of your life? That is nothing, my friend. Nothing at all."

"No," Chayo said. He raised the rifle higher, slowly, praying it did not split in half. "No. It is too much. It is everything we have." It sounded like begging, and he was.

Baseball shrugged and made a face, showing his rotten teeth again. He looked toward the invisible river. "It is no matter. A few days ago, we killed five just like you, but there are always more. The river brings them to us and takes them away again." He sounded tired, a man exhausted by all the things he'd done and all the things he would yet do, but Chayo knew it was useless to ask him why he did such things, if they burdened him so much. He probably didn't know himself anymore. It was just the way things were, and the way they would always be, on the river.

Baseball turned back to Chayo. "I will shoot you and we will take what we want anyway."

Then Chayo was all the way back on the bus in Ojinaga . . . with Castel and all the others dying in front of him.

That hot darkness, the breaking glass. Sparks on metal.

The screaming and the blood.

Ojos de los muertos.

Like the sunglasses of the two *bajadores*.

He and Neva had survived too much, had come too far, to die here, in this place.

Like the *halcón*, they had flown.

Chayo yelled at the top of his lungs, a scream he'd been holding in since that night, and flew again . . .

. . . right at Baseball.

THE *BAJADORES* WERE ABOUT TEN FEET from Chayo and Neva, perhaps more. The broken and empty rifle in Chayo's hand had bought him some time when they'd first appeared, and even now they didn't know whether it was loaded.

It also gave Chayo a longer reach, so he didn't have to close the whole distance.

He caught Baseball off guard by his sudden attack, though he stuck his own gun out in front of him to fend Chayo off, to push him away.

He fired one shot, and Chayo felt the bullet tear the air beside him . . . no . . . *through him*. His body had been set on the fire, and in the still of the desert, the sound of the booming gun was louder than he ever could have imagined, louder than anything he'd ever heard. But still Chayo kept coming, and he brought the rifle around in a long arc, praying again it held together, and caught Baseball in the face with it. It shattered the man's mirrored glasses and he screamed in surprise and pain, as Chayo's rifle flew apart in shards of rotted wood and rusted metal.

A long sliver of that metal remained stuck in Baseball's left eye and it spouted thick blood, high into the air.

Baseball went down and Chayo was on top of him, kicking and still screaming, and drawing the small knife from his belt . . .

THE OTHER, TATUAJE, didn't reach for the machete at his waist, but instead a gun he had hidden in a holster beneath his long shirt. Neither Chayo nor Neva had seen it, and he went for it now, as Neva ran toward Chayo, putting herself in front of Tatuaje's gun. His first shot went low, kicking up dirt and rocks at her feet so that she stumbled and fell, rolling in the scrub. But she got up and kept running, throwing a handful of gritty sand in Tatuaje's direction.

His second went high, lost forever in the sky.

The third wasn't from him at all . . .

. . . it was from Chayo.

He was kneeling over Baseball's body with that man's gun in his hand, and nearly blew Tatuaje's heart out of the back of his chest.

The impact rocked him back and forth and his sunglasses slipped sideways on his head, but he didn't fall.

He said something in both English and Spanish and coughed a thick river of blood, as his eyes rolled up white.

Perhaps he was praying, too.

Chayo's next shot dropped him to his knees, where his gun slipped from his hands into the dirt. He reached down for it but couldn't see it, couldn't find it, his empty hands moving on their own, fingers searching.

Chayo's last shot knocked him backward and put him down.

Still empty-handed.

IT WAS OVER IN SECONDS. When it started, Chayo had never held a gun.

When it was over, he'd killed two men.

Except . . . Baseball was still alive, barely. Dying by the second. There was a splinter of the old rifle deep in his left eye, and Chayo's knife buried in the thin, weathered flesh hidden by the bandanna below his chin. The knife stuck out awkwardly, quivering with each last breath he took. He made gently whispering sounds, like he was telling secrets, like soft wind blowing through an open window. He was kicking his legs . . . back and forth . . . back and forth . . . slowing like a clock winding down.

He was crying bloody tears from his ruined eye, and Chayo held his hand as he died.

Afterward, Neva pulled Chayo up, helping to keep his own legs from buckling. He realized her arms were stained thick with his blood, and when they both finally understood just how bad he was hurt, she helped lay him back down again.

She stood over him looking back the way they'd come, her thoughts unknowable. Chayo wanted to tell her to go, to keep going. The sky was blue above her, framing her with wisps of clouds working their way north, the direction they had been traveling.

He lay in her shadow, and it was cool there.

Then she got to work.

SHE FIRST WENT TO BASEBALL and stripped him of anything useful, searching his backpack. She did the same for Tatuaje, taking the machete. She checked their shoes and belts, grabbed their canteens. She carefully took their guns and extra ammunition and set them aside. Surprisingly, she found a roll of gauze and dirty tape in Tatuaje's backpack and a small bag of marijuana and some yellow pills in a plastic bag, and she used what she could to bandage Chayo's wound and gave him one of the pills with a mouthful of water.

The bullet had passed clean through Chayo's side, leaving a bloody, weeping hole both front and back. He had lost a lot of blood, and there was no way to put it back in again. Either the lost blood or the pill was making him light-headed, like he was leaving a part of himself behind and floating away into that blue sky. He was rising as high as that *halcón* he'd seen earlier.

He truly was flying.

He wanted to lie again in Neva's shadow, but it kept moving, too, racing across the ground too fast for him to catch.

She pulled the bloody rosaries from around Baseball's neck, and put the wooden one around her own and the metal one on Chayo.

She put Baseball's hat on Chayo's head, and tied Tatuaje's bandanna around her hair, keeping it out of her face.

She put one of the guns in her waistband, and the other in Chayo's backpack.

Then she got him onto his feet . . . pulled him standing, and the pain was so bad it made him want to scream and scream again, but he couldn't.

She made him chew another pill.

At the edges of his vision, the world had gone dark and silent and still . . . *dormido* . . . and he didn't want to wake it up.

The sky was full of *murciélagos* showing them the way, or he was dreaming them.

Or instead it was a plane, high above, arrowing to the sort of cities he promised Neva he would take her to. He wondered if the people in that plane were looking down and could see them.

Will they remember them?

He was slowly dying. Tonight, tomorrow.

Will anyone?

What was it Baseball had said? *The river brings them to us and takes them away again.*

Neva had her arm around Chayo and started them both walking again.

===

FORTY-NINE

As Danny finally left the Far Six, Melissa and Zita and Rocky the dog were getting into Javy Cruz's truck. Zita was still wearing Danny's hat, and the sheriff was hovering close to Melissa, helping her and the baby. They were their own gravity, constantly pulling him back to them.

Danny knew Chris didn't want to let them go, even though this was all his idea.

Danny didn't want to leave either, but he had miles to cover and an old friend to meet. He had to get on the road if he wanted to get back by first light.

The whole time, America and Fox Uno stayed up on the porch, watching them all.

HE GOT INTO VAN HORN just before dinner, before they turned on the twenty-five-foot-high neon sign for the historic Hotel El Capitan.

The hotel had been around since the 1930s. Originally a place for ranchers to gather and wheel and deal, the building was turned into the Van Horn State Bank during the 1970s; it was sold in 2007 and remodeled back into a hotel. During the renovations, secret rooms and passageways were allegedly found, including a Customs and Border Patrol holding cell somewhere in the basement. With its great central fountain in the courtyard, terra-cotta- and blue-tiled lobby, and assortment of animal heads staring down from the walls, the old hotel was a museum in this part of West Texas. It was named after one of the higher peaks in the state, a massive limestone edifice rising starkly out of the Chihuahuan Desert, over eight thousand feet high. El Capitan wasn't easy to climb, due to the crumbly rock and the sheer nature of its flanks, but it was a popular bike ride out to the peak in the heart of Guadalupe Mountains National Park from the hotel that shared its name.

Beyond the hotel and the peak, there wasn't much to Van Horn. A few chain restaurants and plenty of liquor stores, a Budget motel and a Presbyterian church and a Greyhound stop next to a Wendy's. The Hotel El Capitan sat only two blocks off I-10, and when Danny checked into his room, which looked out over the fountain in the courtyard, he could hear the big eighteen-wheelers rolling up and down the freeway.

He lay down on the bed with the French doors open to wait, eyes open, letting all that traffic white out his other thoughts, as the sun worked its way behind Threemile and Fivemile mountains and cast looming shadows over the town . . .

ABOUT AN HOUR LATER, he got the call he was expecting from Staff Sergeant Gary West.

Danny met West down in the Gopher Hole Bar, where

West had set them up with two cold bottles of Lone Star. When Danny walked up, West got off his stool and wrapped his arms around him.

"Goddamn good to see you, Danny. I knew you were a cop or something, but I didn't realize you were working all the way down in the Big Bend. Jesus, brother, that's way out there."

Danny laughed and pushed West back into his seat. Last time they'd seen each other in person they'd been kids, razor-thin and feral and dangerous. For a while they'd believed they were immortal, until Afghanistan taught them differently. West had filled out since then, gotten thicker in the face and neck, but the arms he'd crushed Danny with were still strong . . . still dangerous.

West looked closely at the scars around Danny's left eye. "Jesus, you didn't get that back in the shit. As I recall, you mustered out healthy and whole." But the way he said it wasn't entirely convincing. No one came out of Afghanistan completely healthy or whole.

"Well, Staff Sergeant, I've learned that you can get yourself pretty fucked up even when you're not in a war zone."

West raised his Lone Star in a toast, and Danny joined him. "Amen to that, brother."

Danny said, "You shouldn't have gotten these, everything's on me tonight. I'm going to owe you plenty before we're done."

West laughed and drained half his beer. "Hell, I just ordered 'em. I didn't say I was paying for them." He waved at a petite blonde working the bar. "Ma'am, we're going to need another round over here. Actually, we're going to need a lot of 'em. It's going to be an expensive night for my friend."

THEY SPENT THE NEXT COUPLE OF HOURS catching each other up. Danny talked some about joining DPS, and then coming over to work for Sheriff Cherry. He left out some things, including his time with the Earls, and West didn't press.

For his part, West had stayed in the army, slowly moving up the ranks. He'd gotten married to a young Hispanic girl and had two sons: Micah and Jonah. They lived off-base in a small house a few miles from Fort Bliss. He had endless complaints about the military life, but didn't want to do much else with his own. His wife, Letty, was pushing him to get out, take advantage of the GI Bill and get some classes under his belt at UTEP, but he sounded content. He appeared happy.

He was happiest talking about his sons.

Micah was playing peewee football, and West was sure he was the next big college quarterback. Jonah was younger, smaller, but West figured he'd be a hell of a soccer player. West only needed to learn the rules.

"I watch that shit with Letty's wetback brothers all the time, and I still don't understand it, not at all. All that fucking running around. I just yell when everyone else does." And when he said it, Danny caught something in his eye, something sharp and hard, something there and gone again.

I just yell when everyone else does.

He might as well have been talking about Afghanistan.

WEST FILLED HIM IN on how some of the others from
their unit had turned out, some better than others.

"Remember Duran? That fucking little guy? He was
from Puerto Rico, right, or at least claimed he was? Anyway, he completely lost his shit somewhere in Mississippi.
They're calling it that 'death by cop' thing. He goaded
those boys in blue into putting him down right in the
parking lot of a 7-Eleven. His girlfriend was there, holding their baby. He'd been going to the VA, talking to a
counselor, getting meds and all that shit, but nothing
was helping. He couldn't see straight anymore, if you
know what I mean."

And Danny did, more than West would ever know.
Danny remembered Duran. He'd been a funny guy, always trying to quit smoking but never quite getting
there. The sort of guy who had a joke for everything.
They'd been together at both Rumnar and Wanat, and
Danny didn't recall him having any issues on deploy-
ment. But then again, Danny hadn't, either.

Danny wondered if Duran ever quit smoking.

"What about you?" Danny made a small motion toward
West's heart, then his head. "How's it been, since . . . ?"

"Since we got back? Oh, it's been okay, I guess." West
was arranging their empty Lone Stars in soldier-straight
lines on the table. "It's hard now and then. My temper.
I get angry over shit I don't even remember getting angry about. I don't get physical, nothing like that, but it
sure drives Letty crazy. She's threatened once or twice to
leave, but we always work it out. One of her brothers

stopped me on my way to the base, pulled his piece-of-shit Mustang right in front of my ride, and told me if I raised my voice at her one more time, he'd drive me over the bridge to Juárez and fucking bury my ass there. Said no one would ever find me, and I kinda believed him. I think he's a straight-up gang member. Barrio Azteca. Got these tattoos all over him, right up to his neck. Scary, scary shit." West stopped, took a drink of a half-filled beer. "It is what it is."

"You talk to anyone about it?"

West laughed. "Talk to someone? About a short fuse? Fuck all that, look at what talking did for Duran."

"No, I'm serious. Maybe you should. Hell, maybe we both should."

West looked at him closely. "What do you mean? You dealing with some shit, too?"

Danny nodded. "I think we're all dealing with some shit. All of us. How could we not? The things we saw, the things we did." He raised his hand for some more beers. Neither of them needed any more, but then again, maybe they did. "For me, it's these dreams. I've started having crazy dreams . . . about Wanat . . . about Newberry . . . about everything that happened after that, in Rumnar . . ."

West looked away. "Rumnar was some fucked-up shit. We were all on edge after what happened in Wanat, and then Newberry going out like he did. Rumnar shouldn't have happened, but . . . Jesus . . ." West trailed off. "I haven't thought of any of that in a long time. I didn't want to."

Danny nodded. "I know, me either. But maybe we should. Maybe we're supposed to."

THEY TALKED ON INTO THE NIGHT, about things and places they hadn't talked about in years—about things they had never talked to anyone else about out loud—until the Gopher Hole cleared out and it was just the two of them. It was a hard talk, trying to put into words thoughts and feelings and fears that there weren't any good words for, but it was also like clearing the air of thick, dark smoke. Like finding a small shaft of sunlight down in all those black holes Danny had been dreaming of. He felt better just for having tried, and promised to talk to a real VA professional about what he was dealing with if West made the same promise, and he did.

The talk alone was worth the drive, and it almost made Danny forget the real reason he'd come.

But now their bartender, the small blonde named Courtney—with her big earrings and her long hair pulled back—was flipping through a magazine waiting for them to finish up, so she could finally turn down the lights and go home.

The bar reminded Danny of Earlys, which also reminded him of Amé. West was nudging his shoulder. "I think our girl Courtney over there likes you. She hasn't been able to keep her eyes off of you the whole time. I mean, maybe it's me she's looking at, but she's not my type. Too plain Jane, too safe. I evidently like mine Hispanic and crazy and dangerous."

Danny laughed, and started fishing for bills out of his wallet. "Well, looking is free, but these beers aren't. There's this girl back in Murfee anyway . . ."

West went from nudging his shoulder to punching it, three hard shots that sent a shiver down Danny's arm. "Goddamn, we've been sitting here this whole time and you didn't say anything? That's why you've been eye-balling that phone of yours all night, checking for texts. You officially hooked now? She keeping you on a short leash?"

Danny laughed. "I don't know what exactly to call it. It's something. We're close, I guess."

"But is it serious, brother? That's the question you need to ask yourself before Miss Courtney comes over here to collect her tip. Know what I mean?" West had a loopy grin on his face—too much beer, too little food.

"Whatever it is, it's serious enough. Let's leave it at that," Danny said, and tossed all the money on the table. There was no use trying to count it out. He'd had too much to drink—more than he'd had in a long time—but was sobering up fast. Thinking about Amé—why he was sitting with West in the first place, and what he was facing when he went back to the Big Bend—was enough to do that.

West was laughing, too, watching the money pile up on the table. Knowing it was time. He stood up and stretched, and winked and waved at Courtney to let her know they were done, and then he turned back to Danny.

"Well, that's a damn shame, she's easy on the eyes. But I get it, if your girl is like mine, she might cut you just for looking." West reached in his pocket for his keys.

"Okay, soldier, let's do this thing. I got what you asked for. Outside."

Danny stood with him. "I'm not a soldier anymore."

West laughed one final time and threw one of his huge arms around Danny, pulling him close. "That's bullshit and you know it. Hell, that's why you're here. We're always soldiers, Danny boy. Always."

FIFTY

Chris and Amé were standing on his front porch, watching the stars turn on one by one, in almost the same spots he and Garrison had occupied the week before. Fox Uno was inside the house, and Chris could see him through the front window, sitting on the couch, watching TV. The volume was down and the images flashed silently—happy and incredibly good-looking people laughing in a bar of glass and chrome that looked nothing like Earlys—painting the old man's face in weird colors and shapes.

A small breeze had blown down from the mountains, and it was moving Amé's hair around, twisting the trailing smoke from her cigarette. She was careful with her embers, guarding them with a cupped hand, making sure they didn't get free.

Chris hadn't seen her smoke since that day in front of Mancha's.

"Mel didn't do anything crazy, like threaten you or anything like that?"

"No, *nada*." She laughed, although it was forced, only for his benefit. "She talked about Jack."

Chris nodded, unbelieving, but knew he wouldn't get any more out of her. Mel hadn't been willing to share her talk with Amé, either. It had been a long afternoon for all of them, and it was going to be a longer night. He could only hope they didn't have too many more ahead.

"I wish Danny hadn't come out here," Chris said. "I hope he decides not to come back. I don't want him part of this."

"I don't, either, but it doesn't matter what you or I want, or what you tell him to do."

"He never said where he was going?" Chris asked.

Amé brushed hair out of her eyes. "No. But he did mention Eddy Rabbit."

"Eddy? Why Eddy?"

"He spoke with Eddy's girlfriend, Charity. Since he's been released, Eddy hasn't tried to see her or call her."

Chris stared into Amé's smoke, tried to make sense of the shapes he saw there. "That's good for them both. He's not supposed to."

"*Verdad*. But the fact he hasn't tried even once *is* the problem. Danny just wanted to check on him." She picked at some wood on the railing.

Chris shook his head. "If he's going down there, it's because he's still afraid Eddy might have something to do with Fox Uno . . . with what we're doing here. This is about you and me and Fox Uno, not Eddy and Charity."

Amé breathed out smoke. "I talked to her that night after he beat her. She still loves him. She doesn't know how to stop."

"I'm sure," Chris said. "We don't always get to pick and choose. Life would be damn easier if we could, right? Probably wouldn't be half as interesting, though." He thought about Mel and all their tough times together, how they'd always found a way through.

But there was another side of that—was it possible you could ask too much of someone who loved you? He didn't know the answer anymore, if he ever thought he did. Not now, not after forcing Mel and their son out of their home. Not with a man like Fox Uno sitting in his living room.

"Anyway, running out to the canyon shouldn't have taken all afternoon, so maybe that's a good sign." He didn't want to say out loud that maybe it wasn't.

Amé didn't say anything, either. She crushed out her cigarette on the railing, and then swept the ashes into her hand, where she held them tight.

Chris watched the sky deepen, darken. Everything out there was unseeable, unknowable, but it was moving toward them all the same.

The coming night . . . and whatever lay on the other side of it.

"What do you want when all this is over, Amé?"

She thought on that for a while, staring into the same falling darkness that had frustrated Chris. But if she could see through it better than him, she gave no sign.

"I want to be free. I thought I was, until he showed up."

"Fair enough," Chris said. "I want that, too. You will be. And I guess that has to be good enough for both of us."

Chris turned toward the window again to look at Fox Uno. "Look at how calm he is. None of this seems to bother him, affect him. But I can't help wondering if he's changed us."

If America was going to agree, she didn't.

Then they were both silent for a long time, and let the night continue to fall around them.

FIFTY-ONE

They walked out together to West's bright red Camaro, parked in a dark corner of the lot. Away from the quiet and stillness of the bar, they both could almost feel the big rigs passing by on the interstate. A vibration all the way down to their bones, one after another, even at this hour.

The night glowed with their headlights, like lightning from a distant storm.

"Letty once told me I should get a job driving trucks. It was good money, she said. Her cousin Armando did it. I don't know, though. Being stuck in that cab all day? Seems like I might go stir-crazy." West popped the trunk with his remote, revealing something wrapped loosely in a Dallas Cowboys blanket. "She hates this damn car, too. Says we need something more practical for the boys. I know they'll get too big soon to haul around in it, but it's fast, which is a damn nice thought, in case I ever need to make a getaway from those crazy brothers of hers."

West pulled back the edge of the blanket. "Are you gonna need to make a getaway soon, Danny?"

Danny looked at what West had revealed. It was an M110 Semi-Automatic Sniper System, the M110 SASS. It weighed about fifteen pounds, with a flash suppressor and a twenty-round detachable box magazine. It was gas-operated with a rotating bolt, and had a muzzle velocity of at least twenty-five hundred feet per second.

It fired 7.62x51mm NATO rounds.

Not much different from those in his dream.

It had an effective range of over eight hundred yards.

West tapped the retracted stock of the M110. "I also brought those special rounds you requested. I dunno what you're hunting out there in the Big Bend, but this here will take care of it. It'll put it down, *hard.*"

Danny didn't say anything. During all those months working undercover in those various skinhead gangs, his "in" had always been a lie about getting his hands on surplus military weapons. It was the only reason he'd ever gotten close to Jesse Early or his daddy, John Wesley.

In the end, it hadn't been that much of a lie at all.

"I don't suppose you're going to tell me why you really need this, are you?" West asked.

Danny laughed. "Don't worry, I'm not robbing a bank." He reached into his pocket and took out a folded envelope. He'd pulled a thousand dollars out of his bank account that afternoon, after leaving the Far Six. "Here's the money we talked about it. Take it. It's all there. I'll get this rifle back to you in a week."

"If all goes well?"

"Yeah," Danny conceded, "if all goes well."

West looked at the envelope for a long time. He grabbed it, thumbed out a couple of hundred-dollar bills, and pushed the rest back into Danny's hands. "I'll use this to buy something nice for Letty. A good dinner, maybe even get the boys something, too. *You* owe 'em more than you owe me, for dragging my ass out here tonight on such short notice. But seeing you . . . and talking, *really* talking . . . well, that's payment enough for me."

"Thanks, I appreciate it."

"Nah, it's nothing. Don't thank me. Just don't let me read about you in the paper. Not like Duran, right?"

"No, not like Duran."

West looked at him closely one last time, saluted, and then pulled him in for a final, crushing hug. It was like being held by a dozen men, a whole platoon. "But I do feel sorry for the poor bastard on the other end of that scope. Happy hunting, brother."

Danny hugged him back, then lifted the blanket-wrapped M110 out of the trunk. He walked away, leaving West still standing by the open trunk, watching him go.

Eight hundred yards. About the length of eight football fields, which was kind of funny, given that Sheriff Cherry had been a big-time quarterback. But even the sheriff couldn't outthrow the M110.

Eight hundred yards.

With the rifle's Leupold Mk4 3.5-10x40mm illuminated TMR reticle scope and a clear field of vision from the house at the Far Six, Danny would be able to see damn near forever.

All the way to Mexico.

FIFTY-TWO

It was well past midnight, a couple of hours before dawn, when one of Fox Uno's phones rang.

It was the Mexican Telcel, the phone America had spoken to Gualterio on, out in the desert.

America had been holding on to both of Fox Uno's phones to make sure no calls or messages came through they weren't aware of, and when it started beeping, she wasn't asleep anyway. She was still wide-awake, thinking instead about the talk she'd had earlier with Melissa.

What it had felt like to hold the baby, the furious beat of his tiny heart against her chest.

She'd also been thinking about the voicemail she got yesterday from Ron Delaney, the DPS evidence tech. He'd wanted her to know that although they still didn't have any IDs on the bodies they'd recovered from Delcia Canyon, they did have some approximate ages.

The youngest, the boy, had been no more than thirteen years old.

SHE LET THE PHONE RING ON AND ON for several seconds, staring at it in her hand. None of them had expected to hear from Gualterio or his people so soon.

Danny wasn't back yet, and despite what she'd said to the sheriff, she had no idea where he was or what he was really doing.

She'd imagined they'd have more time . . . that *she* would have more time.

Before she could answer it, though, the phone went silent.

She turned it over and over in her hand, then checked the other phone, but there were no calls or messages on that one.

Thirty seconds later, the Telcel started ringing again. She knew it wasn't going to stop. It would never stop now.

America holstered the gun she'd been cradling in her lap, and then slowly got up off the floor of Jack's nursery, where she'd been sitting for most of the night.

She let the phone ring, as she went to find Fox Uno and the sheriff.

FIFTY-THREE

Javy's place was rough, but nice.

The main house was old and rambling—some siding, some wood—within sight of the Christmas Mountains. A good part of his acreage used to be part of the G4 Ranch from way back in the 1880s, before being bought up in 1942 by the State of Texas to create the Big Bend National Park.

Somehow, the Cruz family had come into control of several hundred acres of their own, and they'd been able to hold on to it as the park expanded around them, an oasis in the middle of the desert. It was all oak, mesquite, and chaparral; loose scree on low hills; and plenty of cactus. Javy had long ago abandoned running cattle on the land, instead guiding hunting trips: mule deer, elk, aoudad sheep, javelina, and even mountain lion. Scattered across his land were a couple of bunkhouses without electricity or running water for all the hunters from Dallas, Austin, and Houston looking for an authentic rustic experience.

Javy was a walking encyclopedia of the region. He knew about the Indians who'd settled in the Trans-Pecos more than ten thousand years ago and could point out their middens and their hieroglyphs at the river and creek sites they'd still occupied into the nineteenth century.

He knew the routes the old missionaries and traders had cut along Alamito Creek, places where a dozen ranches and mines had briefly flourished and then failed, most of their names long forgotten or no more than faded ink on old maps.

The hard men who'd named them long gone as well.

It was also rumored that Javy used to work as a smuggler—cigarettes, alcohol, sugar, drugs—and had once been friends with many of the old-time narcos who'd ruled the region.

Javy Cruz—seventy years old—knew a hell of a lot about a lot of things, old and new, including how to make a great cup of coffee. He'd woken Mel up with a big mug of it, although she hadn't slept much anyway, and the chicory and maple smell filled the house, thick as cigarette smoke. Though she'd stopped smoking when she realized she was pregnant with Jack, that didn't mean she didn't crave one now and then, mainly when she was stressed or tired. Like now.

Now she wanted to work her way through a whole pack before breakfast. She wished she had taken more than a couple from Deputy Reynosa.

It didn't help that when Javy brought her his wonderful coffee, he'd had a rifle slung over his shoulder.

HE WAS IN HIS SMALL KITCHEN, making deer sausage and eggs, cooking the thick, handmade tortillas he got from Presidio on a big frying pan. He'd poured some whiskey into his own mug of coffee, and the rifle was laid out on the counter, within reach.

The walls were covered with old pictures and antler racks and trophy heads, not unlike Earlys. The dark eyes of the dead animals stared down at them, glassy and reflective and deep enough to fall into, and she tried not to stare back.

He had a radio on, playing music from a station over the border.

Before settling in the kitchen with him, Mel had checked on both Jack and Zita, who were still sleeping. The night before, Javy had had several long talks with Zita in Spanish, conversations that had left him serious. Deadly serious.

It was sometime after those talks, and before the sun was ready to come up, that he'd gotten out his hunting rifle.

There was also a shotgun standing upright in the corner, near the front door, and a handgun in a holster on his belt, along with a hunting knife. He also had another knife down in his boot, one he always carried there. The same one he'd flashed at the bar when Jesse Earl had come there, threatening her. Now she regretted not taking one of the guns Chris had laid out on their bed. It felt like everyone was armed but her—all the goddamn guns. The last time she'd held one, she'd stolen it from Sheriff Ross's collection. She'd been out in her car, with Chris's blood still drying on the seats all around her, when she'd aimed Ross's own gun at his heart through the windshield.

They'd stared at each other a long time before he'd gone his way, and she'd gone hers. Ross had died a few hours later anyway, but sometimes she couldn't help wondering how things would have been different if Chris had killed him that night, or she had.

She sipped her coffee and watched Javy cook. He had thick hands and wrists, but the practiced ease of a man who'd cooked for himself for a long time. There had been a Señora Cruz once, but Mel didn't know what had happened to her. Javy had a grown son who lived in Albuquerque who came to visit now and then, but no other family she knew of.

He lived out here alone, except for the hunters he guided. He'd started coming into Earlys to drink beer and read the paper after Chris got elected; sometimes he read the Hap and Leonard novels by Joe R. Lansdale, and other books by Michael McGarrity and Craig Johnson. When he was done with them he used to give them to her, and she kept them behind the bar to read in the slow times. They were still there, stacked up in neat rows like the whiskey tumblers, waiting for her.

She wondered if Javy would drink at the bar anymore if Chris lost the election.

She wondered if she would ever work at Earlys again.

JAVY BROUGHT OVER A PLATE for her and refilled her coffee, and then sat down to join her. He didn't have a plate of his own.

"You're not eating?" she asked, embarrassed by all the food in front of her. It was enough for a football team.

"No, I ate earlier."

She looked down at her plate . . . *earlier* would have

been hours ago, not long after midnight. It was still dark outside now.

He must have sat up most of the night, watching over them with his rifle.

"What did you and Zita talk about last night?"

Javy spun his mug in his hands, considered. "She is a bright girl. She told me stories. I listened."

She remembered Zita chattering away, still wearing Danny's hat. If the girl understood what was happening all around her, she didn't show it, but Mel wasn't so sure.

"That's not really an answer."

He smiled, weary, and then hid the remains of that smile behind his mug. "I know."

Mel wasn't hungry anymore, but she took a bite of the eggs and sausage anyway. She pulled apart one of the three tortillas he'd buttered and folded for her, still warm, and chewed that.

"So did you believe her, all her stories?"

Javy had dark eyes and his hair was all white, with a distinct widow's peak. He resembled Fox Uno. They shared the same weathered skin and deep-set eyes fenced off by age lines. He had the faded curves of a tattooed word on his neck, disappearing beneath his shirt, and in all the time she'd known him, she'd never gotten a good look at it or felt comfortable asking what it said. If he had other tattoos, she wasn't aware of them, and she had seen him in shirtsleeves that had revealed his bare arms, veined and muscled from years of hard work. He wore only one ring, a chipped blue stone, on his left hand. He put his mug down and patted her arm with that hand, a father reassuring his daughter. She couldn't remember her own daddy ever doing that, but it didn't make her feel any better now.

"It's going to be fine," he said, taking his mug of coffee and whiskey back up.

Again, another non-answer, but it was all the answer she needed.

The truth was there in his eyes, as dark as those of the trophies on the walls.

He had believed Zita, and that's why he'd stayed up guarding them.

It was why he was walking around his kitchen armed, and had turned his small house into a fortress.

He'd believed every goddamn word she'd said.

FIFTY-FOUR

When the Bronco pulled into the yard at first light, Johnnie yanked Eddy off the couch by his hair.

"Who the fuck is that?" Johnnie asked, dragging Eddy to the window. The others—Ringo, Roman, and the rest—were just awake but moving fast, too, each of them posting up on a window and the back door. All armed. It was early, real early, and it was taking Eddy's brain a moment to fire, like an old engine trying to turn over, and it didn't help that he'd been deep in the middle of a dream he couldn't remember now.

Eddy didn't recognize the truck.

"I said who the fuck is that?"

But Eddy did recognize the driver, when he got out of the Bronco.

"What the fuck is Danny Ford doing here?" Johnnie asked. There was near panic in his voice, like an electric current running through his skull. Eddy could feel it all the way down through the hands holding him up by the window.

"I got no idea. None."

"Johnnie, what do you want us to do?" Ortiz asked. He was the only one who didn't have his gun drawn. The others looked ready to shoot the deputy—Ringo looked in love with the idea—but not Ortiz.

Eddy watched Johnnie think, tiny wheels turning in his head—throwing sparks, generating more of that high-voltage current.

Johnnie's hands were still trembling.

He shook Eddy. "You get the fuck out there and stop him from coming into this trailer. If he finds out we're here, we kill him. Then you, and then that fuckin' whore of a girlfriend of yours. It's as simple as that, amigo."

"How the fuck am I supposed to do that?"

Johnnie shook him again. "I don't know, just do it." Then he pulled him close. "And if you even think about telling him we're here, Charity's gone, got it? First, I will have that big fucker Roman over there rape her. Then the fuckin' crazy Indians will take her down south, put her out to work for a few months, before they finally clip her. And it'll be *hard* work, Eddy, high and hard, if you get my fuckin' meaning."

"I get it. *I got it*. Jesus, let go of me." Eddy pulled away and Johnnie released him. "You keep your fucking animals quiet in here, and I'll take care of this."

Johnnie pointed a finger at him. "You better *be* Jesus and work a goddamn miracle."

Eddy ran his hands through his hair and tried to pull himself together, the thought of that almost making him laugh out loud.

Without another word, Eddy was out the door into the early-morning sunlight.

He nearly ran right into Danny Ford about ten feet from the trailer.

"Goddamn, Eddy, what's the rush?" Danny said, taking a step back.

"Fuck, you scared the hell out of me! I saw a truck I didn't know, and I figured . . . well, I figured all sorts of shitty things . . ."

Danny looked him up and down. "No one's come out here for you, have they? That Apache?"

Eddy shook his head. Since he had no idea why Danny had come out to the canyon, and had no idea what he might be fixing to say, he had to gauge just how much Johnnie and the rest of them could overhear. It took everything he had not to turn around and see if he could catch one of 'em staring out through the busted-up blinds at them.

Instead, he searched around for his cigarettes and lighter in his pockets and kept walking right on toward the Bronco, lighting up as he went, hoping he'd pull Danny in his wake.

He'd been smoking more cigarettes since he'd stopped smoking crank, and was pretty sure they'd kill him just as dead, just not as fast. Not that it mattered, 'cause it would be a miracle if he lived that long.

You better be *Jesus and work a goddamn miracle . . .*

Danny eyed the trailer . . . a good, long look . . . but followed Eddy. "Charity was worried about you."

Eddy blew smoke and leaned against the Bronco. He

hoped it was far enough away. "Well, fuck, you told me not to call her. Threatened me, truth be told. So, you know, I didn't."

Danny came up next to him. "You're right, I did. And I guess you didn't. You're learning."

"Besides, I'm outta minutes on my phone. You might guess that business has been slow since I got popped." What he didn't, couldn't, say was that Johnnie had taken his phone. He'd shoved it away in one of his packs, along with Eddy's spare truck keys, although Charity still had the truck with her.

No calls in or out.

No leaving.

"You look clean, Eddy. You don't look good, but at least you look clean."

Eddy took in Danny's own bloodshot eyes and unshaved face. It didn't look like he'd slept at all last night, maybe not for a couple of nights. "That makes two of us. You look the way I feel . . . like you tied one on last night. Must have been a helluva party."

Danny put his hands in his jeans, rocked back and forth. "What it looks like is somebody worked you over, Eddy. Somebody worked you over bad. You want to talk about it?"

Eddy laughed, nervous. Motioned toward his own face. "This? I got this falling over my junk in the trailer. Woke up to take a piss, next thing you know . . . blam, I'm facedown. At least if I had been high, even drunk, I wouldn't have felt that shit at all. Instead, it hurt like a motherfucker." He tried counting ashes blowing away from the end of his cigarette. "Everything hurts more when you're sober. Maybe that's why I tried so hard for so long not to be. Why'd you come out here, Deputy?"

"I was out this way. I'm going to be out of pocket for a couple of days, taking care of some business."

"Shit, ain't nobody ever out this way unless they're looking for something."

Shadows fought back against the rising sun, most of the canyon still successfully holding on to the dark. "Look, this is important, Eddy. Are you sure none of your friends came across the river? Maybe asked some questions about Deputy Reynosa or anyone else? Is there anything you want to tell me? I don't give a shit what you've done, or what you're doing now, I just need to know." He pointed at the trailer. "You want to let me have a look around in there?"

Eddy shrugged and shook his head, an exaggerated gesture. He hoped those fuckers in the trailer saw it. "You got a warrant this time? Damn, I ain't even slugged you with a frying pan yet." Eddy laughed, trying to pass it all off as a joke. Having first Johnnie show up, and now Danny—both of 'em asking about Deputy Reynosa—was some serious shit. Serious trouble. For Danny, for everyone.

Johnnie's vehicles were hidden around the back side of the trailer, down near the water, but if Danny took a walk around, he'd see them.

And if he walked *into* the trailer . . .

He thought about just rolling the dice and telling Danny everything—about Johnnie and his thugs hiding out in the trailer, about their bags of guns and the old man they were looking for—whatever it took to convince

Danny to just run like hell, the way Eddy used to run when he was under the lights, out on the track.

One foot in front of the other.

But would Danny go for it? Deputy Danny Ford didn't seem like the running type, not at all, and Eddy had never been that lucky.

How far could either of them get?

If Eddy said something now, he'd probably end up getting both of them killed, right where they stood, and then Charity, later.

He pulled hard on the cigarette.

Running in a circle, or worse, caught in a goddamn trap, like a real fucking rabbit.

"C'mon, Deputy, I'm clean here. *Tryin'* to stay straight, not causin' any problems. But if you really want to mess around inside that shithole, go right ahead." He held his breath, swallowing smoke. It was bitter, went down hard. It hurt.

Danny looked back and forth between Eddy and the trailer. Time seemed to stretch on and on . . . the decision hanging in the air. Eddy could almost see it, as clear as the yellow tape he'd found around his trailer, until the phone on Danny's hip suddenly buzzed, an incoming text message. He read it twice and then closed his eyes, shaking his head in obvious irritation. It was some kind of bad news—urgent—and it had distracted the deputy just long enough.

Danny turned his back on the trailer, and Eddy finally let out his breath.

"Okay, okay, I'm not going to fuck with you, Eddy. I didn't come out here to do that." Danny went around and opened the driver's-side door, rummaging around inside. That gave Eddy a chance to get a look at the camper shell on the back of it, where he could see what appeared to be several new, decent-sized holes drilled in the shell, at different heights, covered over with black electrician's tape. Standing back at a distance, the taped-up holes would pretty much fade into the smoked-black plastic of the camper shell, but up close, they were damn visible, and ugly. It seemed like a dumb thing to do to a nice truck, and he was about to say something about it, when Danny turned back to him.

He had a crumpled-up envelope in his hand and was counting some bills out of it.

"Here's a couple hundred bucks. Get your goddamn phone juiced up. Today. Maybe give Charity a call to tell her you're not dead out here. Probably still not a good idea to see her, but one call wouldn't hurt, I guess. And if you see or hear anything, anything at all, you call me next. Got it? I mean that."

Eddy took the money and shoved it into his pocket. With his back to the trailer and the door of the truck in the way, he didn't think anyone inside saw the exchange. "Got it." Then he motioned low to Danny's phone, "Something bad's happening, isn't it?"

"Yeah, I'm afraid so." Danny looked down at the envelope in his hands, which still had plenty of green inside it. "When I was in Afghanistan, I always used to think the calmest days were the ones right before everything went to hell. You always paid for that little bit of peace, no matter what." He handed the rest of the envelope over to Eddy. "Fuck it, take it all."

Eddy did. "She never called you, did she? Charity, I mean. You tried to call me, couldn't get ahold of me, and came out here on your own."

Danny ignored most of what Eddy had said. "You still got my number?"

Eddy searched back . . . remembering the egg carton.

"Yeah, I got it."

"Good, then use it."

Danny got in the truck and turned the engine over, but the driver's-side window was rolled down, and he talked to Eddy through it. The cool, rushing air of the open window had probably done wonders for Danny's hangover, an old trick Eddy knew well. "It's been a couple of nice, calm days. It's getting cooler, with autumn here. I like it. I'm glad to see you're doing okay, Eddy, holding it together. Let's keep it that way, okay? No, Charity didn't call, but I'm sure she wanted to." Danny fidgeted with the keys. "You're going to be all right."

"Yeah," Eddy said, as he turned to walk slowly back to the trailer. "Then how come I feel like such shit?"

JOHNNIE WAS ON HIM the minute he crossed the door.

He punched Eddy in the shoulder, knocking him off his feet. The others were circled all around, except for Ringo. That snakeskin-wearing motherfucker was still up by the window, his black long gun just below the sill, pointed at the floor, his finger on the trigger.

"I think he's gone, Johnnie," Ringo was saying, but he didn't leave the window, and the gun didn't move.

Not an inch.

"What did he want?" Johnnie asked Eddy, his boot hovering to deliver a kick. It looked enormous from the floor.

"Nothin', goddammit, it was a bunch of nothin'."

"Not good enough, amigo. Not even close." The boot swung in, catching Eddy hard in the gut, and cocked back again.

"Goddamn, he wanted to know if I'd seen Charity. He wanted to make sure I hadn't been tryin' to talk to her or nothin'. He was just doing his Dudley Do-Right shit."

"That didn't look like a deputy visit. Hell, that didn't even look oh-ficial. That wasn't his Big Bend truck," Roman said, leaning back against the wall with his arms crossed. He was looking steadily at both Johnnie and Eddy, his eyes flat as river sand. They refused to reflect what little morning light there was creeping in through the blinds.

"What the fuck do you want me to say? I don't plan his work schedule. That's what he came out for, and—" Eddy stopped, sudden, wiping his mouth although it was bone-dry. It was like he'd swallowed a mouthful of that sand. He gave the pause a few extra heartbeats, selling it, but he didn't have to sell it that hard.

"And *what*, dumb shit?" Johnnie asked, crouching down on his boot heels. He'd produced a handgun from somewhere, and it was resting now against Eddy's temple. It was cool, like one of Charity's fingers, against his skin.

"It was . . . bullshit, you know? He caught me off guard, showin' up like he did, but I didn't say nothin'. I played it cool."

"Spit it out," Johnnie pushed, and the gun's barrel pushed, too.

Eddy tried to give him *that* look . . . a look that said . . . *are you sure you want me to say it all out loud? In front of everyone?*

It was a look that also said: *I tried to save you . . . amigo.*

By then, Johnnie had figured it out—it was right there in his eyes, a sudden realization, and a shadow of fear—but it was also too late. He couldn't stop Eddy now, even if he wanted to, not after the little show he'd put on in front of the rest of them.

Not with them watching, waiting.

Johnnie's eyes went wide, wider, that shadow in them lengthening.

Eddy smiled, a bare flicker. A match in a darkness of his own.

Got you, amigo. Got you, you motherfucker.

We're both caught in this trap now.

"He asked me about *you*, Johnnie. Wanted to know if I'd seen you, if you'd been around town. He used both your names: Johnnie, and that other one you go by, Apache. I guess he knows all about you now, and he's lookin' for you."

And then the room erupted.

THERE WAS PLENTY OF YELLING, enough that they pretty much forgot Eddy, who pulled himself off the floor and let it play out.

Ortiz was ready to pack up and leave, right then and

404 ‖ J. TODD SCOTT

there, as was the big fucker, Roman. The other two, Ringo and Chavez, were not as sure. Johnnie kept telling them he had no idea why Deputy Ford would be asking about him, no fuckin' idea at all. And it didn't matter anyway. They didn't have a choice. They had to see this thing through, no matter what.

It sounded to Eddy like Johnnie had been caught in a trap of his own long before he ever walked into Eddy's trailer, and he'd pulled the others right along in with him.

Ortiz said out loud what Eddy knew the others were thinking—*He's just looking for Johnnie, not us. No one knows about us. It's not too late.*

For a moment, Eddy thought Roman might shoot Johnnie right then and there, but Johnnie kept at it, working his side of the story. He sounded like a desperate man pleading for his life, which maybe he was.

"Besides," he finally said, "I got the message this morning, right before that prick Ford was pulling up. We're moving today. It's a go. Today, and then we're done."

Then we're going home.

Eventually they all got calmed down, but the damage had been done. The air was electric, like lightning had gone off inside the trailer. They were all on edge, jumpy, as they checked their packs and their gear. They kept throwing glances at each other, some silent language between them, all behind Johnnie's back.

Maybe Johnnie couldn't see those looks, but he could definitely feel them.

Eddy could.

They probably felt like spiders crawling all over him.

JOHNNIE SIDLED BACK OVER TO EDDY and leaned in close. There was sweat beaded on his forehead, and he stank. "And you're going, too, motherfucker. I may need your help, and I sure can't leave you here alone, now can I?"

"Yeah, yeah, whatever you say," Eddy said. He'd taken his best shot at Johnnie, and maybe, just maybe, he'd bought Danny, and even Deputy Reynosa, some time. Maybe he'd saved Charity, too, for a while longer.

And the day wasn't over yet. Hell, it was just getting started.

Eddy wasn't going to make it all the way to sundown, not in the company of these murderers, but then again, his old amigo Johnnie might not either.

Fair enough.

He pushed Johnnie away, almost daring him to take another swing at him, but Johnnie didn't. He let him go.

There was that feeling of lightning in the trailer again, and it made the hair on Eddy's arms stand up.

Eddy strolled into the kitchenette, not a goddamn care in the world. He was feeling good, loose. He looked over to the others, any of them, except for Johnnie.

"I can't do shit on an empty fuckin' stomach, so I'm gonna make some eggs . . . Any of you sons of bitches want any?"

FIFTY-FIVE

Marco Lucero was almost asleep . . . *again*.

It was the slow-rising heat, the relentless eastern morning sun against the windshield, and the boredom.

That, and the fact he was plain tired. He'd been sitting out here alone since he got a surprise wake-up call from the sheriff at three-thirty a.m.

Marco didn't mean for it to keep happening, but his eyes kept getting heavy. Heavier. There was just *nothing* out here near the Far Six.

He hadn't seen a single living thing move in more than an hour.

Nothing at all, after the coyotes . . .

THERE'D BEEN FIVE OF THEM, moving fast to stay ahead of the retreating night.

After they'd slipped by, he tried to do some Googling on his phone about them—anything to pass the time and stay awake—learning that it was unusual to see coyotes in packs, unless they were hunting a deer or some other big animal. He couldn't imagine what was big enough to hunt out here other than a deer, except for maybe a bored deputy, sitting alone in a crappy truck.

But he hadn't felt any fear watching them, all sleek fur, in tans and grays and whites. Alive, and almost within reach, as they swept around the truck. There was something fast and feral and low to the ground about them, and they'd moved away so silently. They were gone as fast as they'd appeared, except for one—the largest, with a clear white flash along its spine. It had stopped just beyond the truck's hood to look back at him, and where he expected to see orbs as dark as the shadows they were chasing, its eyes had been bright, startling yellow.

Curious.

Those eyes had asked the same question Marco was asking himself: *What the hell are you doing here?*

It had watched him watching it back, before disappearing into a patch of creosote.

SINCE THE COYOTES, time had crawled by increasingly hot and empty, with Marco cooped up in a truck Till Greer had seized from Walter Denbrow, after the old bastard had gotten two DWIs and refused to pay three years' worth of speeding tickets. It had been sitting in the department impound for about six months, and it *still* smelled of Denbrow's cheap cigars and something rotten, like an animal had died inside it. Other than getting out to take a piss against an ocotillo, Marco had been constantly wrapped in that stink, and he was afraid even a good, long shower wouldn't wash it off.

Murfee was safer for not having Walter Denbrow on the road, but he was slowly killing Marco Lucero.

Marco already knew he hadn't brought enough water—his throat as thick and dusty as the tires on the old truck—and he would have gladly killed for an icy glass of lemonade or a sweet tea. He had tucked the old truck up in an arroyo, within sight of the gravel drive that led back to the Far Six, and the sheriff had told him to be on the lookout for *something*, *anyone*, approaching the ranch, possibly that stranger from Earlys—which made him want one of those Cokes that Vianey always poured for him—but with each passing minute, it was only getting harder to concentrate, to stay away awake.

He was starting to think he wasn't cut out for this deputy business after all.

His eyes were just starting to slip . . . *again* . . . when a truck roared up behind him.

MARCO WAS RELIEVED TO FIND OUT that it was only Danny in his Bronco.

Marco had finally broken down and texted the other deputy earlier, wanting some answers, some clarity. He trusted Danny, but the truth was, no one was being clear about what was going on. He knew it somehow involved America, and the old man and girl who'd been staying with her, and Marco figured the sheriff wasn't saying much to protect them in some way. But it sure didn't make his role any easier or make him feel any better about it.

Neither did nodding off, when you were supposed to be the lookout.

Danny slowed way down to get a look at him, and when he rolled down his window, Marco could tell he was visibly relieved, too. Marco had assumed that if Danny showed up, it would be in his department truck. But, then again, Marco wasn't in his duty truck, either—the sheriff had insisted he get Denbrow's—and that had caught Danny by surprise.

He wasn't the least bit angry that he'd almost caught Marco napping. Instead, Danny appeared glad he hadn't needed the gun they both knew was aimed at Marco just beneath Danny's open window.

"JESUS," DANNY SAID. "You really are here."

Marco tried to keep the shakes out of his voice. Danny hadn't said it out loud, but he might as well have: *I almost shot you.*

"I texted you that I got a call from the sheriff last night, asking me to hightail it out here and set up where I could see the access road back to the Far Six."

"Goddamn," Danny said, shaking his head. "He shouldn't have gotten you into this."

Given the look on Danny's face, Marco was starting to agree. "I don't even know what 'this' is. He told me not to do anything, just call if I saw a car or something out here. He made me promise that. I think he has Till and Dale doing drive-bys on America's apartment, too." Knowing how much time Danny spent there, he almost said "your" apartment, but checked himself.

"Okay, okay," Danny said. "It's all right." But Marco could see again all over Danny's face that it wasn't all

right—not at all—and that Danny wanted to tell Marco
to go home, to get as far away as possible from whatever
the hell was about to happen at the ranch. Instead, he
seemed resigned to the fact that the damage was already
done, or that having Marco posted out here wasn't such
a bad idea after all . . .

He clearly wasn't happy about it, though.

"Listen carefully, Marco. No matter what happens, no
matter what you think you hear, do not drive back up to
the house. If another car you don't know approaches you,
you head back to Murfee, double-time. Find Till and
Dale and the rest of them and wait to hear from me or the
sheriff. Got it?"

Marco nodded, now more worried than if he had
never texted Danny at all. He stared into the morning
glare burning on Denbrow's windshield, but it didn't
shine any light on what was really going on.

"Do you have your gun?" Danny asked.

"Yes, of course."

"Good, don't plan on using it."

"What's happening?" Marco asked. "Is America okay?
Does this have to do with that guy in the bar? Just tell
me something, *please*." He was already convinced Danny
would lie to him, and he did, easily:

"Everything's fine, it's probably nothing." But his
eyes—as bright as that coyote's eyes—couldn't help reflecting the truth anyway, just as they had when Danny had
first pulled up next to him and rolled down his window.

Do you have your gun?

Just two deputies in unmarked vehicles on a lonely
stretch of road with their guns drawn.

Things were far from fine. And if both the sheriff and Danny had decided they needed Marco's help, things were a hell of a lot worse than that.

Danny smiled at him anyway, and with a wink told him again it was all going to be okay, as long as Marco tried a little harder to stay awake.

FIFTY-SIX

W *aiting* . . .
  Chris tried writing, but the words wouldn't
come.

He'd lost the thread of the story—the one he'd been
working on in the months leading up to the debate. Words
he'd already written were strange to him now, unfamiliar,
as if they were put down by someone else's hand. He
didn't know these characters anymore, had no idea what
they'd say or what they'd do. He couldn't remember the
original ending he'd been working toward, or how to find
his way there again.

It happened sometimes. Writing was trying to catch
sunlight and shadows in your hands, grabbing hold of
fleeting thoughts and impressions. If you were successful,
each story became a time capsule, a snapshot of your life
right as you put down the words. The problem was, Chris
didn't want any kind of photo of these last few days.

He hoped he wasn't going to have to spend the rest of
his life reliving them.

HE'D PLACED SILENT LOOKOUTS at the Presidio–
Ojinaga bridge and the other Customs and Border Patrol

checkpoints throughout the Big Bend. He'd made a call to Elgin Bartlett, the old CBP dog handler friend of Ben Harper's, who'd since been promoted. He didn't know exactly what Elgin might look for, but at least he gave him the identifiers for America's parents, so if they legally came through one of the points of entry, he'd be alerted.

And as much as he didn't want to expose anyone else in the department to what they were doing out here, he'd had Till Greer and Dale Holt doing regular drive-bys of Amé's garage apartment since last night. They were working from Marco Lucero's rough description of the leather-jacketed man who'd been asking questions about Amé at Earlys, and Marco himself was parked in the shadows of the tiny bridge over the wash at Ranch Road 19, giving him a long eye on the gravel turnoff that eventually led back to the Far Six. Nothing could come down that stretch without Marco seeing it.

Chris had done everything he could think of.

But all his efforts hadn't yielded much. Only Marco texting him to say he'd seen a pack of coyotes—the four-legged kind—crossing 19, skulking over the road and into the scrub on the other side. The young deputy had been surprised, amazed, how the animals had suddenly appeared, and then slid fearlessly past his truck into the dry creek run.

Close enough to touch, and he'd never even heard them.

Marco had grown up in Murfee, but had probably never spent much time way out here. Few people did.

All this beauty, all this raw wildness, sometimes came with a steep price all its own.

Marco's coyotes were a good reminder that even in all this apparent emptiness, you were never truly alone. It was just too damn easy to find trouble you weren't even looking for.

CHRIS PUT THE PEN and yellow legal pad away, grabbed his A5 and the Remington from where they lay in a patch of sunlight on the kitchen counter, and got up to make another endless, useless circle around the house.

FIFTY-SEVEN

D anny arrived at the ranch and immediately disappeared into a bathroom, and when he came back out, he was in his desert camo fatigues.

America had seen them before, hanging up in Danny's closet at his place. He'd brought several pairs of them back from Afghanistan, but he'd never worn them, until now.

He was carrying his department-issued AR-15, but slung over his shoulder was another long gun that America didn't recognize. It must have been what he'd brought into the sheriff's house wrapped in the Dallas Cowboys blanket.

At his feet were two backpacks.

He had his Colt in his holster, too, and she could pick out the bulk of his deputy's body armor beneath the fatigues. Her vest was still leaning against the wall by the front door.

He had magazine pouches across his chest and more on his tactical rig.

Yesterday, he'd refused to drive his department truck or wear his deputy's uniform, and he'd given his Bullhide hat over to Zita. Now, standing in his old fatigues, he'd truly abandoned all pretense of being a sheriff's deputy.

She'd helped make Danny a soldier again.

FIFTY-EIGHT

C hris walked into the kitchen from out back to find both Danny and Amé standing there, and stopped short. He'd run over a dozen things he wanted to say to Danny when he returned, but now seeing his deputy for the first time in his old combat BDUs, armed with a rifle he didn't recognize, he didn't know where to start.

He just said, "Danny, no . . ." and Danny finished for him anyway.

"I'm sorry I've been gone, but I needed to take care of a few things."

Danny moved over to the kitchen window, still talking so Chris wouldn't have to. "Look, I've been thinking about this since yesterday. We've generally got good sight lines from the house windows, but we'll be trapped in here if things go bad, and we have way too many blind spots. With only three of us, we can't cover them all, not if we're trying to keep an eye on Fox Uno, too. Plus, someone's got to expose themselves when Gualterio's men approach, unless you plan on inviting them in for a cup of coffee. I'm going to take up a position outside, out front. I'll have a clear view up the main drive, and most of the west side of the house if they try to flank us. I'll already be burrowed in before they arrive. Just like our cover and contact scenarios . . . you two are contact, I'm the cover."

"Danny, you can't sit out there all day," Chris said.

"I'll sit there long as I have to, just like you're having Marco sit out there right now and play spotter in that old truck." Danny's voice was tight, angry. "You didn't have to do that."

Chris knew Danny didn't like Marco's involvement any more than he did. "Amé got the call early this morning. Too early. It was a surprise. I thought we had another twenty-four hours, at least. I wouldn't give them our location, but they're pressing. Told them we wouldn't do this meet until after daybreak. I had to do something. When they do arrive, they'll have to take that long approach up to the house. That's the only way in or out. And you're right, we will need as much heads-up as possible. That's why Marco's out here. He was also the only one who got a true look at the man in Earlys, if it comes to that."

"You can still send him home, get him clear of all this. I'm here now."

Chris knew he could . . . *should*. God knows, he didn't want to hang any more memorial pictures outside his office. But he also knew it was better for all of them to have Marco sitting right where he was, just like it was better to have someone set up right outside the house, as Danny was now arguing for.

If Gualterio's men did try to ambush them, they could find themselves trapped, pinned down, unable to shoot their way out. The walls would provide some cover, but not enough, not for long. Not if they had to hold out for a while, or if things went from bad to worse.

Duane Dupree's home had burned down around him.

"Marco stays, Danny. At least out there on the road, he'll be clear of whatever happens here. But I can't ask you to do this."

"And you can't order me not to, not now. I've trained for this. *I know this.*"

"That's what I'm afraid of." That's why you really accompanied Amé out here yesterday. You wanted to size up our situation, make a plan. Chris motioned at the rifle he didn't recognize. "Do I want to know where you got that?"

"No, probably not. I'm sorry, I wouldn't tell you anyway."

Chris stared out the kitchen windows, past the scrub, into the sunlight, where he'd been walking a few moments before. Last night he'd stared into the darkness out there and asked Amé if Fox Uno had changed them, and now, facing Danny in his BDUs, facing the decisions he'd made and what they were all about to do, he had his answer. "Okay, we do it your way," he said.

Danny pointed at a bag at his feet. "I also brought our handheld radios and earpieces back from the department, and plenty of extra batteries. The range isn't worth shit, so I didn't even bother giving one to Marco, but up here at the house, we can use them." Danny lifted the bag. "I'm going to go get set up, then we'll test them. You may not have told these men where we are, but they're going to figure it out soon enough."

Chris looked through the windows again. "I figure they're on their way now."

Danny shrugged. "They're probably *already* here. Somewhere close, watching, waiting."

"*¿Por qué?*" Amé asked, the only thing she'd said during the whole conversation.

"They're getting ready. Just like we are," Danny said. And before Chris could say anything, one of Fox Uno's phones started to ring.

FIFTY-NINE

F ox Uno did not know how many people he had
killed with his own hands, or had ordered killed by
the hands of others.

The ways he had conducted these killings were as numerous as the victims themselves: burnings and shoot-
ings and beheadings. He had once planned to take down
a commercial plane with a suspected informant, like the
'89 Avianca bombing in Colombia, but the man he had
hired to prepare the explosives blew himself up in a motel
in Sabinas, killing four others, including two small children sleeping in the room next door.

Fox Uno had paid the families, trying to make things
right. He had always tried to make things right . . . after.

He had even killed a pregnant woman. He strangled
her in a bathtub of cool water in front of her husband,
and what he remembered most was how the woman had
not tried to struggle at all. Instead, she gave herself over
to him, gently. She was at peace. She did not scream or
beg for her life or the life of her unborn child, and she
did not tell her husband to tell Fox Uno what he wanted
to know—the names of two men who had arranged for
the checkpoint outside Saucillo that had claimed Fox
Uno's woman.

She did none of those things, floating in the water with one hand pressed against Fox Uno's heart.

Instead, she said a small prayer, and whispered: *Estamos listos.* We are ready.

And . . .

Oro por su alma. I pray for your soul.

The woman closed her eyes and died praying for him.

As she lay there, he had Gualterio and another man named Miguel Ángel cut the child out of her belly, turning all the water red, and rushed the baby to the nearest hospital. The *niña pequeña* survived, barely, and Fox Uno then paid for new church and hospital records, listing his woman who had been killed in Saucillo as the birth mother. She had been a beauty pageant winner, one of the many women he had bedded and discarded. He ordered all who knew of it to say that it was *she* who had given birth to the baby, and that the child was Fox Uno's.

The dead woman in Saucillo could say no different.

He had the real mother's body burned, along with her husband's, and their ashes and few remaining bones were buried beneath the pavement of a used-car lot.

Eventually, he had the doctors and a Catholic priest who might know the truth killed, as well as others who could have whispered otherwise, including Miguel Ángel.

Even Martino did not know the truth of it. He believed, as did most of Nemesio, that the girl—Zita—was his true half sister.

Su sangre.

Fox Uno had chosen the name Zita because it meant "Little Hope." She had been so small and bloody in his hands, drawing her first breath, struggling to live.

He could not remember the face of Zita's mother anymore, and he never knew her name, but he would always remember her praying for him.

Her hand on his chest, over his heart.

I pray for your soul.

Yo estoy de Muerte . . .

He had watched the one they called Danny walk into the house with all his *pistolas*.

Fox Uno recognized him as a killer, too, born out of one of the *americanos'* many wars. Like Fox Uno, he probably no longer remembered how many men had died by his hand—women and children as well, since that was the way of war. Even this *guerra contra las drogas*, as the *americanos* liked to call it. The sheriff was a man who might kill, but he took no joy in it. But this Danny was no different from the legions of *sicarios* who had murdered on Fox Uno's orders—killing came easy to him, and he was just as dangerous as those that might now be on their way to them.

Coming, a second time, for him.

The ambush had failed at San Carlos, but those who had planned it would plan another, and then another. Was this their next chance, here at this distant *americano* ranch?

If it was, it did not matter that he was in Los Estados Unidos—this country of so many laws—or at the home of an *oficial de policía*.

It would not have mattered to him.

He did not know if Gualterio or Martino—or both—

had betrayed him, but whoever it was would send as many men as it took to kill him and Zita and anyone else in their way.

Men like the one called Danny, or worse.

He watched Sheriff Cherry and America and Danny make their preparations and plans.

He watched them hesitate when his phone started to ring again. They still did not trust the voice on the other end, and neither did he.

Not after all these years, and all the things he himself had done.

He admired them, though, and like Zita's mother had once done for him, he prayed for them.

Even if he did not believe it would do any good.

SIXTY

A mé answered it, listened, and then looked at both Chris and Danny.

"It is time," she said.

"I guess it is," Chris said. He hadn't heard from Bartlett at CBP; he hadn't heard anything from Till or Dale. He'd wanted to do this during the day, but in so many ways they were still stumbling around in the dark.

"Ask how many," he said, "and put it on speaker. I want to hear it, too."

He looked over at Fox Uno, who had joined them. "And you, too, in case you recognize anyone."

Amé switched on the speaker, and a sudden voice—scratchy and distant on the other end—started talking in rapid Spanish. It sounded like more than one person, but Chris could still generally follow the conversation. Amé held up three fingers for Danny, confirming what Chris imagined he'd heard.

"Two people, plus her mother," Chris said for Danny's benefit.

"What are they driving?" Danny asked. "How will we know them?"

After Amé translated Danny's question, there was a long silence from the mysterious caller. When someone finally spoke, he sounded different from the first. Older, maybe. He didn't say much, but this time he was perfectly clear.

"No importa."

And . . .

"Voy a llevar una camisa roja." I will be wearing a red shirt.

The voice, firmer now: *"Ven a nosotros."* Come to us.

Chris had talked with Joe Garrison more than once about how the DEA ran their undercover deals, with Garrison explaining the main concern was always control: controlling the situation, controlling the deal. That was how you best protected the undercover agent. Garrison made it clear they always set up cover teams and *never* let the bad guys dictate the time and place of a meet, which was a lesson Chris had taken to heart, and why he'd moved them all out to the Far Six in the first place. Now this voice—a voice who claimed he'd be wearing a *camisa roja*, a red shirt, when they finally did meet—wanted to change the plan again, just as he'd tried to change it with the surprise call late last night, moving the times all around. Now he was demanding America and Fox Uno come to him, but that wasn't going to happen.

It was never going to happen.

"Is that Gualterio?" Chris asked Amé, but it was Fox Uno who shook his head. "I do not know that man," he said.

"No, se llega a nosotros," Chris said, taking the phone from Amé before she had a chance to say anything else. He stumbled a bit with the translation, searching for the words, but he thought he had it right.

He kept it on speaker, repeating himself. Slower, louder. "No, you will come to the place we tell you." He wanted the voice in the red shirt to understand that if he didn't come to them, there'd be no meeting at all.

Fox Uno spoke, too. There was fury in his voice, an angry command. He shouted over Chris, and when he spoke fast, loud, it was too much for Chris to follow, but still clear enough—something to the effect of "Stop fucking around."

He *thundered*. This was the Fox Uno from Garrison's folder, and Chris knew that voice—it was Sheriff Ross giving a goddamn order.

Fox Uno finished by telling the voice to do exactly what he was told, and Chris understood that completely.

There was a long, long silence, before the voice spoke again. *"De acuerdo, ¿dónde está?"* Where are you?

It seemed that negotiations were over. Chris looked over at Danny and Amé, and then at Fox Uno. He stared down at the phone in his hand.

One way or another, it was time.

IF YOU DIDN'T KNOW THE BIG BEND, there was no easy way to describe how to get out to the Far Six. Not all the roads were marked, some of them changed names depending on if you were traveling east or west, and the gravel strip that ran back to the house from the 19 didn't have a name at all.

Chris had once tried to find his house on Google Maps, only to discover it was completely lost within digitized blocks of green and tan.

It was like it didn't exist at all.

You could find it with grid coordinates, and maybe orient yourself and make sense out of the paths cut through the scrub from the air. You might find it on a southbound flyover, or pick out some of the decaying fencing of the old cattle ranch this used to be. Damn hard, but not impossible. Duane Dupree had known this land like the back of his own bloody hand and drove Chris out here in the dark of night to watch him die, without any problem at all.

Chris took the phone off speaker and handed it back to Amé. Despite the Spanish he'd been studying, he'd never be able to guide someone out to the Far Six.

"Tell him what he needs to know," he said to Amé. "I want to finish this."

But Chris had a gut instinct that the voice on the phone would find them without any trouble at all.

SIXTY-ONE

After the call, America followed Danny out to the porch, pulling him back by the arm.

"I do not want you to do this. You do not have to do this. Please listen to me . . ."

He looked down at her arm, holding him back. "You know, it's weird. I haven't been sleeping well, not for days. But not because of this, not about Fox Uno. It's been all these bad dreams about my time in Afghanistan. They just started up, out of nowhere. They've been getting worse. I don't know why. Why now?"

"I don't know," she said.

"Mostly about this place called Rumnar, a tiny village. We were ordered to conduct a search-and-clear mission there, only one day after one of the guys in our unit stepped on an IED. Blew himself all to pieces. It's not like that had never happened before, or never happened after, but that *one* day . . . sometimes it only takes one day, right? Anyway, we were convinced that someone in Rumnar had planted that device. We finally had someone to blame, or thought we did. It was a bad time, a bad place, and the only thing that mattered was making sure that the man next to you got out alive."

"Danny . . ."

He smiled at her, sad. "When this is all over, I think I need to talk to someone about what happened there. About my dreams."

"That's good. We can do that together."

His smile broadened, almost real. "Sounds like a date. I've really been meaning to ask you out, you know, officially." He looked past her, back through the open door of the house, the smile now faded, gone. "I hope this all goes fine, and this guy with the red shirt shows up with your mother and Fox Uno gets whatever the hell it is that he wants, and he walks out of your life and the Big Bend forever. But if it doesn't go that way, then you want me doing exactly what I'm doing right now. Because if I don't, you and the sheriff will die. I wouldn't let that happen over there, I'm not going to let it happen here."

She searched his face for some different answer. He understood her far better than he even knew, and although there was more she could say, more she wanted to say, there was nothing that would ever change his mind.

They stood silent together, the air around them hot and still, like the entire world was holding its breath. It drew them together like gravity. Clouds bunched around the distant mountains, cool shadows that might never reach them, because on a day darkened by threats, rain wasn't one of them.

He put down his guns and his bags, but not before reaching into one and pulling out her silver gun, the one Fox Uno had sent to her. She didn't want to take it, touch it, but he pulled her to him, *into him*, and slipped the gun into the back of her jeans.

He understood her far better than he even knew.

"You forgot this. I brought it for you, thought you might want it one last time. No matter what happens, this all ends here."

She let him hold her . . . and held him back, just as she had in the dark outside her apartment, when he first said to her: *I'm going to do whatever you want me to, whatever I have to do, so you're never hurt again. I thought you knew that. Goddammit, I'll do anything. I'll go all the way to the end of the world.*

This time was different, though, in every way that it could be.

She tried to ignore the weight of the gun at her back, lost beneath a huge blue sky that went on forever and ever.

To the end of the world.

"I—" she started, but just like he had with the sheriff, he finished for her.

"I know," he said. And then he kissed her.

It was quick, fleeting. She wasn't expecting it, and maybe Danny wasn't, either. He looked surprised, and when she waited for him to do it again . . . when she *wanted* him to do it again . . . he didn't.

He picked up his guns instead.

"I'll see you later," he said. "Don't forget our date."

Then he walked off the porch and into the desert.

PART FOUR

BAJADORES

T he problem between Johnnie and Danny Ford had started eight months before, not too long after Danny had been hired on by the Big Bend Sheriff's Department. Johnnie didn't know anything then about Danny's time with Texas DPS—how he'd been some hot-shit undercover detective for them—or about his years in the army. To Johnnie, he was just another wet-behind-the-ears cowpoke deputy, and fuckers like that were a dime a dozen.

More brawn than brains, and other than the Tejas unit, the sort of guy Johnnie had pushed around for years.

It happened during Operation Violent Tide, a U.S. Marshals nationwide operation. The marshals staged the big fugitive sweep every year, spending a solid week rounding up pervos and murderers and arsonists and other fine upstanding citizens. They always asked for local support, so it had become a lucrative gig for Johnnie and his crew, who spread out around Terrell County and for a small fee let some of the likely targets know that shit was rolling downhill and they needed to get out of its way (and out of town) for a while. They didn't extend the early-warning courtesy to everyone, only those who had the means to buy their way out of the misery. In fact, Johnnie needed some of those guys out and walking around, because they made good snitches and fences for the dope he ripped off. But his boys had always made a fine show of it anyway, busting doors and heads for a few days with the federal government's blessing. It always got them in the paper—trophy pictures—and his daddy liked that.

This year's Violent Tide preoperation briefing was at a Texas Army National Guard armory up in Crockett, and that's where Johnnie ran into Danny Ford. Part of the briefing was given by a young female U.S. marshal, a pretty thing who in the right light reminded Johnnie of Rae, and he made some jokes about that very fact with the other members of the Tejas unit who were there with him—Ortiz and Ringo. Danny, who was sitting behind them, heard it all, and took exception, and said as much in the parking lot afterward as the briefing was breaking up.

At first, Johnnie figured the guy was just fucking with him and was about ready to crack a few jokes of his own about that fine bitch. But it was soon clear Deputy Danny Ford saw himself as some sort of Boy Scout, a real knight in shining armor, and he was definitely most serious about the issue, leaving Johnnie no choice but to laugh it off and tell him—loudly and right to his face—to go fuck himself. He didn't need the opinions or approval of some shit-heel deputy out of the Big Bend.

That might have been the end of it, but Ringo somehow *did* know who Danny Ford was, or at least some of his history. Danny had done all that undercover with DPS on those skinhead gangs popping up all over Texas—real shaved-head, cross-burning, red-bootlace stuff—and Ringo made a crack that Danny's true beef was that he didn't like Mex-ee-cans talking about white women. Specifically, he didn't like Mexicans fucking white women. Ringo said it was a goddamn racial thing . . . racial profiling . . . and then laughed and pushed Danny out of their way.

If he'd only kept his goddamn hands to himself.

Things went downhill fast from there, fast enough that Ringo was on his back before anyone could stop it. Danny did some sort of ninja army stuff, and then Ringo was looking straight up at him from the dirty pavement, breathing hard, blinking furiously. Ortiz, that goddamn pussy, took one big step away, not wanting to be a part of any of it, and Johnnie did the only thing he could think of in the moment . . .

He drew his goddamn gun and pointed it at Deputy Danny Ford.

It wasn't the first time Johnnie had aimed a gun at another cop (and honestly, he knew even then, it probably wouldn't be the last), but never in a public parking lot with dozens of other cops—federal and state—making their way to their cars. He wasn't back in Terrell, and he wasn't inside El Diablo Norte or some other shitty bar. Instead, he was standing across the street from a goddamn library, where Johnnie could see himself reflected in the big mirrored windows that ran along the front of it. All he could think of was a dozen people in there with cell phones, open books forgotten in front of them, filming it all. Filming him. It was ridiculous, and he knew how weak he looked, how weak Danny Ford had made him look—scared, drawing down on shadows. Danny knew Johnnie wasn't going to shoot him right then and there, so he stared down the barrel, not blinking at all, daring Johnnie to do it anyway.

He told Johnnie the next time he pulled a goddamn gun on him, he'd better be prepared to pull the fucking trigger.

Then he let Ringo get up and walked past Ortiz and away.

They stood there for a few moments after, Ortiz calming Ringo down and Johnnie half expecting someone to run over or shout, but no one did. And just like that, it was over.

All over a goddamn girl none of them knew.

Johnnie hadn't planned on crossing paths with Deputy Ford again, until Danny pulled up outside Eddy Rabbit's trailer.

"A RANCH CALLED THE FAR SIX. Do you know it?" Johnnie asked Eddy.

"Yeah, I know it."

"Can you get us there?"

Eddy scratched at his dirty scalp, like he was thinking hard, but he was just delaying.

They were all standing in tall grass around their two vehicles, on an unmarked access road, nothing more than an old cattle trail. Johnnie had made them mount up and hightail it from Eddy's trailer right after Ford left, just in case he came back (and this time with help), so they'd driven around for an hour and found this place, and had been sitting here for another couple of hours, until he finally got the last call.

The Far Six.

The *indios* told him they needed to get to a ranch called the Far Six. That's where the old man was. But like everything else in this damn county, it wasn't easily found on some map. It was here, somewhere.

Ringo was leaning against the Suburban, smoking, whispering with the others. Roman was eye-fucking him, and Ortiz looked like he wanted to shit himself. Only Chavez appeared calm . . . weirdly calm. Ringo had been as put out over seeing Danny Ford as Johnnie had been, and he'd almost shot him through the fucking trailer window just on principle. His pride hadn't recovered from getting tossed on his ass in that parking lot.

What the fuck was going on around here? What had he gotten them into?

He chewed his matchstick and watched the sky. It was no different from the sky over Terrell. The same pretty, pearly blue, scrubbed over with the same gray-white clouds, but home was a goddamn world away.

The wind blew softly over the grass, pushed it down with invisible fingers. It was still louder than Eddy, who hadn't said another word since Johnnie put the question to him.

"Goddammit, I'm not asking again. Can you get us there?"

Eddy relented. "Yeah, it's off Ranch Road 19. Hard to find, but that's not the real problem."

"Okay, then what the fuck is the problem?" Of course

there'd be a problem. There was always a problem. One problem after another, each of them rammed further up his ass.

"The sheriff lives out there. Sheriff Cherry. That's his place."

Of course.

"You're fucking kidding, right?"

Eddy shook his head, and Johnnie could have sworn that fucker was smiling, like he was enjoying this. "No, that's the place. I'm sure."

Johnnie looked at this latest news flash from every angle. What the fuck did it mean? How was Sheriff Chris Cherry tied up with an old narco? Or was it the female deputy?

Danny Ford?

"Juanito, did that piece of shit just say we're going to the *sheriff's ranch*?" Chavez, who'd seemed so relaxed a moment ago, was now loud, suddenly looming over Johnnie. He smelled like dog shit, always like day-old dog shit, like those animals he loved so much.

"Pretty much, that's what he said."

They were now all looking at him, Ortiz shaking his head.

"We're not going to roll up and shoot the Big Bend County sheriff," Ortiz said, not waiting for the others to agree.

"We're going to do exactly what the fuck I tell you," Johnnie yelled. Just like in the bar, he had to get control of this fast. He thought about the empty blue sky above him—these fuckers could shoot Eddy and him and leave them both out here. It might be months before their bodies were found, maybe never.

He drew his gun and aimed it carefully at Ortiz. Just as he'd done back in front of the library, here he was pointing a gun at another cop, and it looked like he'd be doing it again before the sun set. "I don't give a shit what you think, we're doing this. *It's done.*"

He took a step closer to make sure Ortiz got a good look down the loaded barrel. "This changes nothing. We're cops, right? Keep your badges on you. We'll flash them if we need to. We may even be heroes when this is all over. We're the guys who caught the Big Bend sheriff hiding some narco big shot. We're the good guys."

Chavez raised his thick, callused hands. He was all rational again. "We're cool, Juanito. Ortiz was only voicing his concerns. We've all heard them before. We're ready to move when you are."

If the others had anything to say, they didn't share it. Ringo flicked his cigarette into the grass, and after a moment, Ortiz walked over to make sure it was out.

Roman was leaning against the Suburban like Ringo, but his eyes were closed.

It was Eddy who spoke up again, pointing at the Suburban and Johnnie's Charger. "You plan on driving those right up to the front door? I ain't really been out there, but if it's like every other ranch, he's gonna see you comin' a mile away. Hell, for all that, you might as well call him and tell him you're on your way. He might have some cold beers waiting. Or he might not be happy to see you at all, no matter who the fuck he thinks you are."

There was that secret, amused smile again, and Johnnie almost put the bullet he'd planned for Ortiz into
Eddy instead, right then and there. But he still needed
him, at least for a few more hours.

And he did have a good point about their vehicles. A
damn good point. Johnnie didn't know why Sheriff Cherry
was hiding the old man out at the ranch, but knew why
he'd chosen that place.

He must feel pretty damn safe out there.

"Is there anything else out that way? Other ranches,
homes? More fucking trailers like yours?"

Eddy looked skyward, as Johnnie had only moments
before. "Nah, not so much. Nothing I can think of specifically."

"But you can get us close, right? Take us up this
Ranch Road 19 and near to the place."

Confusion passed through Eddy's eyes like the clouds
above them. He didn't know what Johnnie was driving
at, and Johnnie wasn't sure either, but he had the beginning of an idea, something taking shape. If Eddy Rabbit
had been betting they'd stop now because of the sheriff's
involvement, or the issue with the cars, it was a gamble
he'd lost.

"Sure, I can do that," Eddy admitted, unhappy.

"Good enough then, let's go."

But Johnnie didn't holster his gun. He didn't plan on
doing that for a while, not until this was over. Really
over.

The others started getting into the Suburban, as Johnnie tossed the keys to his Charger over to Eddy. "You
drive this time. Lead the way. I'll ride shotgun, and if you

so much as go two miles over the speed limit, I'll shoot you in the fucking head."

Eddy bounced the keys in his hand, letting them catch sunlight. "I got it."

They both walked toward the car.

"Your new friend Deputy Ford didn't happen to mention where he was going after he left your place this morning?"

Eddy shook his head. "No, not a thing." Then he added, "Maybe hunting."

"Hunting, *right*," Johnnie said, and spit his matchstick onto the ground.

He'd bet his last few dollars they hadn't seen the last of Danny Ford today.

But it was okay. Today they were the good guys.

SIXTY-THREE

D anny was having trouble breathing.

It had started slowly at first, a tightening in his chest that had grown fiercer over time, as he lay stretched out on his sleeping bag in the camper bed of the Bronco. It was like a great hand wrapped around him, around his heart, slowly squeezing him to death.

Just like in Eddy Rabbit's trailer, then in Amé's apartment—a hot, crushing darkness descending on him. His goddamn dream. The camper bed was infernal, and although the sun was finally sinking behind the mountains, he was slicked with sweat that was turning his skin to salt.

His bad eye had started to fray, too, like his nerves. A bad lightbulb, winking on and off.

He had to hold it together a little while longer. He just didn't know how much longer he had left.

DESPITE THE URGENCY on the call several hours ago, Gualterio's people were now taking all the time in the world, making them wait, letting a covering dusk fall. It's exactly what Danny would have done, and not very different from when he was working undercover, trying to meet some Hammerskins or Volksfront for the first time. They'd set times and places they all knew no one was serious about, and he'd end up drinking away hours in some shitty bar, only to get a call to move to another, even shittier, bar, or an apartment or motel near a freeway. Maybe he was supposed to meet two guys, and instead eight showed, or no one at all. Other times they'd send a woman, sometimes a teenage kid.

Skinheads, narcos, cops . . . they all played the same game, and John Wesley Earl had been a hell of a real poker player. He used to tell Danny all the time that to win the big hands—to win it all—you had to play patiently, bluff aggressively, and never, ever, be the first one to blink.

During his time with the Earls, Danny had become a pretty good card player, too.

HE'D SET UP THE BACK OF THE BRONCO like a sniper nest.

He had the M110 SASS laid out next to him on the sleeping bag, along with a handful of Clif Bars and a case of Gatorade and two empty gallon milk jugs to piss in. He'd drilled seven ragged holes through the smoky camper shell in three of the four cardinal directions, masking them with electrical tape that he could push away with the muzzle of the rifle or his knife. The raised bed of the Bronco gave him some elevation, the makeshift murder holes presented him clear sight lines and firing angles across the whole front of the property and at least two sides of the house, and the camper shell itself provided cover and concealment.

He'd dropped his AR-15 and some extra mags about ten yards to the south of the truck in a knot of ocotillo, next to the sheriff's Big Bend truck. That was his fallback position once Gualterio's men figured out where he was hiding. If they were good, and he was going to assume they were, he'd probably get about four or five good shots off before they zeroed in on him. Maybe more, maybe less, depending on their number and how distracted they were dealing with the sheriff and America and Fox Uno. Sheriff Cherry had said there was supposed to be three total: two bad guys, and Amé's mother, but it didn't matter what they'd said, only who showed up.

The truth was, anything or anyone could appear down that gravel drive.

And that was fine with Danny, as long as whatever or whoever it was appeared soon, before he fucking suffocated to death.

AMÉ HAD CHECKED ON HIM A FEW TIMES on the radio, and he could tell by her questions that she was worried he might be having a hard time. Struggling. Despite what he'd told her about his dreams, or what she'd already come to suspect on her own, there was no way she could understand how bad it had gotten. But her voice was still a welcome relief—she'd calmed him, giving him space to breathe, as if she was sharing some of her own air.

So far, she'd somehow kept that huge hand from squeezing him in half.

She apologized again and again, promising him she would make things right. She talked about their date, the things they'd do, the places they could go.

All he had to do was hang on.

But she never mentioned that kiss, that quick moment they'd shared on the porch. Neither of them did. He didn't know what to say about it, and maybe there wasn't anything to say.

How had he described it to West? *"It's something . . ."*

And some things just spoke for themselves.

SIXTY-FOUR

Coyotes and Danny.

And the sun.

That had been it, all damn day.

Although the sheriff had called him earlier, leading Marco to believe things were finally starting to happen, the hours after his call had passed in maddening silence and heat. The good-time radio in the truck was a bust—for some reason, Denbrow had knocked it out with a hammer—so he'd had only his own thoughts to distract him, and that hadn't been a good thing at all.

At least now the sun was finally giving him a break, settling lower behind the mountains, turning the horizon pink and orange and blood-red. Eventually the sky would go purple, then dark, before brightening again with stars.

He'd run the AC earlier in the day until the truck had nearly overheated twice, so he'd finally had to shut it off, leaving him to sit with the windows rolled down, tapping his hands on the torn leather steering wheel to keep his focus.

Trying not to think, not to worry.

At least he hadn't drifted off again, not after his talk with Danny, but now he was afraid they'd all forgotten him.

Maybe everything was already over, or the people he was supposed to be keeping an eye out for had changed their minds about showing up, and the rest of them were all up there at the ranch drinking beers and relaxing or something.

Or maybe something bad had happened up at the ranch, while Marco was sitting out here alone in Walt Denbrow's truck.

He was about to grab his phone and just call the sheriff or Danny himself, when it buzzed on its own.

But it wasn't a message or text from Sheriff Cherry, instead it was Vianey Ruiz. She and Marco had started talking some, texting even more, since the debate. She'd sat next to him during the sheriff's bizarre performance—a performance that had all but guaranteed he'd no longer be wearing a badge two weeks from now—and although Marco still hadn't asked her out, he was getting closer.

A lot closer.

She was texting now to find out if he was stopping by Earlys later tonight—the first time she'd ever asked him that—and even though he was thrilled, he didn't know what to say. He had no idea how much longer he was going to be out here, and he still needed to go home and check on Emiliano.

He wanted her to know he wanted to come by, but he couldn't exactly explain what the hell he was doing.

He was still looking down at his phone, smiling to himself and working out different responses in his head, when a van came rolling slowly down the 19.

It didn't come up behind him, like Danny's Bronco, otherwise he would have heard it before he saw it. Instead, it was in front of him, turning into the gravel drive that led back to the Far Six. It was a basic passenger van, nondescript, gray in color, and although it wasn't dark enough for headlights yet, most modern vehicles with automatic lights would have already had them triggered by the coming dusk.

This van's lights were out, though, so Marco didn't even see those reflected in his windshield.

He almost never saw it at all.

It was there and then gone again, disappearing behind some mesquite trees. He caught a flash of it farther down the gravel drive, and then lost it for good behind the cloud of dust it had churned up in its wake.

He had no idea *who* was in the van and could barely describe the vehicle itself. He'd glimpsed it for only a few seconds, but whoever was behind the wheel probably also hadn't gotten a clear look at Denbrow's truck pulled over in the arroyo, either.

He abandoned Vianey's text and instead started dialing the sheriff. He was mad at himself, but at least he hadn't completely fucked up.

At least he hadn't been asleep.

And he did catch the van . . . hopefully in plenty of time to warn the rest of them at the ranch. That was his only job, but after all the long hours, he wanted to do more. He hadn't sat out here forever to make one phone call and turn around and drive home.

No matter what the sheriff and Danny had said.

Although he'd been hot and miserable all day, seeing that van move slowly up the gravel drive had made him go cold. As good as it sounded to head back to Murfee and sit at Earlys with Vianey, he didn't think he could leave his friends behind. He hadn't joined the sheriff's department to run and hide at the first sign of trouble.

The sort of trouble that had cost his brother his sight, and his family their home.

As he waited for the sheriff to pick up, he kicked on the truck's engine.

Denbrow's battered old truck didn't have automatic lights, either, so Marco didn't have to worry about shutting them off, as he turned down the gravel drive to follow the van up to the house.

SIXTY-FIVE

H e was lying on his back, eyes closed, when the radio crackled to life.

It was the sheriff, telling him that Marco had finally seen a vehicle, possibly a van, pulling down the gravel drive.

Danny rolled over and got into a crouch, scanning. Directly to his north was the house itself, about twenty yards out. There wasn't a proper driveway or even a garage, just some crushed gravel and weeds and ocotillo and yucca that served as something of a front lawn, and that's where he'd positioned his Bronco. To the east was the sheriff's truck, closest to the gravel drive that stretched back to the 19, which was flanked for its whole length by the occasional stunted mesquite and acacia. Behind and west of the house was a small prefab storage shed that Danny could see the leading edge of, and beyond that was scrub and cat's-claw and sotol and prickly pear and more yucca all the way to the mountains and the horizon beyond. The sun was also heading west, and his Bronco and the sheriff's truck cast their own long shadows on the ground.

That meant he was a shadow, too, almost invisible behind the smoky plastic of the camper shell. He could see out well enough, at least until he lost the sun at his back. West had thoughtfully included an AN-PVS-22 clip-on night sight that Danny had already tested, but if it got too dark, if things dragged on a little too long, the few tactical advantages Danny had wouldn't mean much. He'd lose control of his battlefield.

He had to make sure this ended fast.

He adjusted the radio earpiece and the mic clipped to his BDUs. He'd folded the rifle's stock to accommodate the small space he had to work in, but now he shouldered the M110 and used its high-powered scope like the spare pair of binoculars he'd brought along. He saw the whole world through a tunnel, things both close and far away at the same time. The scope gave the scene a certain unreal quality, a weird chrome sheen, as if he were looking at a movie.

As if the sheriff's truck and the yucca were shiny props and the house itself were cardboard, easily pushed down with a hand.

The same hand that had been crushing him all afternoon, that was tightening more now.

A house that held people he cared about.

He took a breath, as deep as he could, and forced his hands to stop shaking.

His bad eye was bouncing up and down so he closed it. Working the scope, he didn't need it anyway.

He waited for the van to show itself.

SIXTY-SIX

T hey're here," Chris said, as the van rolled to a stop. It hadn't pulled past his own truck, so there was some ground to cover between it and the house.

Too much ground.

Amé was at his side, with Fox Uno behind her. They were all watching the van idling in the gravel. It was an old Ford Aerostar, the color of pencil lead, rust and primer spotting the wheel wells.

No one got out.

Chris checked in on the handheld with Danny, who confirmed he had eyes on the van as well, and had seen no movement, either.

"Okay, I'm going out there. Let's see who showed up."

"No, let me," Amé said. "I will do it."

"No, you're staying back here, covering me."

Her eyes went hard, reflecting her frustration. She clearly hadn't expected Chris to do this alone. "I have to do this. You won't understand what they're saying."

Chris smiled. "I will if they talk slow enough. I'll be fine. Besides, I'm going to have *him* right next to me." He pointed at Fox Uno. "He can translate." He left the Remington leaning against the door frame, but shouldered his A5, aiming it squarely at Fox Uno, using it to gesture toward the door. "Let's go meet your men and get my deputy's mother."

Amé stepped in front of him, desperate. "No, *por favor*, let me do this . . ."

Danny's voice cut in over the radio: "I got the driver's-side door open and one out. *Just one* . . ."

Chris glanced back through the window, where he also could see the van's door now open, and someone standing there. He turned back to Amé. "It's going to be okay. This is what you wanted. Freedom, right? I'm going to make sure you get that, that we all do."

Chris swapped in the radio earpiece on the handheld hooked to his jeans, and then pulled Fox Uno toward him, ordering him in Spanish to open the front door.

He radioed Danny and told him they were coming out.

Danny's voice came back again, now loud in Chris's ear. "He's got something in his hands, Sheriff . . ."

Fox Uno opened the door.

SIXTY-SEVEN

They'd been walking for an hour, following what remained of the fence line, when Eddy finally picked out the house.

And the sheriff's truck . . . and Danny Ford's Bronco.

Johnnie then had them all fan out and settle in and watch for a bit.

IT HAD BEEN JOHNNIE'S IDEA to abandon their vehicles out by the 19 and hike the rest of the way toward the house, coming at it overland from the southwest, clear and away from the access road that led back to it. Eddy had toyed with the idea of trying to turn them around and getting them lost, maybe walking their asses right into Mexico, but he hadn't been sure he could find the sheriff's house even legitimately trying, so he'd let that plan go.

Now here he was staring at it—a nice little place with green trim and a big front porch—with Johnnie breathing hard next to him.

Johnnie hadn't left his side all afternoon, which had considerably narrowed Eddy's already shitty options. Although Johnnie had destroyed Eddy's personal phone back at the trailer, he'd somehow forgotten about the Apache phone—the one he'd given Eddy during their first meeting—and Eddy had succeeded in slipping that down his jeans before they left the trailer, just like he'd been able to grab Danny's phone number off the egg carton, too, after the deputy had visited him this morning. But so far, he hadn't been able to get free enough to do anything with either of them. And even if he did, Danny wouldn't recognize the unfamiliar number and might not answer the call.

Not if he was tied up with whatever was going on inside that house.

Danny was only a hundred yards away—there in that pretty house, probably with the sheriff and the old man Johnnie had come to kill.

Eddy remembered that the sheriff had recently had a kid with that hot girlfriend of his from Earlys. Would Johnnie and the rest of those fuckers shoot a woman and a kid?

Yes, yes, they fucking would.

Johnnie's boys were spread out in the scrub, all of them in their black ninja gear. They had their badges out on chains, swinging around their necks, easily tucked away at a moment's notice, and Johnnie kept checking a red phone of his own, looking for messages. Eddy didn't know if he was waiting for some signal, or some confirmation, or what. Johnnie was chewing on one of his damn matchsticks, eyeballing the house. To their left, Ringo was using a pair of tiny binoculars to give the place a good once-over. When he was done, he whistled low to Johnnie and flashed a hand signal Eddy didn't understand.

Johnnie nodded and went back to his phone.

Eddy did some math in his head.

He was maybe a hundred yards from the house itself, give or take, and maybe less than that to Danny Ford's truck. At his prime, at his best, he'd been able to do the hundred meters—pretty much the same distance to the house—in about eleven and half seconds. But that was a damn long time ago, and he was far from his prime.

So call it twice that—say, twenty seconds. What were his chances with five pissed-off men trying to shoot him in the back? Next to impossible, and no better than what he'd had with Danny back at the trailer. No way he'd make it. He might get twenty steps before they put him down. His only chance was the Apache phone, which after their little hike felt like it was shoved almost halfway up his ass.

Eddy wasn't proud of many things he'd done in his life, and now was no time for pride.

"Fuck me, Johnnie, my nerves is all shot to hell. I gotta take a shit."

Johnnie looked him up and down like Eddy was on fire, like he'd just burst into rosy flames in front of him. "What the fuck?"

"All this walking . . . those goddamn eggs. Hell, maybe they were bad or something. I think I'm going to shit myself right here."

"The fuck you are," Johnnie said through clenched teeth and his matchstick, as if that order was enough.

Eddy tried on a face that said otherwise.

Johnnie looked around, rolling his eyes, disbelieving. "Goddamn, you are a piece of work."

"Look, you don't need me no more. I did what you wanted. Lemme just move back out of the way."

"I'm sorry to say, amigo, I'm not quite done with you yet. Not by a long shot. And I can't have you stumbling around at our backs. But Jesus, crawl over there, cop a squat. Downwind." Johnnie made a vague motion to some mesquite scrub, well within sight. Not too far away.

But far enough.

Eddy knew exactly what Johnnie meant by not being done with him. After they shot the hell out of the old man and whoever stood in their way, Johnnie or one of the others was going to put a bullet in Eddy's brain pan and leave him behind to take the fall. Nobody who knew Eddy would believe he'd gun down the sheriff or anyone else, but in the bloody aftermath, Eddy guessed he wouldn't have too many friends suddenly standing up to vouch his for goddamn corpse. After all, Eddy's so-called friends had abandoned the very-much-alive Eddy Rabbit after his arrest out at Delcia Canyon.

But not Danny, who'd never been a friend at all.

Eddy crawled a few more feet away, making a show of it . . . fumbling with his jeans, making faces, groaning . . . until Johnnie looked away, embarrassed, shaking his head.

Giving Eddy the chance he needed to slide that Apache phone up into his hand.

He thumbed it on, keeping his eyes on Johnnie. It couldn't have much battery left, only a spark, but he prayed it was enough to get one message out. *Had to be.* He wasn't going to have time to make a goddamn social conversation out of it, or explain much . . . just a few words that he had to make count.

As he waited for the phone to wake up, he stared into the setting sun. That small breeze from earlier had followed them all the way out here, and he could smell flowers, agave and sotol and nolina. He'd been sweating for the whole hike, but in that moment, he was almost cool, relaxed, like he was standing in some nice shade. It wasn't as nice as Eddy's canyon, but it was damn fine, too, in its own way, and he could see why the sheriff might want to live out here.

If Johnnie had looked over at him then, he might have seen his eyes closed and a smile on his face.

Eddy was just typing in Danny's number he'd memorized, hoping he had it right, when Johnnie said something. He risked a glance up, following Johnnie's own gaze.

That's when they both saw an old van roll up and park in front of the house.

SIXTY-EIGHT

T he man in the red shirt did not match the second voice on the phone.

This man . . . *kid* . . . was younger. He had thick hair and the hint of a beard, one of those closely cropped, three-day shadows that took plenty of effort to make look so haphazard. Even at a distance, his sunglasses and dark jeans appeared expensive. It was almost like he'd dressed up for the occasion. He reminded Chris of a college student, a fashion model, rather than a narco, and if Fox Uno recognized him, it was impossible to tell from the old man's face.

The kid had a leather bag or satchel in his hand that he held out from his body. He'd walked about ten steps from the van, but his door was still open. The setting sun was reflecting off the windshield, so it was difficult to see exactly who was sitting in the passenger seat, or if it was even occupied, and based on Danny's voice in his ear, he evidently couldn't get a decent look, either.

Fox Uno walked off the porch and started to approach the kid. Chris followed him down to the bottom step, then held up. He ordered Fox Uno to do the same.

Fox Uno and the kid were about twenty feet apart,

shadows still and dark between them. Chris kept the A5 high, covering both.

"I'm guessing this isn't Gualterio? Do you know who this is?" Chris asked. None of them had truly expected Gualterio to show up in person, but they hadn't expected someone this young, either.

"No," Fox Uno said.

"Tell him we need to see America's mother. Tell him we need to see her *now*."

Fox Uno addressed the young man. Calm. Friendly. He asked him his name.

The kid with the satchel hesitated, like he was waiting for instructions of his own, like he had a voice in his ear the way Chris did. *"Mi nombre es Xavier,"* he said at last, now holding out the satchel to Fox Uno like he was giving him a present. *"Me envió tu hijo, Martino."*

"¿Conoces a mi hijo?" Fox Uno asked. *"¿Has hablado con Gualterio?"*

"No he hablado con un Gualterio," the kid in the red shirt—Xavier—replied, taking a few more tentative steps forward, still offering the bag to Fox Uno, who ignored it. Fox Uno told Xavier that everything was okay, not to be afraid, but the *americanos* needed to see the *anciana*, the old woman, *ahora mismo*, right now, or the man behind him with the shotgun—Chris—would start shooting.

And he would start with Xavier. Fox Uno said it with a serious smile. Deadly serious.

That stopped Xavier in his tracks, and his eyes went wide as he called back to the van.

Chris didn't know exactly what was going on, but it was clear enough that this Xavier didn't seem to know anything about Gualterio. Instead, he kept talking about Fox Uno's son, Martino.

Something was wrong.

The side-panel door slid open and someone got out.

Pushed out.

A woman . . . with gray hair blowing in the breeze.

For a moment, Chris almost relaxed. But he kept his A5 aimed at Xavier anyway, as he stepped down off the porch and joined Fox Uno.

He kept searching the van up and down. There was something about that Aerostar, something familiar.

Xavier started walking forward again, talking fast, blocking Chris's clear sight of the woman standing beside the Aerostar, who was on the side opposite Danny, so he wouldn't have a good look at her, either. The setting sun and the coiled shadows didn't help, so the only one who could see her was Amé, who'd appeared on the porch with Chris's Remington centered on the van's windshield, and her own AR-15 slung over her shoulder.

But she was the farthest away, calling out *"Mama?"* over and over again, across the scrub.

Xavier was still talking to Fox Uno, talking about this Martino, someone who clearly was not in the van, as Danny started talking rapidly—urgently—to Chris, too, his voice suddenly way too loud over the radio in Chris's ear. Danny was saying something Chris couldn't make out, his attention split between Fox Uno and Xavier with his satchel and America at his back.

And the woman with the gray hair—the only one not talking, not saying anything—standing silently on the darkened side of the Aerostar.

Silently . . . not responding to her daughter.

I know that van.

They were all now about fifteen feet apart.

Amé's mother still not saying a word . . .

. . . because Chris could now see the duct tape across her mouth, her eyes crazy with fear.

I know that van.

But before Chris could react, Amé called out, "Sheriff, *no*," and then Fox Uno turned to him and very clearly, quietly, said, *"Corre. Ahora."* Run. Now.

Chris grabbed at him hard, pulling him backward fast. Stumbling, trying to retreat. He was yelling at Amé, too. "Get the hell back to the house!"

And in that space where Fox Uno had been only a heartbeat before, something passed through the air. Chris felt it, imagined he saw it, before he heard the shot itself.

One shot. Two. Maybe a third.

Maybe more.

They echoed over the scrub with voices all their own.

He had no idea where that first shot had come from, but one more step—one more moment—the old man would have taken it in the face.

It was pure luck Chris had grabbed him when he did.

Chris had been shot at before. He'd even been ambushed right here in the Far Six, somehow surviving only because of another moment of that rare, impossible luck, so he knew what was coming for them next: a breathless chaos, time both speeding up and slowing down, the whole world and everything in it reduced to mere heartbeats.

Absolute, heart-stopping terror after that.

He also knew there was no way he had any more lucky

moments saved up. He'd used his last one, maybe the last one for any of them, on Fox Uno.

Amé was still calling out to him:

"That's not my mama!"

Now his young deputy was running forward, not backward, raising the Remington, yelling something about La Tienda.

He understood then why the van had seemed so familiar. He'd seen it around Murfee all the time, most often parked at the little Mexican store, La Tienda.

Who the hell are these people?

Chris ordered Amé back again, screaming, begging—pleading with her just to get to the cover and safety of the damn house.

But not before the satchel in Xavier's hand, the one he had been carrying delicately from the very beginning, turned red and then white and then blossomed . . .

And blew him to pieces.

SIXTY-NINE

TWENTY SECONDS BEFORE THE EXPLOSION . . .

Eddy didn't think his message had worked.

He could see the young guy with the red shirt and the bag who'd come out of the van, as well as the sheriff and an old man who he guessed was the reason for all this shit. They were all kind of milling around in the yard, talking.

He could also see that female deputy, America Reynosa, coming up behind them from the house itself.

She was moving slow, then faster, a shotgun in her hand.

Everyone was in motion, circling each other.

But Danny Ford was nowhere to be seen, and Eddy had a hard time believing that the same deputy who'd chased him through his trailer wouldn't be right in the middle of whatever the hell was going on over there right now.

Johnnie and his boys were moving now, too, raising their own guns and drawing a bead on everyone standing outside.

Badges swinging, catching the last of the light.

No one up by the house knew they were there.

Now they were shooting and Eddy could hear the whip-crack of their rifles, each one a heartbeat late.

For the moment, crouched out of the way, he'd been forgotten.

He looked back the way he'd come, into that last light. This was his chance to run.

But then that radio station in Eddy's head suddenly got a good, strong signal—his Spidey sense firing away—and he remembered those weird circles cut into the camper shell of Danny's Bronco.

A Bronco just sitting there in the middle of everything . . . ignored.

A hunting blind.

Another kind of trap.

Danny *was* right in the goddamn thick of it, like Eddy knew he would be.

One foot in front of the other . . . one foot in front of the other . . .

Eddy Rabbit took a deep breath and started running . . .

===

SEVENTY

TWELVE SECONDS BEFORE . . .

Danny was trying to pay attention to what was going on outside the Bronco, but his phone inside kept buzzing.

He thought it was Marco, maybe warning him about a second vehicle, but he didn't want to take the time to look down at it.

He had the man in the red shirt scoped, and although he didn't have a good angle on the opposite side of the van, he could tell by everyone's reaction that something was happening over there.

His guess was someone else had gotten out on that side.

That made two bad guys, at least.

And Amé coming down the porch, getting in the middle of it.

Things were moving fast, too fast—spiraling out of control—and that damn phone kept buzzing.

But if there was another vehicle, or Marco had seen something, Danny needed to know for sure. It was the whole reason he was out here.

He reluctantly risked a glance downward.

It took him longer than a second to read the few words, trying desperately to make sense out of them, since they weren't what he was expecting. But when they came into focus, he knew exactly what they meant.

A warning. And there was only one person in the world who could have sent it.

Danny pulled away from the man in the red shirt and started to scan the area behind him, checking each direction with sweat streaming down his face and his eye flickering in and out, until he finally saw a second group of men, all heavily armed, moving silently toward the house from the southwest.

They were still far away, but coming up fast.

He counted several muzzle flashes, as they began shooting at Fox Uno and Chris and Amé.

The van had been a goddamn distraction.

Danny keyed his mic and started to tell the sheriff and Amé to get back inside, when he spied another man running like hell across the desert, directly toward the Bronco.

He was waving his arms and running like his life depended on it, and it absolutely did.

Eddy Rabbit.

SEVENTY-ONE

EIGHT SECONDS BEFORE . . .

Eddy ran like he hadn't run in twenty years, and it was goddamn good to run.

For once, he wasn't running in a fucking circle, just running in place. He was free and running as fast and as far as he could go, his thin hair flying behind him. He was fifteen years old again; his entire life stretched out there right in front of him, every shitty decision ready to be done over, every mistake and fuck-up about to be made right.

He was running forward and the world was spinning backward and the sun was going down behind him into an endless blue and black, but he was heading right into a light so bright that he'd never stop running again.

One foot in front of the other.

One goddamn step at a time.

It was like being as high as he'd ever been, but he'd never been so stone-cold sober.

The Bronco kept getting closer, closer, and he was going to make it.

He couldn't wait to tell Charity about this thing he'd done. To tell her he was sorry.

She wouldn't believe it, not a word of it.

So goddamn sorry.

And that was Eddy Rabbit's last thought on earth, as Johnnie Macho blew his heart out.

SEVENTY-TWO

Danny watched Eddy go down.

Blood exploded all over the front of his shirt, and he dropped face-first to the ground without even breaking his fall.

One second he was up and running, and then he wasn't.

That's when Danny realized that it was Deputy Johnnie Machado from Terrell County who'd just shot him.

The last time Danny had seen him was in a parking lot in Crockett.

Before Danny could sight the M110 on him, Johnnie Macho dropped down, too, out of sight. But the other shooters with him were still up and moving. Through the narrow view of the scope, he recognized some of them—other members of the Tejas unit—and they were armed and armored like they were about to swoop down on a drug raid, and maybe in a way they were. They were still focused on Fox Uno and the sheriff and Amé, and they had all three of them dead to rights.

He pushed the muzzle of the M110 out of one of his murder holes and took aim at one of them, a thin guy with a flattop. Danny remembered him from Crockett—he'd been the one who'd backed away from the confrontation in the parking lot. *Ortiz?* Something like that. Ortiz and most of the Tejas unit were wearing full tactical rigs, at least Level III with or without extra plates, which would normally have been enough to slow down the regular 7.62x51mm armor-piercing NATO rounds the M110 fired, except Danny had loaded his with the armor-piercing steel-core specials that West had bought him.

He put the reticle on Ortiz's face. It was clear enough that Danny could see the sweat on the man's skin and the fear in his eyes.

Ortiz, or whoever he was, wanted to be anywhere but here.

Danny didn't blame him, and just before his own vision went black, he pulled the trigger and obliged him.

SEVENTY-THREE

FOUR SECONDS BEFORE . . .

Five things happened, more or less all at once.

First, Johnnie saw Eddy Rabbit go down. Since he was the one who'd just put a bullet in that motherfucker, that was to be expected. On pure instinct, Johnnie dropped down, too, since he'd exposed himself with that shot.

Then, quite clearly, Ortiz's face came apart. A high-velocity round from somewhere drilled straight through the man's skull, his brains and blood flying about ten feet into the air. Before Ortiz even hit the ground, another bullet went through his chest—right through his badge—and then a third tore his left arm in half. Some of Ortiz's mess ended up on Chavez, who'd been taking aim on the old Mexican, and it threw him off enough that his first shot went way wide, and his second didn't prove to be any better, since by then Sheriff Cherry was already pulling the old fucker out of the way.

Chavez's next shot didn't even matter, because the third thing Johnnie saw was a bullet tear a fist-sized hole through the man's armored vest and come out clean on the other side.

Goddamn.

Not a good sign at all.

Fourth, Johnnie finally figured out where all those shots were coming from: the Bronco.

It was glowing inside like a summer storm, one muzzle flash after another, like distant thunder and lightning in low clouds.

That had to be that prick Danny Ford. That was the direction Eddy Rabbit had been running. Johnnie had no idea what the deal was with those two, but Ford was going to chew up and spit out his men one at a time unless Johnnie did something about it. His orders from those goddamn *indios* across the river had been to shoot everyone, and if Johnnie hadn't been so sure about that before, he had no reason to argue with it now.

Finally, number five.

Just as Johnnie was getting to his knees and flipping his H&K MP5 to full auto—to put as many bullets as possible into the Bronco, and hopefully motherfucking Danny Ford as well—the young guy in the red shirt who'd been walking toward the old Mexican and the sheriff blew up.

SEVENTY-FOUR

TEN SECONDS AFTER . . .

C hris wasn't sure if he'd blacked out or not.

Or for how long.

His eyes were open now, though, and bits of rocks and other debris were falling all around. It was like he'd been caught outside in a heavy, dirty rain, and his ears were still ringing from thunder and lightning that had passed by too close.

They blew the kid Xavier up.

That bag had been packed with explosives, and if Fox Uno had taken it, he would have been blown sky-high, too. Instead, he was about five or six feet from Chris, face-down, still unconscious, or nearly so. Amé had already emptied the Remington, tossed it aside, and was now dragging Fox Uno back by the collar of his shirt, using her body to cover both him and Chris from two shooters—*sicarios*—she'd been exchanging gunfire with as Chris had fought unconsciousness. The first had slipped out of the van's front passenger door, and although Chris had no reason to know it, he was the one who'd detonated the explosive, while the second had appeared from the Aero-star's sliding door, pushing aside the old woman with the taped mouth.

She was stumbling, trying to run.

Both *sicarios* were using the open front passenger door as cover, firing through the window and the windshield with abandon. Even through the ringing in his ears, Chris could pick out their stray rounds shattering the front windows of his house, tearing through the wooden porch.

He struggled to sit up, tasting dirt and blood. They were exposed, out in the open, and Amé couldn't shield herself, much less both him and Fox Uno.

He reached for his A5, but it had been blown out of his hands. It was lying too far away to get it, so he unholstered his Colt and started putting rounds downrange, as many as possible, punching the door of the van. He was using his wounded hand, the hand that had been shot clean through when he'd been ambushed the first time out here at the Far Six, so his aim wasn't great—not as steady as he would have liked, since that hand had never regained its full strength—but from his awkward angle sprawled flat in the dust, he did have a good view of the first *sicario*'s boots moving back and forth beneath the door frame, and he zeroed in on them.

He was strong enough for that.

One bullet turned an ankle into powdered bone and blood, another blasted through a bended knee as the *sicario* dropped to the dirt.

But Chris had shot himself dry in the process, and when his slide locked back, he was useless.

Amé was leaning over him, still engaged with the other shooter by the van. The ground around them was erupting with wayward shots, dirt spraying upward and leaving behind deep divots in the caliche, each one making its way haphazardly toward them. It was a horrible, deadly game—one it was only a matter of time they'd lose.

Chris's earpiece had fallen out, so he couldn't hear Danny or key his mic, and it wouldn't have mattered anyway, with the hellacious chatter of guns all around him.

He sat up to use his body to shield America, the only thing he was good for anymore, and wondered if Danny was still alive.

SEVENTY-FIVE

D anny thought . . . imagined . . . *dreamed* . . . he was
under artillery fire.

That's what it had felt like when the satchel exploded, and the concussion of it rocked the Bronco on its
axles.

He never saw it, though, because he'd been entirely
focused on Johnnie Macho. But it did force him to turn
around to see if the sheriff and Amé were still alive, and
that gave Johnnie enough time to recover from Danny's
suppressive fire and start unloading on the Bronco.

Now the truck was coming apart around him, one bullet at a time. Worse, in that one glance, he'd seen that the
sheriff and Amé and Fox Uno were piled up near the
porch—alive—but out in the open and exposed, and under
serious fire as well from other shooters who must have appeared from the side of the van blocked from his view.

Danny closed his eyes and curled up tight and made
himself as small as possible, as the Bronco rattled and
shook from Johnnie Macho's steady assault. He needed
to abandon the Bronco and pull back to the sheriff's
truck, recover his AR-15 from where he'd hidden it. He
couldn't see the shooters bearing down on Amé on the

opposite side of the van, but at least if he was out on foot, he could swing around and flank them.

Yet his body only curled tighter on itself, that great hand earlier that had been squeezing his chest now holding him back, refusing to let him move.

He'd left the Big Bend behind and was now back in Afghanistan—in Wanat—taking RPG fire again from the Taliban guerrillas who'd crept up on his platoon. A group of them had also commandeered the roof of a nearby hotel, shooting down into his men's observation post, their AK-47s talking loudly to each other. He'd forever remember that sound, and all the others that came with it: men screaming and the boom of Camp Blessing's big guns, and the air-bending *whup* of the AH-64 Apaches circling low above them. It had been dawn instead of dusk, but the light had been the same— that diffuse, improbable glow that heralded the day's rising and setting sun.

That only existed on the other side of night.

He'd returned fire with his M-249 Minimi then, the spent brass bouncing all around him, too hot to the touch, like the rounds he'd just been firing from the M110—the heavy brass still rolling around his curled-up body—here and now.

Not in Wanat, but right here at the edge of the Far Six.

No matter what his body and his brain were telling him, no matter what his closed eyes were seeing, he wasn't in Afghanistan anymore. He'd survived that, and if he wanted to survive *this*, he had to fucking move.

Now.

If he didn't move, he was going to die and Amé and the sheriff were going to die.

He punched himself in the head with a closed fist. Once, twice, then over and over again until his vision cleared.

He was crying.

But he willed his body to unclench, cursed at it and spit at it and ordered it to *just fucking move, soldier*, and then pushed down the Bronco's tailgate.

SEVENTY-SIX

Marco had slowly been rolling up the gravel drive, lights off, trying to make sense of what he was seeing, when the explosion occurred.

It was a flash of hot, white light, which had left the sheriff and an older Mexican male down, and America, too, with thick smoke drifting above them, and the scrub still smoldering, as two men abandoned the van, wildly firing long guns. One of them toppled over quick, but the other was still pouring it on, changing magazines with frightening speed. A woman was also running back in Marco's direction, appearing like a ghost out of the hazy smoke, weaving back and forth.

He wasn't sure, but it looked like her mouth was taped shut, and her hands were tied behind her back.

Before she got very far, though, she stumbled and fell, eyes wide, and Marco didn't know if she'd simply tripped or a stray bullet had caught her.

She probably never even saw him, just as wide-eyed, sitting in Denbrow's old truck.

Now he caught a glimpse of Danny also on foot, running low and away from his Bronco, which was throwing sparks from a steady rain of bullets bouncing off its hood and camper shell. Danny was shooting into the side panels of the van, trying to get to the cover of the sheriff's truck parked a few yards away, even as a third armed man was slipping out of the back.

A man neither Danny nor anyone closer to the house could see.

Only Marco could, and if he didn't do something about him, he'd have a clean shot at Danny. He'd also be able to circle around on America and the sheriff.

It was a matter of seconds.

Marco Lucero had never actually drawn his gun on duty, and he'd never aimed it at another human being. Sitting in his lap, it weighed a thousand pounds. He wanted to turn around and drive back the way he came. For the second time that day, he wanted to be at Earlys sipping a Coke and chatting up Vianey Ruiz, watching her tattoos live and breathe under the Christmas lights.

He'd had his chance.

Instead, Marco flipped on the headlights of Denbrow's piece-of-shit truck, pinning that third man in a circle of white light—as hot and bright as the earlier explosion—and then rolled out of the driver's-side door with his gun in his hand.

He hoped he'd remembered to flip the safety off.

He was surprised at how suddenly light it was, as he pulled the trigger again and again.

SEVENTY-SEVEN

America didn't feel the bullet hit her at first.

She was too focused on the *pendejo* behind the van door, who she couldn't get a good angle on. It was next to impossible to shoot at him and shield the sheriff, too . . . and to a lesser extent, Fox Uno, who was groaning and trying to crawl away from her. She also didn't want to accidentally hit the woman she'd seen— the poor, gray-haired owner of La Tienda they'd tried to offer up as her mama.

She'd emptied the Remington and was now using her AR-15, but couldn't get to her extra magazines easily, and the air around her was hot to the touch. Not only from the explosion, but from the passing bullets themselves, scorching the sky as they flew by.

Embers swirled around, close enough she could grab them with her hand, and she tasted bitter smoke.

"Tell me how this ends . . ." That's what Danny had asked her. And although she hadn't known then, still didn't know now, she had to believe it wasn't like this.

She would not allow it to end like this.

She prayed they could hold out for a little longer, as she worked furiously to reload her rifle.

She never felt the bullet.

She thought maybe she'd been kicked or shoved by either the sheriff or Fox Uno.

There was no pain, though, only pressure. A tightening, as if she, too, had been grabbed by the same invisible hand that been holding Danny down only a dozen yards away, although she'd never truly know that.

But when she tried to take a breath, the air wouldn't come, and she looked down just long enough to see the bloody hole torn through her shirt and her heart.

SEVENTY-EIGHT

C hris saw Amé go down.

He had no idea how bad it was; the bullet didn't come from the *sicario* near the van, but off to their right, where Chris could now barely make out two more men moving in the falling dusk. Probably, he guessed, the shooters who'd fired first at Fox Uno. One was huge, heavily muscled, and the other was whip-thin, with dark hair slicked back on his head. They were both in police tactical gear and they were duckwalking, staying low, carefully measuring their shots as they worked hard to stay out of sight of the other *sicario*.

Chris couldn't guess who these men were, or where they'd come from. It was as if they'd magically appeared out of the desert, walking all the way from Mexico.

But they had badges . . . They had to be cops or agents, like Garrison.

He raised a hand and started to call out to them, but as they continued to aim down their barrels, he under-stood they hadn't come to save him.

In that moment, he and Amé were no different from any other narcos to them.

No better than Fox Uno or the *sicarios*.

Amé said something as she fell over him, struggling

for breath, and he caught a glimpse of the infamous silver gun Fox Uno had given her, shoved in the back of her jeans, hidden beneath her shirt.

It flashed in the dying sun, impossibly bright.

He pulled himself up and put an arm around her to hold her close to him.

He whispered in her ear that he had her . . . that it was okay, that she was safe. She started to shake violently.

He grabbed her silver gun and turned it on the cops bearing down on them.

SEVENTY-NINE

D anny was alive first because of Eddy Rabbit, and now because of Marco Lucero.

He never would have seen the shooter he'd flushed out of the inside of the van by firing through the doors and side panels if Marco hadn't lit him up with the headlights and pinned him down with his wild shots. Marco's improbable attack had also kept the son of a bitch's head low long enough for Danny to drop his empty M110 and get to the AR-15 he'd stowed in the ocotillo.

It didn't matter that it appeared the other deputy had missed with every damn shot.

Danny put two tightly grouped rounds into the man's chest before he had a chance to recover, knocking him backward off his feet into the still-open van door. That gave Danny time enough to turn around once more toward where he'd last seen Johnnie Macho and push him back with a few three-round bursts.

Danny then moved fast, swinging around the ass end of the van and putting one more bullet into the shooter already dying there, while clearing the now empty interior by Marco's headlights. Using the big vehicle as cover, he quick-peeked around its side and saw one *sicario* down, but another still up, still firing on the sheriff and

Amé. But this one, having seen Marco's lights, realized he was flanked, and was now switching back and forth, shooting both front and behind, while trying to crawl back up into the van through the open side door.

Danny fired another three-round burst at him, and was about to turn and get into the van himself—planning to shoot him from the inside as he tried to take cover there—when the man disintegrated.

That was the best, maybe the only, way to describe it.

It wasn't like the explosion that had killed the kid in the red shirt, but it was damn close.

A powerful fusillade tore the man apart, caving the side of the van in, blowing the passenger door clear off its hinges.

It flew fifteen feet away, tearing a trench in the gravel.

The entire van bounced up and down, tires exploding, windows shattering.

It was like the great hand that had been squeezing Danny earlier had now grabbed the van and crushed it.

Then Danny truly was back in Afghanistan as a roar washed over him, and the sky lit up with the low, angry pass of a helicopter.

EIGHTY

Johnnie had started retreating even before the helicopter appeared, dropping out of the dusk and strafing the house.

It looked huge, with its giant rotors carving the sky and men hanging out of the open bay doors, shooting at the ground below.

Shooting at *him*.

By then, though, he'd already been shot, and was dying . . .

JUST AS HE WAS ABOUT TO PUT DOWN DANNY FORD, another vehicle's lights had come on—some old truck rumbling down the gravel drive, driven by yet another man with a gun—and since he'd nearly caught one of Ford's bullets with his teeth, and had no idea how many more people were running around, or who the hell was shooting at who anymore, he'd decided he'd had enough.

Fuck those indios *across the river, fuck it all.*

He'd turned tail in time to see Sheriff Cherry shoot Ringo. The sheriff was still down on the ground with the female deputy and the old man, firing some big-ass silver gun, some kind of gangster/narco gun, that even Ringo would have seen the humor in—hell, he would have laughed the loudest—if he'd still had the top of his head.

Following Johnnie's lead, Roman—who'd been right next to Ringo when his head had exploded all over his snakeskin boots—had retreated, too, and they met in the same clump of yucca where they'd first stopped with Eddy Rabbit to eyeball the house, both breathing hard.

Maybe they got lucky and the old man had died in that blast? Johnnie didn't know anymore or care. No one had warned him it was going to be like this. Not even close.

"Goddamn," Johnnie said. "It's a fucking mess. I think it's just the two of us now. We gotta get the fuck out of here."

Roman was checking his rifle, making sure he still had a few rounds left, when he said, "Oh, you're wrong about that, amigo. It's just the *one* of us."

Then he casually shot Johnnie twice.

"What the fuck?" Johnnie screamed. The first bullet hit him in the left thigh, and the second slammed his torso and dropped him backward. He didn't think that one had gotten through his vest, but it hurt like he'd been hit by a car . . . make that a fucking train . . . and there was no way he was running far on his wounded leg.

Tumbling backward, he dropped his MP5, but before he could do anything about it, Roman was standing over him, kicking the fallen gun away. He aimed his own weapon down at the crown of Johnnie's head.

"Are you fucking kidding me? You're gonna kill me over a goddamn whore? Over goddamn *Rae*?"

Roman cracked that big neck of his, rolling it around. He took the badge on the chain around his neck and slipped it beneath his T-shirt. His eyes shone. "Fuck no, not over her. This is for Zam, your wife. I've been fucking her for months now, amigo. She needed a real man. You should have treated her better. I'm gonna marry her and raise up them two boys of yours like my own. Your family, the unit, everything, is gonna all be mine by this time tomorrow. Before long, Chuy is going to ask me to start calling him Dad, after they find you out here and everyone knows what you did."

Johnnie spit, wiped his mouth. He needed a matchstick to chew, something to ground him. Something to set this motherfucker and the whole world on fire. He couldn't believe what he was hearing, and never would have bet on Roman making this sort of move. He never would have bet on *himself* going out this way.

He was goddamn Johnnie Macho.

He stared Roman down. "What *we* did, motherfucker. We were friends. We've known each other our whole lives."

"*Exactamente*, our whole lives, and you've been a prick from day one. I'm done cleaning up your shit and wiping your ass, Johnnie. Adios, amigo."

Roman raised the rifle for the kill shot and Johnnie got ready to die.

AND THAT'S WHEN THE HELICOPTER APPEARED, dropping out of the dusk and strafing the house . . .

It looked huge, with its giant rotors carving the sky

and men hanging out of the open bay doors, shooting at the ground below.

Shooting at *him*.

But as it passed overhead, Johnnie realized Roman was gone.

EIGHTY-ONE

J oe Garrison hadn't run in a long time, but the second the chopper touched earth, bouncing up and down on its struts with its rotors still turning, he followed the FAST guys out the bay door.

He lurched into the heavy wind churned up by the blades, a mess of blowing rocks and dirt and trailing smoke. He bent low, feeling the tightness of his soft vest around his gut. He had his old Winchester shotgun at low-ready, and his badge was clipped up high on the front of his vest.

The last time he'd worn it that way he'd been a young, gung-ho agent in St. Louis. Before Junior Worrell had shot him, and he'd killed Junior.

Garrison and FAST split into two teams, half of them sprinting to clear the wreckage of the van, the rest rushing to where Chris Cherry and the others were spread out on the ground. Danny Ford was running with them, calling out to America Reynosa, who'd clearly been shot, and for one moment Garrison was right next to him, before the deputy pulled too far ahead.

When Garrison got there, Ford and a FAST EMT—an agent originally from Arkansas named Mike Connolly—were already working on her. Cherry was sitting upright, all in one piece, aiming a huge silver gun at an old

Mexican who looked maybe like he'd tried to crawl away in the chaos, but hadn't gotten very far. One of the other FAST agents was flipping him facedown, searching him, putting him in cuffs.

When the sheriff saw him, Garrison started shaking his head.

"Jesus, Sheriff Cherry, this is a hell of a mess you got yourself into." Garrison bent down to gently take the silver gun out of Cherry's hand and help him to his feet.

"I'm probably not the sheriff for much longer." Cherry stood, slow and unsteady. His face was streaked with smoke and dirt and blood. He looked like he was just waking up, and maybe in some ways, he was.

"Well, since I green-lit this operation without the express approval of SAC Don Chesney, I'm not likely to be an agent much longer, either. We're both going to be searching for new jobs." Garrison stared down at the gun; it was silver and etched with skulls and other images he barely recognized, except for one: Nuestra Señora de la Santa Muerte. He had no idea why Cherry would have such a gun, and he handed it off to one of the FAST agents.

"Amé?" Cherry asked, sudden and loud, turning to where his deputy was still laid out on the ground.

"My guys have her, Chris. Let them do their job. Once she's good to move, we'll get her on the chopper. It's going to be okay." Garrison wasn't sure about that, but it was the only thing to say.

"Your guys . . ." Chris echoed, still seemingly lost. "The badges. Jesus, I shot at them, Joe. I had to . . . They were coming for Amé, for me . . ."

"No, it's okay, Chris," Garrison said gently. "You didn't shoot anyone with me. I promise." He put a hand on Chris's shoulder. "What about Melissa? The baby?"

Cherry shook his head, still trying to see how Deputy Reynosa was doing. Still trying to figure out what the hell had happened to all of them. "I sent them away. I need to call her, let her know . . ."

"I've got another group of agents driving to Murfee. I'll have them get her, wherever she is, bring her to you. Wherever you want her to go, just tell me." Garrison pointed at the Mexican in cuffs. "I take it that's the infamous Fox Uno?"

Cherry rubbed his face. "Allegedly. Yes, that's him."

"Goddamn." Garrison whistled. "It's hard to believe . . ." He let it drop, as the old man looked back at him. There was nothing interesting about his face at all, nothing that hinted at the man he was or the things he'd done. Garrison could have walked past him a hundred times and never looked twice. "Sorry it took so long. I was afraid we'd get here too late. I got the message, but I didn't recognize the number, didn't listen to it right away. Then I wasn't even sure I believed it."

"What are you talking about?" Chris asked.

Garrison continued: "We got turned around trying to find you. It was worse in the chopper. From up above, this whole place really does look the same. But without it, we never would have made it in time. We followed the smoke and, finally, the muzzle flashes."

From the air all the shots had looked like brightening stars, one after another after another. Red and white and yellow streaks, blazing away. An entire constellation spread out on the ground that Garrison had used to navigate to the house.

"I didn't call you," Cherry said, shaking his head. "I'm sorry, Joe, but it wasn't me."

Garrison searched the middle distance, where the sun had gone completely down. They were wrapped now in darkness, only the lights of the chopper illuminating the scene around them. "I know."

"Was it Mel?" Cherry asked.

Garrison put a hand on his shoulder again. "No."

EIGHTY-TWO

=====

America wasn't sure if she was dying.

She still couldn't breathe, and pain was galloping through her, trampling her. She couldn't hold her gun, because her hands wouldn't clench it; they fluttered away on their own.

She wanted to stand, but she couldn't find her legs, and then other hands were on her anyway, holding her down.

She couldn't see Sheriff Cherry or Fox Uno.

She couldn't see Danny.

Only the ocean of night above her, deep and dark and cold, and stars rising like a tide there.

She'd been to Miami, once, and had spent nights alone on the beach watching the sea.

A man she didn't recognize was also far above her, yet saying something close in her ear. She tried to fight him, push him away, but she was too weak and getting weaker by the second. He cut away her shirt with bright silver scissors, revealing the Saint Michael pendant Ben had given her—and the armored vest beneath that. He tapped it with a knuckle and smiled, and said something else she didn't catch. He was talking in English, but she kept wanting to translate it back into Spanish, and she got lost with every word.

At last, there was Danny.

EIGHTY-THREE

He held her and brushed her hair away from her face and kissed her eyelids.

Holding her stopped his own shaking.

Holding her, he told her she was safe.

She tried to say something back, but he kept her quiet with another kiss. She'd been wearing her vest, the way the sheriff had always taught them, but there was still blood. *So much blood.* It was possible the round had worked its way past it or underneath it.

As the agent tossed her shirt away, checking her vitals and prepping her to move, something fell to the ground. It had been tucked inside her vest, and Danny grabbed for it, holding it up close.

It was a nearly empty pack of cigarettes. The only thing inside was a tightly folded piece of paper, a single page from a confidential report about Fox Uno. Danny had no idea where she'd gotten it, but there was a cell number handwritten across the top of it. He didn't know the number, either, but could hazard a guess who it belonged to.

He let the page slip through his fingers, let the helicopter's spinning rotors take it far, far away.

Amé squeezed his hand and whispered, *"Lo siento mucho . . . lo siento mucho . . ."* I'm so sorry.

And that he understood.

"It's all over," he said.

They were ready to transport her, but Danny didn't want to let her go.

Holding her, he didn't know how.

EIGHTY-FOUR

CHAYO & NEVA

They followed the rising smoke, and then, as it got darker, they followed the flashing lights.

Neva next saw the *helicóptero* turning in a circle before it dropped low below her sight.

Something was going on out there. And although Neva knew Chayo would want to keep moving, to go around it, she also knew he was hurt and needed help.

El sol was settling behind them, so they still had its rays at their backs. But ahead of them, where they'd both seen the *helicóptero*, it was night. There was still a faint glow over there, a white, smoky smudge against the black to guide them, and Neva aimed them toward it, and Chayo didn't try to stop her or pull her back. She held on to him, dragging him with her, as they stumbled over the scrub. Maybe they'd be caught and sent back to México, but she wouldn't let him bleed to death in Los Estados Unidos. Not for her, not after all he'd done to save her, to save them both.

She was so focused on where they were going, she didn't realize they had walked right up on another *hombre* until he spoke to her.

HE WAS HURT, TOO. At least as bad as Chayo and maybe worse.

He was in strange, dark clothes that reminded Neva of the men who had attacked the buses in Ojinaga, and she thought at first—with the fear rising in her, threatening to wash over her completely—that he had followed them all the way to this place from that night.

He was leaning against a fancy *coche americano*, as dark as the night in front of them. The ground and bushes all around it were torn up, and she could just make out more tire marks in the dust. There had been another *coche* here, but that one was gone. When she and Chayo had walked up, the *hombre* had been trying to get his keys into the lock, but now that they were there, he smiled and slapped a bloody hand against the door he'd been trying to open.

"Well, goddamn, you two scared the ever-livin' shit out of me. You kids look about the way I feel." He shifted against the *coche*, which was holding him up about as much as he was leaning against it, so Neva could see the *pistola* at his waist. He took it out and held it up higher, to make sure she understood.

There was always another *pistola*.

The *hombre* switched to Spanish and his Spanish was good. "I'm going to need you and your boyfriend there to drive me the hell out of here. I don't care what you're doing here, or where you're going, and I've got plenty of money. You can even have the damn car when we're done. I just don't think I can drive. I'm bleeding pretty goddamn good." He shook both the keys and the *pistola* at her, reminding her of that old saying she'd learned growing up—that common refrain in the *narcocorridos* and the *telenovelas* she loved: *Plata o plomo.*

Silver or lead.

That was the offer every narco made.

The *hombre* shook the keys again to keep her attention. "Like I said, I got money and I'll pay, but I'm not fucking asking." He raised the *pistola* in his other hand, and something else, a piece of metal on a chain around his neck. It was a *medalla.* "I am a police officer, get it? One of the good guys. Now get your asses over here, *now.* That's an order, or I'll arrest both of you. I have to catch that fucker Roman . . ."

Neva did not know who the *hombre* was talking about, and most of what he was saying meant nothing to her. He was *policía*, and he was hurt and desperate.

But so was she.

She started to cry, not because she was afraid anymore, but because she was angry.

Angry at the *hombre*, at the *noche.* At the *mundo* that would not leave them alone, or let them go.

He was a *policía* like those who had hurt her, who'd killed Batista.

Policía or narco, it made no difference.

Plata o plomo.

Chayo moved against her, in front of her. He was swaying, unsteady, but he put himself between the *hombre* and his *pistola* and her. *De nuevo.* Chayo didn't say anything . . . his lips were pale and trembling and flecked with blood . . . and the *hombre* laughed at him.

"Fuck me, I'll give you an A for effort, kid. But neither of us are in shape to fight it out. And trust me, I only need fucking one of you. I bet that . . ."

Neva spoke for them both.

"No," she said, barely a whisper. It was the first word she'd said in days. It hurt, moving her mouth, and her voice sounded strange, like it was coming from someone else. She didn't recognize herself.

"*No,*" she said again. Louder, clearer, so loud it was almost a yell, and it rolled across the desert and back to her.

"No," she said, a third time. Soft, final.

And then she shot him with the *pistola* she'd taken off the *hombre* with the baseball hat.

There was always another *pistola*.

She shot him again and again and again until she was done crying, and Chayo took the empty *pistola* out of her hands and dropped it on the ground.

TOGETHER THEY TOOK THE KEYS of the *hombre muerto* and the *dinero* he had on him.

They rolled his cooling body beneath some ocotillo and left it there.

And after she got Chayo settled across the backseat of the *coche*—jumping at the sound of its big engine—she took the wheel and drove them away from the lights and the *helicóptero* and into the night.

EPILOGUE

DÍA

After it was over, they all had to do a hell of a lot of lying for each other.

In the numerous official assessments and inquiries in the days immediately afterward, DEA ASAC Joseph Garrison talked at length about the joint operation he'd been working with the Big Bend County Sheriff's Department. That operation, code-named Arma de Plata, or Silver Gun, focused not only on corruption in the Terrell County narcotics task force—the Tejas unit—but also on the suspected cross-border movements and activities of one of the most feared and wanted narco-traffickers in the world: Juan Abrego Carrión, better known as Fox Uno. The fact that a man believed to be Fox Uno— identity pending—had been arrested *alive* on U.S. soil as a direct result of Arma de Plata was a major coup for both the DEA and the Big Bend County Sheriff's Department. The extremely covert nature of the operation was troubling to some, but it had been necessitated by concerns about local border corruption—as proven by the involvement of at least some members of the Tejas unit—and ASAC Garrison only had to point to the numerous intel briefings he'd conducted and recent inquiries he'd made in Washington, D.C., to validate his version of the events.

SAC Don Chesney, next in line for DEA's Chief of Operations, subsequently confirmed his knowledge of and support for the operation, and noted his thanks for the amazing investigative work of both his agents and the local deputies in the Big Bend.

FOR A WEEK, people from news outlets from all over the world descended on Murfee.

When ASAC Garrison was finally made available to the media, he echoed the sentiments of his SAC, and went a step further: Fox Uno's capture would not have been possible without the fine men and women of the Big Bend County Sheriff's Department. More pointedly, Fox Uno, the infamous cartel leader who had shipped untold amounts of illicit drugs into the United States and who was responsible for thousands of deaths, including the most recent horrific attack on a busload of students in Ojinaga, was in custody *only* because of the foresight and efforts of one man: Sheriff Chris Cherry.

ASAC Garrison said he'd rarely met someone willing to risk so much, for so long, in the pursuit of justice.

EFFORTS, HOWEVER, to interview Sheriff Cherry himself were met with a polite but firm declination.

In the only official statement put out by the department, the sheriff thanked the DEA for its long-running support and commended his deputies—specifically Deputy America Reynosa and Deputy Daniel Ford—for their hard work and dedication.

IT TOOK A JOINT TEAM OF THE DEA, the FBI, the ATF, and the Texas Department of Public Safety more than four days to process the crime scene at the Far Six.

Over 275 rounds were fired during the brief but intense shoot-out.

The explosive detonated in the satchel—identified as a black Cole Haan Barrington Messenger bag—was a traditional C-4 composite improvised explosive device triggered by a Chinese Huawei Honor 5x 4G cell phone that was recovered from the dashboard of the van.

IDENTIFYING THE DEAD was difficult and required the help of the Policía Federal Ministerial, or PFM—the Mexican Ministerial Federal Police—and the Procuraduría General de la República, or PGR—the Office of the General Prosecutor.

The shooters in the van were Joaquín Abarco Hernández, Carlos Gómez Gonzáles, and his brother, Vicente Gómez Gonzáles. They were all on file with the PFM as known *sicarios* of Nemesio.

The young man who died in the explosion was Xavier Alejandro Robles, and he was the only one of the group with any active border crossings on record. He'd most recently crossed on foot two days before the shoot-out, at the Naco port of entry in Douglas, Arizona.

It was unknown how Xavier got from Douglas to the Big Bend, but it was noted in more than one news article that if he'd been picked up by a vehicle at the POE, and that vehicle took Highway 80 over to Interstate 10 (the most direct route to El Paso and then Murfee, beyond), he would have most likely passed right through Tombstone—the historic site of the infamous Gunfight at the O.K. Corral.

Visitors to Tombstone can pay to see a reenactment of the gunfight three times a day.

The older female was identified as María Fernanda Pérez Medina. She was a longtime resident of Murfee, Texas, and owned a small unlicensed clothing and general goods store on the west side of town. The Ford Aerostar van was registered to her.

It was unclear what association she had had with her apparent captors.

It was believed she was shot by one of the deputies from the Terrell County Tejas unit.

THE TEJAS UNIT DEAD included Ernesto Chavez, Edward Ortiz, Thomas Ringo, and Johnnie Machado, son of the Terrell County sheriff, Chuy Machado. Like Sheriff Cherry, Sheriff Machado did not give any interviews, and issued a brief statement denying any knowledge of corruption in his department or in the Tejas unit, and offered no explanation for how or why his deputies appeared to be involved with known *sicarios* from another country.

Both federal and state probes were opened simultaneously targeting the Terrell County Sheriff's Department.

It would be several months later that Sheriff Machado would step aside, citing health reasons, and naming longtime deputy Roman Avila as his successor, until a new election in the spring.

REPORTS APPEARED of a rising tension between the U.S. and a Mexican government that was very eager to see the return of the man identified as Fox Uno.

U.S. government officials, however, were quick to point out that they were under no obligation to return a man whose identity was still in question, who wasn't facing any active charges in Mexico, and who'd apparently come to the U.S. freely, seeking asylum.

These same officials also denied that Fox Uno was cooperating with U.S. law enforcement or that he was receiving treatment for a serious health issue, as some media outlets were reporting.

A FEDERAL INQUIRY was opened regarding U.S. Customs and Border Patrol operations at their checkpoints and points of entry in both Arizona and Texas.

Many people were troubled by the ease with which assassins, explosives and guns, and the notorious head of a Mexican cartel could so easily cross the border.

If such men could, then anyone could, including Islamic terrorists, which were a growing national concern.

And with the capture of Fox Uno, alive, it was also openly asked how a local Texas sheriff and his deputies could do what the combined forces of two governments had failed to do.

———

IN ALL OF THE ATTENTION immediately after the events at the Far Six, one thing happened that merited barely a few lines in the national media, and not much more in the local *Murfee Daily*.

It was such a foregone conclusion, it wasn't considered newsworthy.

Sheriff Chris Cherry was reelected for a second full term.

Word around town was that he won in a landslide.

Charity Mumford had been a pretty woman once, and probably would be again.

Danny could tell she was slowly regaining her color—her *life*—one day at a time.

There were still all the old signs: the faded bruises on her face, the nails bitten to the quick, the old track marks, and the nervous way she looked around as if she expected something bad to happen to her any minute. For her, there were shadows lurking around every corner and under every bed. The way she didn't want to make eye contact was another tiny tic, a poker tell, about the life she'd led and the things she'd seen.

Her eyes were big and wide and a curious shade of blue, and even though more often than not they showed just how afraid she was, at least they were *clear*.

She'd been sober since leaving Eddy Rabbit, and word was she doing well at the women's shelter in Artesia. But she was still a woman who was afraid of what tomorrow would bring, and the day after.

Danny understood that.

SHE'D BROUGHT EDDY'S ASHES in the small box the mortuary had given her, and she scattered them around

Delcia Canyon without much ceremony. The October wind was up, and it caught them and took them skyward, sunward, and for one brief second they were a dazzling white, and then they were all gone.

Charity watched Eddy go as she lit up a cigarette.

THEY LEANED against Danny's truck, talking.

He told her everything that had happened at the Far Six—more truth than he ever told the Texas DPS or federal investigators—about how Eddy had texted him a warning message that only Danny would understand, and how he'd even gone a step further: running right into those killing fields, just to make sure Danny saw him.

To make sure Danny knew what was happening.

Danny had no idea Eddy could run that fast, and Danny would have sworn that he'd been smiling.

Danny told Charity that Eddy had died a hero, but more than that, he'd died clean and sober. And if Eddy could stay clean, so could she. That's what Danny wanted her to know, to remember and hold on to.

That, in the end, Eddy had finally made it through to the other side.

"THANKS," CHARITY SAID, finishing off her cigarette. "It was nice you comin' out to the funeral, and then bringin' me out here for this today. This is what Eddy would have wanted, to be left out here, not some hole in the ground. Thinkin' about stuff like that gave him the creeps." What Charity didn't say was that Danny had been the only one who'd come to the funeral, and Danny had paid for it.

"No, it's fine. I wanted to do this. I *needed* to do this. Eddy did right by me, and I wanted to do right by him."

She stuck her hands in her Goodwill jacket and looked out into the canyon. "He wasn't a bad guy, you know? He meant well. He could be sweet, at times." She shrugged. "He was just kinda broken. He was all jagged-like, but he never meant to cut you. Not on purpose, anyway. It just happened, bein' around him too much, if that makes any damn sense." Danny thought Charity was going to cry, but she only wiped a hand on her dry face, and continued. "I don't know that I'll really miss him, though. Is that a bad thing to say? Does that make me a bad person?"

"No," Danny said. "I don't think so. I don't think so at all."

She smiled, still clear-eyed, and turned away from the canyon. "It's okay, Mr. Ford. I think I'm done here. I don't think I'll ever be coming out here again."

Danny put an arm around her, squeezed her tight. She was small and thin and frail, but he knew her strength was coming back. "All right, then let's get you out of here. I need to get to town to see the doctor anyway. He gets upset when I'm late, wants to charge me extra."

Charity looked at him strange, searching him over. "I didn't think you got hurt in all that shit that happened."

Danny laughed. "No, I didn't . . . I mean, not physically, thanks to Eddy." He tapped the side of his head. "But I got plenty of shit up here to work out from before, when I was in the military. I'm no different than Eddy. I'm broken, too. Hell, we all are, right? Eddy helped remind me of

that . . . how we need to do whatever we can to fix our-
selves, so we don't accidentally cut those trying to hold on
to us."

Charity thought about that. "That makes sense . . . a
lot of sense." Then she stopped, before opening the door
to the truck. "Say, you never told me what message he
texted you, something only you'd understand?"

Danny laughed again. "Yeah, that. It was something
he said the first time we met. 'Tomorrow is a motherfucker.' Then he hit me with a frying pan."

Charity covered her mouth, stopping a laugh of her
own. "He used to say that all the time. Same old shit
Eddy always said. Goddamn Eddy."

Then she was crying, only a few tears at first, which
she didn't bother to wipe away. And when she looked
over to Danny, she was fiercely holding on to a small, but
very real, smile.

"I think tomorrow is gonna be okay for me, Mr. Ford.
I think it's gonna be just fine."

C hris watched her close.

It was Mel's first visit out to the house since the shoot-out, and it was the second time in the last few weeks he'd seen doubt flicker across her face.

The first had been the day he told her about his plan to bring Fox Uno and Amé out here.

She said, "Oh, Chris . . ." and then just stood for a long time with Jack in her arms, taking it all in, while Rocky ran back and forth.

"Yeah," he said, putting an arm around her. "It's a goddamn mess . . ."

THE ENTIRE PATCH in front of the house looked as if it had been chewed up and spit out, all of it torn apart and blackened by the vehicles that had been out to the Far Six.

All the ocotillo and purple sage and mountain laurel was crushed. The damianita daisies that Mel had liked so much were gone, and centuries' worth of yucca had been swept away by the landing skids of Garrison's helicopter. A thick bed of morning glories was scorched and withered, and there would be no fall blooming this year, or maybe ever again. And although all his deputies had been out to the house to pick up the scattered, spent brass from the firefight that hadn't been bagged by the FBI and DPS, Chris could see still see a few stray rounds winking in the cool October sunlight. He knew he'd be finding them out here forever, half buried in the scrub like poisonous treasure.

The front of the house hadn't fared any better. Danny had hammered up boards over the shattered windows, but there were still plenty of visible bullet wounds all across the front face and on the porch rails. Mel walked along the porch and ran a hand over the holes, feeling them as if checking to see if they were real. There were even more *inside* the house, from those bullets that had passed through the broken windows.

There were holes in the roof, and the wind whistled through them.

It was all silent testimony to the furious violence that had occurred here, to just how lucky Chris had been to walk away a second time.

That was the doubt he saw in Mel's eyes. This had been their home, a place she had come to love, but Chris had almost died here, *again*.

Maybe no home was worth so much.

SHE'D BEEN STAYING OUT AT JAVY CRUZ'S, away from the media circus in town, while he'd been living out of the Budget Inn in Murfee. But now that the circus was finally packing up and leaving, it was time to make some decisions.

Bringing her out here was the first one.

He took Jack from her, felt his son's familiar heartbeat and warmth, and let her wander around inside and outside the house. He'd told her what had happened and she'd read some of the news accounts, but none of that had prepared her for this sight.

He gave her all the time she needed, as Rocky—nose down, ears up—traced unseen paths through the scrub, following the steps of the investigators who'd set up shop at his home for days. They'd tried to re-create the shoot-out, to figure out exactly who had been where, at what moment, and although Chris had lived it . . . survived it . . . he couldn't remember many of those exact details.

But I remember I shot at men I thought were cops, agents. I was willing to do that, to save America, to save Danny.

To save myself.

To survive.

Another choice he'd have to live with.

He hadn't bothered to read all the reports and findings. They meant nothing to him. He knew all he needed to know.

Mel walked out slow onto the porch, holding two things: one of his election signs, shot through with two holes, and a broken picture frame. It had been blasted off the wall, shattered, the picture inside ruined. She dropped the sign and turned the frame over and over and then gently put it down on the porch rail. She kissed Chris, and tried a smile that never quite made it to her eyes.

She might have been crying when she was alone inside the house.

"Okay, Sheriff, what are we going to do?"

"We're going to rebuild. That's what we're going to do. I've already talked to Judah Canter about the work."

"Jesus, Chris. The work. Even with the insurance, the money it's going to take . . ."

"I know."

She looked at the picture on the rail, talking to herself. "I can go back to Earlys, steal back some of my hours from Vianey. She'll understand."

"Well, maybe you should think about something other than working in a bar, since you're a mom now and all. We need to keep you respectable." Chris kissed the top of Jack's head; he was awake and blinking. *God, his eyes are beautiful. Like his mother's.* It was almost like Jack knew he was home, too. "I've been talking to Homer Delahunt about his bookstore in town. He's trying to get out from underneath the place. He's looking for someone, anyone. He won't drive a hard bargain."

Mel granted him a ghost of a laugh. "Chris, we don't have the money to fix this house, much less buy a bookstore. I don't know anything about managing a place like that, and neither, for that matter, do you."

"You can learn, and it seems I may have come into some money." He fished around in his pocket and pulled out a folded-up letter. Inside the letter was a check.

Mel read them both. "You sold a story?"

"Yeah, I did. Just a small one, to an even smaller literary magazine in Arizona."

She hugged him and Jack both, tight. "I'm so proud of you. It's great." This time her smile was genuine, but she held up the check and read it again. "I mean, it really is great, Chris, but this barely covers the cost of one of our windows."

"I know. Truth is, short stories don't pay a whole lot. I guess I need to learn how to write a novel now."

"Do you have any ideas for one?"

Chris smiled. "Yeah, a few."

THEY WALKED AROUND for a while longer, surveying the last of the damage together, before making their way back out to his truck. With the true onset of fall, it was getting darker earlier, and there was even a chill, the coming night showing sharper teeth. In another month or so they could stand out here with their breath pluming in the air, frost sparkling on the caliche. But now, although the sun hadn't gone down, a full, silver moon had already risen. It was one of those moments when both sun and moon were in the sky at the same time, fighting for attention, hanging high above the Big Bend and each lighting it in its own beautiful way.

Everything was so clear and illuminated and perfect, the world around them a painting.

"How's Joe?" Mel asked. "Is he still back east?"

"Yeah, he finally got his wish to get the hell out of Texas. He's there overseeing the interviews of Fox Uno. They've got him stashed somewhere, getting treated for chronic myeloid leukemia, and Garrison said he's talking. *Really* talking. He'll live, for a while longer. Long enough. The best damn medical care money can buy."

"Is Joe seeing his daughters?"

"That I don't know, babe. I assume so."

"Is he coming back?" Mel asked, leaning hard into Chris as they both stared up at the sky.

"I don't know that, either, but I don't think so. There's nothing out here for him anymore."

Mel seemed to think about that, as she pulled Jack's blankets around him more. He'd fallen asleep again as they'd walked around the Far Six, and Rocky was at her feet, head on his paws, just as tired from racing around after them.

"But is there something here for us?" she finally asked.

"Well, the good citizens did reelect me sheriff," Chris said.

She punched his arm. "Against your goddamn will, almost kicking and screaming. You didn't want it then, Chris—is this really what you want now?"

And that was the question . . . *What did he want?*

He thought he had wanted his own version of America's freedom.

But what he really wanted were moments like this, with Mel and Jack and Rocky the dog. All of them safe and warm, and the hard truths of the world at arm's length; or even farther, as far away as the sun and moon above them now. Although he wanted to believe he could have those moments anywhere—that he'd finally earned them, by honoring his promises to America Reynosa— he'd tried twice now to leave, and both times had found himself right back here anyway.

Even if he didn't need the Big Bend, maybe it still needed him.

He thought about all his chalk marks still etched across the rocks and trees of El Dorado, that language all his own that spoke so plaintively of his search for Evelyn Ross.

The futility of it, but also its importance.

It was another promise he'd made, this time only to himself, and one he wanted . . . needed . . . to keep.

Because when the rains and the snows washed away all those marks, he'd start again. And again. As many times as it took.

He'd never ask so much of Mel again, but he couldn't ask any less of himself.

He bent down and scratched Rocky behind the ears and then wrapped his arms around his wife and son, careful that the badge and gun on his belt didn't get in the way.

"Ya tengo lo que quiero, aquí mismo," he said. I have everything I want, right here.

And although Mel didn't know all the words, he knew she understood what he was trying to say anyway.

IV

As Chris drove them away from the Far Six, talking again about his ideas for the bookstore, Mel rolled down the window and just let him ramble.

He needed to do this, to talk about something other than what had happened. He needed to move on.

Chris had been worried all along if things would be different for them after Fox Uno, and she'd worried the same thing.

She wasn't sure she had an answer before, or now.

In the days after, she hadn't told him about the young boy and girl she and Javy had found out at his ranch. There hadn't been a right time, or a right way.

Listening to Chris now, that time seemed to have passed altogether.

There were no good ways to lie.

THEY'D SHOWED UP OUTSIDE JAVY'S HOUSE in a stolen Charger, exhausted and gravely injured.

Javy had greeted them with a raised shotgun, only to find the girl had suffered a recent, horrible cut to her face, and the boy a more recent, and serious, gunshot wound. Javy spoke to the girl in Spanish and learned they'd crossed over the river, but they were never at the Far Six.

They knew nothing about Fox Uno or Chris or Danny or America.

They'd seen smoke over that way, a circling helicopter low in the sky, but nothing more.

Their injuries had come from other men.

BUT MEL UNDERSTOOD that their arrival, and their wounds, had everything to do with Fox Uno—and with all the events that were happening at the Far Six and the Big Bend in the days leading up to it. She couldn't draw a straight line between those two things, but it was there all the same. She could *feel* it, as sharp as that splinter of Chris's decision to risk everything to help America.

Fox Uno was a hole, sucking everything down. He'd nearly swallowed Chris and his friends.

Her family . . . the only thing that mattered to her.

By the time the boy and the girl arrived, Mel knew that Chris was okay—she'd heard from him, and then Joe Garrison. But she couldn't, wouldn't, leave Javy to deal with those two injured kids alone. While he settled them in one of his bunkhouses, she called Vianey Ruiz, who in turn reached out to a young Hispanic EMT she knew from Presidio. His name was Lucas, and when he got to Javy's place and took one look at the boy's gunshot wound, he said he needed a hospital. When it was clear he wouldn't go, Mel promised to pay Lucas whatever was needed to treat him at the bunkhouse, and Javy promised to make sure it was done.

Javy also got Zita to promise she would not tell any-one about what she'd seen, and she said she was good at keeping secrets, better than anyone she knew.

Her papa had already taught her how important keep-ing secrets could be.

That night, after Mel shook free from Garrison's agents, she went and bought bandages and pain pills and everything else Lucas had asked for, as well as new clothes for the girl and the boy. For the next five days, she brought them anything she thought they might need and, with Javy translating, learned their entire story.

Everything that had happened to them, and how they had come to the Big Bend.

She cried more than once, holding both their hands, but cried hardest when the girl asked to hold Jack.

JAVY AND LUCAS spent one whole afternoon pulling the police equipment out of the Charger—after their story, and talking with Chris and Garrison, Mel had a damn good idea where it had come from—and they bur-ied it all out on Javy's property. Javy then used a sledge-hammer to put some fresh dents and scratches in the car, and to finish the disguise, splashed some green paint along the wheel wells and the trunk.

He also found a new license plate, but Mel never asked him where he got it.

WHAT SHE WAS DOING was *wrong*, in the strictest sense of the word.

She was, after all, withholding information about a huge federal investigation, helping to hide two illegal aliens, and, in every way but saying the words out loud, lying to Chris. But Mel remembered what she told him only a few days before Fox Uno and America had descended upon their home:

There isn't any real right or wrong here, only what you have to do.

And right or wrong, this thing with the young couple was something she had to do. If she and Chris were going to live with his decision about Fox Uno, then she was going to live with her decision about Chayo and Neva.

She was fine with that.

SHE SETTLED BACK INTO THE SEAT, as Chris continued to talk. She let the wind through the open window hit her face.

It felt good.

Before Chris had brought her out to the house, she'd asked Javy how Chayo and Neva were doing today, and he'd pretended not to know who or what she was talking about.

But he'd said it with a smile.

Neva had talked about having relatives around Murfee, but she'd also talked about Houston . . . Dallas . . . the whole wide world.

The last time Mel had seen Neva and Chayo, they'd been sitting on the bunkhouse bed together, holding hands, sharing secrets of their own.

The future.

And if that was the last time she was ever going to see them, that's how she wanted to remember them.

She reached over and grabbed Chris's hand from the steering wheel.

There were no good ways to lie, but some secrets had to be okay.

Garrison leaned down next to her, close, and told her everything.

They were in the room that overlooked a small ornamental pond, her favorite in the house. One whole wall was perfect glass, with a sweeping view of the bright green slope down to the pond that was ringed with cattails and daylilies and geraniums and sword grass. Beyond the pond was a deeper, darker green of old, leafy trees, and there was a shaded stone bench that they sometimes sat on when he came to visit, but only for a half hour at a time—even on a cooler day like today—because she'd lost so many sweat glands in the fire, and her body did a poor job of controlling her temperature. A hard workout could lead to a heatstroke, so most times they met in this room—bright and beautiful and clean but always colder than the world outside—and just watched that other world together through the glass.

Morgan Emerson's parents had originally relocated to Atlanta so they could get her into the Joseph M. Still Burn Center at Doctors Hospital, in Augusta. It was one of the best in the country, and after the fire that had consumed her in Murfee, she'd needed months of inpatient care at the burn center. When that was done, and they had to move her from Still back home, they decided to stay on in Augusta, and looked for a place in historic Summerville that everyone called "The Hill." Morgan's father was ex-military and knew certain people, and they'd helped him find the house, which wasn't even on the market at the time, and took care of all the arrangements. For a couple of months, a private security firm supplied a twenty-four-hour protective detail on Randall Emerson's daughter, and more than once, when Garrison had arrived to see her, he'd pass a dark SUV or a limousine leaving the residence, the smoked, bulletproof windows hiding the person inside.

Each visit was the same.

Garrison and Randall Emerson shook hands, shared a silent glass of Glenmorangie Signet in the kitchen, and then his wife, Marjorie, walked Garrison just as silently back to their daughter.

HE TOLD HER ABOUT THE EVENTS AT THE FAR SIX, and the surprising phone message he got from Deputy America Reynosa, explaining how she and the sheriff needed his help—that her uncle Fox Uno was hiding out with them, but that men were coming for him and he wouldn't be there much longer. She wasn't sure how much time they had left. She talked about Danny Ford hiding somewhere in the desert, dressed in army fatigues, and voices on phones, and a little girl named Zita. It had all sounded so strange, so unexpected, he almost wrote it off as a bad joke. But the real concern in the deputy's whispered voice, and the very last thing she'd said before the message ended, made him a believer.

She'd said she was calling from baby Jack's nursery at the Far Six.

He told Morgan that he later learned from Sheriff Cherry just what that call had cost the young woman—a choice between the new family she'd found in Murfee and the one in Mexico—and how it was a good thing that damn helicopter had finally gotten repaired, because if it hadn't, he and FAST might never have made it out there in time.

He wasn't eloquent, but described the best he could the terror of flying fast and low over the darkening desert, desperately searching for the house.

Described that resigned but calm look on Fox Uno's face when the cuffs were put on him.

He told her all about the aftermath—the debriefings and the hearings and the interviews. He told her that it had been explained to Fox Uno in no uncertain terms that if he didn't fully cooperate with U.S. investigators, he'd be charged with the death of one federal agent and the attempted murder of another, and be forced to stand trial in a U.S. court on the outstanding RICO charges that El Paso, New York, and San Diego had on him. That is, if he wasn't simply handed back over to a Mexican government that was extremely desperate . . . *too* desperate, most would say . . . to get him back. The government of Mexico had started with promises and ended with threats, but in the end, for Fox Uno, it was one of those choices that wasn't a choice at all.

He also told her something he never revealed to Sheriff Cherry or his deputies, about the men they tracked down after exploiting Fox Uno's phones. Garrison's agents had discovered that Fox Uno had been hiding two SIM cards in his boots, using them to make encrypted calls on a rare Blackphone to Arizona and California during his entire stay in Murfee. Based on the intel request Garrison had put out to the surrounding states, coupled with some high-level phone-tracking analysis, they eventually located three men hiding out in a hotel in Gila Bend, Arizona. They were Barrio Azteca gang members driving a rental car, and inside the car was a bag containing several new phones (including another Blackphone), $250,000 in cash, three guns, and handwritten notes and maps to Deputy Reynosa's apartment in Murfee and Chris's ranch at the Far Six.

They'd made the maps based on Fox Uno's directions, and even as the first shots were being fired at the ranch, they were already on their way to the Big Bend to pick him up.

It never mattered if America Reynosa survived the hell at the Far Six or not. She was already dead.

That's because the men were also carrying two sets of licenses and passports.

One for Fox Uno, in the name of Rodolfo Reynosa, and the other for a girl about Zita's age, in the name of America Reynosa.

Deputy Reynosa had risked everything to save her family and help her uncle, and he'd been willing to sacrifice her, all of them, for next to nothing at all.

The price of a passport.

As Garrison talked, he held Morgan's hand, and although she couldn't cry anymore since her tear ducts had been so badly damaged, he knew she would if she could, but she was also smiling the whole time, too.

HE SAID IT WAS ALL OVER.

DEA couldn't get rid of him now, not with the high-profile nature of Fox Uno's arrest and his role in the Fox Uno debriefings, but eventually he would be moved aside, and then asked, politely, to put in his papers. And he was fine with that, because it was way past time and he was more than ready. There was nothing else he needed to do, and he sure in the hell wasn't going back to Texas again.

Ever.

AFTER HE LEFT MORGAN IN HER COOL ROOM, he sat in his rental car down the street and undid his tie and cried all the tears she couldn't.

Before he'd walked out, he put his badge, #5725, in her scarred hand, closed her fingers around it, and refused to take it back, no matter how hard she'd tried to hand it to him.

All these years, it had been so important. Maybe *the* most important thing, but he didn't need it anymore.

It truly was over.

THE RENTAL CAR came with satellite radio, and he flipped around until he found a station that played those old soft-rock songs he liked. He had nothing but time to kill, since he wasn't due back at the airport for four more hours.

For the first time in a long time, he had nowhere to go, nothing to do. That fire and darkness that had haunted him for so long, that had first taken shape in a field outside Murfee, Texas, had finally and forever slipped away.

An old Gerry Rafferty song came on, "Baker Street," and he couldn't help smiling—a refrain about the sun and brand-new mornings; about finally going home.

He had the rest of his life ahead of him, and no goddamn idea what to do with it.

And that was okay.

He wiped his eyes, feeling foolish, then turned that radio up as loud as it would go.

He was meeting Karen and the kids in Potomac. Angie was coming down from Juniata, and they were all going to drive down to Williamsburg together since Megan had a field hockey tournament, some sort of weekend invitational, and he'd promised to see it.

They were waiting for him.

He was going home.

This was the only time Martino had met Diego Serrano in person, and if he believed before that the man had only sounded like his father, now—up close—he looked like him, too: the same flat stare and thick hands and simple clothes. Diego Serrano carried himself as if he'd walked in from the fields, and when he sat down on the stool that had been put out for him so he could look Martino in the eye, he stank of sweat and beer and dust and cigarettes.

Diego Serrano smiled, showing stained teeth.

He took Martino's hands, which had been tied down to the chair with barbed wire, and held them gently in his own.

DIEGO'S MEN HAD FOUND HIM hiding in the bathtub in a small apartment in Chihuahua City, and brought him here to this warehouse next to the Aeropuerto Internacional General Roberto Fierro Villalobos, after they'd killed six of his men in a brazen mid-morning shoot-out (another ten had given up without firing a shot). After taking him, Diego's men hadn't bothered to hood him or blindfold him—it didn't matter if he knew where he was or where he was going, which was far more frightening—and the thin corrugated walls of the warehouse shook and rattled every time a plane took off.

Until Diego arrived, Martino had offered each man a fortune to put him on one of those planes, but they'd all refused. And they had only hit him once.

They'd grabbed him only two days after the disaster in Murfee, Texas, when he was still trying to figure out what had gone wrong. Not only had the *sicarios* and Xavier failed to kill Fox Uno—Xavier never knew the bag he was carrying contained a bomb, although in the end he might have suspected—his father had somehow ended up alive *and* in U.S. federal custody.

It was an epic disaster. A colossal, fucking mess.

But it hadn't been Martino's failure alone, because there had been a second set of *sicarios* there at the ranch in Texas who'd gotten in the way—a team of corrupt U.S. cops—and Martino Abrego Cabrera had not sent those men.

That had been Diego Serrano's doing: a hedged bet against Martino's plan, or some crazy idea of Diego's. Perhaps, even, a bid to wipe Martino's fingerprints off the killing of Fox Uno. Who knew anymore? But the only way those rogue *policía* would have known to be at that ranch was if someone had told the Serranos where his father was hiding, and that someone could only have been Gualterio.

So it didn't surprise Martino to see that fat traitorous pig appear in the shadows behind Diego, drinking a beer and smoking a cigarillo and laughing with his former

THIS SIDE OF NIGHT ‖ 535

captors, men who days before had answered only to Martino.

The truth of it was, they all answered to Diego Serrano now.

They were all traitors, one way or another.

DIEGO WAS TALKING TO HIM, but Martino was trying not to listen.

Diego had put on leather gloves over his gnarled hands.

Martino knew what was coming next, even if he'd only ever seen it on video.

Diego said something about his name, Tiburón, and how he was going to enjoy pulling this baby shark's teeth out, one by one.

The men behind him laughed, including Gualterio. Martino had already seen the pliers spread out on the aluminum foil, along with the other tools.

Gualterio's day would come soon, too. He'd have his own chance in this chair.

Diego Serrano was a sudden eclipse, blocking out the sun, and he turned the whole world black beneath him.

MARTINO TRIED TO REMEMBER the last time he'd seen his father, the last conversation they'd had, but couldn't.

He had no idea what they had talked about or where they'd been.

Instead, he remembered the cool touch of Xavier's skin against his own, the feel of the man's mouth against his—the way they'd held each other in the dark beneath the sheets, and how it had been as safe as anywhere he could remember.

He drifted back to the ocean view at Manzanillo and the color of the water there—all those impossible sunlit colors, and the towering blue waves crashing against the white sand.

He tried to imagine himself sitting on one of the planes he could hear crossing overhead, flying somewhere, anywhere.

Para volar.

It was the same dream a boy named Chayo Lozano Vidal had held on to when Martino's men had attacked his bus in Ojinaga, although Martino would never know that.

The great noise of those jet engines, and the beach waves in his memory, was not enough to drown out the laughter from Diego and Gualterio and the others, or the metallic coughing sound of the chainsaw.

Martino closed his eyes and put himself on that plane and was finally flying away, as Diego Serrano bent over him and made the first of many cuts.

TWO DAYS LATER, the video was uploaded to the internet.

The whole world watched.

DUSK

America and Danny were supposed to meet Marco and Vianey—sort of a double date—but the other couple hadn't arrived yet, so they waited outside the ice cream place, at the same small tables Danny and Zita had sat at a month ago.

That day, America and Sheriff Cherry had been walking with Fox Uno across the street, watching their reflections in the store windows.

America thought it was too cold for ice cream, but Zita had insisted, and she was laughing now with Danny, showing off the cowboy hat he'd bought her in Nathan so she'd stop taking his. It looked good on her, natural, and although no one knew exactly what was going to happen to her next, for now she was staying with America, and America had come to enjoy having her around. Danny definitely did, and made a big show of buying her presents. It was hard for him to say no to the girl.

Maybe he just understood her.

Zita woke up some nights crying, chased by dark dreams of her time with Fox Uno and the things she'd seen, the same way Danny's sleep had been troubled. He'd started seeing Dr. Harlow, finally talking about his time in Afghanistan, about things he'd only hinted at to

America, and that had been going well. So well that Zita was going to do the same. With America translating for him, Danny promised he'd go with her and sit next to her and hold her hand the whole time if she wanted. He told her it hurt at first to talk about such things, but the more you talked, the easier it became, and the less they bothered you. Although it seemed natural to try to forget and bury all the bad things that happened to you, all those horrible memories, it didn't really work that way. You couldn't ignore them or bury them; instead, you had to get them out of you, like the venom of a snakebite. If you didn't work to heal them, they only made you sicker and sicker over time.

Those bad memories became poisonous dreams. They poisoned everything and everyone you loved.

The sun settled and shadows stretched down the street. The lamps on Main Street were coming on, one at a time. A cool glow, like a dozen tiny, distant stars. Her ribs and shoulder still hurt from the bullet she'd taken. Her vest had stopped most of it, but it had nearly punctured her lung. Most of her chest was still a purple bruise, tender to the touch, and it would be a long time fading.

She'd spoken with Agent Garrison a few times since that night. She'd told him everything about Fox Uno, all the conversations they'd had after he came to Murfee. Garrison had promised his people were looking for her mama and her papa, but so far there'd been no word on them. Fox Uno had been truthful in his debriefings so far, but he hadn't been any more helpful. No one knew where they were, or if they were alive.

Garrison had also sent her back that horrible silver

gun, and she and Danny had driven it out together to the place where Sheriff Cherry had found Rodolfo's body, the place where she'd almost shot Fox Uno, and buried it there as deep as they could.

Danny had said maybe she should talk to Dr. Harlow as well, and she'd said she'd think about it.

He'd told her to think about it *hard*, and then he'd kissed her, helping her wipe the dirt from her hands.

She'd kissed him back, held on to him, and they'd stood there together like that for a long time.

You couldn't ignore or bury them . . . if you didn't work to heal them, they only made you sicker and sicker over time . . .

Even *good* memories, like those America had of her mama and her papa and her brother, could turn into bad dreams, too. All the doubt, the unknowing, the regret. The sadness and loss.

Those memories could be just as hard to heal from.

Maybe when Danny took Zita to Dr. Harlow, she would go with them to check it out. Even if she wasn't ready to commit to anything like that, not yet.

Just as she wasn't committed to responding to Ron Delaney, who'd e-mailed her a bunch of information about the courses she'd need to take if she wanted to pursue forensics. He'd explained that DPS was always hiring and that he'd help her with the coursework any way that he could. She had saved the e-mail, but looked at it only every now and then.

She settled on the bench, with Danny next to her and Zita between them. Zita was chattering a mile a minute and Danny was laughing along with her, still not understanding much of what she was saying, and he had his arm stretched out around them both.

This was the second time they'd made plans with Vianey and Marco, who appeared to be getting serious. Vianey had confided in America that Marco was thinking about leaving the department and going back to school, to be the doctor he'd always wanted to be. He hadn't decided yet, but it was on his mind.

After the Far Six, he wasn't sure he was cut out to carry a badge and gun.

Across the street, a young couple she didn't recognize was getting into a car, one that looked like her brother's old Charger. This one was black, too, all beat up, with some remnants of old green paint. Rodolfo had painted his car with green snakes, and had kept it perfectly clean. He used to spend all Saturday washing and polishing it, so he could drive it over the river for a night in Ojinaga.

She remembered that . . . him waving good-bye to her, smiling, before he left.

The girl kissed the boy and then walked around to the driver's side and got in. She had the window down, and she was laughing as they drove away.

She was happy, *free*, and America knew exactly how she felt.

As they disappeared up the road, America could see reflected in the window of one of the stores behind them—the *librería*—a thin young man in a dark leather coat, with longish hair. He was staring at her, looking right at her, and even in the fading light, he was familiar to her. He matched Marco's description of the man who'd asked questions about her in Earlys, questions that had prompted the sheriff to move them out to the Far Six. But it was more than that. All she had to do was think back, imagine the man in the window glass younger still, wearing a hooded sweatshirt instead of a leather jacket . . .

Lying flat in the back of his Ford Ranger, watching clouds move.

Sharing another endless cigarette, laughing.

A couple, like the pair who'd driven away.

Even good memories . . . could be just as hard to heal from . . .

Caleb.

Marco and Vianey walked up, blocking her view, and by the time she got up from the bench, nearly pushing past them, the young man was gone.

Danny was right next to her, too, asking her if she was okay. After Fox Uno, he was always on guard, always watchful. She still woke up sometimes to find him pacing, checking the windows and doors, and then she had to go to him, hold him, and pull him back into their bed.

Now he was scanning up and down the street, hand unconsciously on the gun at his hip, trying to see what had taken her attention.

Caleb.

She took one last look, shaking her head, and after a gentle touch to the Saint Michael pendant on her neck— reminding herself that Ben would always be there, too— she laced her fingers tight in Danny's, turning him back to the lighted window of the ice cream shop.

Back toward Zita and Marco and Vianey, who were watching them both, trying to figure out what was going on.

She laughed and told them all it was okay.

It was *nada*.

She just thought for a moment she saw someone she'd once known long ago, but that was impossible.

It was only the lengthening shadows of a brand-new night, and those fading memories of the sun going down.

It would come up again tomorrow.

It always did.

AUTHOR'S NOTE

I've spent nearly a decade wearing a badge in the Southwest, and I've seen the best and worst from both sides of the border. If you shared a couple of beers with me now, you might come away thinking those years have left me somewhat jaded—cynical—and you wouldn't be wrong. Maybe there is no way they couldn't.

For the longest time, I also thought those years left me beyond shock, beyond outrage.

I was wrong.

On a rainy night in September 2014, buses carrying undergraduate students from the Raúl Isidro Burgos Rural Teachers' College in Ayotzinapa, Mexico, came under automatic-weapons fire from masked gunmen—some alleged to be municipal police officers—at an intersection in the small town of Iguala, 120 miles southwest of Mexico City.

During the ensuing attack, which spanned multiple locations and several hours, three students were killed outright—the youngest, fifteen years old—while forty-three others were marched off their buses and herded into waiting police vehicles and disappeared.

They haven't been seen alive since.

It was a particularly horrific crime in a conflict where horrors are endless. Despite worldwide condemnation, no one can say with any certainty why those buses were targeted. No one knows who ordered the attack or who, exactly, carried it out. There were investigations. There were clues and theories and even a few arrests, yet maddeningly few answers.

But years later, there remains plenty of outrage . . . as the families left behind continue to protest, continue to seek justice, and continue to question the official reports of what happened that night.

I guess they've become cynics, too.

They also continue to grieve. They'll always grieve.

Eventually, the remains of three of the students were identified from bones allegedly recovered at a mass grave near the San Juan River in Cocula, about twelve miles southwest of Iguala. But even the facts surrounding that are in question, in doubt.

As of 2016, another 130 bodies have been found outside Iguala.

The only truth everyone can agree on is that the discovery of unnamed dead in unmarked graves is far too common.

The fates of the other forty students are still unknown . . .

ACKNOWLEDGMENTS

Third time's a charm, or so they say.

I want to thank the usual suspects: Sara Minnich and Carlie Webber, editor and agent, respectively. Also, everyone at Putnam who makes all this real, as well as Holly Frederick and her great crew, who have worked tirelessly to bring these Big Bend books to a screen near you.

The family: the Scotts and the Martins.

The friends: you know who you are.

The boss: Douglas W. Coleman, who continues to insist I'm the best part-time ASAC and full-time author he's worked with.

The fellow authors, agents, and cops: far too many to count.

The accomplices: all of you who enjoy these stories and continue to support them.

Anyone and everyone else I've forgotten.

And always and forever: Delcia.

Two final things:

I modeled my Librado Rivera and the events that befell Chayo and Neva on the 2014 Iguala disappearances. I leaned hard on Ryan Devereaux's article "Ghosts of Iguala: How 43 Students Disappeared," which was published on *The Intercept*, and on a lengthy, six-part series by Francisco Goldman in *The New Yorker* that thoroughly chronicled the story of the Ayotzinapa school students, and the complicated and controversial aftermath of the attack. My story is fiction, but the well-researched reporting by Messrs. Devereaux and Goldman lays out all the facts, as well as anyone can know them.

For my next story, I'm going to step away from the Big Bend for a bit. I'm finally heading home to Kentucky and I figure Chris, America, and Danny are due for a welcome break.

Trust me, there's still plenty in store for them.

Until then, I hope you'll follow me . . .

TURN THE PAGE FOR AN EXCERPT

Angel, Kentucky: Just another one of America's forgotten places, where opportunities vanished long ago, and the opioid crisis has reached a fever pitch. When this small town is rocked by the killing of an infamous local crime family, the aftermath brings together three people already struggling with Angel's drug epidemic. Over the course of twenty-four hours, loyalties are tested, the corrupt are exposed, and the horrible truth of the largest drug operation in the region is revealed. Angel will never be the same, but a lucky few may still find hope.

LITTLE PARIS

Little Paris Glasser stares right into the dead man's eyes and tries to see himself in them.

Danny, or maybe slow, stupid Ricky, once told him such a thing was possible, but this dead Mexican's eyes are flat and black, reflecting nothing at all.

Truth be told, they're downright creepy, like they're painted right on the wetback's skull.

A dead doll's eyes.

Little Paris *almost* reaches out a hand to rub over one of 'em; to wipe that dead man's coal-black stare right off his skeleton smiling face, smear it on his fingers like fresh paint, like fresh blood, but thinks better of it and takes another hit instead from his little homemade pipe, a GE sixty-watt bulb, and lets that hot taste of crank and CRC Bee Blast Wasp and Hornet Killer mule-kick him hard in the chest.

He flickers and flames, blood catching chemical fire.

He holds a mouthful of acid smoke, and it's like he's done swallowed a whole nest of pissed-off yellowjackets, buzzing around now inside his heart and head and behind his own dark eyes.

Goddamn, he finally breathes out.

Goddamn.

THE SUN'S BARELY UP, just peeking over Crown Hill and hardly casting any shadows yet, but last night still hangs on stubbornly beneath the shingle oaks and cockspurs like a drunk not quite ready to leave the party.

Little Paris ain't sober yet either, has barely slept a wink in three days, with that crank coursing through him and Danny's ghost and all them others calling out his name and his daddy forever pissing and moaning about *this* and Jamie always whining about *that* and Hardy at his too-young-to-know-better age playing the damn fool lately and raising a ruckus.

Everyone looking for a piece of him and a taste of their own, including these here damn wetbacks.

Well, one less, anyway.

When he was older than Hardy is now, but still just a boy all the same, he used to steal a little peace of mind at the family plot beneath Lower Wolf's black cherry trees. Lay himself down on them cool, cracked gravestones, where it was quiet and calm and still, where all them old skeletons and ghosts didn't seem intent on bothering anyone, to watch the bluing sky slow to a stop between the leaves and dream about everything and nothing at all.

Not a care in the world.

But it's never quiet now and the world never stops spinning and even the dead can't seem to keep their goddamn mouths shut anymore.

They talk to him all the time.

He hears 'em calling his name.

Like the Good Book says, there's just ain't no goddamn peace for the wicked.

Little Paris can't even count on his fingers the last time he slept peaceful the whole night through, and though he ain't dead yet, no gravestone pillow for him, he can't help but wonder what someone might see now if they looked hard and straight into *his* goddamn sleepless eyes.

Imagines it ain't no pretty sight anyway—

Maybe a bunch of yellowjackets, big as your thumb, circling and circling and circling.

Angry as hell.

Trying to fly free of his goddamn skull.

THIS WETBACK HERE sure didn't see much of anything when Little Paris blew his fucking brains out four days ago now.

Never even saw it coming.

He and Jamie drove him back here wrapped in some Cabela's camo tarp and he has a vague memory of telling Jamie afterward to toss the whole fucking mess into Rockhouse Fork or even Yatesville Lake, but Jamie's now standing by Little Paris's Mustang, staring down at the dead man like he's never seen one before.

Like this one just fucking magically appeared here flat on its back with two bullets in its skull, turning autumn Kentucky colors and going soft, setting off a mighty righteous stink, where his amigos will soon smell him all the way down in ole *Me-hi-co* or wherever the hell it is they breed 'em.

If Jamie wasn't already his Glasser blood, weak and thin as it might be on his side of the family, Little Paris might find himself inclined to shoot this sonofabitch too.

"What'd I say?" Little Paris asks, toeing the gassy body with one of his boots, but *gently*, so it don't rip like an overripe Granny Smith and explode shit and pus everywhere.

A sweet, crisp Granny Smith is one of Hardy's favorite things.

"What the fuck did I say about *this*?"

Jamie shrugs but won't quite look at him 'cause maybe he really can see all them angry yellowjackets behind his eyes.

"I know, coz. I know. Just ain't seen to it yet." Jamie goes to light a Marlboro, that dumb-ass silver ring of his catching fire with the first of the morning sun. "It ain't like we ain't been busy. That last batch this boy brought is *moving*. I'm still cleanin' up with that."

That last batch . . . the white powder H the dead wetback brought them.

DOA, motherfucker.

Everyone around three states wants a taste of it, but no matter how pure or good it is, smack has never really been Little Paris's thing. It makes him too soft, too fuzzy at the edges. The dope sex is good and all, sweet as pure cane sugar or honey, but he likes the way crank sharpens him right up, a whetstone to a knife, and *that* sex ain't half bad, either.

Rough, angry, although sometimes just a little too much of both.

"If Danny were here . . ." But Jamie stops sudden,

wise enough, or sober enough, anyway, not to hold Danny's name in his mouth for too long. Little Paris has already done heard it a thousand times if he's heard it once—from Daddy out loud and damn everyone else just under their breath—how he ain't like Danny at all.

How Little Paris is gonna be the one to finally let slip through his fingers these mountains that one Glasser or another has held on to with an iron fist for a hundred years or more.

Goddamn.

No, he ain't got the business sense his older brother had, probably never will, but even Little Paris knows a silver dollar when it falls into his hands, so when Jamie told him Danny's wetbacks had started sending their mules out alone, well, then only a damn fool could let *that* slip through his fingers.

Goddamn money for free.

Jamie's since been telling this boy's compadres he got paid and moved on down the highway, like always, but it ain't clear they believe him, although Little Paris figures it might help everyone if they just spoke better fucking English.

It's possible it don't matter quite what they say or even do with him now, since pride all but dictates they gotta come looking for him anyway, but Little Paris don't put too much stock in that.

One dead or missing Mexican ain't worth anyone's trouble, and *no one* comes calling uninvited on a Glasser in these mountains.

Not in Lower Wolf.

Not for a hundred fucking years.

———

ALTHOUGH THE BIG Sandy Power Plant no longer burns the black rock, coal is still in Lower Wolf's bones.

The deep, rolling green of the surrounding hills are knife-cut right down to them old, dark seams. In some places, the land's been blasted away altogether, woods leveled and whole mountains beheaded, hundreds of thousands of years blown sky-high, or so they say.

Strip mining's done left everything raw and exposed, slag scabs and stitches in the hollers. Years back a slurry spill sent a whole mess of arsenic and mercury right into Coldwater Fork and damn near flooded Lower Wolf too.

Damn near poisoned everything, but folks picked up and moved on as they do.

Eastern Kentucky bears such trials and tribulations proudly, wears her scars openly, the way Little Paris shows off all his ink: colorful tats up and down his body that Daddy hates something fierce, so he gets more of 'em, just to piss the Old Man off.

To remind him he ain't Danny and never will be.

Any day of the week Little Paris can run into a third-generation miner grabbing a cold one at the Crow Bar, men who know their way around a Caterpillar D11 or a Komatsu crawler dozer. Not *his* daddy, or even his daddy's daddy before him, but *his* people all the same.

His land too . . . all cut up and forever bleeding and downright poisonous in some places.

When it rains hard, Lower Wolf's colors come back to life.

These here surrounding hills run red and black like old blood.

TODAY'S GONNA BE A REAL CORKER LATER, hot as hell, and somewhere through them trees, tiny bugs are already dipping and dancing off the Coldwater.

Bugs like the ones working away on this dead Mexican.

Little Paris scratches at his naked torso, his latest ink still itching him something fierce, a wolf's head all shot up with arrows.

Now he says, "Seems to me Danny's got no say in it, so you better be cleanin' this up. *Today.*"

And Jamie nods through pale cigarette smoke. "Awright, coz. I got it. I said I got it."

"Damn straight you do," Little Paris answers, as he takes another pull from the bulb, setting them yellow-jackets buzzing angrily again, before realizing it's just his goddamn cellphone.

When he checks the message, he can't help but smile to himself, 'cause this shitty morning just started shining up already.

Jamie eyes the phone. "You comin' on up to the Big House? We still got rest of that shit to deal with."

They need to step on the last bit of the Mexican's H, make it last as long as possible, since they don't know when they're gonna get more in . . . a problem with Little Paris shooting the messenger the way he did. But it helps this batch is so damn strong, damn near killing folks left and right.

556 || J. TODD SCOTT

A little goes a long fucking way, but they always come back for more.

"Yeah," Little Paris says. "But toss me some of that new stuff, I gotta run up the way for a short bit. Just a little errand."

Jamie smiles. Knows just the sort of errand that Little Paris likes to handle on his own, the *only* kind that really gets him out of Lower Wolf anymore. He reaches into his white Escalade, then tosses a bag to Little Paris, who catches it out of the air.

Little Paris roots around in it and pulls out a glassine bindle stamped with a skeleton dancing a jig.

DOA, all right, motherfucker.

And his next tat might just be a handful of those tiny skeletons on the side of his neck . . . a whole family of 'em.

He likes that idea a lot.

"You want me to take Hardy back with me?" Jamie asks, prompting Little Paris to turn to the Mustang's backseat, where a little blond boy lies sleeping.

His own boy, Hardy.

Clutching that little toy six-shooter he's so damn fond of.

A Glasser outlaw, just like his daddy.

Someday, all this will be his. These mountains, these woods and hills—all of Lower Wolf—as long as Little Paris don't let it slip through his fingers.

And maybe someday too his boy will lay up on his daddy's gravestone beneath them black cherry trees and let Little Paris whisper to him.

Little Paris leans through the window and puts the bag on the seat next to Hardy.

"Naw, no need to wake him. He can come on up the way with me. I won't be long at all, and she'll want to see him. Always does."

Danny told him during one of his little Tamarack parties that pussy was gonna be the death of him, but Little Paris figures if that's how he's gonna go, he's just fine with that.

Better than how Danny died, anyway.

LITTLE PARIS CHECKS HIS OWN GUN, a heavy Beretta slipped sideways in his jeans, and stares down at his boy and wonders what he's dreaming and wishes he could sleep just one more day like that.

One last day.

Quiet.

Peaceful.

And not a goddamn care in the world.

DILLON

Dillon Mackey hits his first home run ever, just as his mama, Kara, drops dead in the bleachers.

The ball stays aloft in the hot, heavy air . . . spinning, spinning, spinning . . . even as Kara's on-again, off-again boyfriend, Duane Scheel, falls out right after her.

Looking on, you might think Duane's reaching for Kara—a gentle, almost protective gesture—but you'd be wrong. There's never been anything gentle or protective about Duane Scheel. In and out of Big Sandy RDC since he was sixteen, he once beat a man senseless with a McDermott pool cue.

Once put a blue steel thirty-eight revolver against a Pakistani's jaw in a holdup when he was barely fourteen, and that was ten years ago.

Now tall, thin, wasted, he doesn't look his age but a hell of a lot older. Nothing much left of him at all, a hastily scrawled stick figure, all right angles and sharp edges.

A Punch doll, a bad joke.

So when he tumbles off the rusty bleachers it's like someone's cut all his strings. He goes slack and silly, lifeless and limp, and falls forward with hardly a sound.

DILLON'S ROUNDING FIRST, heading to second, smiling and laughing and raising his arms to the sky and happy for the first time in a long time—least since his real daddy, Ronnie, ran them over to that catfish place in Catlettsburg before he went back up to the corrections for a spell—when Junior Heck's mama, Tanya, starts hollerin' loud like a big ole fire truck.

Dillon passes second, slowing down now and the game long forgotten, as mamas and daddies pull away from the bleachers, a few even runnin' low and covering their heads 'cause they think it's a shooting. Eleven-year-old Dillon knows all there is to know about *that*, what to do if someone angry or strung out or just plum crazy ever bursts into Angel Middle. How you hide when you first hear gunshots. But soon as Tanya Heck started up her hollerin', Dillon knew it wasn't because of no crack of a hunting rifle.

Most of them mamas and daddies have figured that out too, calmly looking for their kids, rounding them up with waving arms.

But some others are just standing around, wrapped up in cigarette or vape smoke, staring down, embarrassed, at something lying on the ground.

Dillon takes one last look back over the left-field fence to see if his ball's still flying high, or maybe rolling instead all the way down now to the water's edge at the Fork, but there's nothing. That ball, and so many other things the boy can't put a name to, lost forever in the deepening dusk, where fireflies pop here and there like campfire sparks, like that one time he and his daddy camped down at Yatesville Lake and what a fire *that* was. It was summer then too and way too hot, but his daddy helped him build it up bigger anyway, feeding it every piece of hickory or black cherry they could find, sitting as close as they dared, his daddy hanging one arm over his shoulder like they were good buddies. They burned hot dogs pitch-black but ate 'em anyway, then laid side-by-side beneath the whited-out stars as his daddy told him stories about the mines and even further back than that, when he was only Dillon's age.

The boy can't remember much of those stories now but still remembers his daddy's hand on his, the warmth of it and the weight of things passed down to him, still gently pressing there.

Dillon never makes third.

He slows down and finally stops altogether between the bases, hands still raised like he's asking a question that's got no answer.

Then he starts up again, shuffling past the pitcher's mound to see for himself what all the damn fuss is about.

HE'S ALWAYS BEEN FINE with Duane whuppin' up on him, but not his mama.

When it happens, and it happens way too much, he knows just how it feels to get angry or crazy enough to shoot up a school full of little kids who didn't do nothin' to no one or burn this whole damn town down.

His whole world.

Duane's no good and it's all just partyin' and fightin' now anyway that his real daddy's gone. This past winter his mama forgot to pay the electric for two whole months, and Dillon had to sleep wrapped up in one of his daddy's old coats but didn't mind so much 'cause it still smelled like him, like cigarettes and beer and aftershave, safe and familiar. He found some old oak leaves and chewing-gum foil in one pocket, two white pills he sold to Junior Heck in the other, and hidden in the lining a never-used Blue-grass Blowout ticket that he still holds on to and believes is worth a hundred or maybe even a million dollars. So much money he can't even guess what it might be, but he's afraid to scratch it off and see, 'cause if he's wrong, it's like he's done scratched away the last bit of something good in his life.

So he just carries that stupid worthless ticket around all the time. Holds it tight the same way his daddy held his hand 'round that campfire and the way he tries to hold on to his daddy's stories and the flickering, fading memories of his face.

'Cause as young as he is, he already knows just how easy it is to forget.

Like when his mama's hurtin' and hard on her medi-cine and she damn near forgets *him*, even though she tells him all the time he looks just like his daddy, so much so it makes her cry. But his face don't mean much to her when she's sick like that, when the hurt is so bad she can't remember anything else, whispering how she needs that medicine . . . *needs it so bad, baby* . . . 'cause that pain's like a toothache and a stomachache and a headache and a whole lotta heartache all at the same time.

It's endless.

She *needs* it something fierce . . . and that means she sometimes needs a peckerwood like Duane to get it for her. She calls Duane *Doctor* like it's a joke and they all have a good laugh at that—good ol' Doc Duane, who never even finished high school.

But other times his mama goes alone to see Little Paris. Everyone calls him the *main man . . . a bad-ass motherfucker . . .* and she's always cryin' after, 'cause he's worse than all the others who've ever come around. Worse than Duane and even that Jerry Dix, who wasn't all that bad, all things considered. He used to high-five Dillon and laugh this goofy cartoon *hi-yuck* and say stuff like *Call me Jere, little bear,* just like they were friends, best buddies. And sometimes when his mama was all partied out, Jere used to sit on the porch with him and share a Marlboro, watching winter stars through the trees.

Jere could even name two or three of 'em, which was more than his daddy could do, until his mama told him that Jere got sideways with Little Paris, so Dillon figures he ain't laughin' now, not ever again.

But on the rare day when his mama's not on her medicine, when she's clear and her eyes shine bright as those stars, bright as that burning campfire, she can be so sweet and gentle it makes him cry, which ain't no grown-up thing to do, although Dillon's watched his mama cry plenty.

A day just like today, when his mama finally felt good enough to come watch him play for the first time this summer and even put on some of that Avon and brushed her hair and found herself some clean clothes and promised him *today was a new day*, just another one of a hundred or million promises that'll never come to anything but somehow still mean everything, a million more lies this boy will always and forever be willing to believe and forgive, 'cause his mama was awake and present and calling him *baby* and he was gonna get in this one good day with her.

Until Duane had showed up stinking of beer and smoke and said he'd done got his hands on some of that new Glasser medicine everyone wants, everyone's been going on about, so why don't he just come on along for the ride and share a little taste?

But at least his mama held *his* hand crossing the gravel lot before the game.

Held on to him.

With that peckerwood Duane trailing a few steps behind, wobbly and barely there, drifting sideways like his cigarette smoke.

DILLON DOESN'T EVEN GET TO where the dirt infield turns to grass before Tanya, her own thick Avon a fresh mess, runs out onto the field, flabby arms wide—

"Oh, Dillon, honey, you don't wanna see this."

She goes to wrap him up in those arms even as he pushes past her, but she grabs at him again . . . calling him *honey, baby* . . . just like his mama does . . . *just like his mama* . . . and that's when he knows it's gonna be bad.

You don't wanna see this . . .

Real bad . . . worse than funny Jere probably takin' a

bullet to the head or his daddy goin' up to the corrections or Duane whuppin' up on his mama and leavin' him with his own bruises.

Like a toothache and a stomachache and a headache and whole lotta heartache all at the same time.

It's gonna hurt worse than all those things for a long, long time.

That's when Dillon Mackey starts running again.

Cryin' all the world for his mama.

J. Todd Scott

"[Scott], a real-life DEA agent, gives you everything you could want in a West Texas crime saga: generational conflicts; the sights and smells of an exotic landscape; the ghosts of monsters and loved ones past."

—*The Wall Street Journal*